BREAKING BEFORE

BOOK 4 OUTLASTING SERIES

LK MAGILL

FIRST HALE PRESS

Copyright © 2020 by Lindsay Magill

All rights reserved. Published by First Hale Press. No part of this publication may be reproduced, distributed or transmitted in any form or by any means, without prior written permission.

This book is a work of fiction. Any references to historical events, real people, or real places are used fictitiously. Other names, characters, places and events are products of the author's imagination, and any resemblance to actual events or persons, living or dead, is entirely coincidental.

Breaking Before/ LK Magill – 1st ed.

Ebook ISBN 978-1-950928-11-8

Paperback ISBN 978-1-950928-12-5

Hardcover ISBN 978-1-950928-13-2

DEDICATION_

To God, thank you for allowing me to write another.

ACKNOWLEDGMENTS_

Beta Readers!!!!

Sara Mae, Emily and Sue - I seriously cannot do this without you guys. Your input and insights are invaluable to this process. Thank you, thank you, thank you.

To my mom (as always) for letting me hide in your bedroom and write while you manage my kids.

Oh… and all the midday baths I stole as well. And let's not forget the meals made, glasses of wine poured, morning phone calls, constant advice, emotional support, the list goes on and on and on and on. Thank. YOU.

PROLOGUE_

THIS IS BOOK 4 IN A CONNECTED SERIES...

If you haven't already, please make sure to start with Book 1, OUTLASTING AFTER.

BEFORE

18 months after the start of the war

SUCKING IN A QUICK BREATH, JAMESON RAN A DIRTY HAND back through his mop of sandy-brown hair. His tan combat boots scuffed against the worn sidewalk. The wide strap attached to his black rifle shifted across his shoulder.

He shouldn't be here... but then again, neither should she.

Lifting his eyes, Jameson took in the sight of his old neighborhood. Large, two-story homes with cracked windows, overgrown yards, and hungry, barking dogs. Little more than a year ago, it would have been considered an upper-middle class haven.

It was mostly abandoned now. The trains hauling

women and children away to the refugee centers had all but stopped running, and most of the men were far away from here, fighting. The ones that remained in the area were increasingly desperate. Electricity was spotty at best. Easy food was becoming a thing of the past.

Internet? Television? Cell phones? Hah. They flickered in and out; staying more out than in these days. The war had been going on for a year and a half now, and there was no end in sight.

Time was running down, counting like a clock ticking backwards. Jameson could feel that particular truth in every inch of his bones.

He was no longer a sophomore in college playing football for the Pac 12. And at this rate he never would be again. Nope. Now he was just a twenty-one-year-old soldier, stomping his way home without permission.

When he eventually returned to his unit, he would pay. Oh, how they would make him pay.

Overhead, the sky was a swirling mass of hazy black clouds. Clearing his throat, Jameson tried to rid the thick smoke from his lungs. The Southern California coastline was burning. Not that this little fact was anything new, it being October and all.

Still, it added to the overall chaos. It added to the sense of impending doom. It's not like there were fire fighters anymore, or policemen for that matter. Those guys were all soldiers now too, like him. They were all South West Side troops doing exactly what they were told to do, and so they weren't here.

Well, except for Jameson. He was here.

Pursing his lips, he gave his head a slight shake. He was breaking about fifty rules by coming to this neighborhood right now, but hey… it was the twenty-seventh of October and there was nothing on earth that could keep him away.

"You came." The female voice seemed to echo down the empty street, causing Jameson's gut to twist and his heart rate to increase.

What the hell was she doing? Standing there on the front lawn of his childhood home, her chocolate-brown hair cascading in curly waves all around her shoulders. Those familiar mossy-green eyes were just staring at him, into him.

She made him *want*… like she always had, and like he always did, he ignored the feeling.

Didn't she see what was around her?

Didn't she see the guy in the house across the street pop his head out the front door? Or the scrawny old man observing them from the home three doors down? Apparently not.

And if she *did* notice them, then Cassandra Roe didn't seem to care. Nope. She didn't feel threatened by these men who reeked of hunger and fear. But Jameson sure as shit did.

How had he let her linger here for this long? Alone. Unprotected.

Narrowing his eyes, Jameson couldn't help his immediate frown. He held one finger up to his lips to signal for her silence as he drew the handgun from his side and flipped off the safety.

"Get back in the house," he called. His voice was rough from all the smoke.

Cass rolled her eyes, but stomped up the steps and slammed her way through the front door anyway.

Temper, temper. She'd always had one. At least, she had for as long as Jameson had known her.

Picking up to a trot, Jameson eyed the guy across the street before shouting, "Mind your own business, and that's not your fucking house!"

The guy didn't respond. He just pulled his head back through the threshold and yanked the door shut. Jameson heard the snick of the lock just as he reached his own front lawn. The grass was overgrown, with massive yellow patches and weeds swirling everywhere. His dad would be so pissed about it, if he'd of been here to see.

Cresting the two steps in one stride, Jameson turned on his heel to do one last sweep of the street before entering his childhood home and closing the door.

"You remembered," Cass spoke hurriedly at his back. "Eli's not here yet, but he will be. He'll come this time."

"Cass," Jameson let her name escape his mouth on a sigh. His shoulders slumped. "It's your birthday, how could I forget?"

Tucking his handgun into its holster, Jameson rotated around to face her before leaning back against the closed front door.

Cass paced back and forth in the living room. Her bare

feet padded across the hardwood flooring. A flash of candy-pink nail polish caught his eye.

"You painted your nails," he commented.

His eyes crawled up her body, taking in her dark skinny jeans and cream-colored sweater. God, she was pretty. She'd always been so damn pretty with that smooth tan skin and all those curves.

"There's nothing else to do here," she snapped. Jameson could hardly open his mouth without her getting defensive. "I know your mom wouldn't mind."

"Yeah." Jameson winced, wondering where exactly his parents had ended up.

They'd planned on going north to his aunt's house outside of San Fransisco, but had they made it? He didn't know. And now they'd been gone for five whole months.

Jameson's eyes focused back on Cass. Of course she had refused to go with them. She was waiting on Eli. She was waiting on her big brother's plan.

"Do you have your things ready?" Jameson asked. His eyes refused to leave her body, even as she nodded her head and gestured behind her.

At the base of the stairs leading to the second floor, there was a pile of stuff. Knowing her, there was probably an ungodly amount of clothing, bolts of fabric, and maybe even her sewing machine. She was artsy like that, the next big designer, his mother used to say.

Jameson frowned. He was going to have to ixnay that last item, even though he knew it would break Cass's heart. The sewing machine was bulky and heavy, and to be honest, she wouldn't need it where she was going. Maybe she hadn't realized it yet, but Jameson was willing to bet his last pair of clean socks that Eli was not showing up today.

If Eli were alive, he would never have left his baby sister here for this long. The thought made Jameson want to throw up. The idea that his best friend in the whole wide world was dead, made him sick.

But even so, it was a possibility that Jameson was now forced to embrace. If Elijah "I'm A Badass" Roe hadn't already broken ranks and scooped up his baby sister on his way out of town, then he was lying dead somewhere. Nothing would keep that guy from protecting his little sister, nothing. Jameson had seen it for himself time and time again.

So that left only one option for Jameson. And Cass was not going to like it.

"You got any food left?" He asked. Setting his rifle to lean against the wall, he shoved off the door. "You've eaten?"

Coming to a stop, Cass cocked her head to one side and eyed him. "Only canned corn and a bag of dry beans. Are you hungry? I can get you something."

"No." Jameson shook his head and crossed to her pile of luggage. "Put on some socks and boots," he instructed even as his stomach grumbled. "I'll load your stuff in the car. It's still here, right? Anyone give you trouble?"

"Yeah, it's in the garage," Cass commented. "And no trouble."

Stooping to pluck up one red suitcase, Jameson grabbed her duffle bag in his other hand and frowned. Sure enough, that damn sewing machine was sitting on the floor too.

Behind him, Cass plopped down on the floor with a pair of tall black leather boots and some ridiculous flowery socks that his own mother had given her. She was the daughter his parents never had, and as soon as Jameson had moved out for college, his parents had moved Cass in.

She'd had two years left of high school back then, and with her brother away on scholarship she'd had no place else to go. Shit, she even slept in Jameson's old bed. Not that he begrudged her the space. With the way she and Eli had grown up, she deserved it.

Moving past the staircase, Jameson hefted her bags down a hallway and through the massive kitchen. The dark granite counters gleamed in the fading light. How many times had he watched his mother stand over the apron-style sink and wash dishes? How many nights had he raided that stainless-steel fridge? It stood empty now. There was no power to keep it running.

Stopping at the door to the attached garage, Jameson dropped the red suitcase to the floor and reached for the handle. It gave easily under his hand and he held back a curse. It should be locked.

Damn it. They'd told Cass to keep every single door in the house locked.

Five months ago, when his parents had fled the neighborhood and Cass refused to go with them, Eli and Jameson had made the rules perfectly clear. If she was going to wait for her brother, then she had to keep all the doors locked and carry the shotgun to every room she was in.

At the time they'd both been stationed close by. Eli had been assigned to a tank unit further south, and Jameson was standard infantry. At the end of every month, one of them would visit. First Eli, then Jameson, so as not to get into too much trouble. They'd bring her food, check on her, see if she needed anything.

Eli had said there was a guy in his unit that knew where an underground bunker was. If things got too dicey with the war, then they were going to defect. At the time, Eli swore he would take Cass with him when they decided to go.

Jameson had believed him. So had Cass. And then two months ago, Eli missed his visit.

The entire tank division had been sent east, out of state. Maybe Eli couldn't make it back because of the distance, Jameson had reasoned.

But that thought was a shred of hope Jameson could no longer cling to. His own unit had finally gotten its set of marching orders. They were leaving the state too, and so this was the last chance he would have to take care of Cass.

"So this is it, right?" Cass's voice sounded just behind him. "We're going to the bunker? You've heard from Eli? You know where he is?"

Squeezing his eyes shut, Jameson bit down on his lip and shoved the door to the garage open. The hinges let out one long squeak as it swung wide. Stepping into the familiar space, Jameson opened his eyes and peered into the darkness. He hated lying to her, despite the fact that he'd become pretty great at it over the years.

"You've never actually loaded my bags before," Cass went on. "So that means we're going, right?"

She matched her steps to his as Jameson kept his mouth shut and moved further into the garage. A few dim rays of light filtered into the space through the decorative windows at the top of the garage doors. His mother's white Mercedes sedan sat under a thin sheen of dust. Just beside it, the space where his father's Range Rover used to park was empty.

"It should have a full tank," Jameson murmured to himself.

Flipping open the small round door to the gas tank, he plucked out the keys just where he'd left them. As he hit the unlock button, two beeps sounded and the headlights flashed once. Good to go. Thank God.

"Garrett." Cass stepped up beside him and put her hand on his forearm. "Look at me."

Fuck. Only his family called him by his first name, Garrett. His mom and dad, his grandma and pops. And then Eli took it up when they'd met in high school (even though everyone on the football team called him Jameson), and what Eli did… well, so did his sister.

"Yeah." Jameson cleared his throat, but continued to avoid her gaze. "We're going this time, so get your stuff in the car."

"You've heard from Eli?" Cass was relentless. "You've heard from him?"

Popping open the trunk, Jameson loaded the duffle bag and turned to walk back for the red suitcase. Cass stepped into his path. Her hands spread themselves out across his chest, and her head tilted up. Her five-foot-six frame was no match for his six-foot-four, but having her so close like this… it always made him feel like the weak one.

Those green eyes of hers were searching, pleading with him and he swallowed once, hard.

"I heard from Eli," he lied. "We're going to the bunker. So just get in."

"I don't believe you." Cass's eyes narrowed as she studied his face. "You're a terrible liar."

Actually, I'm pretty fantastic at it when it comes to you. "I'm not lying. Get in the car, Cass."

"Garrett," Cass warned. "I'm not leaving without him. He said he'd come get me, I just have to wait longer."

Shoving back from him, Cass spun on her heel and began to march away.

Jameson followed, panic rising inside his chest.

"He's too far away," Jameson reasoned. "He can't come back here himself. He sent word with a friend. We've got to go now Cass, so get in the fucking car."

"You are so full of it," Cass spat the words over her shoulder, sending her brown curls bouncing across her back. "I'm not leaving."

The sound of her feminine boots tapping over concrete

filled the garage, followed by the heavy stomping of his own boots as he gave chase. She wasn't thinking clearly. She just didn't understand. It was a war zone out there. Literally.

Their home was no longer safe. This neighborhood had been drained of its people. Women and children were gone. Good men were gone, too. Cass was one of the few holdouts, and now Jameson had to leave. His unit would be heading to Arizona in two days time, then New Mexico after that.

He could no longer ditch for a day or two and take care of her. He'd simply be out of reach. So it was now or never. She had to get somewhere safe, and the fantasy bunker that Eli had talked about was just that… a fantasy.

Closing the distance between them, Jameson grabbed for Cass's wrist and spun her around. She hissed at him and tried to jerk free.

For the first time in his life, Jameson didn't let her. He cinched his fingers tighter around her lower arm, until he was sure she couldn't escape him, until he was sure it would leave a mark.

"You've got to get in the car," he growled. "We're leaving right now."

"Let. Go." Cass glared as she yanked and pulled and tried to break away.

Jameson fought his flood of guilt and dragged her towards him instead, further into the garage. That's when she surprised him, albeit not for the first time.

Cocking back her free hand, Cass stepped into his

space and punched him as hard as she could square in the nose. Instantly, Jameson was seeing stars.

Why had Eli insisted on teaching her how to fight? Shit. That fucking hurt.

Letting go of her, Jameson's hands shot up to his face as blood poured from his nose.

Did she break it? For a second, he wasn't sure. But then he was feeling along the bridge and although it hurt like a bitch, the pain didn't drop him to his knees, so it wasn't broken at least.

"I'm sorry, I just…" Cass's voice was whisper quiet. "You should've let me go."

Blinking his eyes open, Jameson held his slick palms out in front of his face. They were covered in blood. Glancing down, he frowned. His uniform was covered in blood, too. *Shit.* That was going to raise some questions.

But at this point, none of that mattered, Jameson realized. Nope.

This changed nothing. Cass refusing to go with him, changed nothing.

When Jameson's eyes snapped back up to lock on Cass… she ran.

CHAPTER TWO_
CASSANDRA "CASS" ROE

*I*T WAS DARK, SUFFOCATINGLY SO. *H*ER BODY WAS TWISTED AT AN *awkward angle. Even with her knees bent up towards her chest, the top of her head was still smashed against something hard.*

Kicking out, Cass let loose a scream. Her feet didn't get far before they hit a wall. She was lying on her side, her muscles cramping, her body aching.

Twisting now, she tried to rotate onto her back, but there wasn't enough room. Her hands were tied together in front of her. She could feel the rough rope biting into her wrists. She screamed again, and felt her own mix of panic and rage echo dully in the tiny space.

"Let me out!" The words bubbled up her throat. "Let me out! Let me out!"

With each demand she would kick and flail. Her body shifted against thin carpeting. Her knees knocked into what felt like metal. It made no difference. There was no response.

But then her entire body slid to one side and her head

thumped hard against the wall. Her chin tipped down to her chest and her shoulders pressed further into the corner. For a moment, she was almost weightless.

That's when she realized she was moving.

That's when she realized she was stuffed into the trunk of a car.

Sitting up in bed, Cass stifled a scream. Her hands shot up to her throat and she bit her lip. It was that same memory again, clear as day. Of all the things to remember, why was that one stuck on repeat inside her mind?

Running her sweaty palms up and over her face, Cass sucked in a shaky breath. She was okay, she reminded herself. She was safe now.

With a groan, she lifted her head and surveyed her small bedroom. It was the middle of the night, with the moon glowing like a giant orb outside her solitary window.

Tossing aside her covers, Cass swung her bare legs out of her twin-sized bed and stepped onto the thick carpeted flooring. Her short cotton nightgown brushed against her thighs as she blew out a breath and crossed to her small closet. She'd made herself a silky soft robe, and after thumbing through the clicking hangers, she shrugged it on.

The apartment was cool, but mildly so. Although it was nearing springtime in the north, and the nights were cold here, her roommates liked to use the forced air heating to keep things comfortable.

Speaking of which she hoped she didn't wake them. Sometimes, when she had the dream/memory, she would actually be screaming out loud in her sleep. It was embarrassing for some reason, when Shelby or Mia came running in and shook her awake.

Crossing to her small wooden desk, Cass pulled open the thin top drawer and reached inside. It was there. That worn photograph was like a lifeline.

Plucking it up, Cass ran a thumb over the figures in the picture. There were three people in the photo, standing side by side with towering green trees in the background. They were young, maybe in their mid-teens, with youthful, happy faces.

On the left was her brother. He was tall and lean, with her same curly dark hair and tan skin. His hazel eyes nearly leapt off the page at her, he was staring so hard at the camera. Cass sucked in a breath as her brow furrowed.

She only knew the boy in the photo was her brother because that's what she'd been told. Elijah Roe was his name, but she'd called him Eli. He had no middle name apparently, and neither did she.

Blowing out a slow breath, Cass wished she could remember him. She wished she knew where he was, if he was alive, if he missed her.

Clearing her throat, Cass fought the flood of sadness and curiosity. Her nerves were starting to settle a bit, looking at this picture always helped.

Brushing her thumb over the faces in the photograph, she focused on the person standing on the right. He was just as tall as her brother, but his chest and shoulders were much more broad. He was big and strong, even back then, with electric-blue eyes and sandy-brown hair.

Garrett Jameson was his name, and he lived just across the hall now. She had no memories of him either. She had no memories at all, save the one.

"I should know you," she whispered.

Bringing up her left hand, Cass tapped the face of the person standing in the middle of the photograph. It was her, well a younger version.

She was the girl standing wedged between the two teenage boys. Her brother had his arm flung over her shoulders. Jameson had his arm slung around her waist. Her own hands were fisted on her hips, a sassy expression tugging her features.

And while the two boys grinned at the camera, her focus was elsewhere. While the two boys were looking forward, her face was tipped to one side and tilted up. She was staring… frowning? teasing? at Jameson.

"You don't tell me everything," she spoke quietly. "There's more here."

With another frown, Cass tucked the picture into the pocket of her robe before cinching the whole thing tighter around her waist. There was no going back to sleep now. Whenever she had the dream it would shoot adrenaline all through her body. She had a hard time settling after that. She had a hard time letting go.

Padding over to her bedroom door, Cass pushed it open and stepped into the quiet hallway. There were three small bedrooms in their apartment (each girl had their own room) and one bathroom that they all shared.

Turning to her right, Cass walked out into the sparse living room and turned a circle. They were up on the fourth floor of Building Eight and their small balcony looked out onto one of the green spaces. Beyond that, she could see the gleaming metal of the perimeter wall. It was so high and looming in the distance, with its smooth surface reflecting the bright moonlight.

Crossing to the sliding glass door, Cass leaned her forehead against the cold surface and shut her eyes. She'd lived here for four or maybe five years, even though she could only remember the last nine months of it. There'd been an incident involving an electronic microchip that had been implanted in her hand, something about a big computer and a war.

When the chip had been removed, it had affected her brain. She'd lost all of her memories, as had thousands of other people. At least that's what she'd been told. And yet, she felt it was probably the truth. The evidence was all around her. Lots of the other people were getting their memories back. But not Cass. Not yet.

Stepping back, she folded her arms across her chest and stared at her own reflection. If only she could remember, too. If only her mind could grab ahold of her past, but it always seemed to hover on the perimeter of her thoughts, just out of reach.

Sinking her hand into the pocket of her robe, Cass

drew out the photo once again. She nibbled on her bottom lip and stared.

There was one person living here who knew her story, or some portion of it. And although Cass felt like Jameson always held back when they talked, she'd trusted him once. Hadn't she? This picture was proof of that.

Turning on her heel, Cass left her apartment on silent steps. Jameson's door was just across the hall. It was number 401. He was a big deal when it came to running this place so he had a one-bedroom apartment all to himself, though it was fairly small.

Being second in command to Uriah Linfield was gold around here, so it was anyone's guess as to why he wasn't living in the same building as Commander Linfield. Jameson could have an even larger apartment, one with its own kitchen, if he wanted.

Before she could stop herself, Cass was crossing the narrow hall and rapping her knuckles on his door. Immediately, she regretted her decision. What if he was pissed? It was the middle of the night… again. What if he had a girl over?

But then the handle was being twisted and the door was swinging inward. Cass's mouth dropped. He wasn't wearing a shirt.

"Cass?" Jameson's voice was all husky with sleep as he rubbed a hand through his short brown hair. It caused his perfect abs to tighten which drew her gaze down to that V peeking up from his gray sweat pants. "You have the dream again?"

"Um." Cass searched for words, willing her brain to ignore what she was seeing, what she was feeling. "Yeah."

"I'm sorry." He stepped back and motioned her inside. "Come on in."

"No, I'm sorry," she said, and moved past him into the living room. "I just… I just don't know where else to go."

"You should always come here," he assured her. "You did the right thing."

Shutting the front door, Jameson gestured to a long blue couch pushed up against one wall. It had a coffee table in front of it and two arm chairs positioned on the opposite side. Cass cleared her throat and took a seat.

Rubbing a wide hand along the back of his neck, Jameson let loose a sigh and blinked down at her. This wasn't the first time she'd come to him about her memory, although he preferred to call it a dream or a nightmare. She got the feeling that Jameson wasn't convinced it was real. She got the feeling he wasn't convinced she'd actually remembered anything at all.

"You thirsty?" He asked, his blue eyes zeroing in on her. "I've got a jug of water."

"Sure," she squeaked.

Swallowing thickly, Cass glanced at the wall as Jameson turned to leave the room. Out of the corner of her eye she could see the muscles in his back flex as he walked down the hall. She really shouldn't be staring. Was she staring?

Refocusing her attention on the photo in her hands, Cass sucked in a steadying breath. She always came here like this, in the middle of the night, wanting to talk. And

Jameson always obliged her. He would answer her questions, tell her the same stories over and over.

She was like an annoying gnat, coming back to hover around him again and again. She'd of been embarrassed if she wasn't so desperate for more.

But if he had any of those same thoughts, Jameson kept them to himself. He was always polite and friendly, although he was pretty careful when they spoke. If he thought the repetition was pointless, he never said so, and occasionally she would get something extra out of him. Once in a while, there would be a new detail, a new piece of information that he had forgotten to include the time before.

"Here." Jameson returned with a single glass of water in hand.

Stopping in front of her, he offered her the cup. Cass set the photograph on the wooden coffee table and accepted the water. As she pressed the glass to her lips, her eyes flicked up to Jameson's face. He was still standing over her, watching her drink.

Sipping quickly, she set the cup down next to the picture.

"Thank you," she whispered, and swiped at her upper lip with the back of one hand.

Ducking his head in acknowledgement, Jameson retreated to one of the arm chairs and sat heavily. His long legs were splayed out in front of him, his back leaned into the cushion. He stifled a yawn.

"Was it the same dream?" He asked finally.

"Memory," she corrected. "It can't be a dream. It feels too real."

Shifting in his seat, Jameson ran a hand down his face and glanced away before answering, "Alright, Cass. Was it the same memory?"

"Yeah." She bobbed her head. "It was exactly the same. I wake up in the trunk of a car. My hands are tied together. Someone... someone hurt me. I keep screaming."

Leaning forward, Jameson braced his forearms on his knees. Those electric blue eyes of his flitted across her face before settling on the floor. His hands clenched into fists before releasing to smooth along his thighs.

"It sounds like a nightmare," he murmured. "I think you should try to forget it."

"I know."

Reaching for her water again, Cass brought it to her lips and sipped slowly this time. He always said that. When she replaced the glass on the table, her eyes drifted to the picture. Apparently, Jameson followed her gaze.

"Eli loved you," he spoke quietly. "He'd never've let anyone tie you up and throw you in a trunk. And if someone had done that to you in real life, then he would've killed them for it."

"I wish I could remember him." Cass felt the familiar tears prick at the backs of her eyes. "What sort of teenage boy cares that much about an annoying little sister?"

"You guys grew up rough," Jameson stated flatly. "Your mom was... sick. She couldn't work so you guys were really poor. Eli took care of you. It was mostly just you and him."

"And you." Cass frowned slightly, thinking. Her eyes sought Jameson's face and she remembered all of the stories he'd been telling her. "He got recruited to play football at your private school. Then he had you too. You were best friends."

"Eventually," Jameson admitted, dipping his head. "But Eli still took you everywhere with him. You rode the bus together, you sat through his football practices, you went to every one of his games, and not because you always wanted to."

"Because it wasn't safe at our home," she supplied.

They'd had this conversation so many times already; she had Jameson's answers memorized.

"Eli *felt* like your apartment wasn't safe," Jameson qualified. "But that doesn't mean it was actually dangerous. So… this thing in your head that you think happened, it's just a nightmare. A really vivid bad dream. You've got to push it out of your mind. You've got to stop thinking about it."

"But…"

"Look." Jameson stood abruptly. "I've got a meeting first thing in the morning so I can't stay up any longer. You want to take my bed again? I'll stay on the couch."

Tipping her face up to watch him, Cass's brow furrowed and she nibbled at her lip. They'd had this conversation before, too. She knew the outcome.

"Yeah," she said finally. "Thank you."

Tilting back in his black office chair, Jameson shut his eyes and let loose a tired breath. His knee bounced under the conference table. The smell of coffee drifted beneath his nose.

"Is it ready, yet?" Jameson asked, he didn't bother opening his eyes.

"Do I look like your personal secretary?" Uriah grumbled.

The guy was slumped facedown on the tabletop, his forehead pressed into the mahogany surface. They were the only two people in the meeting room, the others hadn't arrived, yet.

"No, if I had a secretary, she'd be way prettier than you," Jameson countered.

Straightening up in his chair, Jameson began to swivel slowly side to side. He needed coffee. He needed it bad.

With each twist of his seat, the chair gave out a long

squeak. The sound made Uriah grimace, but Jameson ignored him.

"Let me guess…" Uriah spoke finally, turning his face to one side. "Your secretary would have curly brown hair, big green eyes, and an ass that…"

"Don't." Jameson stilled in his chair and frowned. "Say it."

Grinning now, Uriah gave him a quick wink before shoving off the table and settling back into his own chair. The guy looked like hell. His golden hair was disheveled and there were bags under those smug brown eyes of his.

"You're lucky I'm too damn tired to call you out on your bullshit," Uriah commented dryly. "Speaking of which, you don't look so spry this morning. Have another late night visitor?"

Pursing his lips, Jameson's gut churned. Late night visitor? Yeah. Cass had come to him again, knocking on his door and making him have war flashbacks like no other.

But it wasn't something that he could tell Uriah about. Hell, it wasn't something he could tell anyone about.

"Baby still got you up?" Jameson deflected. The only way to throw Uriah off these days was to bring up his kid.

"Uhhhhhh," Uriah groaned and ran a hand down his face. "Ian won't sleep. He's eight months old and he's still awake all night long. I don't think I'm going to make it. If the sleep deprivation doesn't get me, Lena will. I'm pretty sure she's tried to smother me in my sleep a few times."

Shaking his head, Jameson shut his eyes and rocked back in his chair. Mission accomplished. For the next undetermined amount of time, Uriah would spew information about his kid. He'd debate the color of poop, the volume of spit up, and lament the use of cloth diapers.

It was a far cry from the respected Commander who shouted orders, strategized ops, and now ran an entire city. Of course, the lack of sleep didn't make Uriah any less formidable. If anything the guy was even more of an asshole.

Lack of sleep could do that to you; lack of sleep and a crappy personality. Not that Jameson minded. If he was being honest, he actually kind of loved the guy.

A knock at the door had Jameson's eyes flying open and Uriah biting off his words.

Throwing Jameson a quick glance, Uriah ran a hand back through his hair before straightening up in his chair. Jameson remained leaning back in his, but stopped with the incessant rocking. Folding his arms across his chest, he composed his face and waited.

"Come in," Uriah called and the door pushed wide.

The smell of coffee grew stronger as a line of men filed in. Each one clutched a steaming hot mug in his hands. Some had stacks of papers tucked under their arms, others did not. They were all soldiers, all men who had served under Uriah in one capacity or another, and had gained his trust.

There were five men in total and as they settled into their seats around the long conference table, Jameson watched them all.

Following close behind them was another man, but this

one was carrying a small tray. On it, were two ceramic mugs, a small mason jar filled with cream, and a tiny bowl of white sugar. The corner of Jameson's mouth twitched at the sight of it, but he immediately suppressed his reaction.

In this room, he was a stone cold observer. He had no weaknesses. None. At least, none that he could show.

"Good morning gentleman," Uriah said as the tray was set on the table in front of him. "How are we today?"

As a chorus of typical responses sounded, Jameson waited for Uriah to snag his coffee first. The guy drank the stuff black, so the moment he removed his mug, Jameson pulled the entire tray over in front of him and picked up the jar of cream.

Ignoring Uriah's frown (coffee is meant to be drunk straight, not full of girly fluff) Jameson poured in the cream with one hand and spooned in heaps of sugar with the other. He wanted this cup to taste like a shot of candy laced with adrenaline. Screw drinking it black, that crap was bitter.

"Any problems overnight?" Uriah asked.

"None," Jones responded. Shuffling through his stack of papers, he pushed a handwritten report across the table. "All patrols came back clear. The woods are quiet, not a lot of movement lately."

Listening distractedly, Jameson lifted the coffee to his lips and suppressed a sigh. So good. It was so freaking good and so freaking necessary after last night. His back ached from sleeping on his own couch, and his conscience ached from being such a lying piece of shit.

"Alright." Ducking his head Uriah studied the paper for a minute before moving on. "What about the interior? Hernandez?"

"A few of the typical complaints." Hernandez handed over his own sheet of paper. "Nothing serious. Some minor theft. No assaults."

"Can you handle it at your level?" Uriah's brow furrowed as he read. "We'll need a judicial system of some sort eventually. Maybe we can select a panel of people to review the more serious disputes."

"I'll put some feelers out in the community and get back to you." Hernandez bobbed his head.

"Speaking of community…" Uriah cleared his throat. "My weekly meeting with several of the more vocal members is scheduled for later this afternoon. Is there anything I should be aware of?"

"Well, we've got some more people talking about leaving," Hernandez supplied. "The weather is getting better for travel again, so I think we'll be seeing this more and more."

Uriah frowned. "Are you still collecting their names?"

"Yes, Sir." Hernandez peeled off another few sheets of paper and slid them over. "We need to start the survival classes again, to give them a fighting chance."

"Agreed." Uriah grumbled as he scanned the list of names. "Jameson, that's your department."

Nodding his head, Jameson set his coffee down on the table and leaned forward. This development was nothing new. Before winter had set in, they'd had several groups of people talk about leaving. It was only natural.

They wanted to set out on their own, escape the confines of the Wall, track down old friends and family members if they could.

It didn't matter to them that it wasn't safe. It didn't matter to them that the world as they'd known it no longer existed. They'd been trapped inside the refugee center while the world around them had burned so they didn't really know what it was like.

You could tell them about the devastation. You could try to describe the fires, the lack of electricity, housing, fuel, food, and general lawlessness, but in the end it didn't dissuade as many people as you'd think. So, Jameson had put together a series of classes.

He and a few other soldiers taught basic survival skills. How to start a fire. How to build a shelter. Self-defense, hunting, food preservation, things like that.

And just five short months ago they'd let seventy-three people walk out of the Wall and into the wilderness. Some of them were women, although the vast majority were men. Without cell phones or the internet, there was no way of knowing what became of them. Were they okay? Were they dead?

Jameson's eyebrows raised as Uriah slid a single sheet of paper in his direction. The next soldier was already giving his report and the others were listening quietly, although their eyes followed their leader's movement.

Reaching out, Jameson tugged at the paper, but Uriah

kept his hand splayed across the page for an extra beat. His index finger gave a purposeful tap on one name in particular before he lifted his hand and removed it to his own lap.

Jameson's eyes danced up to Uriah's face for a moment, but the guy remained focused elsewhere. He was listening to the next report now, and opening his mouth to ask questions. Everyone was moving on.

Gathering the paper in front of him, Jameson's eyes narrowed as he read the name Uriah had indicated. His chest tightened. What in the…?

Blinking hard, Jameson's jaw ticked as he read the name again. *Cassandra Roe.* Cass. Holy shit, she'd signed up to leave.

Swallowing thickly, Jameson breathed through his nostrils. After everything that had gone down, after everything he'd done, Cass was now planning on walking away from the safety of the Wall and straight into hell.

It was all Jameson could do not to crumple the sheet of paper into a tiny ball, set it on the table, and smash it with his fist.

Fuck. Now what?

RUNNING HER HANDS ALONG THE FABRIC, CASS SMOOTHED at the pattern of rich red colors. It was made up of scarlet and carmine and ruby. She didn't know why she knew the names of the exact shades, but she did. Everyone else who worked in the clothing shop just called them light red and dark red.

"Oh, I love that one," Mia cooed.

"I thought you would." Cass smiled to herself and pulled the bolt of fabric off the shelf.

Mia was standing on a raised platform in the middle of the room with strips of material hanging off of her delicate frame. She was the perfect model, the perfect roommate, and also Cass's very best friend.

As Cass approached with the bolt of new material, Mia's brown eyes twinkled. Her short bob of blonde hair brushed against her jawline as she tilted her head to one side and analyzed Cass. Mischief was written all over the blonde's face, so what she said next didn't come as much of a shock.

"So… you weren't in your bed this morning." Mia wiggled her eyebrows as Cass flushed and came to a stop in front of her.

"I had the memory again," Cass offered. "He slept on the couch."

"The couch?" Mia made a mournful face before huffing a breath that sent her blonde locks fluttering. "I swear, I don't know how you sleep in that man's bed without luring him into it. I mean… he's super hot."

Rolling her eyes, Cass set the bolt of fabric on the floor and pulled out her measuring tape. She loved working in the shop. It was the only clothing store inside the Wall and although most of the things that they carried came from one of the big storage warehouses, Cass was allowed to do custom designs. There was something about the hum of sewing machines, the snip of scissors and the pull of thread that calmed her.

"Trust me…" Cass's brow furrowed as she looped the tape around Mia's waist for the fifteenth time. "He's not interested in me that way."

"I don't know." Mia's lips pulled up into a smirk. "He seems pretty interested. You don't see how he watches you walk away."

"Mia." Cass sighed as she dropped the tape and stooped to pick up the fabric. "To you, everyone seems interested, and if I looked like you, then they probably would be."

Scoffing, Mia shifted her hips, causing the material already pinned to her body to sway. "We can always test your theory. You're coming with me to see the band tonight, right? We could dress up, turn some heads."

"And stumble home together?" Cass supplied.

Mia was all talk. She was supermodel gorgeous and the worst kind of flirt, but... she always went home with Cass. Beneath all the sassy talk, Mia was a complete sweetie.

"Hey." Mia swatted at Cass's shoulder. "It's not my fault you're the best pick of them all."

Smiling to herself, Cass kept measuring. And there it was, she thought, the soft center amidst all that confidence and swagger. Mia was a good roommate, and they'd gotten super close, since neither of them could remember the time before.

Shelby, their other roommate, had a few flashbacks here and there. Mostly they were snippets from her childhood, at least that's what she always said. But some of the other people they hung around with, Nolan and Levi and Maggie, they all remembered everything.

"That's all I need for now," Cass said. "You can get dressed."

Dipping her head, Mia turned away as Cass reached up to undo several of the pins that were holding the summer dress together. It would be so pretty when she was finished, she could already picture the final product in her mind.

Stooping to tuck the bolt of red cloth beneath her arm, Cass walked to the far side of the room and set everything down on a large drafting table. It was warm in this part of the shop, with material lining the walls and the sun shining through several skylights overhead.

Plucking up a piece of white chalk, Cass unrolled the red fabric and began making marks. She would use it as an accent. Some along the bottom edge of the skirt, a thin ribbon around the waist, straps that tied into bows over the shoulders.

"Have you asked him yet?" Mia came to stand beside Cass and played with a box filled with pins. They rattled around as she sorted through the different colors.

With a groan, Cass flicked her eyes over to her friend and then returned them to her work. "Not exactly, but I will soon."

"Cass." Mia clucked her tongue. "You've got to ask him."

"I know." Cass cleared her throat and fought the twist in her belly. "I will. It just hasn't been the right time. He already told me the name of the state and the city, so…"

"But the address is crucial," Mia reasoned. "Nolan says he can get us down to Southern California, but it's a really big area. If we're going to find your old house, then he says we have to get the address… and that's *if* your home is even still standing. Are you sure you want to do this?"

Pausing in her work, Cass squeezed the white piece of chalk between her fingers and closed her eyes. Did she want to do this?

Yes. No. It was complicated and dangerous and messy. She'd been told the world beyond the Wall was not safe. It didn't have electricity anymore and the people living on the other side were oftentimes violent. But…

Her brother was on the other side of that Wall. And something inside of Cass knew that he was alive somewhere. Something inside of her knew she had to find him. If she found Eli, then she'd find her memories. Cass was sure of it.

"Yeah," she exhaled the word finally and opened her eyes. "I've got to at least try. You don't have to come with me."

"Of course I do!" Mia exclaimed with a laugh. "You don't get to have an adventure without me. Besides I already signed us up. We're official. We're going."

A knock at the far door had both Cass and Mia looking up. They were shut in the back part of the store, where only employees and the occasional client went. Up front was the retail side, with racks and racks of clothes and shoes set out on display.

Anyone who lived inside the Wall could come and buy clothes here. Everyone was given a monthly allowance which Cass and her coworkers had to keep careful track of. They would pull the person's paper file and write the amount that was spent each time the person came in.

If the person worked a job, say at the farm or as a nurse, then they were allocated more credit to spend. Credits were paid out in the form of money, which was just a slip of colored paper with Uriah Linfield's signature on it.

"Come in," Cass called.

It was probably one of her coworkers coming back to use the machines or grab more stock for the front. They knew she had a client back here and wouldn't want to barge in with Mia half-dressed.

But when the door swung open and a familiar head poked in, Mia released one of her knowing hums. Cass nibbled at her bottom lip. It was Levi, one of the guys they hung around with a lot.

When he spotted them, Levi gave up a wide smile that had his dark eyes sparkling. Stepping further into the space, he kept one hand on the doorknob and ran the other over his short crop of black hair.

"Ladies," he said, before flicking a thumb back over his shoulder. "They said I could knock. I'm not interrupting, right?"

"No, no," Mia answered. Giving Cass's shoulder a quick squeeze, she crossed the room towards him. "We're all set. I was just heading out."

"Oh, alright." Straightening, Levi stepped aside and let Mia slide past him. "You both still coming tonight?"

"Wouldn't miss it," Mia called over her shoulder, and then she was gone.

Clearing his throat, Levi stepped further into the space and let the door swing shut behind him. He was a soldier, like so many of the other men living here, but he was off shift today. His hands found the front pockets of his blue jeans and as Cass ducked her head to study her work, he continued to stroll towards her.

"New project?" He asked.

"Yeah." Cass felt heat warm her cheeks as he came to a stop at her side. "A dress for Mia. It'll be summertime soon."

"Is it gonna be short?" He asked, and when she nodded yes, he laughed. "Nolan is gonna freak."

Furrowing her brow, Cass glanced up at him from her work.

"Why?" She asked. "She's going to be so beautiful in it."

Blowing out a breath, Levi scrubbed a hand over his short beard. For a few moments, he simply stared at her. The blush on her cheeks deepened, but this time Cass refused to look away. Levi dropped his hand and tapped his fingers against the edge of her work table.

"He likes her," Levi admitted finally. "And that dress is only going to increase his competition. That's all."

"Oh." Cass released a breath and dropped her eyes back to her work. "Everyone likes Mia."

"Not everyone," Levi mumbled.

Ignoring him, Cass finished up her chalk marks on the back of the scarlet fabric and set the entire piece to one side. Leaning up, she reached for her scissors and the box of pins. Levi watched.

"So, Nolan tells me you and Mia are looking to leave."

Glancing up, Cass caught his furrowed brow before she refocused on her work.

"Yeah," she confirmed before starting her first cut.

"You still can't remember anything?" He asked, maybe for the hundredth time.

"Nope." Her lips popped on the "p" sound.

She was getting pretty tired of that question actually. Especially since Levi and Nolan had all of their memories back. It was hard not to be a little bit bitter, and perhaps a lot frustrated.

"But you remember that you lived in California," he stated. "In Newport Beach."

"That's where Jameson said we lived," Cass offered, keeping her eyes trained on the silver scissors as they snip, snip, snipped their way through the material. It all felt so crisp and perfect in her hands.

"Jameson says," Levi repeated, using that tone that told Cass he wasn't happy.

"Yeah." Cass's eyes flicked up to scan his face before they darted back down to her work. "You don't like him?"

"No, he's fine. I mean, I don't interact with him much, but he's just…"

"Just what?" Setting her scissors down, Cass gave Levi her full focus.

"Nothing." Levi made a face and shook his head. "That's not why I came to see you anyway."

"Oh?" Cass's brow raised. "What's up?"

"I just wanted to see if you were really leaving." Levi shifted closer. "And to let you know that if you are, I'd like to come, too. If that's alright with you."

Cass pursed her lips and blinked up into Levi's face. After a moment, he grinned.

"Would that be okay with you?" He reached down to brush one of her curls back over her shoulder. "If I tagged along?"

"Um…" Cass swallowed.

Her throat was suddenly dry. Why was it dry?

"Sure," she answered finally. "The more the merrier."

THE BABY FELT HEAVY IN HIS ARMS. HOW COULD SOMETHING so little, feel so big?

Cradling Ian's head in the crook of his elbow, Jameson stared into the little guy's soft round face. He had dark hair like his momma and brown eyes like his daddy. But for now the kid's eyelids were blessedly closed, his pink lips were pouty, with a line of drool leaking out one corner.

Lifting his own head, Jameson eyed the exhausted couple sprawled on the other side of the room. Lena was sitting at her dining room table, shoveling food into her mouth with her bare hands, while Uriah was lying on the floor beside her feet. He was flopped onto his back on the beige carpeting with one arm flung over his eyes.

"I don't know what you two are complaining about." Jameson reclined on their sofa and grinned. "He sleeps just fine for me."

Lena's hand stilled on the plate in front of her as her

blue eyes swept up to shoot daggers at Jameson. Uriah's hysterical laughter could be heard bubbling up his throat.

"Oh my God," Uriah wheezed, his chest bouncing. "You're gonna die. She's gonna kill you, but then we'll have no way to make Ian sleep."

"I could strangle you," Lena growled, then glanced down at the array of nuts and stale bread piled on her plate. "But I'm too hungry to get up."

"Don't get up." Jameson shifted on the couch, propping both of his feet on the coffee table with a loud clunk.

Lena tensed and Uriah lifted his head in horror.

Ian didn't even stir.

"You guys are being too quiet around him," Jameson offered. "He can sense the tension."

"When did you become such a damn baby expert?" Uriah scoffed, and let his head flop back down to the carpet.

"It's a gift," Jameson countered. *And my mom made me volunteer at a children's hospital twice a week the second I turned fourteen. I've spent over four hundred hours holding babies and playing with sick kids. Practice makes perfect and all that.*

"I love you and hate you all at the same time," Lena murmured between bites. "Is that possible?"

"You aren't the first." Jameson let his eyes fall back to Ian's face. "And you won't be the last."

"Speaking of which..." Uriah groaned and pushed up onto one elbow. "The answer is no. I'm not blocking Cass from leaving."

An invisible hand pushed its way deep into Jameson's chest then, and gripped his heart. The beats it gave out became strained and slow. He could feel the thump… thump… thump, thudding against his ribcage.

"You're telling me this while I'm holding the baby?" Jameson's jaw ticked, but he fought to keep his breathing even, his arms relaxed.

"Absolutely." Uriah bobbed his head, his face serious. "I'm not the source, Jameson. I'm not in the business of locking people up inside this Wall, no matter how badly I would like to."

"I'm not saying for forever," Jameson gritted out. "I'm just saying there should be a rule about getting your memory back first. She doesn't know what's out there. She can't possibly be making a sound decision."

"It's been over nine months," Uriah continued, lifting a palm up placatingly. "If she doesn't have her memory back by now, then she may never get it. You want me to hold her here against her will?"

"Yeah." Jameson nodded his head. "That's exactly what I want you to do."

"Not going to happen." Uriah pushed all the way up to sitting and sighed. "I have enough on my plate with the community members as it is. I'm not going to prove them right and show them I'm some kind of evil dictator. You and I both know that would be a huge issue."

"But…"

"Right now people can walk in and out of that Wall

anytime they want. Unfortunately, that includes your little *not girlfriend.*"

Uriah's air quotes around those last two words had Jameson's eyes narrowing, but before he could open his mouth to speak, the guy kept talking.

"And look… she'll have to get the training like everyone else. You can oversee it yourself, and then she'll get to make her own decision after that. There's nothing you can do about it."

"Says the man who locked his own woman and sister up in his bedroom for three days," Jameson gritted out.

"That was different," Uriah scoffed and had Lena rolling her eyes. "This chick is neither your woman, nor is she your sister."

"Easy," Lena hissed. Kicking out with her little foot she nailed Uriah in the side.

"Ow." Grabbing his ribs, Uriah turned to glare at her over his shoulder.

"Your jerk level is at a ten right now," Lena pointed at him. "Tone it down, Linfield."

Sliding his feet off the coffee table, Jameson stood easily from the couch and glanced down at the baby in his arms.

"No. He's right. She's not either of those things to me," Jameson said. *More like a weird combination of the two, but whatever.*

Crossing the room towards Lena, Jameson studied Ian's features a little more. He was healthy and safe here, with a fleet of nurses, doctors and medical equipment to check and monitor his every milestone. The Wall, after all, had been a breeding facility first and foremost. Why would anyone in their right mind want to leave?

Because they weren't in their right mind. The answer came to haunt him as he thought of Cass, and what he might have to do to her… again.

"Alright Mommy." Jameson forced a grin and leaned down to lay Ian gently in Lena's waiting arms. "Your turn."

"Look what you did," Lena hissed at Uriah as she cradled her son. "Our baby whisperer is leaving because of you."

"Whatever." Uriah groaned and shoved to his feet. "Our baby whisperer is a pussy."

Closing the distance to his friend, Jameson cocked back his fist and gave the guy a solid thump in the chest. "Anyone ever tell you what a dick you are?"

"All the time," Uriah countered and with a quick shove he pushed Jameson towards his front door. "Tell Cass I say hi, by the way. Let's not pretend you're not going to hunt her ass down right this minute."

"Screw you, Linfield," Jameson mocked.

Wrapping his hand around the silver doorknob, he let himself out of the apartment, but was careful to close the door behind him with a soft snick. Not that it made any difference. He didn't get two steps down the hall before he heard Ian start to cry. Better get gone now, he figured, before Lena came charging after him.

Quickening his steps, Jameson fled Building One with its spacious family-style apartments and stepped out into the darkness. The air that hit him was crisp and icy. It might be springtime now, but they were situated firmly in the mountains of the north, and that meant there were many more cold nights still to come.

Stuffing his hands in the pockets of his jeans, Jameson listened to the tap, tap of his own boots hitting the concrete sidewalk. He'd spent the entire day assisting Uriah with his endless meetings and so Jameson's mind was still on overload.

Admittedly, it'd been hard to concentrate given the shock of the morning's information. Cass planning to put herself in danger (actually this shouldn't surprise him now that he thought about it) had sat front and center in his brain. The need to try to talk her out of it was so strong, he could feel that familiar panic working its way into his bones. Last time shit had blown up on him though... big time.

So when Uriah had finally been able to wrap things up, Jameson knew he had to play things with Cass differently, persuasively, covertly.

Before he could track her down however, Lena had shown up with circles under her eyes and a screaming baby clutched to her chest. She needed his help, so he'd grabbed a quick shower at his apartment, changed his clothes, and then hustled on over to her place.

By that time Uriah had brought them all dinner back from the cafeteria, and while Jameson had eaten one-handed, Lena had cried through a shower of her own before going face down in the bedroom for about an hour.

Ian snoozed easily in the crook of Jameson's arm the entire time.

Uriah, for his part, had passed out on the living room floor. He probably would've still been sleeping there except that Lena had "accidentally" tripped over his body on her way back to the dining room table. After that, Lena went back to sucking down snacks like a vacuum with a satisfied smile tickling her lips.

Shaking his head now, Jameson glanced up at the sky. It was bright tonight, with a big yellow moon and a scattering of stars. Maybe Lena and Uriah didn't realize it yet, but they were actually the perfect little family.

What they saw as never-ending chaos was actually just life. They were both healthy and together and in love. Their son was a strong little sucker with enough lung power to wail for hours on end. Back at the hospital where Jameson had volunteered, there'd been so many babies that could barely manage a few squeaks.

With a sigh, Jameson guided his steps towards the recreation building. Music floated through the air, punctuated every so often with the sound of laughter. There was a live band playing tonight and Uriah had given the okay to sell a stock of beer and wine out of one of the warehouses. He wanted people to relax into life here, and alcohol tended to help with that.

So, if patterns held true, Cass's little roommate, Mia, would've definitely dragged her over there. The tall blonde was a knockout, and with Cass by her side, the entire room would be salivating. Jameson was willing to bet money on it.

As he approached the front steps of the building, the deep strum of a base guitar spilled out. It was followed by the beat of drums, the chords from a lead guitar, and finally a man's voice singing. The band was good. Even Jameson had to admit it, though he wasn't big on music, not since the war.

Cresting the wide stone steps, Jameson yanked open one of the double doors and let the sound from inside invade the night air. The large room was dim, with just a few overhead lights shining down from the vaulted ceiling. People packed the space, talking, drinking, dancing. Laughter rippled everywhere, overwhelming and overpowering.

It stole Jameson's breath a moment.

If you would've asked him just last year if he'd ever see this sort of thing again in his life, he would've said no. Not just no, but never fucking ever. Music was dead. Women were dead. Dancing was dead. Life was dead.

But yet here it was. After the years of fighting, and killing, and starving, and surviving, here was a blast from the past like no other. A fucking party.

It was just like before. It was just like back in high school.

And just like back in high school, Jameson's eyes searched for Cass.

When they lit on her figure swaying to the music in the crowd, Jameson's whole body tensed. She was with Mia alright, and the two of them were taking turns spinning each other. Around and around and around. Cass's head was thrown back, the ends of her short flowery dress fluttering against her thighs.

God, she was pretty. She'd always been so damn pretty.

Rolling his shoulders, Jameson coached himself to relax. She was still here, safe and sound, and having fun. It was okay for her to have a little fun. That was how her brother had always played it back in high school.

Eli. Fuck. If only Jameson could go back.

Weaving through the crowd, Jameson headed for a long wooden table that was serving as a bar. It was backed into a corner with a few servers hustling around, grabbing bottles of beer from large coolers filled with ice. Slapping the bottles onto the table top, they'd wait for their customers to hand over a few Linfield Dollars and be onto the next person in line.

Jameson waited his turn behind several other guys. His fingers curled around a few bits of paper in his back pocket that served as money. Every so often, he threw a glance over his shoulder, searching for Cass. She slipped in and out of his view as the people crowding the dance floor shifted and swayed.

When he finally got his beer, Jameson found a long wall to lean back against. Pulling one foot up to rest against the wall, he brought the beer to his lips and took a long drink. It was icy and cold and fucking perfect. Hissing out a breath, he scanned the room once more and found her.

This time, she wasn't with Mia.

Clamping his jaw shut, Jameson's fingers curled tighter around the bottle in his hand. It was that guy Levi. He was standing over her, his hands on her waist, his face tipped down close to her. He was saying something, and she was listening.

There was a drink in her hand now where there hadn't been one before. Levi must have bought it for her.

How many had he already bought? How many drinks had the guy given her tonight?

Jameson's brow furrowed as the beer lingering on his own tongue turned sour. Levi Harris. He was a Nor Side soldier somewhere in his late 20s that had lived behind the Wall before the raid. Along with his many companions, his memory had been wiped clean by the source on its way out of existence.

But after a few months, like thousands of others, everything had returned to him. He had all of his memories back. He knew who he was, and who he'd been before, and what had happened to him. He was capable of working as a soldier again, so now Levi had a guard shift patrolling the community grounds five nights out of seven.

The guy didn't report directly to Jameson (because he was too high on the food chain for that) but still, Jameson knew everything about him.

Why? Well, because Levi hung around Cass like a damn dog.

And the other reason? The bigger reason? It was because the guy *claimed* that Cass had been his girlfriend. Levi Asshat Harris *claimed* that before Cass's memory got swiped, everyone had called her Sandy (not Cass) and she'd been happy to let good ole' Levi into her life *and* into her bed.

That tidy little "fact" alone had Jameson wanting to go all hulk smash on the guy. And in reality it's not like it would be all that hard. Levi was about five foot ten inches tall and maybe 170 pounds at the most. Jameson was a solid 240 pounds of muscle packed into six feet four inches of anger.

Hulk. Fucking. Smash.

But as much as Jameson liked to fantasize about picking Levi up and snapping him in two, he couldn't. Because if he did, then Cass would want to know why.

She'd want to know why her brother's old friend was stomping the shit out of her new little buddy. That's right... her buddy. Because Jameson wasn't the only one keeping a few secrets from Cass.

For all of Levi's claims of a relationship, he hadn't managed to confess any of them to Cass herself. So thankfully, he'd been friend-zoned for now. Cass was vulnerable, and Levi wasn't pushing it... yet.

Closing his eyes, Jameson blew out a slow breath and tried to calm himself. After all, watching Cass flirt with some other guy at a party was nothing new. In fact, Jameson had become pretty expert at it over the years.

Some big brothers are super protective, overly so. They regulate their sisters dating lives into non-existence. Unfortunately for Jameson, Eli had not been that kind of brother. He'd been the more reasonable kind, the fucker. If he was dragging Cass along everywhere he went, then he wanted her to have fun too… reasonably so. And if anyone liked to have a good time, it was Eli.

But for all of his partying ways, Eli did have a few rules. Cass was allowed to dance with guys as long as they weren't too grabby. She could have a couple drinks (no more than two). She could even sneak away and maybe make out a little, but absolutely no second base. If the guy's hands started to wander, then he was in for a beatdown.

Jameson had lived for the beatdown part, and he'd been more than happy to deliver on several occasions.

Opening his eyes now, Jameson rolled his shoulders again in an attempt to ease his tension. The beer in his hand came up automatically to his lips and he took a few long pulls. Swiping the back of his hand over his mouth, Jameson refocused his gaze on Cass.

She was looking up at Levi now, a smile blooming across her pretty face as he said something to make her laugh. Fuck that funny asshole, Jameson thought. But then she was glancing back over her shoulder.

Cass's mossy-green eyes flitted around briefly before settling decidedly on Jameson. She blinked once, slowly, before her brow furrowed.

Jameson's heart picked up the pace, pumping harder as he held perfectly still and let her look at him.

Tilting her head to one side, Cass narrowed her eyes a moment, then gave her head a little shake as if to clear it. Now it was Jameson who was frowning. Something was wrong.

Kicking off the wall, he stormed towards her through the crowd. She was pressing one hand to her forehead and squeezing her eyes shut. That dumbass Levi was letting go of her waist and plucking the drink out of her hand. He had no idea what was going on.

Shoving bodies out of his way, Jameson heard people all around him grunt and protest as he passed, but he didn't turn to look. He had to get to her. Something was wrong.

But even with all of his hustle, Jameson was too late. He was not three steps away when it happened. And before he could reach out to catch her, Cass's eyes rolled back in her head and she dropped like a stone to the floor.

THE GLASS BOTTLE FELT COLD IN HER HAND. THE ROOM FELT hot. Tilting her head up to peer into Levi's face, Cass gave him a smile. This was the third beer he'd brought her...no wait, fourth?

The drink had tasted bitter at first, but it wasn't so bad anymore. Nope. It wasn't as hard to drink now. The liquid just slid right down her throat, leaving her feeling bubbly and light.

"You gonna share that one with me?" Levi teased, he had to raise his voice to be heard over the music.

Laughing, Cass pressed the bottle to her lips and sipped quickly. She felt good. This was fun.

Nolan had swept Mia further into the thick of the crowd. From this position, Cass could just see them dancing. He had his arms around her body, holding her close as she flipped her short hair and rotated around to give him her back. Shooting a look over her shoulder, Mia's eyes twinkled as she spied Cass.

Raising her beer in the air, Cass gave Mia a flirty wink. With a shake of her head, Mia rotated around again and shouted something over the crowd. Cass couldn't hear a word she said, so she laughed.

Rolling her eyes, Mia pointed a finger at something behind Cass and mouthed the words slowly... *Don't. Look. Now.*

Frowning, Cass glanced over her shoulder in the direction Mia had indicated, and froze. Blinking, she stared at Jameson. He was leaning back against a far wall, his white t-shirt spreading over his broad chest, one leg kicked back, a beer in hand.

He was so causal and so cool and so hot all at the same time. And he was staring. He was staring right at her. Cass's belly flipped and uncertain tingles shot to her fingertips.

This wasn't the first time he'd made her feel this way. And this wasn't the first time he'd looked at her like that.

Giving her head a little shake, Cass felt a painful throb in her temple. When she narrowed her eyes at Jameson, the room changed.

Jameson was still standing against a wall, a white t-shirt on, a beer in his hand. But this time, he wasn't alone. Nope. He was younger, a bit thinner in body and fuller in the cheeks. And he was surrounded by pretty teenage girls. Because he was in high school. They all were.

Pressing her hand to her forehead, Cass gasped. Then

the memory swallowed her up and all the pain in her head was gone.

"THAT'S YOUR SECOND DRINK RIGHT?" ELI ASKED.

He was standing just beside her, his large hands splayed over the granite counter top as he nodded his head towards the drink in Cass's hand. Lifting the red solo cup to her lips, Cass hid her smile. It was her third actually and it tasted pretty awful.

Eli narrowed his eyes as she slowly sipped, but he didn't say anything. They were standing at the center island in a massive kitchen in some rich kid's house. A vast array of half drunk liquor bottles were spread along the granite surface in front of them and the kitchen was filled with people.

Music pumped from the living room next door. Girls giggled. Guys laughed.

"Yes," she answered finally, after setting the cup back down. "It's my second drink."

"That's the last one then." Eli elbowed her gently in the ribs before lowering his voice and whispering in her ear. "I'm gonna do a little shopping, so don't worry okay? You've just got to buy me some time."

Shopping. That's what Eli liked to call it.

Ducking her head, Cass eyed the empty backpack wedged between their feet. Eli kicked it with the toe of his shoe so that it crumpled further in on itself. When he said "shopping" what he actually meant was stealing. He was going to sneak into this rich kid's pantry when no one was looking and take as much food as he possibly could without getting caught.

Because...?

Because they were actually that poor. Or maybe because Eli was just that proud. He could've told Mr. and Mrs. Jameson how empty their fridge was at their apartment. But he didn't. Without a doubt Garrett's parents would have fed them dinner tonight.

Hell, the Jamesons already had them over to dinner three nights a week. But no. Eli was all about handling it himself. He didn't like charity. He liked to earn it, or he liked to steal it.

And since it was nearing the end of the month, the time to steal was now. Eli worked a few hours each weekend at the liquor store near their apartment, but the money from that had already run out.

So here they were, about to stock up again. And with the kitchen being as crowded as it was...it was up to Cass to run interference.

With a sigh, she let her shoulders sag a moment. She was tired and hungry. Neither of them had eaten since lunch was served at their school earlier in the day and her brain was getting all fuzzy from drinking alcohol on an empty stomach.

Eli nudged her side with his elbow again. He was getting impatient. Garrett wasn't in the kitchen right now so undoubtedly Eli felt this was the best time to execute his plan.

Lifting her gaze, Cass swallowed down her embarrassment and plastered a fake flirty smile on her face. She stuck her cup straight up in the air and glanced around the kitchen.

"Who wants to dance with me?!" She squealed, and was rewarded with a round of girly hooting from the crowd.

As the kitchen emptied of partygoers, Cass lingered beside her brother, cup in hand. Someone was already turning the music up in the living room next door. The speakers were pumping so hard that the air was vibrating all around them.

Stooping to pick up the backpack, Eli's usually easygoing expression was replaced by something harder, angrier.

Varsity quarterback. Life of the party. Homecoming King. Thief.

"Watch yourself," he warned, and shooed her out the door. "Garrett's on guard duty now, and you know he thinks of you like a sister too. Don't get anyone's ass beat tonight. Okay?"

Grumbling at the thought, Cass lifted her cup in salute before shoving through the kitchen door and into the living room. The space was packed.

Long leather sofas and wooden end tables had been pushed up against the walls to make room for more bodies. Kids were dancing, drinks raised in the air, spilling drops all over the hand-scraped bamboo flooring and each other. Bodies were grinding against bodies. Hands were where they shouldn't be... lips were, too.

Pausing a moment, Cass stood still and let her eyes travel the room. Everyone was having so much fun, like they didn't have a care in the world. Brushing one hand over her homemade dress, Cass worried the pale green fabric between her fingers. That's when she saw him.

Garrett was leaning against the opposite wall, a beer in hand, a harem of groupies hanging onto his every word. When he looked up and spotted her, Cass's tummy did that stupid flutter thing. She felt her whole body tingling as heat rushed into her cheeks, turning them pink. Ducking her head, she tucked an impossibly curly hair behind one ear and moved into the crowd.

Garrett was handsome. He was good looking and kind and popular. He had his own car, was the captain of the football team and was a really good running back on top of it. He had these killer blue eyes, thick brown hair, and was completely 100% not interested in Cass.

He was her brother's best friend, and he thought of her like an annoying little sister. It damaged her already fragile ego like no other.

"Hey, you're Cass right?" A boy from another school stepped into her line of sight and stopped with a grin.

"Yeah." Cass flashed him a smile and sipped her drink.

The whiskey and soda burned on the way down. All around them, bodies swayed.

"You wanna dance or what?" He asked and when she gave him a nod, he pulled her in close.

Rotating in his arms, Cass rubbed her body against his, and let him rub his body against hers. The speakers thumped, causing her ears to hum and her heart to match the fast beat. She tipped her drink back and chugged this time. The boy laughed. Cass's smile widened.

Before long his hands were roaming. He put his lips to her neck and kissed her skin, then sucked. Cass grabbed his shoulder with one hand and tried to brace her drink with the other, but ended up spilling all over the floor. She let him kiss her and she let him touch her.

She enjoyed the fact that he so obviously liked her. That was good enough, right? It didn't matter that she didn't tingle under his touch.

"Yeah, that's gonna be enough of that," Garrett's voice boomed loud just over Cass's shoulder.

Turning her head, Cass was just in time to see Garrett reach a giant hand down between them and shove the guy she'd been dancing with to the floor. Said guy tumbled into about three other people on his way down, causing the room to gasp and partygoers to scatter.

"What are you doing?" Cass seethed as embarrassment flooded her.

"Nope." Garrett gave his head a shake and grabbed her hand. "You know the rules. That asshat was crossing the line. Let's go."

"Garrett," Cass growled as he tugged her towards the kitchen. "You're overreacting! That wasn't even close to second base."

"That was grabby as fuck," Garrett countered. "It's time to go. Where's Eli? He in the kitchen?"

Cass's stomach dropped and a line of sweat beaded on her brow. Her brother had to be done by now, right? She'd been out here a long time, hadn't she?

The one person Eli would absolutely not want to catch him stealing was Garrett. Her brother would die before he let Garrett know Eli couldn't take care of them. Eli was so full of pride.

"Come on," Garrett urged, refusing to let go of her hand.

"No, Eli's not in there," she claimed, as Garrett came to a stop at the door to the kitchen and twisted the knob.

Cass's heart leapt into her throat. The door swung wide.

But then there Eli was, making out with some redheaded girl he'd shoved against the refrigerator. Cass's eyes quickly dropped to the black backpack resting on the floor by her brother's feet.

It was full now. It was zipped up tight and completely full.

Thank God. Relief catapulted through Cass's system. They had more food. She could eat. She felt a little lightheaded at the thought.

"Yo." Garrett let go of her hand and snapped his fingers in the air at Eli. "Let's go, man. Party's over."

Breaking his kiss with the girl, Eli leaned back and flashed Garrett a wide grin. "You're such a buzz kill, Jameson."

"Yeah, yeah, yeah." Garrett crossed his arms over his chest. "Your sister thinks so, too."

"That right?" Shoving back from the redhead, Eli grabbed his backpack and hefted the thing over his shoulder. "You good, Cass?" He asked, his eyes communicating his success. "You alright?"

Huffing out a breath, Cass watched the other girl straighten her dress and walk away with a smirk.

Beside her, Garrett jabbed an elbow into her side before repeating, "Cass, you alright?"

"I'm alright," she sighed. "Thanks to you two jerks, I'll always be just alright."

"YOU ALRIGHT?" JAMESON'S VOICE BROKE AS HE LEANED HIS face in close to Cass.

He was on his knees in the middle of the floor with her limp body pulled onto his lap. The band had stopped playing, people had stopped dancing, and a small circle had formed around them.

"She just passed out or something," Levi murmured.

When he reached in to lay a hand on Cass's face, Jameson shoved him away.

"No shit, moron," Jameson bit out. "Did you give her something?"

"What?" Levi was crouching down next to them, with Mia pacing just behind him.

"Did you slip something into her drink?" Jameson gritted out. This guy had a death wish, seriously.

"What?" Levi was incredulous. "No way. Where would I even get that stuff? It's after the war remember?"

"Fuck," Jameson spit out the word and let his eyes fall back to Cass's face. He'd forgotten.

She'd been dancing one minute. Laughing and drinking and flirting with the idiot. Then the next second, she'd dropped to the floor and taken years of Jameson's life with her.

Pressing two fingers to her throat, he assured himself for the fifth time that she had a pulse. He could feel the steady beat beneath the pads of his pointer and middle finger. As her lips drew in air, he sucked in oxygen too.

She was breathing. Her heart was beating. She was alive, just unconscious. This wasn't the first time in his life that Jameson had checked Cass for a pulse. He tried to push the memory away.

"Cass, you alright?" Jameson cleared his throat as a tremor snaked into his voice.

When she stirred in his arms, her forehead scrunching, her body turning, he exhaled in a whoosh.

"I'm alright," she mumbled, her eyes were still closed. "I'm always just alright."

"Thank God," Mia squeaked, drawing Jameson's eyes up to her.

People all around them began murmuring and shuffling. Then that Levi idiot had the nerve to smile.

"Who's on shift tonight?" Jameson barked at him, and caused the guy to frown. "Who's working patrol?"

"Uh..." Levi glanced around the room at the gawking crowd before narrowing his eyes on Jameson. "Randy, I think."

"Good." Jameson huffed a breath as he worked one hand under Cass's knees while keeping the other beneath her upper back. Hoisting her in closer to his chest, he rocked up onto his feet. "Go get him. Tell him to wake the on-call doctor and meet me at the med center."

"Uh…" Levi continued to stare dumbly as Jameson held Cass in his arms.

"I think the words you're looking for are: *Yes, Sir,*" Jameson supplied, shooting the guy a glare.

Levi was just a low level grunt in the Linfield Army, Jameson was an Officer sitting at its head. When Jameson said jump, this guy should be touching the fucking ceiling.

"Uh, right." Levi nodded, seeming to come back to himself. "Yes, Sir."

Before the guy had a chance to scurry off, Jameson began stomping his way towards the exit doors with Cass held in his arms. The crowd parted for him, and after a beat, Mia jogged ahead of them to hold open one of the large double doors.

With Cass just beginning to stir, Jameson pushed out into the moonlight.

When the crisp night air hit the bare skin of his arms, Jameson clutched Cass a little tighter to his chest. She was murmuring now, and as he glanced down into her face, her mossy-green eyes fluttered open and locked on his.

"Garrett?" She croaked.

He nearly tripped and fell right then.

He hadn't heard someone call him by his first name in years. It had his gut twisting and his throat wanting to close up on him. Did she remember what happened? How much?

Forcing himself to remain upright, Jameson puffed out air. He pointed his feet towards the medical building and worked to compose himself. After a few beats of silence, he glanced down at her briefly and answered.

"Yeah, Cass? You had us all scared back there. You feeling okay? Anything hurt?" Swallowing the lump in his throat, Jameson kept walking.

"Did you know?" She whispered.

Her hands came up to his chest, her fingers clutching at the fabric of his white t-shirt as her body sagged in his arms.

"Did I know what?" He asked carefully, his heart hammering.

"About Eli," she said and turned her face away from him. "Stealing the food."

For a second, Jameson swore his heart stopped beating. She remembered that? *Shit.*

Sucking in a long breath, he blew it out slowly as his legs kept pounding the ground. Behind him, he could hear Mia struggling to keep up in those high heels of hers. They were crossing a wide stretch of lawn now, the medical building was just coming into view.

But Cass remained limp in his arms as he walked. She wasn't wriggling. She wasn't fighting like a cat to get away. She was embarrassed, yes, but she wasn't angry. So she hadn't remembered *everything*… at least not yet.

"Stealing is a strong word," Jameson admitted finally.

"So you knew," she croaked.

Everyone knew. Why do you think it was so easy for you to clear out a kitchen?

"He was hungry, Cass," Jameson murmured. "You were both hungry."

By the end of Senior year, any kid that gave a party made sure to stock their pantry with extra food. They'd of given their star quarterback anything he wanted, all Eli would of had to do was ask. But Eli had always been too full of pride. So every kid at that school looked the other way while he took the food that they all bought just for him.

So was that stealing? Nah. And anyway, Eli had earned it. He'd given their school the championship they'd wanted three years in a row. The least they all could do was feed him some nights.

"Did he ever find out?" Cass asked quietly. Her brown curls bounced as Jameson walked. He tried not to stare. "That you knew?"

"No." Jameson frowned. "And it's nothing to be ashamed of Cass. Now what else did you remember? Tell me everything."

"There was a party," she said and shifted in his arms. "You can put me down, by the way. I think I can walk."

"Not a chance. Now tell me what else," Jameson huffed and gripped her tighter.

The last time he'd held her like this, she'd been screaming her hate for him. He wanted to replace that memory with this one, even though he knew it was selfish.

"You were there, watching me," she admitted. "I was dancing with someone else."

"You're gonna have to be more specific than that." Jameson smiled. "That happened a lot."

"Eli was in the kitchen, taking food." She sucked in a ragged breath. "You pushed the guy I was dancing with, and he fell. You made us leave."

"Hmmm." Jameson crested the stone steps of the medical building and came to a stop at the darkened doors. "That happened a lot, too. Did I wail on the guy or just slam him down?"

"Seriously? How many of my dates did you beat up?" Cass huffed a sassy breath and pushed her hair out of her face. "And you can put me down now, this is ridiculous."

There she is, he thought. And for the first time in half an hour, Jameson felt like he could breathe. The tightness in his chest loosened and he almost sighed. Cass was okay, like she was *really* okay.

Off in the distance, a few figures came jogging into view. Jameson squinted his eyes as the three bodies rounded the corner of an apartment building and headed their way. That must be the on-call doctor, and the soldier on duty... Ronald? Randal? And someone else, probably Levi.

Staggering up the steps now, Mia clutched her black heels in one hand and gave Cass a once over.

"How're you feeling?" Mia's brow furrowed as she held her free hand out between them. "How many fingers am I holding up?"

"Stop." Cass batted the hand away and then glared up at Jameson. "Put. Me. Down. This is embarrassing. I'm fine. I just passed out."

"And had a memory," Jameson qualified. "You're getting checked out."

"You remembered something?!" Mia squealed and clapped her hands together as her heels clattered forgotten to the ground. "That's amazing! Yay! What was it?"

Sighing, Cass covered her face with her palms. "I was at a party with my brother in high school. That was it. Nothing special."

"Ooohhh, I want one too," Mia whined. "What do you think triggered it?"

Cass's eyes flitted up to Jameson's face a moment before dropping to his chest. A faint pink tinged her cheeks, but then she was glancing away again.

"I don't know," she mumbled finally.

Shifting her around in his arms, Jameson fought the burn in his muscles and the curl in his belly. It was him. He was the common link. He'd been standing in the room with her when she'd dropped and he'd been in her memory too.

He only wished he could see exactly what she'd seen.

He only wished he could undo some of the things he'd done.

But then the three figures from far off were cresting the wide stone steps and puffing out oxygen. Jameson's initial assessment had been correct. There was the on-call doctor

(Collette something), the clinger (Levi), and one of the patrol guards (Randy something).

The doctor and Levi were up the steps and fluttering all over Cass in less than a second, while Randy pulled a set of master keys from his pocket and unlocked the medical center doors. It was all Jameson could do not to step back and take Cass out of their reach.

"Let's bring her into exam room one." Collette motioned Jameson though the doors first and then kept pace behind him. "It's further down on the right."

The sound of shoes squeaking on linoleum filled the empty hallway. Someone was flipping on overhead lights as they went. Off to the left, there was a receptionist area with a series of empty chairs and short tables piled with old magazines. On the right, was a length of blank white wall. Then doors started popping up.

Jogging around him now, Collette pushed open one tall door and held it wide. Turning his body sideways, Jameson hefted Cass through the threshold as she swatted at him and muttered in protest.

There was a padded blue table along the back wall, and so Jameson headed for it as Collette flipped on another light.

"Just set her right there," the doctor instructed.

Laying Cass carefully on the table, Jameson found he couldn't help but grin as she continued to glare up at him. She had her arms folded across her chest and her brows pulled tight. Behind him, Jameson could hear the running water of a sink, the washing of hands, and the shuffling of feet.

"This is unnecessary," Cass hissed, and made the layer of disposable paper beneath her crinkle when she tried to sit up. "I'm fine."

"I'll be the judge of that," Collette announced. "Now, the rest of you… out."

"What?" Jameson's own brow furrowed as his gaze snapped to the doctor.

She was collecting instruments from a wooden drawer by the sink, a blood pressure cuff, a stethoscope, one of those light things they use to look in your ears. Glancing up at him, she made a shooing motion. That's when Jameson noticed Mia and Levi lingering near the door.

"You heard me," she stated. "Everybody out."

Snapping his jaw shut, Jameson exhaled through his nostrils as he stalked out of the room. He hadn't realized Mia and Levi had both crowded in as well. It was good Cass had friends, he reminded himself. Mia was fine of course, but that Levi idiot hanging around was a bit harder to swallow.

When the exam room door closed behind them with a click, Jameson found himself in a deserted hospital hall-way. Mia, Levi and Randy were all standing there, too. Waiting.

Turning to Randy, Jameson tipped his head towards the entrance.

"Go do another sweep," he instructed. "Then come back to lock up when we leave."

"Yes, Sir." Randy bobbed his head like a good little soldier and scurried out.

"You can leave, too." Jameson turned his attention to Levi. "Go back to the music, or whatever. I'll get her home."

"Not a chance... *Sir*." Levi shook his head as he tipped back to lean against the opposite wall. "She was with me at the party, I want to make sure she's okay."

"That's right..." Jameson took a giant step closer to Levi and cocked his head to one side. "She *was* with you when she fell. How many drinks did you give her?"

"Not enough to make her pass out," Levi countered. Rolling his eyes, the guy ran a quick hand back through his raven-black hair.

Beside him, Mia cleared her throat and nibbled on her bottom lip. Her chocolate-brown eyes danced between the two men. Her hands clutched her pair of black pumps again, she must have picked them up before coming inside.

Creeping even closer to Levi, Jameson folded his arms over his chest. This. Guy. He'd fed her alcohol and then let her melt to the floor like a puddle. He was right there and yet he hadn't even made a grab for her before she fell.

Suddenly it felt super crowded, like the hallway had shrunk all around them.

"Oh?" Jameson's brows raised. "And how many is that? Would you know?"

"Of course not," Levi sneered and shifted against the wall. "What's your deal? It's not like you're her boyfriend or anything."

"Yeah well, neither are you." Jameson's chest rose and

fell with his breathing. He kept his arms crossed, his muscles tense, his neck tight. *Don't hit this prick just yet. Keep it dialed in.*

Mia's mouth dropped a fraction as her gaze continued to flit between the two men. Jameson stared at Levi. Levi stared right back.

Bringing one slender hand up to cover her mouth, Mia cleared her throat a second time before backing a step. Her bare feet were silent on the flooring.

"You're trying to make me into some kind of bad guy here and I'm not," Levi protested. Putting his palms out between them he vented his frustration. "Cass and I were together before, and I just want to see if we can have that again. That's it."

"You were together?" Jameson spat, his mouth grew sour around the words. He'd heard the rumors, but never straight from the guy's lips.

"Yeah." Levi bobbed his head.

"Does she know that?" Jameson asked, quirking a brow.

Swallowing, Levi glanced to the side. His body sagged and his hands came down to tap against the wall behind him. After a beat, he shook his head *no*.

"What are you so afraid of?" Jameson hissed. "Why don't you want to tell her?"

"I just..." Sucking in a breath, Levi returned his gaze to Jameson. "I'd rather her remember everything on her own, okay? I'd rather not have to tell her myself."

"Tell me what?" Cass's voice came from behind them. It had both men jumping.

Glancing over his shoulder, Jameson eyed the doctor and Cass standing together in the hallway. The door to exam room one was still drifting closed behind them.

In the silence, Mia cleared her throat for a third time. It was becoming quite the annoying habit.

Stepping to one side, Jameson unfolded his arms and focused his attention on Collette. Before Levi had a chance to shove his foot further into his own stupid mouth, Jameson released a barrage of questions.

"That was quick. How is she? Everything check out alright? Is the brain scan next? Will you do an MRI?"

Holding up her hands, the doctor shook her head and frowned. "Cass is fine. Her fainting spell is a fairly common side effect of regaining memory. I've seen it a lot over the past several months. There's no need for a scan."

"But it wouldn't hurt to have one done," Jameson countered.

"It's not necessary." Collette waved him off. "And to be honest we haven't turned that machine on since the electronics ban. I would need Commander Linfield to authorize it personally."

"Not necessary." Jameson sliced a palm through the air. "I can authorize it."

Rolling her eyes, Cass huffed a breath before stomping off. Dr. Collette took a step closer.

"That's right... *Officer* Jameson, you do have that sort of authority, don't you?" The doctor placed a soft hand on his forearm and held Jameson in place. "As it happens, I have several other things that need approving around here."

Stifling a groan, Jameson's eyes snapped to Cass as her figure retreated down the hallway. Her arm was linked through Mia's, but her steps appeared steady.

Beside the girls, Levi had both of his hands stuffed into the pockets of his jeans. He was telling them something, although what exactly he was saying was hard to make out.

"She'll be fine," Collette assured him quietly, seeming to track his gaze. "I treated her before her memory loss and Cass is perfectly healthy. She was cleared for breeding by the source. Believe me, if she had a brain tumor or cancer of any kind, we would know."

"Wait." Jameson frowned, as his focus returned to the doctor standing before him. "Breeding?"

"That's right." Collette heaved a tired sigh. "I believe Levi was her partner, from what I can recall."

Jerking his head up once more, Jameson's gaze shot right back down that hallway. He was just in time to see Levi holding the exit door open while the girls navigated through it.

Breeding. Cass. Levi. *Partner.*

The words slammed into his chest like punches, making him want to charge after the guy and beat the living shit out of him. Levi had been with Cass like that? Like they were trying to have a baby together?

The realization had Jameson's head swimming. Suddenly he was down right winded. Shit. It was like he could hardly breathe.

Beside him, the good doctor kept chattering away. If she noticed something was up, she didn't mention it. And that's when Jameson realized he was in the exact same position now that he'd been in before the war. Actually, scratch that. It was worse this time, because of what he'd done.

Jameson had no right to feel jealous over Cass. None. He'd sworn an oath to his best friend in the whole wide world. He'd made a promise to Eli, and just because that man was now gone, didn't make things any different. If anything, it made his promise that much more important.

Squeezing his eyes shut, Jameson exhaled a breath. Suddenly, it was like he was standing beside Eli all over again. In his mind, he could see the memory of them as boys together play itself out.

"I want to come to one of those parties with you, Garrett, but I'm not leaving Cass in that fucking apartment with Wendy," Eli said.

Eli always called his mother by her first name. It was Wendy. Never mom.

Because Wendy was sick with something a little different than cancer. Yeah, truth was, Eli's mother was a desperate drug addict. Any money Wendy got from the State went straight into her arm, or up her nose, or down her throat.

The only reason the three of them could keep their crappy apartment was because it was rent controlled. Wendy's government benefits were direct deposited there first.

"So bring her," Jameson suggested.

They were jogging along the track at the high school, puffing out air with about a hundred or so other seventeen-year-old boys.

It was football season, and Cass was parked on the bleachers doing her homework.

Jameson worked hard not to glance her way.

"But if she comes with me, I don't want her to spend the whole time nagging at me to leave," Eli reasoned. "So we've got to let her have a little fun, too."

Eli's eyes darted over to Jameson a moment before returning to the rough reddish astro turf beneath him. "Not too much fun," he continued. "Like we have to keep an eye on her, you know? She can dance and maybe have one drink."

"Yeah." Jameson huffed air before pursing his lips. Keeping an eye on Cass wouldn't be a problem. In fact, the issue was in trying not to look at her.

"'Cause I know you think of her like a little sister, too," Eli went on, his eyes popping back up to lock on the side of Jameson's face. "You'll protect her just like me. You'd never fuck that up, right? You swear?"

Keeping his arms pumping, Jameson swallowed the lump that wanted to form in his throat. It was like his whole body fought against the words he now had to say. His entire being knew they were fucking lies. But he had to do it. He had to make this promise, or risk losing them both.

After a beat, Jameson nodded his head and answered, "Yeah, she's like a sister to me, too. I'd never cross that line. Cool?"

With a fat grin spreading over his face, Eli ducked his head and replied, "Yeah. Cool."

HER HEART WAS HAMMERING IN HER EARS AS SHE RAN. HER black boots flew across the wooden floor of the kitchen, then down the narrow hall.

She hadn't meant to do it.

She hadn't meant to... but she'd done it just the same.

Letting loose a scream, Cass tore through the living room and slammed out the front door. She could hear him coming behind her. She could sense him gaining.

Overhead, a thick cloud of black smoke rolled through the sky. Her eyes scanned the neighborhood with its familiar line of two-story homes. They were all but abandoned now. There was nowhere to go. There was no one to help.

Adrenaline raced through Cass's system and kept her legs moving. She ran across the yellowish lawn, aiming for the cement sidewalk, though she wasn't entirely sure why. Instinct, maybe?

She had no plan.

She had only fear and rage mixing inside of her.

So when his arms wrapped around her body, when he lifted her so high up off the ground that her feet were cycling through the air, Cass let loose another scream.

"Let me go!" She cried out, her throat was raw from it. Her soul was raw from it. "Stop!"

Then she was scratching. She was tearing at his arms and thrashing her body and throwing her head back until it crunched against his flesh.

The last thing she heard was his grunt of pain.

Then she was falling. She was wriggling and screaming and rotating in the air and then the back of her head hit the gray cement. Hard.

After that, all the lights went out.

Sitting up in bed, Cass cradled her head in her hands. A new nightmare, or memory, or whatever. It had her chest heaving and her stomach rolling. It hurt. It felt so real that she physically hurt.

Rubbing at the back of her head, Cass reminded herself that it wasn't real. She hadn't just been knocked out cold from a fall. There was no crack in her skull. There was no blood.

With a groan, Cass glanced up to stare out her window. It was daylight. The sun was up in a pale sky filled with racing clouds. She'd slept in.

She couldn't remember the last time she'd slept in, but then she'd been out late listening to the band and drinking and dancing with Levi. Then she'd had the memory of the other party…

Oh yeah. That.

Drawing in a breath, Cass threw back the covers and climbed out of bed. Shaking her hands in the air, she tried to rid herself of the angry tingles still running through her system. It wasn't real.

Well, maybe it had been real, but it was over now. She was alive and safe right here behind the Wall.

A soft knock at her bedroom door had her glancing over her shoulder. Crossing to her small closet, Cass shrugged into her robe and cinched it around her waist. She was wearing her pajamas, but still, there was a coolness to the air.

"Come in!" She called finally and was relieved when it was only Mia who opened the door.

"Hungover much?" Mia groaned. Her hair was disheveled, her flannel pajamas wrinkled.

"Not bad," Cass admitted, as Mia pushed inside and flopped down on the bed.

"Lucky you. I feel awful." Mia groaned as she ran her hands back through her short hair.

"Hmmm, how many drinks did Nolan give you?" Cass questioned, strolling back to her bed, she took a seat beside Mia and looked her over.

"I don't know," Mia huffed, and rolled onto her side. "He was pretty upset when I left him there, too."

Frowning, Mia let her gaze hop up to Cass's face. "But I

wasn't going to just let them take you away. Not after you passed out like that."

Flushing at the memory, Cass brought her hands to her lap and twined her fingers together. Pretending to study them, she let the embarrassment wash over her. If she was going to have a memory, then why did it have to be right then? Why did she have to faint in the middle of a packed room with everyone watching?

"But hey, it had a plus side right?" Mia hoisted herself up and ran a hand down Cass's arm. "Not only did you remember something, but Mr. Hot Stuff himself was right there to swoop you up and carry you away."

"Ugh, don't remind me." Burying her face in her hands, Cass felt her already warm skin burning red.

She didn't know what was worse, the memory of her brother at that party or the memory of Garrett holding her. It was like she could still feel where his hands had gripped her. It was like she could still feel the steady beat of his heart in his chest. His extremely nice, extremely strong chest.

Ducking her head down to peek into Cass's face, Mia wiggled her eyebrows tauntingly.

"I don't know why you get so embarrassed," she commented. "He was the one refusing to let go of you. Plus, you should have seen him and Levi fighting over you in the hall. It was beyond sexy."

"They were not fighting over me." Cass's hands dropped to the bed and she gave Mia her best glare.

"Pffft." Mia waved her off before sitting up straight and flashing a knowing grin. "Yes, they were."

"Garrett is just super protective over me," Cass explained, thinking back to her memory of the party in high school. "He's like a big brother. He and Eli were best friends."

"Garrett?" Mia's eyebrows raised.

"Oh." Frowning, Cass gave her head a little shake. "That's what I called him then. Jameson is his last name."

"Riiight…" Mia drew out the word so it lingered in the air. "Well, you didn't see the look on Mr. Hot Stuff's face when Levi mentioned he was your boyfriend, or ex-boyfriend, or whatever."

Groaning, Cass slapped a palm to her forehead and flopped backwards onto the bed. She'd forgotten about that part, the Levi former-boyfriend part. After she'd been given the all clear from Dr. Collette, and Garrett had proceeded to jump down said doctor's throat, Levi and Mia had walked Cass back home.

That's when Levi had made his confession. They'd been together. It was during the war, they were both living inside the Wall, and according to him they had dated… exclusively. Try as she might, Cass couldn't remember any of it.

And when she'd looked at Levi, standing there under the stars, his hands reaching for hers, she didn't *feel* anything for him either. Nothing bad. Nothing good. Just… blah. Friendly blah.

"So are we going to talk about the part where he asked you to dinner?" Mia murmured.

"No. No, we are not."

Squeezing her eyes shut, Cass blew out a slow breath. That hangover feeling was actually starting to creep up on her now. Her stomach was rolling uncomfortably and her skin was feeling too hot. They'd slept past breakfast in the cafeteria, but if they left now they'd probably make it for lunch.

"What about the part where you said the word 'yes' like it was a question?" Mia teased.

Rolling to the side, Cass gave Mia a quick thump on the arm and had her yelping. She shouldn't have said yes to Levi, she knew that. But at the time he'd looked so hopeful and he was so nice, she just couldn't muster a no.

"Someday Miss Mia," Cass warned with a smile. "I'll be the one teasing you about guy troubles."

"Oooo." Mia cackled and rolled off the bed. "I hope that day is soon."

Six pairs of boots echoed in the massive bunker. Blowing out a breath, Jameson rubbed the back of his neck with one hand and tilted his head up. He'd seen it before, more than once, but still…

"All aircraft are accounted for, Sir." Hernandez gestured to the rows of helicopters, fighter jets and drones. "They should be fully functional, but of course we've never actually tried to fly them."

"Good." Uriah bobbed his head and moved off down the line.

The officers did this walk-thru once a month, but the pilot division came here daily. Per Uriah's instructions, they kept all aircraft clean and in working order. Once a week they were authorized to flip everything on briefly to make sure that it still worked. But that was it. They weren't allowed to fly them.

Uriah didn't want to draw attention to their position by

putting anything up in the air, not to mention that they had a limited supply of jet fuel. It's not like there was an oil refinery up and running ready to make more of the stuff.

Plus, nobody knew what was still out there in the rest of the world. The other refugee centers were supposed to have been constructed with the same plan and stocked with the same stuff, but were they? Uriah didn't know. None of them did.

And up until very recently, Uriah wasn't willing to risk finding out.

"The equipment I'm interested in should be somewhere over there." Pointing to the far wall, Uriah indicated row upon row of steel shelving.

Keeping pace beside him, Jameson frowned at the sheer magnitude of it all. The sturdy metal shelves reached almost to the ceiling and contained box upon box upon box of sealed equipment. It was all labeled and categorized, but still. The volume of items was overwhelming, and they were looking for just one box. Just one labeled PRC-511.

Coming to a stop, Uriah rubbed at his chin while one of the other soldiers hustled off to get the forklift. Jameson stood next to Uriah and sighed. Back when the source was still functional, the system had all been automated, driven by barcodes being entered into an electronic tablet. Now they were left to track everything down by hand.

"I just hope there's some of the older technology in there, too," Uriah murmured. "I don't want to use tablets and shit if I don't have to."

"You really think the source might be lurking around in

some computer somewhere?" Jameson turned to eye his friend. "Like if we turn it on, the thing might come back and somehow take over?"

"I don't know." Uriah shrugged as the forklift fired up several rows away. "But I'm not ready to chance it if I don't have to."

Nodding his head, Jameson began his slow search down the aisle to their right. Uriah took the one to their left and the other soldiers all split off in a similar fashion. PRC-511. PRC-511. Inside that box there should be well over two dozen military grade portable radios.

And not just the short range walkies they'd used back in Utah. No. These were the kind that came in a backpack with a foldable antenna you could set up. If they worked like they should, then they would extend Uriah's communications reach up to 500 miles.

That distance wouldn't quite get them to the old city in Utah, but it would definitely get them to the compound where Uriah's sister lived. And if they used that spot as a halfway point, then they could relay information down into Utah, no problem.

"Found it!" A voice called from several rows over.

Stopping short in his own aisle, Jameson scanned the containers before him as the forklift rumbled its way towards the other voice.

Ammunition, spare parts, weapons, survival equipment. Cocking his head, he took a step closer and ran his right palm over the yellow letters. Inside these boxes were water filters, flares, fire making kits. The people living here now didn't need these items, but any people leaving the Wall to strike out on their own could really use them.

Hmm. Jameson tapped a finger on one of the boxes. It was definitely something to think about. Maybe they should have a send-off pack. Maybe when a person wanted to leave, they should have the option of taking some of this stuff with them.

Stepping back, Jameson tipped his chin up and scanned the containers on the shelves above him. Surely there were some boxes filled with sleeping bags, pop-up tents, lengths of rope, canteens. Important stuff. He'd talk to Uriah about it, when he got a chance.

"Third shelf, seventh box from the left!" A soldier called, lifting his voice to be heard over the rumble of the forklift.

Smiling to himself, Jameson abandoned his aisle and followed the sound of the motor. It was still so damn beautiful. Whenever he heard the roar of the machine it had his chest filling and his feet tapping. He missed driving. He missed the smell of exhaust and the squeal of tires on pavement. He missed that part of humanity. The part they could never quite get back. Not in his lifetime at least.

No more cars were being manufactured. No more gas was being produced. They'd killed that knowledge. They'd killed that capability. It would take decades upon decades of hard work and education to get it back.

Thankfully, it was possible.

The source had compiled a library of textbooks in another

one of the warehouses, so all human knowledge hadn't been completely wiped off the planet. Uriah was working with some of the community members to organize a college of sorts, but that was on the back burner for now. Learning how to refine oil was just not as important as farming.

Food first, and all that.

"Whatever you do," Uriah called. "Do not drop that box."

As the tines of the forklift slid beneath the container, everyone held their breath. The soldier operating the machine hadn't dropped one yet, but still... there was always that chance. It wasn't until the box was set safely down on the concrete flooring that the forklift operator shut off the machine and leaned back in his seat.

Swiping a hand across his brow, the guy flashed them a quick smile.

"All good, Sir," he said. "Didn't even jostle it."

"Great." Uriah grumbled and strode towards the box.

Matching his pace, Jameson pulled a set of bunker keys from his pocket. While Uriah ran his hands over the dusty yellow letters, Jameson grabbed for the padlock and twisted the squat silver key inside it. With a click, the lock gave way and he pulled it free of the container and stepped back.

Pulling the top of the metal container open, Uriah's face lit when he spied what was inside. Bingo. It was just the technology he'd been expecting to see, all perfectly organized and awaiting use.

"Now." Uriah hefted one of the backpacks out and unzipped it. "We've got to see if it works."

"Are the batteries stored elsewhere?" Jameson asked. Reaching for an antenna, he rotated it in his hands.

"Oh yeah." Uriah's brow furrowed and his eyes jumped from the bulky box radio inside the pack to Jameson's face. "They are. Shit."

Just then the walkie talkie attached to Jameson's side beeped with an incoming call. Frowning, Jameson reached for it and held it up to his lips. Depressing the side call button, he gave the okay to proceed.

"Officer Jameson, this is Soldier Malpas at Entry Door Two," the soldier recited.

"This is Jameson, go ahead."

"Yes, Sir." Malpas drew in a breath. "I've got a vehicle on approach."

Shooting a look at Uriah, Jameson's brow furrowed. "Repeat that."

"Sir," Malpas again. "I've got a vehicle on approach at Entry Door Two… like a driving one… it looks like a Jeep."

"Are you taking fire?" Jameson asked.

"No, Sir."

"Then hold your fire, but keep them outside the Wall," Jameson instructed. "We'll come to you."

"Roger," Malpas recited and clicked off.

"Expecting anyone?" Jameson replaced the radio at his side and carefully wedged the antenna back in the box.

Huffing an indignant breath, Uriah zipped up the backpack he'd been holding and set it down. Of course he wasn't expecting anyone. They were never expecting anyone, especially someone with a functioning Jeep.

"Hernandez." Uriah's eyes jumped to one of the soldiers. "Lock all this up and put the forklift away. The rest of you, come with me. We've got a vehicle to inspect."

FLIPPING THE JEEP'S SUN VISOR DOWN, DAVEY TRIED TO shield his eyes. It wasn't that it was especially bright out, but the sun had managed to peek through the clouds at just the wrong moment. Now it reflected against the massive shining metal wall in front of him, making it hard to see, making it hard to focus.

"Everyone just play it cool," Cole was saying. He was slowing the Jeep down, keeping one hand on the wheel and the other on the shifter. "We'll just ask for Uriah and that should be it."

They'd broken free of the woods now and were entering the dead zone between the forest and the Wall. Here, the SUV was completely exposed. There was no cover, nowhere to hide. They were just bumping along straight towards a line of heavily armed soldiers who were guarding a large hole in the bottom of the perimeter wall.

It made Davey nervous. So many eyes, so many weapons, none of the protection their team usually traveled with.

"A lot can change in a few months," Liam commented. He was sitting in the back, one hand on his pistol, the other bracing against the empty middle seat. "When we left, there were thousands of people living here that couldn't remember their own names."

"What's that supposed to mean?" Hannah snapped.

Her tone had Davey glancing back over his shoulder. He was just in time to see her little fist lash out and strike Liam on the upper arm. At the impact, the deadliest guy in their crew cringed and managed to look apologetic. *Apologetic.*

It almost made Davey smile. Keyword there being almost.

He hadn't actually smiled in over a year. He didn't remember what that felt like. And truthfully, he didn't want to remember. What right did he have to smile when his baby brother was lying dead in the cold mountain ground? None.

"Sorry Han," Liam murmured quickly. "I didn't mean you."

"But I didn't remember my own name then," Hannah spat. Then her lower lip started to tremble and tears pooled in her eyes.

"Um..." Liam cleared his throat and glanced up to the rearview mirror. "Are you actually going to cry right now?"

"No!" Hannah huffed a breath and crossed her arms over her chest. Whirling away, she glared out the rear passenger window. "I don't know. I mean, I don't know what's wrong with me. Something's wrong with me."

Davey shifted to his left to look at Cole, but their fearless leader was busy staring at the rearview mirror. His own eyebrows were raised in question. He was looking at Liam, who (surprise, surprise) remained silent.

After a beat, Cole gave his head a quick shake.

"You're fine Han," he assured her. "Everything's going to be just fine."

Refocusing his attention out the front windshield, Cole gripped the steering wheel tighter. Davey did the same, except his hands tightened on his weapon.

There were more pressing matters at hand, like the dozen soldiers currently studying their approach. And it's not like this whole thing with Hannah was a complete surprise.

After all, she was the reason they'd made the trip in the first place. Something was wrong with her. She needed to see a doctor.

In front of them now, one of the guards was stepping forward and motioning with both of his hands for them to stop. The other soldiers standing all around him were holding their weapons close. It was clear they weren't going to just let them roll on through the wall unchecked.

Working the clutch and gear shifter, Cole slowed the SUV to a crawl before easing on the brake. He may have come to a stop where instructed, but he did not switch off the engine. Nope. In fact, keeping a foot buried in the clutch, Cole shifted into reverse, just in case.

With a classic Cole smile spreading across his face, the guy then proceeded to roll down his driver side window. Before the soldier standing on the outside had time to open his mouth, their fearless leader was spewing all kinds of information.

"Hey Soldier Malpas, right? How ya been? Great weather for travel, don't ya think? Is Commander Linfield around?" The questions kept right on coming, helping to ease the tension in the surrounding men.

You see, there was definitely a reason why Cole was Strike Team Three's leader and Liam was not. It was all in the charm.

Working to clear the tension from his own muscles, Davey kept both of his hands on the black rifle laying across his lap. Cole may have the soldier currently hovering at his window chuckling, but that could all change in a split second. Davey'd seen it before… maybe too many times. Laughing one minute, bleeding out the next.

So if Davey needed to kill a dozen people right now, then it would only take him a second to get his weapon up and firing. He was fast and he was ready. He was always ready.

In the backseat, Hannah shifted around and sniffled quietly. Beside her, Liam remained perfectly still. No doubt he had his own weapon at the ready as well.

"Well, yeah I remember you Officer Tanner, Sir. But we've been instructed to hold this Jeep here until Officer Jameson can arrive to inspect it. Give me a sec though, and I'll radio him again," Malpas said.

Straightening, the soldier plucked the black walkie from his hip and held it to his lips. His thumb depressed the button and his mouth began moving, but Davey never heard what it was that he said.

The echo of *that* name kept thundering around in his brain, filtering into his soul, leaving him straining.

Officer Jameson.

Jameson. The man who'd conducted the raid on their compound not so very long ago. The man that had come to steal Hannah and Lena, in the snow, in the night. The man that killed Flynn and Trey and Chan and... and Ryder.

A black pit opened in the center of Davey's chest. His hands clutched at his rifle. Sweat beaded on his brow.

Blinking, he tried to clear his vision of what he saw. His brother dead, lying flat on his back on the cold wooden floor, his body riddled with bullets. A pool of dried blood caked beneath him. His eyes frozen open. Those blue eyes that were so like his own.

Fuck. Shit. He wanted to rage and stab and scream and kill.

But then the Jeep was shifting into gear. Cole was shouting something out the window and they were lurching forward. The soldiers who had been blocking the blown out entrance to the Wall stepped calmly aside. The Jeep was passing through.

In the backseat, Liam was grumbling something, and Hannah was rolling down her own window and Davey was fighting to keep control. Now was not the time. He couldn't lose it right here, not when his target was so very close at hand.

Breathing in slowly, Davey closed his eyes and cleared his mind of the pounding rush of blood. Focus. He had to focus on something else. Hannah was talking. Cole was answering. The Jeep was coming to a stop and shutting off.

"I'm only asking for an hour," Hannah whined. "Don't tell Uri until I've had a chance to see my nephew and Lena. I just want to see them first."

Davey's eyes flipped open and he shot a look at Cole. In the back, Liam was yanking at his door handle and shoving out of the Jeep. Hannah was leaning forward, her arms wrapping around Cole's shoulders as she held him lightly against the drivers seat.

"He's going to ask why we're here," Cole reasoned. One of his hands came up to circle gently around Hannah's forearm.

"Just an hour." Hannah worried her lip a moment before continuing. "Then you can tell him about everything, okay? He'll make me go straight to the doctor the second he hears and I want to hold Ian first."

"You'll sit down when you hold him?" Cole asked, turning his head in an attempt to look at her face. "Just in case you get dizzy or fall again?"

"Of course." Hannah smacked the side of Cole's cheek with a kiss before releasing him and fleeing the vehicle.

"It's a deal then!" She called to Liam. "Ian first!"

Letting loose a long sigh, Cole sat still a moment in the quiet car. Beside him, Davey did the same. Hannah was brushing at her golden hair and smiling in triumph at Liam who had both of his arms folded over his chest now. His rifle was slung over his shoulder, his pistol was tucked into the holster at his hip, and the look on his face said it all. Not happy.

And Davey could understand why. Hannah had been getting some of her memories back over the past several months, but she'd also been fainting. She got dizzy spells a lot, had trouble controlling her emotions, and she'd even fallen a few times.

Once, she'd hit her head so hard she'd been unconscious for over three minutes. Davey knew because Ace had counted the seconds... out loud. They'd been in the middle of serving breakfast at the time so it was an absolute shit show.

The entire compound had freaked, and Ace, with all of his medic experience, could only guess at the reason for her issues. She needed a real doctor, he'd said, one with access to medical equipment.

When Hannah had finally come to, and tried to brush them all off, Cookie had gone on strike. No more meals until she agreed to get looked at back at the Wall. Period.

So here they were. Cole, Liam and Davey. Her small escort. Her worried escort. Even Davey, with his currently empty heart, couldn't deny his concern. After all, what would happen to Liam and Cole if Hannah was really sick? What sort of men would they become if... if she died?

"You alright?" Cole asked. His fingers were drumming on the steering wheel, his eyes focused straight ahead. "It's a lot to take in here, I know."

Swallowing, Davey's brow furrowed. He hadn't even noticed their surroundings. Clearing his throat, he bobbed his head *yes* and shoved out of the Jeep. When he tipped his face up and looked around, his mouth went slack.

Holy mother of...

Humanity.

Pristine buildings. Rolling grass lawns. Winding cement sidewalks. Lush trees.

And people. Lots and lots of people. Men and women and even small children. They were riding bikes, walking, chatting together. Laughing.

All of their clothes were clean. All of them had shoes. Hardly any carried weapons. It was a blast from the past... an unwelcome one.

How had all of this safety and security and peace been right here, while Davey's little brother had suffered not two hundred miles away? While they'd all marched and bled and killed and been killed and starved and burned... for *years*. It wasn't fair.

It. Just. Wasn't. Fair.

"Hey." Coming over, Liam laid a heavy hand on Davey's shoulder and peered into his face. "Put the safety on that thing and strap it to your back. You're making everyone nervous."

Looking down at the shining black rifle in his hands, Davey sucked in a shaky breath. Out of the corner of his eye, he noted a line of soldiers lingering. They'd followed the Jeep inside through the wall and were watching.

"You'd still get to it faster than they'd get a shot off," Liam whispered, seeming to follow Davey's train of thought. "But in here, you won't need it."

Nodding his head, Davey met Liam's intense stare a moment before flipping the safety on and sliding the strap over his shoulder. When the rifle was secured to his back, he rolled his neck and shoved both hands into his pockets.

There, he thought, cool as a cucumber. And in a moment, it was true. Ice flowed from his dark heart into his veins. He felt numb. Same as always.

So when the entourage of soldiers came stomping around the corner of a nearby building, Davey didn't even flinch. When Hannah squealed and threw herself into one of the guy's arms, Davey's face remained impassive. When she called him Uri and he laughed and spun her around, Davey merely observed in the background, like he had countless moments since his brother's death.

It was like he was floating next to his own body. He would tilt his head to one side and his brain would register what should have been going on in his heart, but its like the rest of him just didn't get the message. There was no curiosity, no amusement, nothing good.

Then Liam was stepping up to shake hands with some of the other soldiers and Cole was flashing one of his smiles and it was clear that they all knew each other.

Which made sense, seeing as how both Cole and Liam had lived with Uriah Linfield for months while Davey was back at the compound, digging an icy grave. Cookie had told him all about it.

But Davey was good at going through the motions. He would step forward (when asked) and offer his hand to shake (when it was appropriate) and give them his name (if necessary).

So it came as a bit of a shock when Cole introduced Davey to that big bastard with the brown hair and blue eyes. Because the moment Cole said the guy's name, Davey froze. He couldn't speak. He couldn't offer a hand to shake. He couldn't breathe.

All he wanted to do was scream. All he wanted to do was jerk the knife from his waist and slide it across the soldier's throat until the red rushing down the guy's shirt was the same curtain that currently clouded Davey's vision.

Jameson. His brother's killer.

He was standing here alive and well. And apparently everyone expected Davey to be okay with it.

Well... he wasn't okay with it.

Not by a long shot. But it's not like he could murder the guy right here. If Davey really wanted a chance at him, then he had to bide his time. He had to get him alone. He had to act normal.

Giving his head a purposeful shake, Davey did the most difficult thing that he'd ever had to do in his entire life. He forced a small smile to appear on his lips, stuck his palm out in the air, and he clasped the hand of the man that stole everything good from his life.

"Name's David Wells," he said. "But people call me Davey."

HOLDING THE LARGE WHITE PLATE IN HER HANDS, CASS stood patiently beside Mia. They were at the meat carving station in the cafeteria and there was always a bit of a back up here.

Inhaling, Cass took in the delicious scent of ham and roasted chicken. The farm was producing a greater variety of food all the time, though it was not without effort.

Staring down at her mostly full plate, Cass salivated over the portion of fresh corn, mashed potatoes, green salad and tiny muffin. There was even a bit of butter melting into a puddle in the potatoes.

"Just wait a few more months," Mia commented. "We'll be harvesting asparagus, broccoli and my personal favorite, peaches."

"Asparagus." Cass let the strange but familiar word tickle on her tongue as a green image worked to form in her cloudy mind.

This happened sometimes, and other times not. She would either know things, or she wouldn't.

"It's yummy and good for you," Mia explained, before stepping up to the carving station.

Holding out her plate, she spoke to the server, "One of each please."

"It's green," Cass offered finally, her brow furrowing as she attempted to summon the memory.

"It is," Mia confirmed, then she stepped aside so Cass could offer her own plate to the server. "You should come with me to the greenhouse. I'll show you a few of the plants. I think there's even a picture of an asparagus on some of the seed canisters."

Nodding, Cass accepted a serving of ham and backed away.

Mia worked on the farm, mainly growing food in one of the huge greenhouses. She was good at it apparently, and had been given her own section to manage. The corn currently on Cass's plate was part of Mia's jurisdiction.

Making their way over to one of the long wooden dining tables, Cass followed Mia's lead. The tall blonde flashed a smile and ducked her head at more than one greeting as they passed. Behind her, Cass couldn't help but roll her eyes. Mia turned heads everywhere they went.

When they finally settled near the end of a mostly empty table, Cass chuckled and gave her head a shake.

"Must be hard to be so pretty all the time," she teased.

"Have you checked the mirror lately?" Mia countered.

"If you weren't so oblivious, you'd notice not all of those guys were looking at *me*."

"Whatever." Cass waved her off, then huffed a breath. "What do you want to drink? I'll grab us some silverware, too."

"Water's fine." Mia tucked a loose strand of hair behind one ear. "I'll guard your plate."

Crossing to the far corner of the room, it didn't take long for Cass to retrieve what they needed. She stuffed some silverware in her back pocket and balanced two plastic cups in her hands. When she approached their table, she quirked a knowing smile. What had been nearly empty before was now definitely crowded. In fact, her seat directly across from Mia's was the only open one left.

Nolan, Levi, Junior, Tucker, Kent. They were all talking and laughing and turning in their seats to watch her approach. Cass felt a flush of unwanted heat creep into her cheeks, but sucking in a breath she placed the cups on the table and dug the silverware from her back pocket.

Levi stood up beside her and pulled out her chair. Mia wiggled her eyebrows. Cass mustered a small nod.

"Thank you," she said as she took her seat.

"So Cass..." Nolan cleared his throat from across the table as Levi dropped back to the seat beside her. "Heard you had a flashback the other night."

"Um, yeah." Ducking her head, Cass picked up her fork and scooped up some corn.

"Still lookin' to leave this place?" Nolan continued, his hazel eyes were zeroed in on Cass, she could feel it.

Scrunching up her face, Cass's fork paused on its way to her mouth. She'd been planning on leaving for a few months now, but that was when all she had was a picture of her brother and a recurring nightmare. Now she had more memories.

But without her entire memory intact, Cass continued to feel insecure. It was like she was playing a game for the first time, while everyone else around her had practiced for years. If she could just go home, then maybe all of her memories would return. And if she got her whole self back, then maybe, just maybe, she'd be able to track Eli down.

Because no matter what Garrett said, Cass knew her brother was still alive. She could feel it way deep down in her bones.

So did her flashback from last night change things? If she woke up tomorrow and could remember her entire life, would she still want to leave the Wall?

"Yes," Cass answered finally and lifted her head to look Nolan in the eye. "I want to go with you guys when you leave. As long as you'll take me to Southern California, like you promised."

Smiling, Nolan bobbed his head and threw a quick glance at Levi. The other guys were all talking and eating.

Mia was distracted, her head bent, listening to Tucker whispering something in her ear. After a beat, she covered her mouth prettily and laughed. Nolan's jaw ticked momentarily, but then he was ducking his head and stabbing at his own plate with his fork.

"We'll take you to So Cal," Levi assured her. Bumping

his shoulder lightly against hers, he peered into her face. "I guess there's some classes we all have to take before we can go, and Nolan has been looking at some old maps, trying to plan a route. We'll aim for Newport, but it's a big place. We need an exact address to get you home."

Relief burst in Cass's chest at the use of that word. Home. She was going home. And from there she would find Eli.

Heaving a giant sigh, Cass let a smile overtake her face.

"I'll get you an address," she told Levi. "Soon."

"YOU SHOULD'VE TOLD ME RIGHT AWAY," URIAH GROWLED.

Pacing the cramped hallway in the medical center, the stocky guy ran a frustrated hand back through his already mussed golden hair. Beside him, Lena bounced a fussy Ian on her hip. The dark-haired baby gurgled and grabbed chunks of her pink shirt in his little fists. Jameson sighed.

"She wanted to hold *your* son." Cole's words were clipped, he'd given this explanation three times already. "Besides, it's been going on for months already, what's one more hour going to change?"

Stopping short, Uriah turned to face a tired Cole and a pissed off Liam. The two of them were standing side by side, both their backs pressed against the blank white wall of the medical center hallway. Where one was tall, the other was even taller. Uriah had to tilt his head decidedly up to glare at Liam.

But Liam, as usual, remained unmoved.

The other soldier that they'd brought with them, David Wells, was leaning against the opposite wall. His hands were stuffed in his pockets, his blue eyes were locked on the linoleum floor. Just to his left, tucked away behind the closed door to exam room number four, was Hannah Linfield. Dr. Collette had dropped everything to come see her right away.

For Jameson, it was eerily similar to the night before. He couldn't help but think of Cass. The fainting. The falling.

Thank God she hadn't slammed her head as hard as Hannah supposedly had. But maybe that was next, Jameson thought. His gut gave an extra twist.

He'd *known* it wasn't just memories coming back. Damn it, she'd needed that head scan.

"If anything is wrong with my sister," Uriah gritted out. "I'm holding you two idiots personally responsible. You never should've taken her away in the first place."

"Noted," Liam bit back. "You think you're the only one worried, Linfield? Take a fucking number."

Sucking in a sharp breath, Uriah's chest puffed up. The florescent lights were shining down and the baby was really beginning to cry now and a line of soldiers was watching everything from the far end of the hall.

Shifting Ian to her other hip, Lena stepped between the two men and placed a hand on Uriah's chest. If anyone could diffuse the situation it was her. She'd always been the peace keeper when they'd all lived together in the bunker down in Utah. Hopefully that role would work once more.

"She's going to be just fine," Lena murmured quietly. "But when she comes out of that room, she's going to need her brother *and* her guys on the same team. Understood?"

Pursing his lips, Uriah kept his gaze focused on Liam. Jameson watched his friend's jaw tick and his fists clench. He was just another big brother drowning in the idea that he'd failed to protect what was his. It was so damn familiar. Too familiar.

Squeezing his own eyes shut a moment, Jameson fought the flood of memories that wanted to assault him. Eli had been just that same way, when things had gone down, right there at the end. The difference here was a life saver, though. This situation had witnesses.

Popping his eyes back open, Jameson moved from his position in the center of the hall and looped a hand around Uriah's elbow. With a firm tug, he walked the guy backwards until Uriah was able to break eye contact and turn away.

Lena's head dropped in relief and Cole dragged both of his hands down his face with a groan. Liam didn't move. He didn't flinch. His face didn't fall in relief or glow in triumph.

He was stone. Stuck in one spot like a statue, staring at the door to exam room four.

"Let's wait to hear what the good doc has to say," Jameson whispered to Uriah. "They couldn't travel in winter anyway. They came as soon as they could."

Shooting him a patronizing look, Uriah folded his arms across his chest. His mouth stayed pressed in a firm line. His brown eyes were filled with a mix of fire and fear.

"Anyway, it wasn't so long ago that you tried to choke me out for rescuing your sister and Lena," Jameson offered, he kept his tone light, trying to ease the tension. "Let's give this a bit more thought first."

Huffing a breath, Uriah's gaze danced to Jameson and softened. "Well, your idea of rescue involves handcuffs and chloroform," he countered. "You had a beat down coming."

"Maybe so," Jameson admitted.

Come to think of it, he *did* have a slight history of forcible rescue. And that shit always came around to bite him in the ass. Maybe Uriah wasn't the only hot-head that needed to give things more thought before acting.

Just then the door to exam room four cracked open. Everything stopped. Even Ian quieted for a second. His mouth closed as his wide eyes still dripped with tears.

Standing on the threshold, Dr. Collette had an unreadable expression on her face. Quickly, she glanced between the men as if looking for someone in particular. Damn doctors and their expert poker faces, you'd never know what terrible truth simmered between their ears.

"Can I get Cole and Liam to come in here, please?" She asked.

Shoving off the wall, Liam was through the door first, followed quickly by Cole. Jameson looped an arm around Uriah's shoulders and hugged him tight. Before the guy could utter a single protest, the doctor was ducking back inside and closing the door. The hallway was silent once more.

Well, for another moment anyway.

Then Ian began to cry. Again.

"*I* should be in there, not those assholes," Uriah growled.

"Those assholes are married to your sister," Lena countered.

"God, don't remind me." Uriah pushed away from Jameson and paced to the other wall. "Fucking weird."

Jameson cracked a grin. Yeah, it was fucking weird. Definitely an unorthodox situation, but for some reason it seemed to work.

Hannah and Cole and Liam were all together... and although Jameson couldn't figure out how that didn't result in a daily brawl, it didn't matter. They were all consenting adults and this was after the war. There was no one left to care. Well, except for Uriah.

Behind Jameson, the door to exam room four popped open once more. That was quick, he thought.

Glancing over his shoulder, Jameson frowned as Liam shoved out of the room and stormed off down the hall. His head was bent towards the floor, his long legs eating up the distance as people parted to give him space.

"Uh-oh." Lena exhaled a breath.

"That's it," Uriah announced.

Crossing to the door, he ripped it open. Cole was helping Hannah off the exam table and the doctor was busy putting away some equipment.

"What the hell is going on?" Uriah practically shouted as Jameson craned his neck to get a better look inside.

"Liam will be fine." Cole kept his hands on his wife's arms and eased her to standing. "He's just scared."

"I don't give a shit about him!" Uriah gestured angrily down the hall where Liam was quickly slipping out the front doors. "What's wrong with my sister?!"

"Uri, calm down. You're embarrassing me. The entire hospital can hear you." Hannah sighed and attempted to push a hovering Cole back a step. The guy didn't budge.

"Then tell us what's going on," Lena urged, bouncing a wailing Ian in her arms.

"Well…" Hannah's hand shifted down to cover her belly as she glanced up into Cole's face. The guy was beaming. *Beaming.* "I'm pregnant."

"Oh my God!" Lena squealed.

Handing a wriggling Ian off to Jameson, the little dark-haired pixie pushed past her husband and threw herself at Hannah. While Cole protested and Uriah gaped, the women hugged and rocked and laughed.

Hannah was… *ohhhh.* That's complicated.

Jameson's brow furrowed as he swung Ian up above his head. Walking a few steps away along the hall, Jameson made the kid giggle. Up and flying, then slowly back down. Up and flying, then slowly back down.

It wasn't long before the baby began to settle. After a minute, Jameson was able to cradle Ian in his arms, facing out. The little guy shoved a fat fist in his drooling mouth and sighed.

"I don't know which one of you to kill," Uriah managed finally. "This is so fucking weird."

Flashing the guy a giant grin, Cole rocked back on his heels.

Beside him, Lena was chattering excitedly as Hannah supplied all sorts of information. She hadn't known. She hadn't even suspected. She'd spotted just last month, but apparently that can be normal for the entire first trimester.

Wait… *eeeew*. TMI. Jameson's face screwed up and he gave his head a slight shake.

"What about the fainting?" Uriah cornered the doctor as she squeezed by everyone on her way back to the hall. "The dizzy spells?"

"Some of that is memory recurrence," Collette explained. "And some is just hormones and a little dehydration. We'll get her on prenatal vitamins and manage her diet and she should be just fine."

"*Should* be?" Uriah pressed.

"Yes." Collette nodded sagely before turning to leave. "Your little niece or nephew is just fine too, by the way. Healthy and right on track."

"Niece or nephew?" Uriah gaped, as the realization hit him. "I'm going to be an uncle."

"Oh my God!" Lena tightened her arms around Hannah's neck. "I'm an auntie!"

Taking a step back, Jameson rotated Ian in his arms and began walking around with him again. The kids big blue eyes blinked heavily a few times before his lids gave up the fight altogether. Ian's chubby fists were loosening and his little kicking legs went slack.

For a moment, Jameson stared down at the baby. Hannah was getting dizzy spells. She was fainting. And yeah, she was getting her memories back finally, just like Cass. But now Hannah was also pregnant.

So… what if… what if Cass was…

The idea alone had Jameson's whole body tensing. She wasn't with anyone. *Right?*

He'd watched her as closely as he could over the past several months, but still, he had to work each and every day. There were lots of times when he was busy, when he didn't see her come home or leave in the morning. Was she dating someone he didn't know about? And then there was that Levi fucker.

Shit. Jameson's chest was constricting and his throat was bobbing. In his arms, Ian's little face was scrunching up. Uh-oh. Don't wake the baby, he thought.

Inhaling through his nose, Jameson shut his eyes and purposefully made himself relax. Breathe in. Breathe out. Don't lose it.

He couldn't let his thoughts carry him away just now. He couldn't afford to go there, not with Ian in his arms and Lena needing him.

"So it was probably you then," Uriah stammered, pointing an accusing finger at Cole. "That's why Liam left? He's pissed and so he's going to kill you now for me."

"Uri!" Hannah huffed and shot him a glare. "Stop."

"Um, we don't know whose it is actually," Cole offered, again with the grin.

Glancing down to Hannah he frowned before continuing, "And I don't think we should do DNA or anything, do you? Does it matter?"

"No." Hannah shook her head. "It doesn't matter. You're both the dad."

"Dude." Uriah bit down on his own fist and heaved out a breath. "This is so fucking weird."

"You asked." Hannah smirked and patted her tiny belly.

Now that Jameson looked closely, it *was* sticking out just a bit. Tilting his head to one side, Jameson said the first thing that came to his mind.

"So what's with the disappearing act?" He asked.

A pained look crossed Hannah's face. Reaching out, she stroked a hand down Lena's arm. For a few silent seconds, the two women stared at each other, then the little dark-haired pixie nodded and stepped away.

"I'll go talk to him," Lena offered.

"Are you sure?" Hannah asked.

Beside her, Cole grabbed for her hand and squeezed.

"Absolutely." Turning, Lena left the exam room and crossed back into the hall. "You good for a bit with Ian?" She asked, as she passed Jameson.

"I'll follow you, but I'll stay back." Jameson began walking behind her. "Just in case Ian gets hungry."

"Alright," Lena agreed, but kept moving towards the exit doors.

. . .

OUTSIDE THE MEDICAL CENTER, EVENING WAS APPROACHING. The air was cooling off, the sun was easing down between the western mountains. Hugging the baby closer to his chest, Jameson trailed behind Lena. Her little black boots were stomping along the sidewalk, her hands were shoved into the pockets of her light jacket.

Lifting his head, Jameson scanned the area for signs of Liam. The guy could be anywhere. Sure, he was tall and under normal circumstances he stuck out. All that dark hair and dark eyes and brooding energy seemed to create ripples around him that attracted attention.

But then again, the guy was a hunter first and foremost. A killer. A stone cold stalker of men. So if he needed to fade, to blend, to disappear, then he absolutely could.

"Where would he go?" Jameson lifted his voice to reach Lena's ears, but not so much that anyone else would hear.

They were crossing an expanse of green lawn now. The rec center was way off to their left, a number of housing apartments were to their right. Lena didn't slow and she didn't glance around. It's like she knew exactly where she was headed.

"He had a spot," she offered over her shoulder. "Back when Hannah didn't remember him. I used to find him there sometimes."

Nodding, Jameson fell silent.

Ten minutes later, he found himself climbing a set of narrow metal stairs inside the massive metal perimeter wall. Lena was ahead of him still, her breath puffing out, the sound of their steps echoing all around them.

When they got to the top of the stairs, she leaned her back against the lone exit door and worked to catch her breath. Jameson stood quietly in front of her with Ian still passed out against his chest. His own lungs hungrily gathered air and his arms were aching, but he didn't show it.

"Just hang by the door," Lena breathed finally.

Jameson nodded.

Turning to face the metal door, Lena yanked at the handle and had the heavy thing swinging slowly inward. A rush of cold air hit them as she slipped out onto the narrow walkway. They were on top of the wall here and it was a long way down.

Before the door could close all the way, Jameson crossed to the threshold and wedged the toe of his boot in the frame. From his vantage point, he couldn't see anything except the dusky gray skyline and a forest of small darkened trees shooting out as far as the eye could see. He could hear them talking though. They were close.

"Hey," Lena's voice came first, quiet, tentative.

There was no answer.

Jameson could only assume Liam was there and maybe nodding his head. Or maybe the guy wasn't doing anything at all. Maybe he was just staring off into the distance as nighttime took over the sky.

"This is good news, you know," Lena again.

"Is it?" Liam's deep rumble came to fill Jameson's ears.

"Yeah, it is." Lena sighed. "The baby's healthy. Hannah's healthy. She's remembering you, this is good. This is what you wanted."

"What if something happens to them?" Liam's voice was so low Jameson had to strain to hear it. "Women die in childbirth all the time."

"Not here," Lena countered. "We haven't lost one yet."

"Yeah, but this is me we're talking about," Liam hissed. "I've done too much wrong to live happily ever after. Fairy-tales aren't real Lena, and my karma is coming. What if this is it?

What if I'm the reason they… they don't make it? I should leave. I should go, and then maybe they'll stand a chance. Cole deserves this, not me."

"You swore you wouldn't run again," Lena reminded him. "And I don't think that's the real issue here. What are you really afraid of, Lee? You need to say it out loud."

Pause. Silence.

Then finally, Liam spoke.

"You already know," he said.

Jameson could hear his own heart beating in his ears.

"You aren't him." Lena's voice came finally. "Liam… you could *never* be him."

"I've *always* been him," Liam whispered. "What if… what if I…"

"Look at me," Lena commanded. "Lee. You. Are. Not. Your. Father. You would never hurt them. Never. You'd cut off your own hand first."

"Fuck, Lena," Liam's voice broke and Jameson could almost feel the guy crumbling. "What am I going to do? I don't know how to be a dad."

"Yeah you do," Lena corrected. "You're going to be the best daddy around. I know it, Lee. I *know* it."

"I'm going to be a dad," Liam repeated. "Holy shit. Lena, I've never been more scared of anything in my life."

"Yeah," Lena again. "That's how you should feel, Lee. That's normal."

Then there was some sniffling.

A cleared throat.

Muted crying.

Slipping his toe back from the door, Jameson carefully, slowly, waited for it to snick closed. His heart was tapping in his chest and his gut was sinking.

He'd learned something about Liam today that he hadn't ever known, hadn't ever suspected, and he felt sorry at his intrusion. He shouldn't have eavesdropped.

Looking down into Ian's peaceful face, Jameson studied the baby a little bit more closely. Was this the scariest thing in the whole world?

When he thought about Cass, he nodded his head. Maybe. Maybe.

Pressing her right palm to the cold window, Cass blinked out into the pouring rain. The school bus bumped along the road, they were nearing her stop.

Huffing a sigh, Cass squinted through the foggy glass. The dirty cement sidewalks and cracked asphalt streets looked even worse wet. Wasn't rain supposed to wash everything away? Wasn't rain supposed to make things clean?

Sucking in a breath, Cass dropped her hand to her lap and wedged her icy palm between her legs, searching for warmth. Her jeans were a size too small, and the fabric was thinning from years of wear, so it didn't offer her much protection against the weather.

The dingy gray sweatshirt she had on wasn't much better. It was a hand-me-down from Eli who'd gotten it from the thrift store on the corner of Fifth and Main three years back. Better than nothing though.

As the brakes on the bus squealed, Cass and thirty other kids *rocked forward, bracing themselves against the worn brown vinyl of the seats in front of them. Time to get off. This was her stop.*

Pushing to her feet, Cass climbed over the grumbling girl who sat beside her. You'd think after riding the same route day after day, they'd of at least exchanged names, but no. They were in middle school now, a place of cliques and small groups, where people noticed if you wore the wrong clothes or hadn't showered in a few days.

Shuffling down the aisle, Cass made her way off the bus and into the rain. Before she had a chance to glance around, the bus doors were snapping closed behind her and the engine was revving. Standing still on the street corner, with her backpack strapped firmly to both shoulders, Cass waited for the hot blast of exhaust to hit her. It was the last bit of warmth she would feel until she returned to school the following day.

Usually, she would take a seat on the nearby bus bench and wait for another two hours until Eli arrived. She wasn't allowed to walk home by herself, it wasn't safe. At least that's what he always said, but Cass knew the real reason. Her big brother didn't want her to be alone with Wendy.

Holding out her hand, Cass watched as fat drops of water pooled in her palm. Her hair was getting soaked and her clothes were beginning to stick to her skin. She couldn't wait here today, alone, in the rain.

And up until this year, she hadn't ever had to wait at all. Because before this year, she and Eli had always gone to the same school and they'd always ridden home on the same bus.

But now Eli was at that rich kids private school, on a full scholarship for football. Between the bus ride out of their crappy neighborhood and after school practice, Cass's brother would be hours behind her.

Dropping her hand, Cass glanced around at the empty street. No one was lingering out here in the rain. She'd be just fine walking the two blocks home.

Picking up her feet, Cass sloshed through a million tiny rivers of water that flowed over the sidewalk. Her worn sneakers absorbed the wet, making each step she took squishy and uncomfortable. The skin on her body prickled as she gripped the straps of her backpack and bent her head down low.

Ten minutes later, she arrived at their apartment building and stomped up the cramped stairs.

Brushing her dripping locks from her face, Cass stopped on the second floor landing and pushed into the hallway. Noise assaulted her, the walls were so thin. Tucking her hands under the straps of her backpack, Cass listened to the mix of muted music, the crying babies, the screams of an adult argument.

When she got to apartment 206, she rummaged around in her back pocket and produced a copper colored key. Sliding it into the lock, Cass twisted the handle and entered her apartment.

It was dark, which wasn't surprising. They were nearing the end of the month now so the electric bill had been cut off and they didn't have power. If she opened the fridge, she'd find a jar of old mayonnaise and maybe a few slices of stale bread.

Tossing her sodden pack on the floor, Cass swung the door shut behind her and fastened the lock. A shiver ran through her. She could take a shower, but the water would be lukewarm at best. The entire apartment shared the same water heater and the *best time of day to get hot water was in the middle of the night, when most people were out partying or passed out.*

"Cassie, my baby," Wendy rasped from the kitchen table. "You're home, early. You remember Neal, right?"

Turning slowly, Cass peered through the dim apartment. Her mother was sitting where she always was, at the rickety wooden table near the kitchen. Beside her, sat a man. Neal.

He had greasy light-brown hair tucked beneath a black ball cap and almost gray-colored eyes. He was her mother's part time boyfriend, and full time drug dealer. If he was here, then that meant Wendy was getting high. Again.

Dipping her head, Cass averted her eyes. She could hear Neal lick his lips and her mother flick a lighter.

"Yeah, Mom," she said finally. "I remember."

"Where's your brother at?" Neal asked.

"Practice," Cass answered quietly. Eli was going to be so pissed that she didn't wait for him.

"Well, alright then." Neal cleared his throat and drew Cass's attention back over to him. "I brought some dinner. Come eat, darlin.'"

With a nod of his head, Neal indicated a collection of fast food bags littering the table. Cass frowned. They didn't have electricity, it was the end of the month, her mother's disability check wouldn't get here for another six days. So how the hell was she paying for this visit from Neal?

Flicking her eyes up to the man in question, Cass sucked in a quick breath. The scent of drive thru hamburgers and hot French fries filled her nose. Her stomach grumbled loudly.

"Someone's hungry." Neal chuckled and patted the seat to his right. "Come eat."

Making her way over to the table, Cass sat heavily in the chair. Her jeans were beginning to itch and chafe her legs, her sweatshirt was dripping water onto the floor. She didn't dare remove it.

Reaching for one of the brown paper bags, Neal shoved it in Cass's direction. Without looking at him, she grabbed a hamburger and unwrapped it quickly. Her hands were shaking and her body was shaking, but as soon as she took that first bite, everything else melted away.

Her mouth exploded with flavor and warmth. It was so good. So much better than the tiny sandwich and red apple they gave her at school. Saliva flooded her mouth as she took bite after bite after bite.

Across the table, her mother's leg bounced and bounced. She was always like this, anxious to get her hit.

Cass tried to ignore her as Wendy bent forward and inhaled something from a tiny glass pipe. Neal shifted in his seat, shoving his hands deep in the pockets of his loose pants as he watched.

Usually he was reaching across the table, grabbing the pipe as soon as Wendy was done, but this time he only tilted his head and waited. Cass kept eating.

"It's good right?" Neal asked, his gaze focused on Wendy. "I gave you a little extra. You'll feel better now."

"Yeah." Wendy exhaled and leaned back in her chair. "That's good."

Reaching for a bag of fries, Cass dragged them closer and began shoveling them into her mouth. They were salty and a little soggy, but they tasted amazing on her tongue. Chewing quickly, her eyes scanned the table.

Bags of half-eaten food. Wrappers. Napkins. Straws.

A lighter. A pipe. Tin foil. A tiny plastic baggie with cloudy little crystals inside.

Then... bingo. A pair of disposable cups.

Standing up, Cass leaned forward and grabbed one of the drinks and a nearby straw. Soda. She hadn't had soda in a really long time.

"You like coke?" Neal snickered. "Get it? Coca-Cola... coke."

Forcing a tight smile, Cass nodded her head and rocked back down in her chair. Neal was such a loser. He couldn't afford coke. At least, that's what Eli always said.

Ripping open the paper wrapper, Cass shoved a straw into the drink and took her first long pull. It was sweet and syrupy and had her lips smacking together at the taste.

Across the table, Wendy slumped forward. Her sickly thin arms spread out on the wooden surface, her head flopped to one side, her mouth parted in a sigh. She was out already. That was fast.

"So Cassie." Neal threw his arm around the back of her chair and stared at the side of her head. "You all grown up now, right? You ain't a little girl no more."

Swallowing hard, Cass's brow furrowed and her tummy flipped. She was twelve... almost thirteen. Did that make her a grown up? She definitely didn't feel like a kid anymore.

Shrugging, Cass stopped drinking long enough to answer, "I guess."

"Nah, you are." Neal bobbed his head and leaned closer. "I can see it."

Setting her drink down on the tabletop, Cass swiped the excess soda from her lips. All of a sudden, her stomach was hurting.

Glancing at Neal, she felt a deep sinking sensation. She wanted to throw up. She was going to be sick.

"You want to take a hit?" He asked, his grayish eyes were cruising all over her body. "Just a little one to take the edge off. It'd do you good. Your mommy sure likes it."

"No." The word was out of Cass's mouth before she even had to think.

Her eyes popped up to Wendy, then over to the front door. Eli would lose his mind if she ever touched drugs. Lose. His. Mind.

And anyway, it's not like Wendy made the experience look all that tempting. She spent most of her time passed out. The rare moments that Wendy was actually awake, she was tortured, always twitching and picking and worrying, forever hunting for that next piece of relief.

Cass never wanted to be like that. She never wanted to end up like her mother. Wasting her life. Starving her own children.

"Oh, come on." Neal chuckled and scooted closer. His arm dropped from the back of Cass's chair to loop around her shoulders. "It'll feel real good. Have you ever felt real good before?"

Shoving back in her chair, Cass pushed away from the table and stood up. Her heart was pounding and her throat was closing up on her. She didn't like him touching her. He'd never touched her before.

Neal's gaze tracked her as she turned towards the bathroom. She could feel his eyes on her almost like the touch of a hand.

"Hey now," he called and stood up to follow. "You don't have to go running off. I'm not gonna hurt cha.'"

A million words wanted to come out of Cass's mouth. Go away. Stop. I don't believe you. But between her twisting stomach and her racing pulse, she couldn't make her mouth utter anything at all.

Before she got to the bathroom door though, Neal was grabbing her. She felt his bruising grip on her elbows as he spun her around and pressed her back against the wall. Cass gasped, her eyes popping up to lock on his face.

Neal smiled... slowly.

"There now, Cassie." His stinking breath spread itself over her face. Cigarettes and stale beer. "There are other ways to make you feel good. I can show you. I can be the first one to show you."

Wriggling in his grasp, Cass's eyes widened as his mouth came down to cover hers. His fingers dug into her arms, his body smashed her against the wall. She froze, locked there as a thousand silent screams clawed at her throat.

But then a key was twisting in a lock and the front door was banging open.

Neal jumped back and ran a hand over the brim of his ball cap. Cass looked at the door.

Eli was standing in the threshold now, his short brown hair dripping water, his shoulders heaving, as if he'd run a mile.

"What." Eli stepped into the space and slammed the door behind him. "The fuck. Neal."

"Hey now, Eli boy." Neal puffed up his chest and turned to

face the fourteen-year-old. He had to look up. "You may have grown a few inches the past year or so, but that don't mean you can talk to me like that."

"Oh yeah?" Eli's eyes shot to Cass, then back to Neal. "Get in the bathroom Cass."

"I..." Cass's mouth dropped and she began to shake.

"Bathroom, Cass." Eli shucked his backpack on the floor, followed by his duffle bag full of football gear. "Now."

Ducking her head, Cass did as she was told. She slipped into the tiny bathroom and locked the door behind her. It was pitch black. The only line of light she could see was leaking around the door frame.

Hugging herself, Cass shifted her weight from one foot to the other. She didn't know what to do. She couldn't calm down.

"You put your filthy fucking hands on my sister?" Eli's voice came through the door, only slightly muffled. "She's twelve you sick fuck."

"Hey," Neal's voice grew cocky. "She came after me."

"Yeah, right," Eli scoffed.

The sound of his footsteps squeaking along the worn linoleum floor echoed for a moment. He was moving closer. She could hear him come to a stop just in front of the bathroom door.

"You need to go," Eli's voice was low. "Get your shit and get the fuck out. I don't wanna ever catch you back here again."

"Nah, boy," Neal countered. "Your mama still owes me for tonight. She ain't paid, yet."

"I said get out," Eli again. "You're not getting that kind of payment anymore, not from her and definitely not from my sister."

"Oh, you wanna step up to me, boy?" Neal chuckled and had the hair on the back of Cass's neck standing on end. "You may have a bit of height to ya, but you're scrawny as hell. Back up, junior, before you hurt yourself."

Squeezing her eyes shut, Cass sucked in a ragged breath. Eli was six foot two already and stronger than he looked, but Neal was right, he was skinny and underweight, mainly because he didn't get enough to eat.

"Leave, old man," Eli was whispering now, Cass had to strain to hear him.

"I'm gonna come back for my payment," Neal hissed. "You can't watch that little sister of yours all the time. Hell, maybe I'll have 'em both. Huh? What do ya think about that?"

That's when the first hit came. Cass could hear it. A fist slamming into flesh. A grunt of pain.

Then another hit. Then another.

Rushing for the door, Cass hesitated with her hand on the knob. Eli'd said to stay in the bathroom. He wanted her to stay inside, but should she? What if he needed her?

Then something slammed into the door itself. Hard. Loud. Cass yelped and jumped back.

More hitting. More grunting. Muttered curses.

Were they from Eli? Or Neal? She couldn't tell. Something slammed into the door again, over and over. The thin wood heaved with each hit. She thought maybe it would break.

Then it stopped.

Silence.

Creeping back towards the door, Cass gripped the handle once more. Her heart was clamoring to escape her body. It was *like the thing wanted to leap out of her throat. That's when she heard the gurgling... the choking.*

"Eli?!" She called. Her hand shot up to clutch her own throat.

No answer.

More gurgling.

Another thud against the door, lighter this time.

"Eli!" Cass screamed it now as terror licked up her spine. "Eli! Answer me!"

Pacing away, Cass stomped through the dark bathroom. Three steps forward and her toes were kicking the old cracked tub. Turning abruptly, she rushed back to the door and rested her forehead against it. She could hear someone breathing. Only one person's ragged breathing.

"Eli," Cass's voice wavered as she squeezed her eyes shut.

"Yeah, Cass." Eli sucked in air between his words. "I'm here."

"Oh thank God."

All the oxygen left Cass's lungs in a whoosh. She felt light-headed and woozy and sick. Flipping the lock on the handle, she pulled the door open and stopped short.

Eli was sitting on the floor just on the other side. His knees were drawn up and his head was hanging down between them.

Not one foot away, lay Neal. He was flopped on his back. His limp arms were spread wide. His glassy eyes were open even wider, staring, unblinking.

"Don't. Look." Eli panted. He didn't raise his head.

Covering her mouth with both hands, Cass simply stared.

"Just get back in the bathroom." Eli coughed and shook his head. "I'll take care of this."

"Eli..."

"Just stay where I put you!" Eli screamed the words now, his face still tilted towards the floor.

Retreating into the bathroom, Cass shut the door once more and flipped the lock. Her hands were trembling and her heart was racing. Tears pooled themselves in her eyes. Hot and fresh and guilty.

"When I tell you to stay," Eli continued quietly. "Just. Stay. I will always come for you, Cass. Always."

SITTING UP IN BED, CASS GRIPPED HER THROAT AND TRIED like hell not to scream. Her whole body was shaking, convulsing now with the vivid memory.

When I tell you to stay. Eli's words pulsed inside her mind. *Just. Stay. I will always come for you.*

Throwing the covers aside, Cass launched herself out of bed and ran for the door.

THE POUNDING ON THE DOOR IS WHAT WOKE HIM, BUT HE didn't know that at first. Sitting up in bed, Jameson dragged a hand down his face and smacked his lips together. It was the dead of night and he'd been in a stone cold deep sleep.

Then it came again... the pounding. It wasn't knocking, there was no polite rapping of a knuckle on wood. No. This was desperate hands slapping at his front door, over and over.

Stumbling out of bed, Jameson tripped in his tangle of sheets before staggering to his nightstand. Wrenching open the drawer, he pulled the black handgun from its spot and gave his head a quick shake. All the while, the noise continued.

Making his way to the front door, Jameson peered through the peep hole and exhaled in a whoosh. Shit. It was Cass.

His heart was hammering like a staccato drum in his chest as his head tipped back and his eyes closed. God, she'd scared the crap out of him.

After a beat, he tucked the gun into the pocket of his sweats and refocused on the door. Another nightmare? Another memory? His stomach sank and he blew out a short breath. Had she finally remembered everything? Was it time for his confession?

Yanking the door open, Jameson tripped backwards as Cass threw herself at him. She was crying, sobbing and shaking as he wrapped her up in his arms.

"You okay?" He murmured the question into her hair as the front door swung shut of its own accord. She felt so good up against him. Too good.

"He killed him," Cass's voice trembled and hitched. "He killed him. Did you know he did it? Did you know?"

"Wait, slow down." Jameson's brow furrowed. Stepping back he held Cass at arm's length and peered into her face. "Who killed who? Are we talking now, or is this a flashback?"

"A flashback. A flashback." Cass bobbed her head as tears filled her eyes. "Eli. He... he..."

"Slow down," Jameson urged, squeezing her upper arms gently in his hands. "I've got you. You're safe."

"It was because of me," Cass continued, her eyes darting about the room. "It was my fault he did it."

"Hey... hey..." Jameson ducked his head, trying to get her to make eye contact.

When Cass finally looked at him, her face crumpled.

Her eyes squeezed shut and she did that thing girls do where their noses turn red and tears streak down their cheeks. Her mouth parted and closed, parted and closed as strangled cries began to bubble up her throat.

Watching Cass fall apart was like having someone punch Jameson right in the center of his chest. She was in pain and there was nothing he could do to take it away. Looping his arms around her body, he pulled her into his chest once more and held on.

Cass continued to cry.

Jameson wasn't wearing a shirt, so he felt the dampness of her tears against his skin. Her body was shaking and her hands were up between them, covering her mouth. Reaching up a hand of his own, Jameson stroked the length of her hair. It was so silky beneath his fingers, just like he'd always imagined it to be.

"Whatever you remembered," Jameson began quietly. "It's in the past. Whatever happened, it can't hurt you anymore."

"He wanted me to stay, and I didn't," Cass whispered.

Jameson's gut dropped. Sucking in a breath, he willed himself to calm down. He willed himself not to go back there, not to feel the regret and the guilt and the sorrow. He had his own memories to battle, and he'd do well to follow his own advice. It's in the past. What happened is gone now. You can't go back.

"You're still shaking," Jameson murmured, and tightened his hold on her. He shouldn't be doing this, the hugging, the holding. "Are you cold? Let's get you into bed."

When she didn't answer, Jameson looped one arm beneath her knees and scooped her into the air. Carrying her down the short hall, he shouldered his way into the small bedroom and crossed to his bed.

His body hummed where it contacted hers. It was like his mind knew he needed to let go, but his body was screaming that it was all wrong. He needed to keep touching her. He *needed* to.

Pursing his lips, it was all Jameson could do to lay her on the mattress and step back. He ran both hands through his mess of dark hair and blew out a breath. She had her hands up over her face as she continued to sniffle and shake.

Turning away from her, Jameson retrieved the gun from his pocket and replaced it in the nightstand drawer. He slid the drawer shut slowly and glanced to his left. Cass was beginning to settle down now. She was reaching for the covers and blinking away the tears.

All the times she'd come to him with her nightmares, it'd never been this bad. He wondered what she'd remembered. He wondered what Eli had done, but he didn't want to push it. A sick sort of selfish part of him didn't want her to remember anything at all.

"I'll take the couch," he said quietly.

"Why didn't you tell me?" Cass asked, her eyes bobbing up to lock on his.

"Tell you what?" Jameson swiveled to face her and jammed his hands in the pockets of his sweats. There were so many things he hadn't told her, he couldn't even begin to guess.

"You said my mom was sick," Cass continued. "That was a lie."

Huffing a breath, Jameson's face tipped up and he stared hard at the wall. *Liar.* It wasn't the first time she'd called him that. But Cass was just too damn beautiful, lying in his bed. The blankets were pulled up to her waist, her hair was a tangled mess on his pillow. It stopped his heart from beating, if only for a second.

"She *was* sick," he tried finally, but Cass shook her head.

"No." Pushing up to sitting, her eyes filled with anger. "She was an addict. A horrible druggie, loser, addict. Why didn't you tell me? Why lie?"

Why lie? Jameson fought the scoff that wanted to escape him. If she only knew the extent of his lies. She wouldn't be sitting here talking to him, that's for sure.

"I'm sorry I kept it from you," he said. "I guess I figured if you never got your memories back, then why burden you with it. Why not let you live with a sick mom instead?"

In an instant, Cass's eyes melted from anger to sadness. Her hands came up to cover her mouth again and fresh tears welled in her already red-rimmed eyes.

"Hey." Jameson stepped to the bed and sat down beside her. "Don't cry anymore, okay? Don't cry."

Reaching out a hand, he brushed a wayward curl from her face. Cass's eyes popped up to his and she leaned into him… *seeking* him. His heart jumped in his chest.

"There was a man," she whispered. "His name was… was… Neal. Did you know Neal?"

Climbing further onto the bed, Jameson gathered Cass close to him and made to lie down. He knew he shouldn't do it. He *knew* he shouldn't, but he did it anyway, and she even made room for him.

With his head propped up on the pillow and Cass pressed against his side, Jameson tucked one arm beneath his own head and held back a sigh. Her face was nestled close to his chest, her body running the length of his, their legs were touching.

"No," he answered her. "I never met anyone named Neal."

"Eli didn't mention him?"

"No." Jameson's brow furrowed as his stomach clenched. "You said he killed someone. Did you mean Eli?"

Cass's head nodded against his chest and for the next several minutes, Jameson had to hold his breath as the whole sordid story poured out of her mouth. Her mom. The drugs. Neal.

What Eli did…

And Cass was *twelve* at the time. She was just a kid, just a baby really, and Eli hadn't been much older. Shit, when Jameson was twelve his biggest concern was not getting the video game console he wanted.

All this time Jameson had known Eli's life had been hard… but… Fuck. It made what happened between them in the end that much more awful.

Squeezing his eyes shut, Jameson fought his own flood

of emotion. He wanted to save Cass. He wanted to protect her from everything, from himself even, just like Eli had done. God, if he could only go back. What he would give to just go back and make different choices.

But he couldn't go back and undo what was already done. And Cass was going to remember everything eventually. Maybe he should just tell her now.

"I'm sorry," Cass whispered. Her head was still on his chest, her hair tickling his shoulder and arm.

"You've got nothing to be sorry for," Jameson rasped. His throat wanted to close up on him.

"You were right," she continued. "I hate thinking about it. I hate knowing what happened. Every time I close my eyes I see them, I *hear* them. I wish my mom really had been sick, Garrett. I wish we were just poor and that was it."

Exhaling through his nostrils, Jameson reached down with one hand to pull the covers further up Cass's body. He wished they'd had a different truth, too. He wished it for Cass and for Eli and even for himself.

Rolling up to one side, he began to scoot out from under her. He should get going now. She was clearly worn out and this was a place he didn't belong, a place he didn't deserve to be.

"Wait." Cass raised her head and frowned at him. "You're leaving?"

"I was gonna take the couch," he reminded her. "You're tired. You should get some rest."

"Can't you just stay?" She asked, those mossy green eyes

blinked up at him. "I feel like we've done that before. Have we done that before? It feels familiar, is all. I miss familiar."

Pausing, Jameson looked down at her. Had they done that before? Laid together in the night, with their bodies touching? No. Not even close.

Elijah Roe had waltzed into Jameson's life on the first day of football practice Freshman year with a chip on his shoulder and a throwing arm that wouldn't quit. He was the dirty kid from the wrong side of the tracks and Jameson was the bored boy who'd been given everything he ever asked for. The difference in their backgrounds was like… insta-glue.

Their pieces fit together, and that was it. They became best friends. Brothers. It was them against the world.

But then about halfway into the year, came Cass. All of sudden, she was at every practice, in the background, waiting. Eli took her everywhere he possibly could. She started coming to dinner at Jameson's home, spending time with his mom, hanging out on weekends. And as soon as Eli could negotiate her way into their same school, she was with him then, too.

So it was Jameson and Eli.

Or Cass and Eli.

Or the three of them together.

It was never Jameson and Cass. Never.

"We've never slept in the same bed together," Jameson offered. "But you slept in my bed at home three nights a week for years. My parents set me and Eli up with bunk beds in the guest bedroom. By the time I moved out for college, you were living with my parents full time."

"Oh." Cass's face fell. "It just feels…"

Jameson's eyebrows raised as he waited for Cass to finish her sentence. He was halfway out of the bed, but still partially in it. She was tipped up on her side, her head on the pillow, her cheeks turning a soft shade of rose.

"It feels what?" He prompted as his heart tapped at him and his body screamed to crawl back in beside her.

"Comfortable," she said finally. "Because I'm like a sister to you, I guess. That's how you feel about me, right? Like family."

Exhaling, Jameson slipped out of bed. "Yeah, Cass," he answered. "Just like a sister."

Lies.

So many lies.

Gripping the fabric in both hands, Cass kept her foot pressed down on the floor pedal as she guided the material carefully through the sewing machine.

The dress was coming along nicely. She loved the feel of the crimson fabric as it slipped beneath her fingers. She could imagine how it would hang on Mia's frame, the perfect display for weeks worth of work.

Furrowing her brow, Cass focused on the silver needle. It moved so quickly, it was just a blur really. But this part required her complete attention, she wanted the stitches to be even and organized and tidy. Unlike her mind which, after her latest night spent in Garrett's bed, was cluttered and confused and messy.

What was happening in her brain wasn't matching with the feelings in her body. And it was that exact imbalance that left her feeling vulnerable and unsure. Being close to Garrett felt... *good*.

But not like the brother-sister sort of good that he was feeling. Nope. Nothing like that.

Blowing out a breath, Cass lifted her foot from the pedal. The needle stopped whirring and, leaning in closer, she checked her work. It was perfect. Cass let a big grin spread itself across her face. She kicked ass at this.

A soft knock at the door to the workroom had her head lifting with curiosity. She didn't have any clients left to see today. She didn't know who it could be. But before she could utter a sound the door was swinging inward and Levi stuck his head inside.

"Hey," he said and smiled. "I tried you at your apartment, but Mia said you were probably still here."

"Um, yeah." Cass ducked her head and returned her attention to the sewing machine. She had another few hours left of work before the dress would be ready for its first fitting.

"So... are you ready to go?" Levi asked, as he stepped into the room.

Cass's eyes flitted back up to him and she frowned. "Ready to go where?"

"Dinner." He chuckled and shook his head. "It's after five and I made reservations at the restaurant... remember?"

"Ohhhhh." Cass released the fabric and sat back in her chair. Dinner. *Right.*

"Let me guess, you forgot," Levi supplied, then ran a hand back through his thick crop of black hair.

"No." Cass frowned, then covered her face with both hands. "Yes. I'm sorry."

"That's alright." Levi's voice was making its way closer as he talked. "We can still make the reservation if we leave now. Are you hungry?"

Peeking at him through her fingers, Cass exhaled on a sigh. If he hadn't interrupted her, then she'd still be sewing, but now that he was here, her stomach was grumbling. And he was a nice enough guy, a former boyfriend even, according to him. She must have seen something in him before, felt something before. Why not try again?

"I don't look very date-worthy," she commented, letting her hands drop to the table.

"You look great." Levi beamed as he came to a stop in front of her. "But you always look great."

"I'm in jeans and my hair's a mess…"

"You make jeans look like a mini-skirt and your hair is sexy as hell." Extending a hand to her, Levi wiggled his eyebrows. "Come eat with me. It'll be like old times."

Eyeing his outstretched hand a moment, Cass searched herself for clues. There was none of that spark she felt when she was with Garrett, but there wasn't any fear either. No butterflies lighting up her insides, but also nothing bad. He was a friend. She felt like he'd been a good friend before, like Mia almost.

"Okay." Cass reached for his hand and let him help her up. "Let's go."

. . .

On the way to the restaurant, they talked about his day. Levi joked about his guard duty shift and told her about the recent return of two former officers in the Linfield army.

The evening air was crisp, but not overly cold. Halfway there, he threw his arm around her shoulders and drew her into his side. Cass let him.

Beyond the metal perimeter wall, the sun was sinking low in the mountains. The sky was bursting with creamy oranges, soft yellows and burning reds. All Cass could think was what a beautiful fabric it would make, all those colors bleeding together.

"So they've issued a schedule of survival classes," Levi said, as they approached the building with the restaurant in it. "You've got to pass six out of nine in order to leave. You still want to go, right?"

"Yeah." Cass thought of Eli. She couldn't shake the feeling that he was out there. She had to get to him, if she could. "I want to go."

"Alright well, we can do them together if you want."

Cresting the stone steps, Levi kept her tucked beneath his arm until the very last moment. He only released her so that he could pull open one of the large glass doors and usher her inside. A blast of heat hit her first. Heat, then noise.

Glasses clinked, dishes rattled, people laughed and talked. It was rather dim, with music playing like a distant echo in the background.

Cass's mouth dropped open and she stared. She'd never

been inside the restaurant, at least not since she'd lost her memory.

Stepping up to a wooden podium with a pretty woman standing behind it, Levi leaned forward and spoke to her.

"We have a reservation for two. It's under the name Harris."

The woman nodded politely as her gaze flipped down to a sheet of paper on the podium and then back up to the two of them.

"Of course," she said. "Right this way."

Taking Cass by the hand, Levi followed the hostess (because that's what she was called... a *hostess*) as they weaved between crowded tables. Cass stared down at their connected hands as she walked. Her mind was working on overdrive, absorbing and stuttering, supplying her with new words or old words (depending on how you looked at it).

When Levi glanced at her over his shoulder, Cass tipped her face up and couldn't help but smile. It came naturally. She felt her pulse jump slightly and it made her wonder. Could she like Levi? Like really, *really* like him?

Because this was fun, enjoyable even. It was warm and pretty and smelled good in here. She was having a nice time.

But then the hostess was coming to a stop and gesturing to a small table with two chairs positioned around it. There was a small flickering candle in the center with a pair of white napkins placed opposite each other.

Beside them sat a pair of water glasses and then another

set of goblets for wine. Fancy, Cass thought suddenly, this was *fancy*.

Their silverware glinted in the low flame of the candle, and then Levi was stepping over to pull out one of the chairs for her. It made her feel good, like he liked being with her.

That's when Cass's eyes flitted over to the large table just beside them. The large table that was overflowing with people who were talking and laughing. The large table where Garrett was sitting wedged between two women, with a sleeping infant in his arms, and eyes that were focused entirely on Cass.

Crap.

Instantly Cass's tummy exploded with a million tiny tingles and she felt her cheeks tinging pink. Garrett did not look away. He just sat there and stared at her. Cass was forced to glance down.

Soooooo… there was *enjoyable* and then there was lightning inside your body, she thought. Levi was enjoyable and Garrett was like lightning. Forbidden. Sparking. Lightning.

Quickly taking her seat, Cass tried to focus her attention back on Levi. He was making his way over to his own chair with an easy smile on his face. When he sat, he accepted their menus from the hostess and passed one over to Cass.

"Your waiter will be with you in a moment," the hostess announced.

"Thank you," Levi replied before she breezed away.

Gripping the single sheet of paper in both of her hands, Cass blew out a slow breath. Her face was hot and her belly was flipping but she willed herself to calm down. She couldn't have the lightning (because she was like a sister to him), but maybe she could have enjoyable.

Yeah, maybe that's how it was supposed to be anyway.

"Of course they had to sit us next to my boss," Levi muttered and had Cass glancing up at him. "But it looks like they're almost done, so…"

"Your boss?" Cass's brow furrowed. Did she really know so little about him?

"Well, more like my boss's boss's boss, but still." Levi shrugged and let his eyes drift back to the menu in front of him. "Commander Linfield, Officer Jameson, Officer Tanner, Officer Byrne. It's a freaking convention over there."

"Oh." Cass willed her eyes not to dart over to Garrett, but of course they had a mind of their own.

Yep, he was definitely still looking. Cass swallowed. Well… scowling was more like it.

Returning her gaze to her own menu Cass deliberately read off the choices. Garden salad. Caesar salad. Potato soup. Roast chicken and rice with a vegetable medley. *Medley…* hmmm. That word didn't ring any bells.

"Would you like a glass of wine?" Levi asked. "It looks like they have Chardonnay or Merlot."

Pursing her lips, Cass focused her mind on the words

instead of on the nerves cruising through her body. She'd had beer before and that hadn't been hard to remember, but Chardonnay… Medley… Merlot. Her mind swirled and she pressed one hand to her forehead in an attempt to make it slow down. The proper memories were in there, and its like they were fighting to burst out, but in the end, they just wouldn't come.

"You okay?" Levi asked and reached for her across the table. "Cass?"

Popping her eyes open, Cass lifted her face to look at Levi. His brown eyes were awash with concern and he'd cocked his head to one side. Giving him an embarrassed smile, Cass lowered her right hand from her forehead and watched as Levi's thumb stroked along the back of her left.

"I'm fine, it's just…" Huffing a sigh, Cass rolled her eyes before admitting, "I don't know what those words mean."

"Oh." Levi gave her hand a little squeeze, but didn't let go. "Which words?"

"The wine words."

"Okay, this isn't a big deal," Levi assured her. "Chardonnay is a type of white wine and Merlot is a type of red wine. You always chose the white when we came here before."

Dipping her head, Cass sucked in a breath and withdrew her hand. "Then that's what I'll have," she announced. "Thank you."

"Great." Levi beamed as the waitress walked up to their table.

After they placed their order and the wine was brought

out, Cass's nerves began to settle. She could do this. She could enjoy this dinner date and act like a normal person.

Levi talked about the survival classes they had to take, hunting, fire-making, shelter building, food preservation, self-defense. He and the other soldiers who would be going with them already had a background in most of those things, but it was important for Cass and Mia to learn as much as they could.

Easing back in her chair and sipping on her wine, Cass just listened. She knew she had a lot to learn. She'd been told that living outside the Wall was nothing like living inside of it, but still... that same old underlying pull nagged at her. No matter the discomfort or danger, she had to go. She had to try.

When she was nearly done with her wine, Cass felt relaxed and easy. Before their dinner arrived, she figured she better use the ladies room.

She wanted to run her hands through her hair and check her reflection in the large bathroom mirror. All of a sudden, she wished she'd dressed up, she wished she'd made more of an effort.

Standing from the table, Cass threw a glance at Garrett on her way to the bathroom. His eyes weren't on her anymore. No, they were staring directly at the side of Levi's head.

Frowning, Cass brushed off the odd ripple that fact caused in her belly and made her way to the back of the restaurant. For some reason, she didn't have to ask where the bathroom was... she already knew.

Stepping into the ladies room, Cass had to smile at the bustle of activity inside. There were three women leaning close to the bathroom mirror, applying lipstick and running combs through their hair. Another woman was washing her hands and they were all talking.

All of them. At one time. Giggling and gossiping and filling the space with the echo of their voices.

After using the bathroom, Cass went to wash her hands and stopped to stare at her own reflection. Her soft brown curls were a frazzled mess and her face was smooth, but plain.

Letting out a grunt of displeasure, she drew the attention of all the other women in the space over to her.

"What's the matter?" One of them asked. "You okay?"

"Yeah." Cass washed her hands and went to dry them. "I'm just a mess is all."

"Ohhhh, we can fix you up real quick," another offered, and had Cass's brow lifting.

"You can?" She asked.

Yes. The answer was yes, apparently, they could. Because literally one minute later, Cass's hair was brushed and sprayed, her lips were glossed a sinful shade of red and a coat of dark mascara had her green eyes popping.

With a satisfied smile and a quick thank you, Cass was back in the restaurant and making her way over to her table. She looked good now and so she felt good too, and that's when she realized something. She really needed to let Mia help her out in the makeup and hair department.

There was more to this girly thing than awesome clothes, which of course she already had.

Brushing her hands down her white blouse, Cass came to an abrupt stop when she saw what was waiting for her at her table.

Garrett was standing over Levi, his balled fists braced on the tabletop, his mouth spitting words she couldn't quite make out. In the background, a baby was crying, the one that he'd been holding earlier, and a dark-haired woman was bouncing the little guy helplessly on her hip.

Every table in the vicinity had dropped into silence. Swallowing, Cass willed her feet to move forward as her brows drew together. What in the…?

"Is everything alright?" She asked as soon as she was close enough.

The sound of her voice had Levi glancing up at her over his shoulder and Garrett's mouth slamming shut. The former was a touch pale, the latter a touch flushed.

Before either of them answered, a handsome man with chestnut hair wedged himself between her and Garrett and stuck out his hand.

"Everything's just fine," he chuckled and bumped Garrett to one side with his back. "I'm Cole, by the way. We've never formally met, but I'm guessing you're Cass."

"Um…" Cass's brow furrowed deeper as her eyes danced from Levi to Garrett and then back up to lock on this Cole guy. "Yeah, I'm Cass."

"Well great." He laughed and shook her hand. "It's great

to meet you. But as you can see we were all just leaving. I'm sure we can catch up another time."

"Oh." Cass sucked in a breath as he dropped her hand. "Sure. Okay."

"Okay," he echoed and smiled.

Turning, Cole gripped Garrett by the arm and began to march him out of the restaurant.

The size difference between them was almost comical, and its not like that Cole guy was small. Garrett was really just that big. His broad shoulders were tense as he walked, his steps long and deliberate. When they reached the exit, he yanked his arm out of Cole's hand and slammed a wide palm on one of the doors, causing it to fly open.

Looking down at Levi, Cass's mouth dropped and her eyebrows lifted.

"What was that about?" She asked.

"Nothing." Levi blew out a breath and gestured to her empty seat. "It was about nothing. Ready to eat?"

Glancing at the table, Cass realized their food had arrived while she'd been gone. Nodding her head, she stepped to her chair and sat down. There was no way that exchange between Garrett and Levi was about nothing. She may not be all there in the head, but Cass wasn't stupid. Whatever had just gone down, it was about her.

She remembered the flashback she'd had about the high school party. About how Garrett had shoved her date to the ground and dragged her back to Eli. Maybe this was more of the same.

Garrett was taking his watch dog duties a little too seriously.

Well, she would have to put a stop to it. She wasn't a little girl anymore and she could date if she wanted to.

Yeah. She would just have to tell Garrett to back off the next chance she got. The next time she saw him, she'd tell Garrett to leave Levi alone, and she'd finally ask him for their home address so she could give it to Nolan before they left the Wall.

COLD WATER SPRAYED STRAIGHT INTO JAMESON'S FACE. HIS eyes were closed, his palms were braced on the white tile of his shower wall.

Go cool down. Cole's words were on repeat inside his head. *It's not that guy's fault you didn't make a move. She doesn't know she's your girl... therefore, she's not your girl.*

Blowing out a breath, Jameson willed his body to relax, to let go. Fuck Cole for being right. Fuck Uriah and Liam, too. But they just didn't understand.

No, he had not made a move on Cass, at least not one that she could remember.

And although his buddies couldn't understand why, there was a good reason for that. They thought he was just a pussy, afraid of rejection, but it was so much more. They didn't know what had happened before, they didn't know what Jameson had done.

They couldn't comprehend the cost of her remembering, and what a strange mix of emotions that brought out it him. It's like a part of him wanted her to know, to get it off his chest, to get rid of the guilt and regret, but then another part of him dreaded it.

Squeezing his hands into fists, Jameson pushed off the wall and rotated around in his shower. Cold water poured down his shoulders and back. Keeping his eyes closed, he saw the memory in his mind… clear as day.

Cocking back her free hand, Cass stepped into his space and punched him as hard as she could square in the nose. Instantly, Jameson was seeing stars.

Why had Eli insisted on teaching her how to fight? Shit. That fucking hurt.

Letting go of her, Jameson's hands shot up to his face as blood poured from his nose.

Did she break it? For a second, he wasn't sure. But then he was feeling along the bridge and although it hurt like a bitch, the pain didn't drop him to his knees, so it wasn't broken at least.

"I'm sorry, I just…" Cass's voice was whisper quiet. "You should've let me go."

Blinking his eyes open, Jameson held his slick palms out in front of his face. They were covered in blood. Glancing down, he frowned. His uniform was covered in blood, too. Shit. That was going to raise some questions.

But at this point, none of that mattered, Jameson realized. Nope.

This changed nothing. Cass refusing to go with him, changed nothing.

When Jameson's eyes snapped back up to lock on Cass... she ran.

"Cass!" Jameson shouted her name as she shoved through the garage door and slammed it behind her.

Picking up his feet, he ran to the door and pushed it wide. Entering his childhood kitchen, Jameson shot a quick glance to his right and assured himself of what he already knew. She'd gone left, towards the front of the house, not out the back.

Charging after her, Jameson's heavy boots pounded against the expensive hardwood flooring. He could hear a scream bubble up from her lips as she skidded to a stop at the front door.

Struggling for a split second with the knob, she didn't look back. She didn't even glance over her shoulder.

Jameson's breath was coming in bursts now as he narrowed his eyes on her and moved faster. Didn't she get it? This was not a game. This was life and fucking death. If she stayed here, then she would die. He knew it in the most real part of his soul. He had to save her... even if it was from herself.

Before he could reach her though, the front door was swinging wide and Cass was darting out across the yellowing lawn. She'd had a bit of a head start on him, but even so, he wasn't far behind her now. Shit, she didn't stand a chance.

"Cass, damn it!" Jameson shouted again as he flew out of his house.

She was almost across the lawn, her girly black leather boots were slipping just a little. Jameson didn't break stride. He saw nothing but her.

Pumping his arms, he quickly caught up just as she hit the cement sidewalk. Grabbing her by the waist, he hoisted her up in the air and held her tight to his body.

"Let me go!" She cried. "Stop!"

Then she was thrashing, kicking and scratching. He felt her fingernails rake across his forearms, felt the blood well out of the fresh lines in his skin. Nope, he thought, he wasn't letting go that easy.

But then she threw her head back and it connected with his nose... again. Pain exploded in his face and his arms loosened of their own accord. Staggering back, Jameson didn't see her fall.

No. He heard it. He felt the impact of her skull against the cement sidewalk in every inch of his body.

When his eyes finally flew open, Jameson dropped to his knees.

"Cass!" He screamed. "Oh fuck. Shit!"

Her eyes had rolled back in her head and her body was lying in a crumpled heap.

Crawling to her, Jameson laid a shaky hand on her neck. It took a few counts before he felt her pulse. All the breath exploded from his lungs and tears welled in his eyes. She was alive.

Shit, he'd fucked up. He'd fucked up so bad.

That's when he felt the barrel of a gun pressing into the back of his skull.

The cold metal was accompanied by a familiar sort of clicking. Someone was holding him at gunpoint and they'd just cocked the damn thing.

"Get away from her," the voice was shaky, but there.

Holding his hands up, Jameson kept his eyes wide.

"Take it easy," he said. "This isn't what it looks like."

"Yeah right," the voice again, male, older. The guy from across the street? Or the old guy from three houses down? "She's been screaming bloody murder for the past five minutes."

"I'm only trying to help her," Jameson said. "I'm going to need you to put down the gun."

"I can't," the voice again, raspy, unsure.

"You can, and you will," Jameson's voice remained steady even as his heart beat a furious pace in his chest. "Put the gun down now and we can talk about this. I can explain."

"No... No." The voice wavered as the barrel of the gun pressed harder into his skull. "I... I'm going to have to put you down. We can't have your kind here."

"This is a misunderstanding," Jameson coaxed. Adrenaline shot through him and he lowered his arms just a little. "You need to put the gun down... now."

For a moment, time slowed.

All of Jameson's senes narrowed, focused, as the past year of training kicked in. He could feel the gun shift against the back of his head, he could almost see the guy's trigger finger slip down, making ready to pull.

What happened next was fast. It was all self-preservation and instinct and training wrapped up together.

Ducking his head, Jameson spun on his knees. His right hand came down to jerk his own gun out of its holster, his left hand came up to swat the other man's weapon aside. Then he was firing. Two shots.

Pop. Pop.

The old man's eyes flew open in surprise. He didn't even get a shot off.

Then the guy was falling, gripping his belly where the bullets had landed, and groaning.

Jameson's heart skipped a million miles an hour inside his chest. It hurt, it was beating so fast. Maybe he was having a heart attack, Jameson thought. He didn't know. All he knew is that he felt ill. Absolutely fucking sick.

Crawling over to the old man, Jameson shook his own head slowly. The guy was still groaning and writhing around on his back, shifting helplessly from side to side.

Blood was oozing out from beneath him, painting the sidewalk in a bath of deep crimson. He was in pain. The shots had landed too low. His death would be a slow one.

Blinking down at the old man, Jameson felt a flood of sorrow hit him. Why? Why did this have to happen?

"I couldn't let you kill me," Jameson rasped finally.

The old man merely shook his head. Tears leaked from his eyes.

"I would never hurt her," Jameson again, sniffing.

Then bringing his gun up, Jameson sucked in a breath and did what he had to do. There was no way this old man was going to survive. There were no more hospitals, no ambulances and no emergency room doctors.

Pressing his weapon to the center of the old man's forehead, Jameson pulled the trigger.

Pop.

The guy's body jumped once and his feet flopped apart. There was no more movement after that.

"Fuck," Jameson spat the word as his chest heaved.

Glancing around the street, he noted there was no one else around. No eyes were watching him. No guns were pointed at him. Looking back over his shoulder, Jameson spied Cass. She was still unconscious, thank God.

THE NEXT HOUR WAS A BLUR. JAMESON SCOOPED CASS UP AND loaded her into the trunk of his mother's pristine Mercedes sedan. He bound her wrists together, just in case she came to during the drive, and tried to escape. Then Jameson backed out of his parent's garage and into the street.

The trip north to the train station was eerily silent, so he flipped on the radio. It was all static.

There were no other cars on the road... or at least, none that worked. There were plenty of abandoned ones left clogging the roadways, sidewalks and intersections. Thankfully someone else had come through this way before. There was a path of sorts, where vehicles and been moved just enough to sneak a single car through.

After forty-five minutes, Jameson arrived at the train station.

Unlike the rest of the area, this place still had people in it. Mostly, they were soldiers. It wasn't until Jameson put the car in park and flipped off the ignition, that he heard her. Cass. She was awake, and she was pissed.

Resting his forehead on the cream-colored steering wheel, Jameson sucked in a steadying breath.

He was covered in blood, his own and the old man's both. All of sudden, he was tired. So fucking tired. He wanted to lay down *and go to sleep for about a thousand years. But he couldn't. Nope. He was too close now, his task was almost complete.*

Yanking the keys from the ignition, Jameson shoved them deep in his pocket and popped open the driver side door. Not 100 yards away, a line of women were being loaded into one of the train cars. It wasn't a passenger car like he'd hoped. It was a cattle car. The entire train was made up of cattle cars.

Walking around to the trunk, Jameson moved quickly to pop it open. Before Cass could come springing out to destroy him, Jameson leaned down and kissed her square on the mouth.

The kiss was meant to stun her, to throw her off balance, and it worked.

It also set off a million bells in his own body. He had to work hard to stop. He had to work hard to pull away, and when he did, he found he was out of breath.

Staring up at him, Cass's mouth was still parted. Her lips were pink and pouty. Her green eyes were wide and wondering. The anger was gone.

"What was that?" She whispered. "Why are you doing this?"

"Because I love you," the words were out before Jameson could think about them, truth was funny that way. "I fucking love you Cass, and this is the only way to save you. This train will take you to a refugee center."

"Garrett-"

"Eli isn't coming back," he insisted. "And now I've got to leave, too. I need you to get on this train, Cass. For me. Please."

Squeezing her eyes shut, Cass bit at her bottom lip. Jameson felt his stomach sink and his heart crack. Whether she agreed to go or not, whether she loved him back or not, this was goodbye.

Goodbye hurt. It hurt a hell of a lot more than he'd thought it would.

When Cass's eyes flipped back open and they locked on his, he had his answer. When she nodded her head and offered him her bound hands, he felt a flood of sweet relief. She would go. She would go on the train for him.

Taking his knife from his pocket, Jameson flicked it open and cut the rope from her wrists. Then she was sitting up and throwing her arms around his neck and his whole heart shattered.

"Find Eli for me," she whispered. "I know he's out there, Garrett. I just know it."

STANDING STILL IN THE ICY SHOWER, JAMESON'S EYES FLIPPED back open and he let loose a groan. Cass had gotten on that train that day, and ultimately, it had saved her life. But it was what had happened after that, that haunted Jameson the most.

The thing was… he *did* end up finding Eli. Or rather, Eli found him.

CHAPTER SEVENTEEN_
CASS

FOLDING HER ARMS OVER HER CHEST, CASS GLANCED around. The sun was high overhead, with not a cloud in the brilliant blue sky. Even so, the air was cool. She'd put on a pair of tight blue jeans and a short sleeve gray blouse, but maybe long sleeve would have been better.

Beside her, Mia fisted one hand on her hip while she twirled a lock of her short blonde hair with the other. More than thirty people were ranged around them in a semi-circle. Mostly, they were men, with a few women thrown in here and there.

All eyes were focused forward, on the three imposing soldiers standing up front, facing the crowd. Cass's eyes locked on the one in particular that she hadn't seen in over a week. Garrett. He was making a speech, or giving a lecture, however you wanted to phrase it.

At his back was a large single-story cement building. It had no windows and only one door.

Cass could only guess what was inside as she'd never been to this part of the Wall before. They were wedged far in the back, where only soldiers went. All she knew was that day one of survival class was about to begin, and it was titled: Self-Defense.

"All of you are here because you've got it in your heads that you want to leave," Garrett was saying.

His voice lifted to drift over the crowd as his bright blue eyes swept each and every face. Well, except for one face. He skipped Cass. It was like she wasn't even standing there.

"And since Commander Linfield is all about freedom, I'm not here to convince you to stay," Garrett continued. "My function, instead, is to help prepare you for what you will encounter once you leave the safety of the Wall. Not what you *may* encounter, mind you. But what you most definitely *will* encounter."

Pausing for effect, he continued to scan the crowd.

"On the other side of that wall, there are no rules. There are no laws, no policemen, and no soldiers to help you."

Stepping forward, Garrett gestured with his hands as he talked. Cass's eyes tracked him.

Beside her, Mia popped a hip and sighed. Lowering her voice, the blonde ducked her head and whispered in Cass's ear.

"Mr. Hot Stuff can get pretty intense, no?" She teased, and had Cass suppressing a chuckle.

Ignoring them, Garrett's lecture continued.

"For those of you that are soldiers, you already have a

pretty good idea of what you're walking into. But for those of you that are civilians, the world on the outside will come as quite a shock.

No one will be making your meals for you. There will be no grocery stores from which to buy food. Everything you eat, you'll have to either hunt, gather, grow, or steal."

Coming to a stop, Garrett planted both feet and glared.

"The men that you will come across out there are no joke. They've managed to survive a massive civil war, followed by famine, and the loss of society in general. And no matter how nice they may appear, I guarantee you, they've killed at least one person in their fight for survival… probably more like a dozen.

And believe me, killing *you* will always be in the back of their minds.

Maybe it will be for your boots. Maybe it will be for the food in your pack, the water in your canteen, the knife in your pocket. Or maybe it will be for the woman who walks beside you.

It won't really matter why they decide to kill you. All that matters is that you're ready for them when they do."

Lifting a hand, Garrett gestured to the building behind him.

"Which brings me to why you're all standing here today. Inside this building is a shooting range. Who here has fired a gun before?"

Glancing around, Cass noted over half of the crowd raising their hands, Levi and Nolan included. When Cass looked at Mia, her friend merely shook her head slightly and began to fiddle with her hair. This was beginning to feel serious.

"Good." Garrett nodded his head, and people lowered their hands. "You are all dismissed from this class. Our ammunition supply is limited, so we won't be wasting any of it with practice shots for guys that already know what they're doing. This class is for those of you that have never fired a weapon before."

Murmuring amongst themselves, the crowd began to shift as some of the men separated out from the others. Levi made his way over to Cass, with Nolan aiming for Mia. That's when Garrett's voice boomed again.

"There's no time for chit chat," he stated flatly. "Those of you that are left will be split into three groups. We're lucky enough to have Officer Tanner and one of his strike team soldiers, David Wells, here to assist us today. Let's not waste their time."

Cass's eyes snapped over to Garrett who was pointing to the two soldiers that had been lingering at his side. The green-eyed man Cass recognized from their encounter in the restaurant. His name was Cole, so that would make the blonde with the blue eyes David Wells.

All three men had handguns strapped to their hips, but only David Wells had a rifle slung across his back. When he locked eyes with Cass, she frowned.

His expression was empty, lifeless, like there was no one inside of him to peer back out.

"If everyone could just make their way inside," Garrett was saying. "Then we'll get you split up and start training."

Starting forward, Cass looped her arm in Mia's elbow only to have Levi step in front of them. With a quick smile and a flash of white teeth he reached out to run a hand down her upper arm.

"Sorry we won't be able to train together," he said. "Can I catch you after? Another dinner maybe?"

"Um..." Cass's eyes flitted to Mia who merely grinned.

"It would be in the cafeteria, though," Levi added quickly. "I don't have reservations for the restaurant."

Bobbing her head, Cass suppressed a yelp as Mia pinched her side.

"Sure," she squeaked finally and then they were off.

Pushing past Levi and Nolan, Cass practically dragged Mia to the door of the range. It wasn't that she didn't want to have dinner with Levi, they'd actually been hanging out pretty regularly for the past week. It was just that she'd wanted a little break, just a bit of time to breathe and to think.

Slipping into the building, Cass and Mia joined the crowd of bodies standing off to the right. They were in a well-lit rectangular room that was considerably smaller than the building itself. A single long countertop ran the length of one wall with a pair of soldiers standing behind it.

At their backs hung a collection of equipment. Different types of guns, small red and gold boxes labeled with numbers and letters, sets of plastic eye glasses, and army-green colored earmuffs.

Cass gaped at the array of weapons. Mia tightened their already linked arms.

"There's eighteen of you total," Garrett was announcing. "So you'll split into groups of six. Ladies, since there's five of you, let's have you all form one group together, plus one more guy…"

A hand shot into the air and a red-haired man shouted, "Me!"

The room broke into a round of chuckles as Garrett rolled his eyes and dipped his head in acceptance. Cass released a breath, feeling the tension ease all around them.

"Please form lines and step up to the counter." Garrett gestured to the pair of waiting soldiers. "These guys will help get you fitted with eye protection and ear protection. When you're all set, file through this door to my left and into the range."

As people stepped up to the counter, Cass kept her eyes on Garrett. He was folding his thick arms across his chest and leaning back against the wall. Just beside him, the door to the range remained closed.

On his other side, Cole (or Officer Tanner if she was being super respectful) angled his head in closer and began to talk. It was impossible to make out what exactly he said, because so many other voices were now filling the small space, but Cass found herself watching anyway.

Ducking his head, Garrett appeared to listen intently. Then all of a sudden, his eyes popped up and they locked immediately onto Cass. *Crap.*

Looking quickly away, it was all Cass could do not to

reach up and press her palms against the hot flush on her cheeks. Damn the butterflies now exploding in her body.

"Uh-oh." Mia clucked quietly. "Busted."

Biting back a groan, Cass tugged Mia closer to the counter. It was almost their turn, and if she had any luck at all, Officer Tanner or Soldier Wells would be conducting their training. Garrett had done a pretty good job of avoiding her this past week, so why would anything change now?

TEN MINUTES LATER AND CASS'S THEORY GOT BLOWN ALL TO hell.

Garrett would be the women's trainer. Of course he would.

When the group of women (and one happy redheaded male) entered the narrow range, Garrett was waiting for them at the far end.

Shooting Mia a pathetic look, Cass mouthed the word: *Why?*

Her friend merely winked, and mouthed the words: *I told you so.*

Coming to a stop in front of him, their little group clutched their protective glasses in their hands. Their plastic earmuffs were looped around their necks.

Garrett had on a pair of his own earmuffs and motioned for them to put theirs on as well. After they did, he spoke to them in a normal tone of voice. And much to Cass's surprise, they could all hear him.

"These are known as shooter earmuffs," Garrett explained. "They will cancel out the loud noises, but allow us to talk back and forth without shouting. Now, if you look to your right, you will see a sheet of paper hanging about ten yards down range. It has a silhouette of a man on it and that is your target."

One woman raised her hand and Garrett nodded at her to speak.

"That seems pretty close," she said.

"We're starting close," Garrett explained. "But the most you'll practice at is about twenty yards. When you use a handgun, you'll want to wait until your target is close to you. This is an intimate weapon. You'll see the guy blink and hear him breathe. That way, you have a better chance of putting a bullet somewhere vital. Got it?"

Swallowing, Cass nodded her head along with the rest of her group. Somewhere vital. Because the idea was to stop the other person from blinking, to stop them from breathing.

Closing her eyes, she remembered Eli and Neal. She'd heard Neal stop breathing, and now that she remembered, she'd never forget it.

For the next several minutes, Garrett introduced them to their weapon. Holding up a single black handgun he explained that it was a Smith and Wesson MP Shield. This version was slightly smaller than the standard, and therefore easier for a woman to grip.

Nine millimeter was the size of the ammunition. Here was the safety. Here's how you load it. The magazine holds eight rounds. Here's how you put them in. Here's how you take them out. Here's how you cock it. Here's how you aim. Here's how you fire. Again. Again.

One by one, the women all around Cass were called forward to practice. Some of them were better than others.

Glancing to her right, Cass watched the rest of the men shooting in the range. Officer Tanner was taking up two lanes with his six guys and Soldier Wells had the next two lanes down.

Not Garrett though. He was going one by one, and thereby taking a lot more time than the others.

By the time it was Cass's turn, all the other shooting in the range had ceased, but no one had left. All eyes were on her. She hated him for it.

"Come on, Cass." Garrett gestured for her to step up beside him.

The gun was lying flush on the short countertop. A fresh silhouette target was hanging in its spot down range. Willing her body to stop shaking, Cass sucked in a breath and walked up to him.

All of a sudden the space they both occupied seemed extra cramped, intimate even. There was a solid barrier on her immediate right and a wall just to their left. Although she knew everyone was watching, Cass could no longer see any of them. It was just her, the gun, and Garrett.

"Your gun is not loaded," Garrett spoke quietly. "But I

want you to check it anyway. Get in the habit, whenever you pick up a gun."

"Okay," Cass exhaled the word and did as she was told.

"Good." Garrett bobbed his head. "Now load it. Remember, only point the barrel down range or at the ground. I'll move just behind you."

Clearing her throat, Cass picked up the magazine and slid it into place. Raising the gun, she flipped off the safety and pointed it at the target. Her hands were trembling slightly, and it embarrassed her. Why did she feel so unsteady?

"Take your time," Garrett whispered. "Aim like this. Look at the sight. You see it?"

Maybe Garrett had been standing close to her before, but it was nothing to what he did next. Cass felt his entire body envelope hers. Garrett's arms came to wrap around her arms, his chest was pressing against her back, his hips were brushing against her butt.

"Now just, keep your eye on your target," he continued calmly. She could feel his breath exhaling against her neck. "And gently squeeze the trigger. One fluid motion. Let the shot surprise you when it happens."

Biting at her lower lip, Cass tried like hell to focus on the black silhouette hanging motionless exactly ten yards away. He hadn't done this with anyone else, had he?

No. She'd watched each and every lesson, and sure he'd corrected the others with a hand here, or a shoulder shift there, but not with his entire body.

His entire, sexy body. The one currently sending a

million sparks zinging through Cass. Lightning. Damn the lightning.

"You okay?" He asked quietly. "No pressure, but fire anytime."

Sucking in a ragged breath, Cass's hand jerked and she pulled the trigger. The shot went wide. It didn't even hit the edge of the paper.

"That's okay," Garrett breathed, still behind her. "Just, aim and try again. Ease your finger against the trigger. Try not to jerk your hand."

Closing her eyes, Cass pressed her lips together. Her tummy was dancing and her chest was constricting and her hands were shaking. Everyone. Was. Watching.

She couldn't do it. Everyone was watching her fail and with Garrett so close, she couldn't concentrate, she couldn't calm down.

"No." Cass bit out the word as her eyes shot open.

"No?" Garrett asked, she could hear his confusion.

Giving her head a violent shake, Cass set the gun down on the counter and slipped out from beneath his arms. Keeping her head down, she ripped off the earmuffs and fled down the aisle in the range.

She had to get away.

She had to get out.

As she ran past them, she could hear people murmuring. Bodies were shifting and boots were shuffling. There were twenty-one sets of eyes on her right now, of that she was certain. She'd never been more embarrassed in her life.

Picking up her feet, Cass abandoned all composure and

ran. Her lungs were tight and her cheeks were bright red. It wasn't until she burst out of the building entirely, that she could breathe again. Her lungs sucked in air, but her feet kept right on pounding over the grass.

Glancing over her shoulder, Cass assured herself no one was racing after her. The door was swinging closed and no other bodies appeared. Not Mia and not Garrett. Even still, her heart raced up into her throat and she felt the need to keep running.

She had to get away. She had to escape.

Her body urged her on, even when her mind knew there was no practical reason to keep running. Overhead, the sun was still shining and the sky was still blue, and that's when it hit her. The deja vu. The intense feeling that this had happened before, that Garrett had chased her before, that running from Garrett was… familiar.

CHAPTER EIGHTEEN_
JAMESON

Standing at the bottom of the flight control tower, Jameson looked up. It was tall, the highest structure that had been built inside the Wall, and thanks to Uriah's paranoia its power cable had been dug up and disconnected months ago.

Beside him, Cole held a hand up to shade his eyes and frowned.

"What happens if there's an incoming air strike?" He asked.

Huffing dismissively, Jameson gripped the two straps currently digging into his shoulders and adjusted the heavy pack on his back. It contained a PRC-511. It was time for a little test.

"Where would an air strike come from?" Jameson asked finally and stepped forward to unlock the door.

"Oh, I don't know," Cole sneered. "Maybe one of the

other refugee centers? Who knows what the hell's out there."

"I guess Uriah's willing to take that risk," Jameson offered. "At least until we have a better handle on the source, and if it has the ability to come back."

Grumbling under his breath, Cole adjusted the pack on his own back and threw a glance to his buddy, David Wells. The blonde had yet another PRC-511 strapped to him, but he didn't seem at all bothered by the weight. In fact, the guy didn't seem particularly bothered by anything. He just shadowed Cole, all quiet and watchful and steady.

Twisting the silver key in the lock, Jameson opened the heavy metal door and stepped back. The interior of the tower was dark, with a single elevator at the bottom and a narrow set of stairs off to one side. No power equals no elevator so they had quite the climb ahead of them.

With a last glance to the empty air strip that lay just behind them, Jameson motioned the pair of soldiers inside. The plan was to haul these three units up to the top and turn them on. Uriah had sent Hernandez and five other soldiers to various points outside the Wall. If the radio units worked as they should, then life as they knew it would begin to expand. They'd have long range communications again. The possibilities were encouraging.

Walking over to the elevator, Cole jammed one finger on the button impatiently.

"Doesn't it have a backup generator or something?" He groaned.

"It does, but that takes fuel," Jameson reasoned. "No sense wasting any when we can climb."

Cole's gaze drifted over to the stairwell and he sucked in a breath. Jameson narrowed his eyes.

Cole almost died in a stairwell just like this one not so very long ago, hence the small limp he couldn't quite hide. Maybe he shouldn't be going up with them after all. Maybe it should just be him and Davey… David Wells.

"Hey." Jameson cleared his throat and nodded at the stairs. "You good?"

Giving his head a purposeful shake, Cole stepped around to yank open the door to the stairwell himself. Gesturing for Jameson to go first, Cole rolled his eyes.

"After you," he stated flatly and had Jameson grinning.

"You're a tough bastard," Jameson commented as he began to climb. "I'll give you that."

"I don't know what you're talking about," Cole replied.

Davey, as usual, remained silent.

For what seemed a long time, the sound of their steps filled the space. It was dim, but not terribly dark, with high windows positioned on each and every landing. The air was slightly stale and tasted of dust.

As their boots continued to stomp, the pack grew heavier on Jameson's back. He felt the straps pressing down into his shoulders as a trickle of sweat slipped along his spine. His breath puffed out of his lungs and his thigh muscles burned. It was an almost pleasant feeling, the exertion.

When they reached the top, Jameson shoved through

yet another door and into the control room. The large space was in the shape of an octagon. Every wall was made up of windows. The view was… surreal.

Crossing to one of the many desks that sat in neat little lines in the center of the room, Jameson slipped the equipment off his back and laid it down. Beside him, Cole and Davey did the same.

"Alright, let's set them all up first, then we can turn them on one at a time and do a check," Jameson stated, then turned to Davey. "You got the frequency list?"

The blonde soldier swung his gaze almost reluctantly over to Jameson before nodding his head once. Those light-blue eyes of his were piercing as he stared hard for a moment, but then Davey was shrugging off his own pack and turning away.

A man of few words, Jameson figured. And more than a little strange.

Focusing on the task at hand, Jameson got out the large box radio, the retractable antenna and the battery packs. Somewhere approximately five miles away on a neighboring mountainside, sat Hernandez and Malik. They were just one of three teams with the same equipment waiting for a signal test.

Pursing his lips, Jameson arranged his equipment and hoped like hell this worked.

"You still want our help for the next survival class?" Cole asked.

He was setting up his PRC-511 a few tables over. With Hannah pregnant, the trio had decided to stick around, at least until after the baby arrived. Liam was freaked out as it was, so they figured there was no need to throw a home birth at him.

Lena had told Jameson all about it. She was pretty gossipy when he came to hold Ian.

"Yeah," Jameson answered as he fumbled with his own antenna. The piece of equipment was pretty big actually so it would need a table all its own.

"You gonna keep sabotaging Cass, or will you let one of us work with her this time?" Cole asked casually.

"Excuse me?" Jameson's brow furrowed as his eyes popped over to Cole.

The guy was chuckling softly and shaking his head.

"Don't think I don't know what you're doing," Cole said, his hands kept working even as he talked.

"Oh yeah?" Jameson's frown turned into an outright scowl. "And what's that?"

"Come on…" Cole turned to him and grinned. "No one could get a shot off with your big ass humping them in front of everyone."

Jameson's brows rose and his mouth dropped open. Cole continued to eye him with a knowing look plastered across that smug face of his. Jameson sputtered and reached for a response.

"I was helping her balance," he tried finally.

So what if the weight of his arms had thrown off her aim. If she stayed behind the Wall, she'd never need to know how to shoot. *And* if Cass couldn't pass any of the survival classes, then she couldn't leave the Wall.

Boom. Problem solved.

"Is that what they're calling it these days?" Cole teased. "I'll tell Hannah that the next time I try rubbing my dick all over her ass in front of twenty people. I'm sure it'll go over real well."

"Hey, fucker." Jameson dropped what he was doing and rotated fully to face Cole. "I was not rubbing my dick on her. Was. Not."

In fact, it'd taken quite a bit of concentration from Jameson not to get hard, thank you very much. So in the end, he was actually pretty proud of himself. Cass was now afraid of shooting. She'd run away and thereby failed the course. *And* she had no idea how good it'd felt for him to cover her like that so… no harm, no foul.

"Whatever," Cole huffed and raised his voice. "What do you think Davey boy? Is Jameson full of shit?"

Glancing over his shoulder, Jameson shot a look at the blonde soldier. He was standing a few tables over, setting up his own radio. His eyes were focused downward, his hands moving methodically over the equipment. For several seconds, he gave no indication that he'd heard them. Then finally, his jaw ticked once and he swallowed hard.

"Yeah." Davey nodded his head but he did not look over. "He's full of shit."

Jameson returned his gaze to Cole with his eyebrows raised in question. In response, the other guy's shoulders sagged and he let loose a low sigh. Something was off with Davey. Something was definitely off.

Lowering his voice, Jameson took a step closer to Cole and frowned.

"That guy ever joke around?" He asked.

"He used to," Cole murmured his response. "But he hasn't been the same since his brother died."

"Oh." Jameson's frown eased, and he felt that familiar pinch you get when you hear about that kind of thing. "I'm sorry."

Cole's eyes darted up to Jameson's face then and he opened his mouth to speak. His green eyes were searching and his expression was grim. But then at the last moment, he seemed to reconsider.

Giving his head a slight shake, Cole's mouth snapped shut and he exhaled through his nostrils.

"Remind me to tell you about that," he said finally. "Some other time."

Pulling her hair off the back of her neck, Cass gathered it into a ponytail and held the thick mass of curls in one hand. She should've tied it up before they came in here, but it hadn't been nearly this hot outside.

Blowing out a breath, she felt a line of perspiration beading on her brow. Above them, the massive green-tinted glass of the greenhouse distorted the color of the sky.

"Look, just don't worry about it," Mia sighed. "It was only one class."

Letting loose a pitiful whimper, Cass released her hair and dragged both of her hands down her face. Only one class? Easy for Mia to say, she hadn't taken off like a crazy person in front of twenty-one witnesses.

Speaking through her fingers, Cass uttered the words she'd repeated for the past two weeks, "I'm still so embarrassed."

"Don't be," Mia insisted. "Besides, you've been good at everything else so far."

Coming to a stop at one of her orange trees, Mia knelt in the dirt and began sinking her fingers into the soil. Cass fisted her hands on both hips and watched. They'd been working in the grove for several hours already, and by *they* she meant, Mia worked and Cass hid from Levi and Garrett and everyone else she knew.

But soon it would be time for another survival class. She couldn't skulk around in Mia's orchard forever. And Cass dreaded it.

Okay, so maybe dread was a strong word, but she wasn't looking forward to it, that's for sure.

"You passed the fire-making," Mia said absently, still tending to the dirt beneath her tree.

"Only because you lent me your flint," Cass reminded her. "Mine wouldn't work."

"Yeah, but you got the fire to light in the end," Mia continued. "And the food preservation class went well."

"Except my first set of jars didn't seal because the lids were all defective," Cass cut in. "I swear, it's like someone's sabotaging me. How am I ever going to get to California if I can't even fire a gun?"

Rocking back on her heels, Mia dusted at her hands and shoved up to standing. After giving Cass a patronizing look, she pulled a folded sheet of paper from her back pocket along with a pen. Brows furrowed, Mia scribbled a few notes before replacing the items and walking to the next tree.

"You can fire a gun," Mia reasoned. "You just can't hit anything with it. Besides, it's not like we own a gun anyway. Levi and Nolan will be with us and they both have guns. We'll be fine."

Nodding absently, Cass trailed Mia to the next tree. It was true, just because they wanted to leave did not mean they would be issued a weapon. Garrett had explained that guns were in limited supply, along with ammunition. Any soldiers that wanted to leave could keep their weapons, but civilians were basically out of luck.

Cass and Mia could try to buy a gun, but Commander Linfield wasn't selling any of his army's stock and none of the soldiers were willing to part with their's either.

Frowning, Cass fought the swirl of nervousness this idea brought on. The fantasy of going to find her brother was one thing, and this violent reality was turning out to be another. If it was really that dangerous outside the Wall, then she'd definitely need a way to defend herself.

Coming to a halt beside her friend, Cass watched Mia reach up to rub a few green leaves between her fingertips. Mia's eyes twinkled as she murmured something under her breath. Cass had no idea what exactly she was doing, but she figured the same could be said of Mia when Cass was making her dress. Did it matter the process? The end product was perfection.

Inhaling, Cass took in the scent of the oranges hanging all around them. They smelled tart and sweet all at the same time. Coupled with the humidity inside the green-house, the air was heady... almost overwhelming.

"So what do we have left?" Mia asked absently, her face tipped skyward as she examined the green canopy above them.

"Um..." Cass tugged on the front of her blouse in an attempt to get more air. "Build a shelter, processing meat from an animal, hunting, and two more I can't remember."

"So that's what, like another month maybe and we'll be looking to leave," Mia reasoned. "Have you got the address yet?"

Sucking in a breath, Cass glanced down and stubbed the toe of her boot in the dirt. She'd been avoiding Garrett, dealing with her own nightmares and trying to let go of her very physical reaction to him. That lightning thing, complete with tingles and heat exploding everywhere, yeah, she had to get rid of that somehow.

"Not yet," she admitted finally. "But I will. I'll get it from him."

Rolling her eyes, Mia huffed a laugh and reached for her back pocket. After scribbling some more things on her paper, she proceeded on to the next tree.

Cass trailed her like a sweaty, damp, apologetic puppy. Perspiration trickled off her skin, she didn't know how Mia did this day after day.

"It is miserable hot in here, you know that?" An unfamiliar voice had both women stopping in their tracks.

Turning around slowly, both Mia and Cass's mouths dropped open. There was a pretty golden-haired woman standing just behind them. She had one hand propped on her hip and another fanning her flushed face. She was clearly the source of the voice, but that wasn't what had Mia and Cass gaping. Nope.

It was the tower of tall dark and intimidating that stood still just behind her. The man was as tall as Garrett, but slightly leaner. With his black hair, olive skin and chocolate eyes, he was everything dangerous and handsome and sexy put together.

And he was staring right at them... looking both interested and bored all at once, if that was possible.

Unfazed by their gaping, the woman kept right on talking. There was something vaguely familiar about her, but Cass couldn't quite place it.

"You're not the easiest person to find," the woman was saying. "But Liam's a little bit good at tracking things down so, bingo, here we are."

Cass blinked. Mia blinked. The woman grinned and offered her hand for a shake.

"I'm Hannah, by the way," she said. "I know you're Cass so that must make you Mia."

"Um..." Cass's brow furrowed as she shook the woman's hand. Glancing quickly to Mia, she noted her friend's eyes were drifting slowly up to the scary/sexy dude's face. "Yeah. I mean yes, I'm Cass."

"Oh, don't mind him." Hannah gestured easily behind her. "He's in stalker mode, but I swear he's harmless."

At her comment, Liam raised one eyebrow and snorted. Mia's mouth snapped shut. Cass swallowed.

"Anyway..." Hannah huffed a breath and let one hand slip down to stroke at her belly. "I was talking with my husband and he mentioned some issues with you in your survival classes."

Cass's eyes flipped from Hannah to this Liam dude before narrowing. How would that guy know anything about it? She'd never met him before.

"Oh not that husband." Hannah waved a hand. "I mean Cole. You know Cole."

Cass's brows hit her hairline as her gaze popped from Liam back over to Hannah. Beside her, Mia choked. Not *that* husband... as in... more than one...?

"Wait, wait, wait," Mia managed finally. "What's going on?"

"Cole said you're having a bit of a problem with Jameson," Hannah explained. "And I'd like to offer my assistance... or rather, Liam's assistance."

"I don't understand." Cass shook her head.

Frowning, she looked once again to Mia for help. Her friend simply splayed her palms out in a helpless gesture and shrugged.

"You need to learn how to shoot," Hannah supplied. "You need to know how to defend yourself, to kick some ass. Right?"

Nodding her head, Cass ran a nervous hand back through her tangle of brown curls. Yeah, she needed to know all of that.

"Liam's what you would call an expert at that sort of thing," Hannah continued. "He can teach you how to shoot and instruct you on some hand to hand stuff. He's also pretty handy with a knife. Are you interested?"

"But... why?" Cass's eyes flitted past Hannah to settle on Liam. Mr. Sexy Danger just stared right back at her. "Why would you help me?"

Stepping forward, the guy laid a large palm on Hannah's shoulder.

"There was a time when Jameson was extra helpful to Hannah," Liam explained. "He helped her to leave a place when I wasn't willing to let her go. Everything worked out in the end, but let's just say... I'm looking forward to returning the favor."

"But, I'm not Garrett's girlfriend..." Cass offered, then realizing her error, she corrected, "Jameson. I mean, I'm not Jameson's girlfriend. So why do you care?"

Smirking, Liam gave his head a little shake.

"Semantics," he responded. "So are you interested? I'll want to work with you every day for a few weeks, maybe even every day until you go."

Huffing a breath, Cass brought both of her hands to her hips and pursed her lips. She did need to know these things, and even if she'd never met this Liam or Hannah before, it wasn't like she was getting any other offers.

Plus, they'd mentioned Cole and he'd been one of her instructors for the past several weeks. He was always professional and charismatic and sometimes down right charming. She felt she could trust him. Actually, she *did* trust him, and if this was his wife then...

"Alright," Cass said finally. "I'd really appreciate that. I mean, thank you, I'll do it. I'll do whatever you tell me to do."

Rubbing his hands together, Liam grinned. It was the first hint of softness that he'd shown and Cass had to admit, his already handsome face lit up with the expression.

"Perfect," he said. "Let's start first thing tomorrow."

ROLLING OUT OF BED, JAMESON RUBBED AT THE BACK OF HIS neck and stifled a yawn. The sun was shining outside his small bedroom window. It was mid-morning already, he'd slept in.

This wasn't part of his normal routine. Usually, he'd of been up by dawn. That gave him time for an early run to loosen his body and center his mind. Then he'd hit the gym for maybe an hour before reporting to work.

But last night had been a late one.

Uriah had called him over to their apartment. Ian had his first cold. Lena hadn't slept in two days and Uriah couldn't miss his morning meetings, so until about two a.m., Jameson had let the both of them sleep.

He'd stayed awake, holding Ian upright, listening to his pitiful little coughing until Lena had roused and taken over.

So here Jameson was, oversleeping and a touch groggy.

But when he planted his bare feet on his gray carpet, he was ready to start his day, only about four hours behind schedule.

Shuffling to his closet, Jameson pulled out a pair of black sweats and a white t-shirt. After getting dressed, he left his room, used the bathroom quickly, and skipped the shower.

He'd use the one at the gym after he was done. He kept a spare uniform in a locker there, as well as a pair of boots.

After lacing up his running shoes, Jameson shoved out of his apartment and tried not to focus on the door just across the hall. Was she in there? Was she already at work?

It wasn't a survival class day, so the chances of seeing Cass were pretty close to zero. He told himself he didn't miss her. He told himself it was just habit. And the fact that she hadn't come to him with any of her nightmares for the past three weeks absolutely did not bother him. *Right.*

He didn't miss the smell of her on his sheets when she left in the morning. He didn't miss the look of her in those tiny pajamas, or the sorry excuse for a robe she wore (it didn't hide anything, by the way).

Nope. He relished his space. This was good for him. He needed this.

Especially since she hadn't been giving that Levi asshole the time of day either. Jameson knew. He'd checked. And that wasn't one bit stalker-ish. Nope.

Anyway Jameson figured Cass was avoiding him now. The idea both stung and set him at ease all at the same time.

Maybe it was finally sinking in for her, the reality of life beyond the Wall. Maybe she would finally give up, reconsider, stay home. He'd put in enough effort at humiliating her by now. Any normal chick would've been properly scared off.

The thing about Cass was, she had grit, she didn't scare easy. And she got it from Eli, damn him.

Jogging down the stairs, Jameson kept his body loose and let his muscles work. He needed this run to center his mind, to brush off thoughts of her. Pretty soon, he was slamming out into the sunshine and picking up the pace.

The grounds were serene. Late-spring was in full swing now, with summer just around the corner.

At this time of day, the colors seemed brighter, the sounds more brash. He heard the squeal of children, the gossip of women, the laughter of men. The grass was greener, the trees taller, the sky a more crisp shade of blue.

Again Jameson's mind wandered back to Cass. He thought about high school, about all of those years of her being so damn close, but so frustratingly untouchable at the same time. He thought of all the boyfriends he'd scared off, and all the girls he'd screwed drunk, trying like hell to rid Eli's little sister from his system.

Shaking his head, Jameson dismissed the irony. Here he was, right back to square one. Him wanting Cass, and her not knowing which way was up. His conscience ate at him daily, with Eli hovering at the back of his mind. And yet his body kept making its demands.

"Stop it," he murmured to himself.

His chest was expanding and contracting with his measured breathing, his thighs burned pleasantly and his feet kept pounding along the cement sidewalk. The gym was just up ahead, and he'd be primed and ready to hit it hard. Nothing like a little pain to push away the thoughts, to eliminate the desires.

Cresting the stone steps, Jameson tugged open the single glass door and slammed his way inside. Sucking air, he took in the scent of rubber mats and the tang of body sweat. There was a line of treadmills off to the right, weights against the far wall and a variety of equipment spaced in the center of the room.

Normally, guys (and gals) would be busy using said machines, but today it was virtually empty.

Stopping short, Jameson's gaze was drawn to the far left, where a crowd of people were standing around the boxing ring. Strange, he thought, someone must have a friendly competition going on.

Bracing his hands on his hips, Jameson wove his way through the various machines until he reached the group of people. Their cheers and boos filled the space. All of their attention was directed at whoever was fighting in that ring.

Being tall, it only took Jameson a few blinks to lock in on a familiar figure standing in the corner of the ring. It was Liam, and he was shouting instructions at whoever was sparring.

Although the platform itself was elevated, the people who were fighting were on the ground, which made it difficult to see them. Jameson's eyes jumped to another familiar figure standing just behind Liam, but on the opposite side of the ropes. *That* particular person caught Jameson's stare.

Oh. Shit. Cole mouthed the words as they locked eyes.

Jameson frowned.

Liam was oblivious. He was too caught up in calling out moves to notice anything else.

"Now stab him!" Liam called. "Yeah! There. Again! Fucking quick, damn it! Like I showed you."

The crowd around the ring groaned, and then Jameson was wedging his body through, pushing people aside as he went.

He heard a few guys protest, but like most times he tossed men around, they shut the hell up when they turned and took a look at him. Jameson didn't even glance their way. He kept his eyes on that ring.

And suddenly, he was standing at the ropes and everything came into view. There was Cass, in shorts so fucking tiny they were more like panties, and a damn tank top. She was straddling some guy on the ground, clutching a fake wooden knife in her hand and grinning.

She looked like an avenging angel. A murdering goddess with wild hair and flushed skin.

And she was on full display, with a hundred eyes looking.

"What. The. Fuck." Jameson growled the words. He could feel them rumble around inside his chest before they burst from his throat.

Whipping her head around to look at him, Cass's mossy-green eyes were glowing as her chest heaved in and out. She had head gear on and a mouth guard protecting those pearly white teeth of hers, but damn if Jameson's heart didn't trip in his chest just a little.

Of course, her momentary distraction was all the guy beneath her needed. Without hesitating, he reversed their positions, flipping her onto her back and pressing her into the mat.

It was Levi. And although he didn't hurt her, Jameson felt all the blood in his body rush to his head where it swirled and clouded his vision.

This guy again. Seriously?

Hulk. Fucking. Smash.

Before Jameson could leap between the ropes and make good on his body's threat, Liam was stepping up to the pair inside the ring and yanking Levi off of her. The guy tripped back a few feet and swiped at the sweat on his brow.

Ignoring him, Liam knelt down and continued with his instruction as Cass drew her knees to her chest and tried to catch her breath. Her mouth was parted and she was panting, but the whole time Liam talked, her eyes were locked on Jameson.

"That was good," Liam was saying. "You got him in the kidneys, but that's a slow death. I want him to die quicker than that next time. He had time to get on top of you. That's a no go."

"Alright," Cass answered between breaths and finally

ducked her head.

Reaching for her, Liam helped her up to her feet and shuffled her back to the far corner of the ring. Jameson's hands gripped the ropes of the boxing ring and tightened as he watched. But then Cole was crossing in front of him and squatting down, effectively blocking his view. Apparently, that last part was deliberate.

"You're here late." Cole tilted his head to one side and offered one of his most charming grins.

Jameson glared. Fucking traitor. The desire to wipe that smirk off of Cole's face suddenly became quite strong.

"What the fuck, Cole?" Jameson accused.

"Hey." Cole held up his hands in defense and chuckled. *Chuckled.* "She's a natural. Liam hasn't even been working with her all that long and she's pretty damn good."

"Yeah. That's because this isn't her first rodeo. Her brother taught her how to fight." Jameson sucked in a breath and tried to dial himself in.

There were a ton of witnesses here. He couldn't exactly go Hulk at the moment. He had no good reason.

"That so?" Cole's eyebrows raised.

"Not with a knife," Jameson qualified, thinking back. "But with her fists, her body. She packs a hit."

"You speak from experience?" Cole again, his voice teasing.

Tapping his own nose, Jameson's expression was grim. "She broke this once."

"Ouch." Cole smiled. "I'm sure it was deserved."

"Look asshole," Jameson hissed. "I've been working

awfully hard to make sure she never has to use that shit again. Now you go behind my back and train her?"

"Not me." Cole shook his head and pressed a hand over his heart. Mocking son of a... "But the wife had other plans."

"Hannah." Jameson shut his eyes and tipped his head back.

He should've known someone would talk. If not Cole to Hannah, then Uriah to Lena. They were all conspiring against him. They just didn't understand.

"Alright," Liam's voice boomed in the noisy room as he clapped his hands together. "We're going to reset. Cole, move your fat ass."

Grumbling good-naturedly, Cole stood up and climbed through the ropes to the ground. That's when Liam's gaze locked on Jameson. And it was only one second before those calculating dark eyes of his sparked.

Jameson's gut sank.

Oh. Shit.

"Jameson," Liam called. "Why don't you step in for Levi. He's getting pretty worn out. My fighter needs someone fresh to destroy."

"That's not necessary," Levi protested, running a hand back through his hair. "I feel fine."

"Nah." Liam shook his head, but he didn't even glance at the guy. "Go sit."

Gritting his teeth, Jameson's eyes danced from a departing Levi over to Cass. She was standing in the far corner, her skin glistening with sweat, her curly hair springing wildly out of her high ponytail. As he watched, her chest puffed in and out, working for air, but not overly so.

Behind her, her little blonde bombshell friend was handing her a water bottle and whispering something suspicious. Mia and Cass were way too much trouble. After a beat, the two girls giggled. *Giggled*.

Jameson's jaw ticked. Why was everyone so damn cheery? Didn't they get that this was a fucking funeral?

Climbing reluctantly up through the ropes, Jameson rose to standing in the elevated ring and rolled his shoulders. He towered over Cass. Towered over her.

Walking along the edge of the ring, he let loose a breath and eyed Liam. His old "sort of" friend let the corner of his mouth twitch up just a hair. He was enjoying this.

So obviously this was payback for helping Hannah escape Utah and get to the Wall. But still… the nerve of this jerk, helping Cass to leave, helping her get ready to go. It was infuriating.

And sure, maybe the guy thought he was doing Jameson a favor, setting up this little wrestling match, but in reality he was just bending Jameson over… big time. Because there was no way that he could wrestle around with Cass and not trigger a memory. It simply hit too close to home. But nobody else knew that.

With a satisfied smirk, Liam grabbed some head gear and a fresh mouth guard from Cole and tossed them at Jameson.

"Let's start with you attacking her from behind," Liam

stated. "Just approach her from the back and try to pin her."

Ducking his head, Jameson tried to hide his grimace. Of all the attack positions for Liam to choose, it had to be that one. Karma. Fucking karma.

Shifting on his feet, Jameson adjusted his gear and then jumped up and down, trying to shake off his nerves. Cass was walking to the center of the ring, with her fake knife tucked into her waistband and a playful look on her face. When she turned her back on him, he stopped jumping.

For a moment, he just stared at her. Whose idea was it to have her in those damn little shorts? It killed him. She killed him. And if he really did trigger a flashback right now, then she was *actually* going to try to kill him.

"Before we start," Cole announced and had everyone quieting. "How about a little wager?"

Holy. Shit. Jameson's stomach clenched. Could this get any worse?

"If Cass wins, then Jameson has to let her retake the shooter class," Cole continued. "Without humping her this time."

The room rippled with laughter and Cass threw Jameson a look over her shoulder. Her cheeks flushed and her lips twitched.

He tried to swallow then, but his mouth had gone bone dry. *This is maybe the last time you're going to look at me like that... like I'm your friend.*

"And if Jameson wins," Cole cut in. "Then Cass has to give him a date."

Closing his eyes, Jameson sighed.

That did it. If the room had rippled with indulgent laughter before, it exploded with catcalls now. The crowd was hooting and Cass was clearing her throat and Jameson was trying not to melt through the floor. His friends meant well... really, they did. But could a guy not catch a break?

Of course, he was the one with the secret. They couldn't know how badly they were fucking him over right now.

"Alright! Alright!" Liam was shouting. "Let's get it! Kill his ass, Cass!"

Jameson's eyes flipped open and he licked his lips. Liam motioned for him to go.

Stepping forward on feet that didn't feel like his own, Jameson approached Cass from behind. His mind kept alternating between the two very distinct times he'd allowed himself to do this. The first time, he'd been short of breath, running, angry. He'd scooped her up against him so fast, he hadn't even had time to feel her pressed against him.

The second time, had been at the gun range. He'd been controlled, focused, and just a touch ashamed. He'd taken his time, enjoying the way her smaller body fit against his. He'd kept his hands on her arms then, and he'd drawn it out for as long as he could.

So this time... it'd be different. He expected her to act quickly. He expected her immediate refusal, her immediate attack.

Walking up behind her, Jameson wrapped his arms

around her body and pressed his chest into her back. One of his palms splayed itself out over her stomach, the other one crossed over her body and gripped her opposite arm.

He was nervous, worried, scared. He kept his face tilted to the side, anticipating her signature move. He didn't want the back of her skull to crush his nose a second time.

But as they stood there, nothing happened. He felt her chest drawing air into her lungs. One beat, then another. His heart was pounding in his chest and his lips were parting and the sparks shooting themselves from his head to his toes were almost unbearable.

Why was she waiting? Why wasn't she moving? The questions blurred together in his mind until all he could sense was her butt pressed against his hips and her softness beneath his hands. He wanted to move his mouth to the back of her neck and brush his lips against her skin.

"You alright?" He whispered. His voice was a rumble, coming from somewhere deep down in his body.

Ever so slightly, Cass tilted her head to one side. Her curls brushed against his face, tickling his lips and making him want to flip her on her back right now. He wanted her beneath him, and all alone.

But then she was moving. One second, he was thinking *those* thoughts, and the next she was rolling him easily over her shoulder.

He landed on his back with a whoosh of expelled breath and wide eyes.

Then she was on him. Jameson felt the point of her fake wooden knife press into the skin at the base of his throat.

With a little more force and a real blade, she could shove the thing all the way through to his spine.

Which was the point, really. He would be dead in seconds, his brain effectively severed from the rest of his body.

Boom. Deadly. Done.

Panting, Cass kept her hand steady as her legs straddled his chest. Her dark curls were tumbling forward now and they swayed slightly between them.

Jameson blinked. It was almost like a dream. She was that beautiful. She was the most beautiful angel of death he'd ever seen. And a part of him wished things could end just like this, in a split second, before he ever had to make his confession.

"Guess you didn't really want that date," she said quietly before shoving off of him and striding away.

Tucking the wooden knife back into the waistband of her shorts, Cass exhaled a shaky breath. Her bare feet padded along the surface of the boxing ring, heading back towards her corner. Sweat trickled down her forehead, burning her eyes and causing her to blink furiously.

"You're worthless Jameson," Liam sneered. "Get your big ass up and let's re-set. You've actually gotta try this time."

Behind her, Cass could feel the whole ground shift as Jameson moved to get up. Her heart was pounding and her lungs were heaving. She wasn't sure if it was from the training or from being this close to him again.

Suddenly, a water bottle was being thrust in her face. Flicking her eyes up, Cass accepted the drink and eyed Mia. Her friend was smirking mercilessly as she lowered her voice and leaned over the ropes.

"He's staring at your butt right now," she snickered. "Just thought you should know."

Huffing a breath, Cass fought the trembling in her hand as she removed her mouthguard and clutched the water.

"He didn't even try," she murmured back. "He let me flip him on purpose."

"Don't be so sure." Mia wiggled her eyebrows and reached in to tip the bottom of the bottle up so Cass would actually take a drink. "Mr. Hot Stuff just doesn't know what to do with himself."

Gulping some water, Cass pushed the drink back at Mia and swiped the back of her hand over her mouth. Liam was in her face now, giving her a once over with those intense brown eyes of his.

"That was good," he said. "But this time it's for real. He's a big boy, so when he goes to grab you, you're gonna need to act quick. It may have felt easy to flip him before, but he's got a good hundred pounds on you and it's all muscle. If he doesn't want to be flipped, you won't get him over this time."

"So what do you suggest?" Cass's brow furrowed, her hands coming to fist on her hips.

"Hit him fast and hard." Liam bobbed his head. "Remember his sensitive spots."

Reaching a hand between the two of them, Liam poked a finger at her throat, her nose, then her eyes. Cass bobbed her head and jumped in place a bit, trying to shake off her nerves.

Why was she nervous all of a sudden? She'd been all

confidence and swagger when she'd been fighting with Levi.

"Use your entire body," he reminded her. "Get to your knife first thing. A gut shot might get him to drop you, but be ready for the fall and use it to your advantage. Get on him and hit a kill spot right away… more than one if you have to."

"Okay." Cass nodded her head and popped her mouthguard back in.

Straightening up, Liam looked over her head and shouted. The noise in the room quieted, but only slightly. Everyone was still talking and laughing all at once.

"Same deal as before!" Liam called. "But you gotta try this time jerk off or I'm gonna bring her little dinner date back in here instead. Got it?"

In response, the crowd let out a collection of taunts and hoots that had the corner of Cass's mouth twitching. Avoiding Garrett's stare, she stalked back to the center of the ring and gave him her back. Closing her eyes a moment, Cass inhaled deeply and then let everything go.

She'd been training with Liam every day for a few weeks now, but it hadn't taken her body or mind all that long to get in line. It was like this was familiar. The hitting and the wrestling and the adrenaline all spoke to her, woke something inside of her up.

When she opened her eyes, the room was silent. Looking around, Cass saw people moving their mouths, nodding their heads and talking to one another. It wasn't that they weren't making noise, it was just that her ears had turned them all off.

Giving a slight nod, Liam clapped his hands once and she knew what was coming. Her body could sense him… Garrett… start to move. She could feel his energy collecting behind her, even over the sound of her own breathing, and the beat of her own heart.

The ground shifted, but only slightly, he was being extra light on his feet this time. It took a lot of will power not to glance at him over her shoulder, but they were supposed to be simulating a surprise attack so she kept facing forward. Even so, all of her senses were on high alert.

And this was important. Winning was important.

Cass had a plan in mind. A series of steps, if you will. So when Garrett's hands grabbed her and he hauled her up off her feet, instinct took over.

Throwing her head back, Cass intended on crushing his nose with the back of her head. But all she met with was empty air. He'd ducked off to one side, saving himself. Cass's legs were kicking out in front of her now and so she twisted her body. She was wriggling, writhing, and trying desperately to break free.

Then her brain blitzed on her. It was like static. She felt a scream bubbling up from between her lungs.

One second, Cass was in a boxing ring, in the middle of a gym, inside the Wall. The next second, she was on sidewalk in some suburban neighborhood. The man behind her was gripping her tight, refusing to let go. It was her nightmare. It was her memory.

Sucking in air, Cass tasted a mix of heavy ash and smoke. Something, somewhere was burning.

"Let me go!" She cried, her throat was raw from it. Her soul was raw from it. "Stop!"

Then she was scratching. She was tearing at his arms and thrashing her body...

Garrett. It was Garrett behind her. It was Garrett holding her against her will. She was scratching his arms, making him bleed, fighting him.

Static. Cass's brain flashed forward, to now, to the boxing ring.

Opening her mouth, she whimpered the name of the man from her nightmares, the name of the man in her dreams.

"Garrett," she gasped it, her eyes popping open wide at the realization.

Then she was falling. She was wriggling and rotating in the air and then her head hit the floor. Was it the cement of the sidewalk? Or was it the springy floor of the boxing ring?

Static.

Her brain flashed back again, and her eyes were rolling in her head as the memory sucked her under.

Anger filled her chest.

Garrett, damn him. She was locked in his mother's trunk, her hands tied together, her head throbbing.

"Garrett!" She screamed her frustration. "Let me out!"

Kicking hard with her legs, she slammed her boots against the inside of the trunk, again and then again. They'd come to a stop finally. The engine had shut off.

How dare he? How dare he haul her out of that house (so what if it belonged more to him than to her) when she didn't want to go? Eli had told her to stay and she knew he would come for her.

And before, Garrett had always done exactly what Eli wanted. Why in the hell was he changing course now?

Damn him for always loving her brother more than her. Damn him for always keeping her trapped in the friend zone, the little sister zone. Damn him for never noticing how badly she needed his approval, his attention, his anything.

But then the trunk was springing open and the man himself was looming over her.

Before Cass had a chance to curse him, he was leaning inside and covering her mouth with his. He was... he was kissing her.

Kissing. Her.

Cass's eyes slammed shut and her heart exploded. His lips were on her lips, his tongue sneaking in to lick against hers. She felt her entire body responding to him, to what she had imagined, to what she had wanted for years.

But then he was pulling away. He was taking a step back and staring down at her. Those blue eyes of his were pleading, begging. He was covered in blood. Crimson stains were splashed all over his face and his clothes.

"What was that?" She whispered. "Why are you doing this?"

"Because I love you," Garrett whispered back. "I fucking love you Cass, and this is the only way to save you."

STATIC. HER BRAIN FLASHED FORWARD... THEN BACK. Forward, then back.

It was like a rolodex in one of those old time movies. Do you remember those? Flipping, rotating, pausing so you could read a card, read an address or a name. Only... when Cass's mind paused, it didn't upload a phone number or an address... it uploaded memories. So. Many. Memories.

She remembered everything now.

Childhood in that shitty apartment. Her mother using. Her brother hiding them in the bathtub. Going hungry. Eli weeping quietly in the corner.

Eating at the shelter. Wearing boys clothes that were too big for her. Getting soaking wet in the rain. Always being cold.

Then high school. Private school. Eli in his football uniform, smiling. His laugh. Meeting Garrett. Living with

Garrett's parents. Mrs. Jameson giving her her first sewing machine. Finally feeling safe.

The war.

Their neighborhood burning.

Garrett coming for her… Garrett loving her.

After that, all the lights went out.

"You can't be in here," Dr. Collette was telling him.

"Like hell I can't," Jameson spat. He'd just laid Cass's limp body on the exam table, there was no way he was leaving.

"How long has she been unconscious?" The doctor asked, while leaning over Cass.

She held up one of those little pen lights as she lifted Cass's eyelids. One lid, then the other. There was no response. No blinking. No movement.

Jameson's heart flipped inside his chest.

"Minutes," he answered.

Running his hands roughly back through his hair, Jameson yanked until he felt pain all along his scalp. He'd sprinted from the gym all the way here with Cass swinging like a rag doll in his arms. Her eyes hadn't opened once. His breath was coming in gasps now. He felt sick. He was going to throw up.

"Did she hit her head?" The doctor again, as a few nurses pushed their way past Jameson and headed for the exam table.

"Yes," Jameson gritted out the word and squeezed his eyes shut. "We were at the gym sparring. I... I dropped her."

"Okay." The doctor dipped her head and then glanced to one of the nurses, a guy. "Help Officer Jameson to wait in the hall."

"What?! No." Jameson's eyes swung to the male nurse who was a good head shorter than he was. "It was an accident."

"I don't doubt that," Collette again, holding her fingers on Cass's wrist. "But you're a distraction, and Cass deserves my full attention. Out. Now."

As the male nurse approached him, Jameson felt panic bubbling at the back of his throat. It was the same feeling that had shot through him in the gym the second Cass had started screaming. That's why he'd opened his arms like an idiot and let her go.

Instead of landing on her feet, like he'd figured, Cass had collapsed to the ground and hit the side of her head. He could still hear the thump of it inside his mind, echoing. It was just like before on the sidewalk.

Squaring his shoulders, Jameson looked down on the nurse now standing in front of him. He could kick this guy's ass without issue, but then where would he be? Taking the doctor's attention away from Cass, which he absolutely did not want to do.

But still… indecision ruled him. He knew he should leave, but he just couldn't bring his body to move.

Then suddenly, he felt a pair of large arms wrap him from behind. Liam's voice was sounding against his ear just as his friend began dragging him from the room.

"Come on," Liam was coaxing. "We can wait out here. Come on."

Shaking his head, Jameson's eyes widened. He didn't want to let her out of his sight. He needed to see her, to watch her, to make sure she woke up.

Raising his voice, Jameson began shouting his demands to the doctor.

"Test her for everything this time!" He called, thinking of her symptoms and how similar they were to Hannah's. "Cat scans, MRIs, everything! Check if she's pregnant, too!"

The nurse was nodding at him then, and the doctor was hovering over Cass. But then the door to the exam room swung shut in his face. Liam's arms continued to pull him backwards. Jameson's bare feet slapped against the linoleum floor of the medical center's hallway.

He hadn't even thought about putting his shoes on. When she'd passed out, he just scooped Cass into his arms and fled the gym like he was on fire. He still felt like he was on fire. Hell, he was burning.

Spinning suddenly in Liam's arms, Jameson turned to face the guy. Placing a large palm on Liam's chest, Jameson shoved him hard and felt all of his own terror transform itself into a ball of anger.

"You," he accused. "Fucker."

"Hey, man." Liam held up one palm placatingly, while keeping the other hand braced firmly against Jameson's shoulder.

There would be no easy shots here. If Jameson wanted to throw down, then Liam would be ready.

"We didn't know you were together," the guy kept talking. "We didn't know she might be… you know… *pregnant.*"

"We're not together," Jameson spat the words out and brushed Liam's hand from his body. "And if she is pregnant, then it's not mine. But you're still training her behind my back. This is *your* fault. The fact that she's in here right now, is *your* fault."

"Hey, I'm not the one that dropped her," Liam countered. His brows raised as Jameson's lowered.

"That's enough," Cole hissed.

Wedging his body between the two men, he kept his green eyes locked on Jameson. It took another few seconds of shifting before he managed to create some space.

But then, as if on cue, Liam faded back against the wall that ran the length of the hallway. He clasped his hands behind his back loosely, like nothing had even happened. His dark eyes were still trained on Jameson though, and they were no longer apologetic. It made Jameson want to blame the guy all the more.

Glancing down at Cole, Jameson sucked in a breath. This was not the man that he wanted to fight. And if he was being honest with himself, Liam wasn't that guy either.

Clenching his fists tighter, Jameson backed a step from

Cole and let his eyes take in the rest of the people crowding the space. Standing beside Liam was the little blondie, Mia, and on the other side of her was that asshat Levi.

Of course he would be here. The guy was like bedbugs, freaking impossible to get rid of without chemical warfare or fire. Cocking his head, Jameson's eyes zeroed in on Cass's ex-boyfriend. Fire, he thought. That might just work.

"If it makes any difference," Mia spoke finally. "She's not pregnant. She hasn't been with anyone like that… um, at least not since I can remember."

At her words, every male in the hallway turned to fix his eyes on the blonde. Her cheeks tinged pink and she nibbled on her lower lip a moment before clearing her throat and glancing down. It was the first time Jameson had seen her even slightly embarrassed.

Exhaling through his nostrils, Jameson pursed his lips. Something that had been coiled up deep down inside of him slowly unwound itself. No one had been with Cass. Not him, and not Levi either.

"Soldier Harris," Jameson stated flatly as he gestured to the end of the hallway. "You're dismissed. Go."

"Wha… what?" Levi stammered and shoved off the wall. "You can't just… I'm not leaving."

"I believe that was an order from a superior officer," Cole chimed in. "Go."

Levi's mouth dropped open and he simply blinked at them a moment. Jameson folded his arms across his chest and glared. He was just itching for someone to take out his frustration on. Just. Itching.

But then swallowing suddenly, Levi's mouth snapped shut and his shoulders tensed. Turning on his heel, he stalked off down the hallway. The squeak of his sneakers sounded against the flooring. The glare of the fluorescent lights shone off his shiny black hair.

Just as he slipped out the double front doors of the medical center, Uriah slammed in. There was an entourage of soldiers with him, like there always was. Malik, Hernandez, Kimley, Jones.

Motioning for them to stay in the reception area, Uriah's eyes locked on Jameson. There was worry crawling all over his face. He'd heard about Cass.

Jameson's jaw clenched and he glanced back at the still closed door to exam room number five. *Come on, Cass baby. Don't do this to me. Wake up. Be okay.*

"What happened?" Uriah's voice sounded out in the narrow hallway as he jogged to a stop in front of Jameson.

After a brief pause (wherein Jameson refused to answer the question) Cole cleared his throat and spoke quietly.

"Jameson and Cass were sparring in the gym. She had some kind of episode and lost consciousness."

"I dropped her," Jameson bit out, turning his back on Uriah, he faced the exam room door and stared. "She hit her head."

Another awkward pause ensued in which Jameson could feel everyone exchanging glances behind his back.

"It wasn't a hard fall," Cole supplied. "She was wearing

headgear and it was more like she collapsed feet first before folding down to the mat. I think she was out before she hit her head."

Whipping around to glare at him, Jameson's jaw ticked. "You don't know that," he growled, and narrowed his eyes further when Liam rolled his.

"You got a problem?" Jameson tipped his chin at Liam, who scoffed.

Stepping between them, Uriah slowly pivoted Jameson around and thereby managed to break the tension. With a tight grip on his friend's shoulders, Uriah gave Jameson a little shake.

"Save all this energy for her," Uriah said. "She's gonna wake up and be just fine, and then you'll probably have some groveling to do or something. Do you know how to beg? I've gotten pretty fucking good at begging Lena."

With a groan Jameson dragged both hands down his face. If only it were that easy. If only this was what everyone else thought it was, Jameson wanting Cass, but being too big of a puss to tell her. Hah. They had no clue.

Just then the door to the exam room swung open and Dr. Collette stepped out. Everyone straightened and fell silent. It seemed like time stood still.

Craning his neck, Jameson caught a glimpse of Cass sitting up on the examination table, rubbing her forehead with her fingers before the door clicked closed again.

All his breath left him in a whoosh and he felt instantly woozy. She was awake. She was alive and okay and sitting up and holy shit. He was seeing stars.

"Our patient has regained consciousness," the doctor was saying. "And it appears she has no lasting negative effects. I believe this is just another memory recurrence episode and is consistent with everything that I've seen over the past ten months in other patients."

"I was told she hit her head," Uriah responded, while Jameson tried to focus. "Does she have a concussion or TBI? Is there anything else we should know?"

"There's a little redness on the side of her head, but other than a mild headache, she doesn't appear to have any issues," Dr. Collette offered. "I think it's safe to judge she didn't hit her head all that hard, so I'll be releasing her without any restrictions."

"Wait." Jameson held up both hands. "No MRI? No Cat scan or CT scan or whatever the hell you guys call it? Did you check for pregnancy? Hannah was pregnant. Is Cass? Did you check for anything? You weren't in there all that long."

"Easy," Uriah murmured, laying a hand on Jameson's shoulder.

"Officer Jameson." Dr. Collette pursed her lips a moment and stared up into his face. "Are you the patient's husband?"

"Uhhh…" Jameson blinked as his mouth dropped open.

"Are you her next of kin?" The doctor pressed. "Because the last time I checked, my patient's condition is still considered private."

"Oh really?" Jameson sucked in a breath as his brain began to function again. "Because the last time *I* checked,

HIPPA and all that legal privacy bullshit is dead. Aren't you even going to keep her overnight? Just to monitor her? She was out cold for a *long* time."

"No, it's unnecessary."

"If it's a staffing issue," Jameson continued, waving a hand. "Then I can sit with her. I'll stay up all night."

"It's not a staffing issue."

The doctor's brows drew together as she continued to stand firmly in the doorway. Sure, she had to tip her head decidedly up to look into Jameson's face, but his size was doing nothing to sway her. She was like a little stone fortress, with armor made out of baby-blue scrubs and running shoes. Jameson was still barefoot. But he could care less about that.

Just as he was opening his mouth to argue another point, the door to the exam room cracked open once more. Cass poked her head out and those mossy-green eyes of hers came to rest briefly on Jameson's face. His heart slammed into his ribs a few times before the doctor stepped to one side and let Cass out.

"It's okay," Cass was saying. "He has a way of bullying you into getting what he wants. He might as well be next of kin. Isn't that right, Garrett?"

"Uhh…" Jameson's brow furrowed as he looked down at Cass.

"I'm fine by the way," she said, fisting one hand on her hip and staring up at him. "Just remembered a few things."

"Oh." A shot of adrenaline licked through him. *What things exactly?*

Shoving past him, Cass began to walk away down the hall. After a beat, Jameson shook his head and squared his shoulders. Not so freaking fast, hot shot, he thought. She'd been dead weight in his arms not an hour ago.

As if sensing him jogging up behind her, Cass threw him a look over her shoulder but didn't stop walking.

"Oh, and I'm not pregnant," she called. "Since that seems to be *such* a concern for you."

Gritting his teeth, Jameson lengthened his strides until he was pacing beside her. Okay, so maybe he hadn't been the most quiet person while discussing her case with the doctor. Sue him for being concerned.

Glancing up ahead, Jameson frowned. They were almost to the exit doors. Was it him or had everyone else in the place suddenly gone silent?

Closing his wide palm around Cass's elbow, Jameson gripped her gently. To his surprise, she did not yank away. He figured that was a good sign. She probably hadn't remembered him shoving her into the trunk… yet. Goody.

"Hey, slow down," he murmured, ducking his head close to hers. "What if it happens again? You need someone to watch you."

"And I guess that person is you?" Cass's eyes flipped up to his face. She was searching him for something, he wasn't sure what.

"Yeah." Jameson swallowed and felt his mouth go dry. "I can watch you, but I think you need to lie down. I think you should rest for awhile."

Coming to a stop, Cass crossed her arms over her chest

and looked away, out through the double glass doors and into the sunshine.

Reluctantly, Jameson released his grip on her. Tucking both of his hands into the pockets of his sweat pants, he waited. He couldn't touch her anymore. He shouldn't even be trying. Shit, he was such a wreck. His nerves were bouncing all over the damn place.

"What do you suggest?" Cass asked finally, her gaze shooting back up to his.

"Come stay with me." The words were out before Jameson could even school himself.

"At your place?" Her brows drew together. She was watching him again.

"Yeah." He swallowed, hating himself but unable to help himself all at the same time. "At my place. I'll take care of you, make sure you don't fall again."

"Okay," Cass whispered the word and bobbed her head before she started walking again. "If that's what you want."

STANDING AT THE BOTTOM OF THE STAIRWELL, CASS HEAVED a sigh and looked up. They both lived on the fourth floor and there were no elevators. Garrett was hovering just behind her, a silent ball of tension, just as he had been for the entire walk over from the medical center.

"I can carry you," he stated, and she felt his hands brush against her waist.

Without a word, Cass stepped quickly out of his grasp and began marching up the stairs. As her bare feet slapped down against each step, she had to admit that the soles of her feet were sore. But as much as she'd like a free pass to the top, Cass's mind was still processing. She was reeling from all the memories and the flood of emotions they brought on.

Now that she remembered her brother, *really* remembered him, it made her mourn the loss of him all that much more. Because knowing Eli, he would definitely have come to get her during the war, just like he'd promised. And because he hadn't showed, that meant one thing… he was just what Garrett had warned her he was, Eli was dead.

Pausing at the second floor landing, Cass braced one hand against a wall and closed her eyes. Ugh, then there was that whole thing with Garrett sort of kidnapping her (that he then clearly lied about, by the way).

Had he told her he loved her just to get her on that train? Or had he meant it? And even if he had meant it at the time, that was years and years ago now. She didn't know what to make of it. She didn't know what to do.

"This is ridiculous," Garrett spat, and suddenly Cass was being lifted off her feet.

"Garrett!" She warned, but by then it was too late.

In one swift motion, he flipped her around and tossed her over his shoulder before continuing up the stairs. Her hair was swinging wildly and she had to brace her palms on his lower back in order to lift her head. She was treated to a view of the steps as they continued to climb, as well as his particularly nice butt.

Firming her lips, Cass averted her gaze, or tried to… mostly.

She could fight him, she figured, if she had more energy, but what was the point of struggling? She didn't want to pitch them both down the stairs just to make a point, and this was just so typical of him. This act right here was so unbelievably typical of Garrett. Damn him and his sexy savior complex.

When they got to the top, there wasn't even a question

as to which apartment he turned to. He didn't ask her if she'd changed her mind, or offer to get her any of her things, even though her place was literally just across the hall. Nope. He just twisted the doorknob to his own apartment and ducked low to cross inside.

"Don't you lock it?" She asked, he was still holding her balanced on one shoulder as he turned and closed the door behind them.

"What for?" He countered, before walking her directly to his bathroom and setting her gently on the closed lid of the toilet seat.

Huffing a sigh, Cass avoided his gaze. Of course he wouldn't think to lock it. He was a big guy living alone with next to no vulnerability. Locked doors weren't a necessity for him.

"Would you like a bath?" He asked and had her eyes flipping open.

He was squatting down just in front of her now, his head cocked to one side. His large hands braced on her knees.

"Um..." Cass was at a loss for words. He was suddenly so close, blinking at her with those impossibly blue eyes of his.

"I won't watch you, I swear." He held up both palms then, and had such a serious expression on his face that she wanted to laugh, or maybe to cry. "We can keep the door open and I'll sit with my back to you."

"You're going to be in here while I bathe," she clarified. "Naked."

"I'll sit in the doorway," he reasoned. "I just need to listen, in case you pass out."

"I could shower," she pointed out.

"No." He shook his head, frowning. "You could fall in the shower."

Pushing up to standing, Garrett dismissed her entirely. Discussion closed, just like that.

Leaning back against the toilet, Cass folded her arms over her chest as he bent over and plugged the tub. It wasn't a large bathroom so his shoulder brushed hers as he turned the water on and adjusted the temperature.

Despite her best intentions of being standoffish, Cass's eyes traveled over the shape of Garrett's arms beneath his white t-shirt. The fabric stretched across his biceps before hugging the muscles along his shoulders and back.

Inhaling, she took in the scent of him. Completely male and uniquely Garrett. If there was one smell in the whole wide world that she knew best, it would be his. After all, she'd slept on his sheets, in his bed, for years.

Closing her eyes, Cass fought the tingles bursting all over her body. Unlike over the past few months these tingles shot straight to her core, using a past filled with the quiet lust of a teenage girl to propel them.

How many times had Cass stared at Garrett only to have him ignore her? How many times had she watched him slip into some back bedroom at a party with someone else, someone older, prettier, more experienced than she was. Too many.

When the tub shut off, she opened her eyes only to find

Garrett staring at her over his shoulder. His face was hovering not eighteen inches from hers. Cass's breath caught in her throat. Seemingly unaware, Garrett's eyes zeroed in on her lips a moment before shooting quickly back up to her eyes. Swallowing, he turned his head and scooted away.

"I'll grab you a towel," he murmured. "Don't undress yet."

Nodding her head, Cass remained silent as he disappeared out the bathroom door. There was a warmth to the air now, a humidity. Glancing at the water, she watched a few bubbles stir over the surface. He must have poured in some soap for her, while she was focused elsewhere.

A few moments later, Garrett returned with a perfectly folded white towel and a tall glass of water. He set both items on the sink before crossing the few steps to the threshold of the bathroom door.

Turning away from her, he plopped down on the tile floor. His long legs were pulled up in front of him. His massive arms were draped around his legs.

"I thought you'd be thirsty," he said finally. "I know I am."

Oh yeah, she thought. The sparring in the gym, then all the running around to the medical center and hiking them both up here. He must be just as achey and tired as she was.

With a sigh, Cass stood up and peeled off her clothes. The little booty shorts went first (Mia's choice of workout wear), along with her thong, tank top and sports bra.

Dipping a testing toe in the water, Cass let out an involuntary moan. It was hot. She loved it hot.

Clearing his throat, Garrett drew her attention back over to him but, true to his word, he did not turn around.

Glaring at his back, Cass fought the fifty million things she wanted to say to him. A part of her wanted to come out with everything all at once. She wanted to demand answers, clarification, confessions. But the other part, the entirely female part, preferred to trap him. She wanted to give him some rope to play with, and see if he chose to loop the end around his big dumb neck and hang.

With a feline smile, Cass stepped into the tub and slowly eased all the way inside. The water stung her skin for a few seconds before the pain was replaced by ecstasy. So good. Why did a bath feel so amazingly good?

"You alright?" Garrett asked, his head tipped up. He exhaled at the ceiling.

Ignoring him, Cass brushed the bath water up and over her chest. Again. Then again. She loved the sound of it, the feel of it.

"You're going to have to say something," Garrett sighed. "Or I'm going to turn around."

"You said you wouldn't look," Cass reminded him. "You promised."

Chuckling, Garrett leaned to his right and rested the side of his head against the doorframe. "That's all I wanted," he said. "To make sure you're okay."

"Why?" Cass bit at her lower lip and held her breath.

"Why what?"

"Why do you care if I'm okay?" Cass let her gaze travel over to settle on Garrett's back. His muscles were flexing beneath his shirt.

"How much do you remember?" He asked quietly.

"Enough to know you've lied to me," she offered.

Pushing off the doorframe, Garrett cradled his head in both hands and blew out a loud breath.

"I'm sorry about that," he said finally. "I didn't know what else to do."

"How about the truth?" Cass blinked up at the ceiling as her hands continued to stir the water in the tub. *Come on, Garrett. Give me something.*

"What was I supposed to say?" His voice raised a bit before cracking. "Don't worry, Cass... the scary fucker in your dreams doesn't hurt you, he's just shoving you into a trunk to save your life. Oh, and by the way... it was me. I'm the bad man tying you up. But I swear I didn't force myself on you, even though you can't remember that part. Yeah right, that'd of gone over real well."

"You could have told me you believed me," she countered. "Instead of making me feel like I was crazy, like it wasn't real."

Hanging his head down low, Garrett sucked in a breath.

"Yeah, okay. You're right. That's what I should've done. But if you hadn't already noticed, I'm not very good about doing things the polite way. When push comes to shove I just... shove harder. And I'm sorry about all that, truly I am."

Glancing over his shoulder, Garrett's pleading eyes met

hers. "Shit, Cass. I've done so many things that I'm sorry for, okay? There's shit that I did during the war... shit I should tell you about, but *fuck*. I don't even know where to start."

Rolling onto her side, Cass hid her naked body against the side of the tub and peeked over the edge at him.

"You think I'm mad about things you did during the war?" She asked, her brows furrowing.

"Cass..."

"No." Cass gave her head a quick shake. "I remember it all now, Garrett. I know it was bad. War is bad. It makes good men do terrible things. I don't want to hear about what you did."

"But..."

"Did you rape women?" She asked suddenly and watched his face screw up in disgust.

"Hell no, I..."

"Did you kill children?"

"No. Cass..."

"Then I don't want to know," she cut him off. "I just want you to answer my original question. That's all I want."

"What?" Turning around to face her, Garrett rose to his knees in the doorway, his confused eyes fixed on her face. "What question?"

"Why do you care if I'm okay?" Sucking in a breath, Cass held it.

Closing his eyes, Garrett's face fell. "If you remember everything now, then you already know why."

"That was a long time ago." Cass shifted in the tub, gripping the porcelain side with one hand.

She wanted to hear him say it again. Garrett was the only person in her entire life who'd ever said those words to her. The. Only. One.

She didn't come from a family that talked about that kind of thing. Even Eli had never said it. Her brother had never told her that he loved her, he showed her instead. So yeah, she wanted to hear it again. She wanted to hear it from Garrett.

Exhaling slowly, Garrett's eyes popped open and he looked at her for a moment. The water was still warm, but a wave of goosebumps prickled along her skin. Swallowing, Garrett pushed up to standing and turned his back on her.

"Yeah, it was a long time ago," he admitted. "But now that you've got your memory back, you'll remember that I told you how I love you… twice."

Taking a step forward, Garrett walked through the open doorway of the bathroom, keeping his back to her the entire time. Cass's heart was thundering in her chest as she shoved up to sitting in the tub. Where was he going?

"You'll also remember," Garrett continued, reaching to one side to grip the door in his hand. "That you never said it back."

And with that, he swung the door shut.

Cass's mouth dropped, but no words escaped her.

After a brief pause, she heard his footsteps walking away.

Jameson sat on the edge of his bed and stared at the floor. His chest was aching and his jaw was grinding and he was fighting the turmoil twisting within him. He'd told her how he felt. Three. Freaking. Times. And she still hadn't said it back.

His ego was bruised, his conscience was crying, but his body was still making its demands. After all, looking down on her in that bathtub, he'd had a perfect view of that round ass of hers. And it was everything his imagination had figured it would be, maybe more. His mouth had begun salivating, his hands itching to reach out and touch.

So that's why he'd had to get the hell out of there. Fast.

After closing the door on her, he'd stomped over to his bedroom and took a long drink from the jug of water he kept in his closet. He was thirsty, sure. But when he was done chugging he hadn't felt settled. He hadn't felt satisfied. Nope. He was still thirsty, just… not for water.

Swiping a hand over the back of his mouth, he'd paced aimlessly around on his sore bare feet for a minute before finally wandering back over to the bathroom door and pressing his ear up against it. She was okay. He could hear her splashing around in the tub. It sounded like she was washing up.

That's when he'd realized that she would need something to sleep in, so he'd come back to his room and found her one of his t-shirts. Taking a seat on the edge of his bed, Jameson had let loose a long sigh (maybe it was half groan) and hung his head low. What in the hell was he going to do now?

He'd tried to tell Cass what he'd done. He'd tried to explain what had happened during the war. The truth, the awful fucking truth, was on the tip of his tongue, but she'd cut him off. She didn't want to know. She didn't want to hear it.

Part of him (the old part that still had morals and integrity) knew he needed to confess to her anyway. But the other part (the part that currently had the majority vote) wanted to stay silent. That part wanted to keep his secret, take it to his damn grave with him, never let it see the light of day.

After all, what had gone down was done. He couldn't take it back, no matter how badly he wanted to, and no one else on this planet knew what had happened. It was the perfect awful crime actually, one that was burning a hole in his already bleeding heart.

His heart that was bleeding because of her. His heart

that had three huge rips in it from the times he'd told Cass what she was to him, only to be met with silence.

So why did it still beat for her? What made him not care? What made him continue to want her anyway? He didn't know. He couldn't make it stop and he couldn't figure it out. He just knew he still wanted her. He just knew he still loved her.

When the door to the bathroom swung open, Jameson's head shot up. From his position on the bed, he could see directly across the hall. Cass was walking towards him, wrapped in nothing but a damp towel. Her wild dark hair was wet and dripping. Her smooth skin was slick with moisture. She was crossing the threshold into his room.

He swallowed once, and licked his lips. He couldn't help it.

"I'm sorry," she said and came to a stop directly in front of him.

She was so close, she was standing between his knees. Jameson had to straighten and lean his head back just a touch to look at her face properly. With her standing and him sitting they were almost exactly the same height. She was so damn pretty. Too pretty, with a scattering of freckles over the bridge of her nose.

His mouth dropped a fraction and he clutched the extra t-shirt he'd been holding closer to his lap. He was still in sweats and a shirt, there wasn't much material to hide what she was doing to him. The smell of his soap on her skin was intoxicating. She was intoxicating, making his thoughts slow and his body react all on its own.

"It's just…" she was talking, saying things he should be hearing. "No one's ever said that to me before. I don't know how to say it back. It's not just a word to me, you know? It's a big deal."

It took a while for her words to sink into Jameson's brain (he was a little light on blood flow at the moment). During that time, his eyes wandered of their own accord. He took in the pink pout of her lips, the line of her neck, the swell of her breasts beneath the towel. He wanted to reach out and touch her. He wanted to put his hands all over her and his mouth too.

But then his conscience kicked in and he was sucking in a breath and trying like hell to steady himself, to rein himself in. He clutched the shirt tighter against his body, it was almost like a protection against what he wanted to do to her.

Clearing his throat, he gave his head a little shake. Focus. Focus.

"Eli loved you," he said finally. God, saying *that* name stabbed Jameson right in the heart.

"Yeah, I know he did," Cass acknowledged. "But he never said it out loud."

"Oh." Jameson frowned, as his blue eyes skipped up to lock on her green ones. "My family said it all the time."

"I know." Cass smiled and huffed a laugh. "I heard them. I heard you all saying it. It was just never directed at me. So saying it now is… hard. Harder than I thought it would be. I don't know why the word is so scary, but I do feel it for you. I felt it on that train coming here, and I felt it the years before that, and all the years after that too."

"Cass." Jameson's heart was picking up the pace as his eyes searched hers.

"It'd be easier for me to show you," she whispered and wet her lips with the tip of her tongue. "Can I show you?"

Then she was stepping into him. She was pressing her mouth to his, her lips against his, her tongue licking out to meet his. A bolt of electricity shot straight through him. Jameson dropped the shirt to the floor. His eyes slammed shut and his hands wrapped her body as he pulled her up against him.

She felt soooooo good. Tilting his head to one side, he deepened their kiss, exploring her mouth, enjoying her tiny gasp and the curl of her lips as she smiled.

"Cass," he groaned her name as her hands came up to lock around the back of his neck.

The towel that she'd been holding slipped slowly down between them. Jameson's hands helped it of course. His fingers skipped over the skin of her shoulders, down her spine, to her lower back. When he cupped her ass, he let loose a long groan and slowly squeezed her soft flesh in his hands.

Then she was climbing onto his lap, sitting astride him. Their mouths were locked together, still kissing, nipping and teasing. Her chest rubbed against his chest, her arms cinched tighter around his neck and Jameson felt himself leaking into his sweat pants.

"It's not fair." Cass broke their kiss a moment and had Jameson's eyes flying open. "You still have your shirt on."

Smiling, Jameson released her only long enough to tear his shirt off over his head. Cass giggled, rocking back on his lap to give him room. He felt the moment her hot core brushed against him. He was hurting now, he wanted her so bad.

"There," Jameson announced, as he gathered her back up against him. "Fair enough for you?"

"Mmmm," Cass hummed and shook her head side to side.

She had a teasing small smile on her lips as she used the weight of her body to tip him backwards onto the bed. Jameson's back hit the mattress with a soft thud as he brought her down with him. Her breasts squished between them. He could feel the press of her nipples against the skin of his chest and he wanted so badly to put them in his mouth, first one, then the other. But she wasn't giving him the space or the time for that.

Slipping her hand under the waistband of his pants, Cass wrapped her fingers around his hard length and squeezed. Jameson's eyes shot open and he released a string of muttered curses. At this rate, she'd have him finishing before they even started.

"Cass," he warned.

Her name rumbled from somewhere deep in his chest. It only made her smile wider. Well, two could play at that game, he thought.

Looping one arm around her waist, Jameson flipped

their positions. One second she was on top, and then the next, she was on her back beneath him. Pressing his hips down between her legs, he pinned her to the mattress and cocked an eyebrow.

"The only action I've seen in the past six years is from my own hand," he stated. "You're going to have to let me take the lead on this, or I'll be done in thirty seconds."

Laughter bubbled up Cass's throat as she laid her palms flat on his pecs. Her cheeks were flushed, her eyes twinkling.

Damn. In that instant, Jameson was gone. If he'd had any chance of escaping her before, he was officially done for now.

"It's alright if you're quick," she said. Her hands were traveling down to his stomach again. Those mossy green eyes of hers followed their path. "I just want to be with you, like all those other girls were with you."

"Whoa up." Jameson moved to block her hands with one of his own. He was bracing most of his weight using only one forearm now. "Firstly, those other girls were a distraction because you weren't an option. Secondly, I can't be with you like that, I don't have any protection."

"What?" Cass's eyes popped back up to lock with his. He could feel her frustration as she tensed beneath him. "I'm clean, no diseases remember? Are you?"

"Yeah, but that's not what I'm worried about," he reasoned. He'd never been with a woman without a condom before, and as much as he wanted to feel Cass in that way, he still wanted to protect her, too. "I can make you feel good without getting you pregnant. Just let me show you."

Again with the soft feminine laughter. This time he was the one frowning. All the tension melted from Cass's body and in an instant it was replaced with something altogether different. Her lips came up to find his neck, her hips shifted and rolled against him, the tips of her breasts teased against his chest.

Jameson's brain blitzed on him. His muscles gave out and he collapsed down on top of her. Groaning, he rubbed himself shamelessly against her core. Only his sweatpants separated them now and he could literally feel just how hot she was.

"It's okay," she murmured, her lips kept moving along his neck. "I won't get pregnant. Levi and I tried for a year. Something's wrong with me."

"Fuck." Squeezing his eyes shut, Jameson stilled and sucked in a breath. "Don't tell me that shit. I want to leave right now and go smash the guy's face in."

Again with the giggling and the wriggling and the kissing from Cass. Lifting his head up a bit, Jameson stared down at her. If she kept moving like that, he might just go off in his damn pants. He didn't think his ego could stand for that, so he was going to have to change it up.

Why was it so hard to take control with this woman? She was like half his size and yet she was dominating him.

With a knowing smile, Jameson shoved up and started retreating down the length of her body. It was time to switch things up. It was time for her to feel breathless because of him.

He let his mouth drag a damp trail from the base of her throat to each one of her breasts, circling and sucking. Taking his time, he waited for her to arch into him and moan before moving lower, to her soft belly.

When Cass tried to sit up and reach for him, he pinned her gently to the bed with one hand. He'd wanted to do this to her for as long as he could remember. It was time to wipe all those fucking thoughts of Levi out of her mind and replace them with him. Just him, and what he could do to her.

Settling his wide shoulders firmly between her thighs, Jameson gripped Cass's hips with both hands and pulled her closer to his face. She looked exactly right. She smelled exactly right, and he bet she tasted exactly right, too.

Picking up one of her legs, Jameson set her right knee over his shoulder. Cass gasped a bit as he dragged one finger down and began to touch her. He heard a few nervous phrases fall from her mouth. Something along the lines of: *You don't have to do that* and *Are you sure you want to?* before he buried his face and got to work.

It wasn't long before she was coming. He felt her fingers thread and grip in his hair. He listened to her whimpering turn to moaning, then finally to the sound of his name on her lips. He fucking loved it.

He loved it when she cried out, when she pushed herself against him, encouraging him, demanding more, higher.

So he took her higher. He took her higher until she shattered all apart for him. Then he did it to her again, adding his fingers, suckling, licking. She was gone for him now, the same way he'd been gone over her.

When she was limp and panting and wide eyed, he stopped. Crawling up her body, he stared into her face and watched her blinking up at him. She was stunned. He felt like a million bucks.

"I still want you," she whispered. One of her hands came up to stroke the side of his face. "I want to feel you inside of me. Please."

Dropping his head a moment, Jameson felt his body leap and lunge at the chance. He wanted that too. He wanted it so fucking bad.

Shoving his pants down, Jameson lowered himself between her legs and carefully pushed himself inside of her. She was small. He was… not. And although that fact felt insanely amazing to him, he didn't want to hurt her. He wanted to protect her. He would pull out, he told himself. He wouldn't risk her.

But then she was gasping and wrapping her hands around his body. Her hips rolled against him, helping him sink deeper. Then he was seeing stars. His arms went weak and he collapsed down flush with her and pushed the rest of the way inside. It was so completely different without a condom. It was so completely different being with her.

His heart was hammering and his lungs were burning and the pleasure was so immediately intense. Jameson's body worked without his direction. He was rocking into her, pulling out, then pushing back in again. She was moaning beneath him and he heard himself moaning now, too.

Then everything became too much. It was too good. It felt way too good and he'd wanted her for way too long and before he could stop himself, he was coming. He slammed his mouth down on hers and released inside of her, where he said he wouldn't go. But he couldn't stop.

He gasped against her mouth and fisted her hair in his hands. That's when he heard it. That's when she finally said it, and it lit his whole body on fire.

"I love you," Cass whispered. "I love you, Garrett."

CHAPTER TWENTY-FIVE_
CASS

"You're distracting," Cass murmured. It was the next day and they were in her workshop.

"Am I?" Behind her, Garrett grinned. Cass didn't have to turn around to see it, she could feel the smile blooming on his face.

Clearing her throat, Cass tried to balance on his lap while working the sewing machine at the same time. Her right foot depressed the pedal while her hands gripped the red fabric of Mia's dress. It was almost ready for its final fitting. Mia would be here any minute.

Shifting in the chair, Garrett continued to lay a trail of kisses along the back of her neck. He held her hair off to one side while his mouth puffed warm air against her skin.

Brows furrowed, Cass tried to concentrate on what she was doing, but it was impossibly hard right about now. Her body was tingling and Garrett wasn't stopping. Not that she particularly wanted him to, but still.

"Shouldn't you be at work?" She exhaled the words, trying to keep the pant from her voice. Damn this sexy man.

"Yes," he admitted. A chuckle rumbled in his chest as he leaned in closer. "Yes, I should."

"Mia will be here any minute," she protested.

Okay, so it was a weak protest, but it counted for something, right?

"Mmmm-hmmm," Garrett hummed, moving his face slowly side to side.

She could feel the scrape of his five o'clock shadow against the top her shoulder. He hadn't had time to shave this morning. They'd been busy. Really, really busy.

"What if she walks in here and sees us?" Cass asked.

Pausing, Garrett lifted his head. "You don't want people to know about us?"

"No, it's just..." Huffing a sigh, Cass stopped the machine and twisted to look at him over her shoulder. "This is brand new, I don't know what we are. Is there an us?"

Tilting his head to one side, Garrett worried his bottom lip a moment. "Do you want there to be?"

"Do you?" Cass countered.

He was not getting her to admit it first. Was. Not.

"Yeah, I do." Garrett nodded his head before sliding his hands around her waist. "I want there to be an us. And I especially don't want there to be a you and anyone else."

"Is that right?" A feline smile crept across Cass's face as she returned her attention to her sewing.

"That's right." Garrett pressed a few more kisses to her neck. "And I want a whole lot of other things, too."

"Like what?" She asked.

Her foot returned to the pedal. The machine started up again. Just a few more stitches and she would be done.

"Like I want you to move in with me," he said. "And I want everyone to know about it. And I don't want you to leave. Ever."

Brow furrowing, Cass focused on the dress. The seam was coming along nicely. Just… a few… more… inches…

"Move in with you. Everyone knows. No leaving," she repeated absently. "Got it."

"Cass," Garrett warned. "Are you listening?"

"Hmmm?"

Cass worked to tie off the stitches before stopping the machine and sitting up straight. A grin burst on her face as she held the dress up to the light. Yes. It came out even prettier than she'd imagined, if that was possible.

"No leaving," Garrett repeated. His fingers pulsed around her waist, emphasizing his words. "As in… no more trip beyond the Wall. I want you to stay here with me. I don't want you to go."

Pushing back against him, Cass forced Garrett and her rolling chair back just far enough so that she could stand up. She bit the extra thread off the seam of the dress and then stepped to one side where she flipped the entire thing outside in. Giving it a brisk shake, she held it up in front of her once more. Mia was going to love this thing.

"Cass." Garrett rose to standing and stepped towards

her. Looping his hands around her body, he brought her in close so their foreheads were touching. "Promise me you won't leave."

Closing her eyes, Cass let his kisses overwhelm her. Garrett's mouth came down to hers and he made the rest of the world disappear. Her heart was hammering and her thighs were clenching and she couldn't believe she could want him again so soon.

"I promise," Cass relented between kisses.

She hadn't had a lot of time to consider it, but the only reason she'd wanted to leave was to get her memories back and find her brother. Now that she had the one, it made her realize she'd never get the other. Eli was gone.

"Well, well, well… what do we have here?" Mia's voice burst into the room and had both their heads whipping up.

Pushing through the door, the tall blonde sauntered towards them, eyebrows wiggling, a knowing smirk plastered on her lips. Cass couldn't help but smile back. Her best friend just had this special energy about her, it made you want to laugh, it made you want to play too.

"Looks like you're feeling better," Mia stated before coming to a stop in front of them. "Guess now I know why you weren't at breakfast… or lunch."

Chuckling, Garrett gave Cass an extra squeeze before releasing her. Mia's eyes were twinkling and Cass's cheeks were heating and she was at a loss for words. But then Mia's gaze settled on the red cloth still clutched in Cass's hands and her mouth dropped into an O shape.

"Is that my dress?" She squeaked, clapping her hands together like a small child. "Is it finished?"

Beaming, Cass smoothed at the fabric and held it up.

"Yup," she answered. "Ready to try it on?"

"Absolutely!" Mia snatched at the dress and pressed it against her body. "It's amazing. Cass, you're a genius."

"The next big fashion designer," Garrett added. "My mom always used to say that."

Slanting her eyes up at him, Cass caught the flicker of sadness that moved across Garrett's face. She wondered what had happened to his parents. She wondered what had happened to her own mother.

There had been mass evacuations at one point during the war, and she'd assumed her mother had made it onto one of the trains. Mr. and Mrs. Jameson had fled in their SUV a few months later. They'd begged Cass to come with them at the time, but she'd refused. Cell service was all but extinct at that point, so that had been the last she'd heard of them.

Reaching out, Cass ran a hand down Garrett's arm. He gave his head a quick shake and glanced over at her. A smile returned to his face.

"I've got to get to work," he said. "But you'll have dinner with me, right? Then we can start moving your stuff over."

"Um…" Cass's brow furrowed as Mia's eyes widened.

"Moving your stuff?" Mia looked from Cass to Garrett. "You're stealing her from me?"

"Yes, ma'am." He nodded sagely before leaning in and covering Cass's mouth with his. He was making a statement and he knew it. "Meet me at the restaurant at sundown, okay?"

"You're a bulldozer." Giving him a quick shove, Cass tried to catch her breath after that last kiss.

"Dinner," he repeated, while Mia cleared her throat loudly.

Stepping back, Garrett gave both women a wicked grin before turning on his heel and leaving the room. When the door swung shut behind him, Cass drew in a deep breath. Mia threw her head back and laughed.

"Mr. Hot Stuff is living up to his name," she said between giggles. "You should see the look on your face."

"He's always been like that." Cass pressed her palms to her cheeks, willing the pink to recede. "You should've seen him in high school. There wasn't a cheerleader around that could resist."

Stripping out of her clothes, Mia hummed to herself. She'd been wearing tight jeans and a low-cut blouse. Her hair was styled, her makeup was done.

As Cass watched, she cocked her head to the side and remembered. She remembered some things Mia had told her when they'd first arrived at the Wall. She remembered how Mia had been dressed, so many years ago, when she'd stumbled off that train and into Cass's life. Mia deserved to know. She deserved to have something from her past.

"I've got my memory back," Cass said quietly.

"All of it?" Mia's head tipped up as she wriggled into the dress.

"All of it," Cass confirmed.

Stepping up to her friend, Cass tugged at the fabric and worked the zipper up the back. The dress fit perfectly. It hugged Mia in all the right places. The length was short, just how the blonde bombshell had wanted it. The scalloped ends teased around her long thighs.

"I'm happy for you," Mia chirped.

Sucking in a breath, the blonde straightened and smoothed at the fabric with her hands. There was a full length mirror hanging on one wall. Walking over to it, Mia exhaled slowly and did a turn in front of it. She looked like a model, Cass thought and nibbled at her lip.

"You told me things," Cass offered. "About where you're from. Do you want me to tell you what you said?"

Closing her eyes, Mia's throat bobbed for a second. Her fingers curled and then uncurled.

"Is it bad?" She asked finally.

Mia's eyes were still shut. Cass watched her best friend hold her breath.

"No." Cass frowned and stepped up to fuss and fluff at the dress. "Nothing bad."

Mia's chocolate-brown eyes opened then and Cass watched them in the mirror. Mia looked nervous, unsure, but then she squared her shoulders and nodded her head.

"Tell me," she said and forced a shiny smile.

"You, um…" Cass wasn't sure how to begin. "You lived with your uncle and aunt on a farm. It was somewhere in central California."

"Oh." Mia frowned. "I guess that explains my job here… and why I know so much about plants."

Dipping her head, Cass went on. "I don't know what happened to your parents. You never really mentioned them."

"Alright." Mia swallowed. "No parents."

"You're uncle was very strict." Cass let her fingers stroke along the dress. "I think he was your mother's brother. I think you said that once. Anyway, when you first got here, you were wearing a long dress. It covered your whole body, from your wrists to your ankles. Your hair had never been cut, the ends were past your waist. You weren't allowed to use makeup, or wear pants."

"Oh… shit." Mia's mouth dropped open.

"And you definitely weren't allowed to curse." Cass popped a grin.

"Wow, that sounds…" Mia trailed off, her eyes soaking up her current attire in the mirror. "Awful."

A laugh burst from Cass's lips. Slapping her hands over her mouth, she tried to suppress it, but then Mia was laughing, too. The two of them just lost it. They were standing in front of the mirror, tears rolling down their cheeks as they tried to stop the giggling. It wouldn't stop.

Pressing her hands to her aching tummy, Cass gulped in air and let out laughter. Mia braced one palm on the mirror and shook her head. After a few minutes, the giggles subsided and Mia sucked in a breath.

"Don't ever let me go back to that," she warned. "If I suddenly remember everything, don't let my fashion sense die such a horrible death."

"You're not helping." Cass stifled another round of

giggles and wiped the happy tears from her cheeks. "And I don't think you're in danger of that. As soon as you could, you cut your hair. You came in here and spent your first monthly stipend on clothes and makeup alone. You had to sneak food from the farm because you didn't have money left over to eat at the cafeteria."

"So that wasn't me." Mia fisted her hands on her hips and stared at her reflection. "Whoever my uncle made me into, that wasn't the *real* me."

"No." Cass shook her head and laid a hand on Mia's shoulder. "I don't think that was the real you at all."

After a few more twirls before the mirror, Mia shimmied out of her new dress and back into her jeans. She still had another couple hours of work left on the farm and Cass had a new order to work on in the shop. They chit chatted a bit while Cass folded the red dress and placed it neatly in a cloth sack.

"So you're moving in with him?" Mia's eyes sparkled as they assessed Cass.

"I guess so." Cass shrugged and felt her belly filling with butterflies. "Yeah. I guess I am. It's only across the hall."

"So… no more adventure beyond the Wall?" Mia cocked an eyebrow.

"No." Cass nibbled on her lip. "He wants me to stay. Are you still going?"

"Without you?" Mia scoffed and grabbed the cloth sack. "Nah, you were the only reason I was leaving in the first place. You're my bestest most goodest friend. I go where you go."

Smiling, Cass shook her head. "You're mine, too. I'm glad you're staying."

Nodding, Mia spun on her heel and sauntered back out of the room. The energy she took with her was similar to Garrett's. Electric. Cass wondered how she'd gotten looped in with such dynamic people. She herself felt so small in comparison.

She only wanted quiet time to create. She only wanted the hum of the sewing machine and the slip of new material through her fingers. Sighing to herself, Cass selected a bolt of fabric off the wall and got to work.

WHEN SHE LIFTED HER HEAD A FEW HOURS LATER, THE SUN was setting. Skylights set into the ceiling revealed a mass of clouds painted in pinks and purples. Rolling her shoulders, Cass leaned back in her chair and tried to ease the cramping in her muscles. How long had she been bent over the machine?

A soft knock at the door had her rubbing at her face. Dinner. Crap. She'd totally forgot.

"Come in!" Cass lifted her voice and let her hands drop to her lap.

The man that entered was not who she expected. Where Garrett was towering tall, this man was of average height. He stuck his head in first, his brown eyes lighting as they zeroed in on her. Cass felt her shoulders fall and her heart dip just a little. Levi. She owed him an explanation.

"Feeling better?" He asked as he stepped into the room. "I tried you at your place this morning, but no one answered. I didn't want to wake you."

"Yeah, I wasn't…" Cass pursed her lips before continuing. "I didn't spend the night there."

"Oh." Levi frowned. "Did they keep you overnight in the med center? I should have gone back there, I'm sorry, I just…"

"Not there," Cass cut him off and searched for a way to do this gently. Levi was a great guy. He'd always been a great guy, but now she knew the truth. "I got all of my memory back."

"You did? That's great!" A smile lit his face as Levi crossed the room to her.

Cass gave him a smile back, and sighed.

When she'd first been delivered to the Wall, Cass had been genetically tested and placed in breeding phase one. At that time, she hadn't known what it meant, none of them had. But eventually that phase number made her one of the first women required by the source to get pregnant.

And after months of stalling (while she'd been unable to choose a man for herself) the source stepped in and selected one for her. Levi.

He'd been just like he was now, good-looking and nice and kind. But she hadn't been the one to choose him, so he'd always felt more like a friend than anything else. Levi was the man that she *had* to give her body to, over and over, for a year. And yeah, he was really sweet about it, but still. He'd always felt like just a friend to her, nothing deeper, nothing more.

"I'm sorry," Cass blurted, holding up her hands in surrender. "I don't know how to say this."

"Say what?" Levi's face fell as he studied her.

"I… um…" Cass glanced to the side. "I'm with someone else. I met someone else. I'm sorry."

All his breath whooshed from his lungs and Cass cringed as Levi's shoulders slumped. Shoving his hands in his pockets, he stared at the ground for several seconds.

Swallowing, Cass fought the flood of guilt and sadness that hit her. Levi didn't deserve this. He deserved someone who loved him, someone who only wanted him. She just wasn't that person.

"It's Officer Jameson, right?" Levi's head tipped up and he cleared his throat. "He's been after you for months, he finally got what he wanted?"

"Levi." Cass locked eyes with him. "I knew him from before. We grew up together, we have history."

Nodding his head, Levi looked away and stuck his tongue in his cheek. He was upset and disappointed, she got that. She understood.

"Tell me this," he said finally, his eyes coming back to settle on her face. "Was he always this pushy about you? Because he seems like a pretty controlling guy."

"Um…" Cass's mouth dropped. She was at a loss for words.

"I'm just worried, Cass." Levi stepped forward. "That he's bullying you into this."

"He's not," she assured him. "Like I said we have history. It's complicated."

"Alright." Levi ducked his head. "Did he want you before you were one of the last women on earth? Because if he didn't choose you before you were the only option, then he doesn't deserve you now. You get that, right? If I'd of seen you before the war, I'd of done everything I could to be with you. Did he?"

"Levi."

"Because where I'm from, when a girl says things are complicated, it usually means the guy she's seeing is a douche." Sucking in a breath, Levi removed his hands from his pockets and ran them back through his raven-black hair.

"It's complicated because I was thirteen when we met and he was my older brother's best friend," Cass explained. "He's not pressuring me into this, I promise."

"Okay." Levi blew out a breath and took a step back. "Alright."

"I'm sorry," Cass tried again, leaning forward in her chair. "Really... I..."

Waving a hand, Levi huffed a breath. "I don't want you to be sorry. I want you to be happy. I guess that's just not with me."

Swallowing her words, Cass felt her throat tighten and tears burn the backs of her eyes. Why did this have to happen? Why was life so damn unfair?

Turning around, Levi stalked to the door. His shoulders were tight and his movements jerky. When he placed his hand on the knob, he stilled and looked back at her over his shoulder.

"You're probably not coming with us then?" He asked. "We're leaving in another few weeks. I'll still take you to California, no strings attached, if that's what you want."

"I appreciate that." Cass bobbed her head and gave him a half smile. "But I'm staying now."

"If you change your mind," Levi said, before twisting the knob and opening the door. "Then you know where to find me."

Slipping out the door before she could answer, Levi disappeared without another word. Resting her head in both hands, Cass blew out a long breath.

"I know where to find you," she whispered finally. The words hung by themselves now in the silent air.

THE SOIL BENEATH HIS BLACK BOOTS WAS DARK AND RICH. Crouching down beneath the grove of orange trees, Davey ran the tips of his fingers through the dirt. Inhaling, he took in the scent of ripe fruit, green leaves and heat (if heat indeed had a smell).

Sweat trickled down his spine where his rifle pressed against his back. There was plenty of moisture in the air too. Being inside one of the massive greenhouses was like stepping into a different climate. But weather didn't matter. His rifle was always strapped to his back, just like his knife was in its sheath on his belt and his handgun was tucked in its holster on his hip. He was ready. He was always ready.

Lifting his head, Davey blew out a breath and rose to standing. He was down to a short sleeve t-shirt and blue jeans. He was even second guessing his ball cap. The thing was soaking through on his forehead, but it did work to keep that strange greenish tint of sunlight out of his eyes, so there was that.

Reaching for the bill, Davey adjusted his hat and began to walk once more. He had no reason to be in here, other than it was a sort of escape. He needed a break. He needed to get away from them for just a little while.

It was hard to wrap his mind around his so called friends. Cole and Liam. The bastards actually *liked* Jameson. They joked around with the guy, were comfortable turning their backs on him. It was like nothing had ever happened. It was like Trey and Flynn and Chan and Ryder had never happened.

Even Lena and Hannah, the very same women that Jameson had *kidnapped*, seemed to like the guy. They left him alone with the baby... often. The baby that was supposedly named for Chan. Hah.

They let Chan's killer hold his namesake. How fucked up was that? Didn't they remember that part? Didn't they remember the raid?

Grinding his teeth together, Davey continued to stalk quietly through the orange grove. He weaved around the trunks of trees, even though they were placed methodically in nice neat little rows. Occasionally, he dragged a palm around a trunk, felt the rough texture of the bark against his skin.

He was behaving as best he could, keeping his head down and not making a fuss. Every opportunity he got, he volunteered for work with Jameson. If he was going to kill the fucker, then he had to be close to him.

It was hard. It was really, really hard listening to the guy laugh and joke and cuss and breathe when Ryder was dead and cold in the ground.

But Davey was being patient. He was biding his time.

He needed to get Jameson alone, that was the key. Although it would be simple enough to put a bullet in the guy's back in a crowd full of people, that wouldn't provide Davey with the satisfaction he required. He needed to look into Jameson's eyes. He needed the guy to know why he was dying. He needed the name *Ryder* to be the very last thing echoing in that big ass head of his right before the asshole bit the bullet.

So... self-discipline... patience... focus. That was the mantra playing itself out in Davey's mind, over and over, every single day.

There wasn't room for anything else. Then again, there wasn't much competition in his vacant little soul. The numbness dominated him. It was like he was walking along the bottom of the ocean. The weight of the sea was above his head and all around him, pressing down, silencing any noise.

Davey found himself in a great empty void. He also found he didn't necessarily mind it.

There was no light down here. No intensity. Time passed. The clock kept right on ticking (hypothetically speaking) and although Davey discovered that time didn't exactly heal all wounds, he found that it *could* dull them.

He didn't feel the depth of pain like he had when he first saw his brother's lifeless body. It no longer felt like his heart was being sucked out of his chest through his ribcage. Nope. Now he felt nothing. And nothing kept him functioning, so there was that.

Coming to the edge of the grove, Davey leaned against a tree trunk and folded his arms across his chest. He was in the shade here, it was the last long row before the other crops started. There were people in the distance, walking along the far edge of the greenhouse, or tending to other things.

Davey let his eyes scan each person, taking in their features, cataloging them in the way a hunter might note things about the herd he was stalking. This one is weak. This one is strong. But then his gaze settled on a familiar figure and he frowned.

The blonde. Mia. She was on her knees in the dirt between two rows, pulling weeds from a line of crops. They looked like asparagus.

For once there was no crowd of hungry boyfriends surrounding her. There were no men competing for her attention. Her short blonde hair hung forward, the tips just reaching below her jawline. As she worked, she hummed quietly under her breath. Davey didn't recognize the tune.

She was wearing a tank top, her slender shoulders were lightly tanned and smooth. Davey's eyes followed the line of her body, absorbing the details of her trim waist, round ass and long legs tucked beneath her. She was wearing faded jeans that were covered in dirt and a pair of short brown boots that barely reached her ankles.

It was the first time that he hadn't seen her all made up

and flirting. It was the first time he'd seen her all alone. She was… beautiful.

For a split second, Davey forgot. He forgot about the war. He forgot about the training and the marching and the shooting and the killing.

In that moment, Davey was back in Wisconsin. He was a boy in a field, looking at a girl in a field. The corner of his mouth tweaked up just a touch.

Then she was straightening and glancing over her shoulder at him. Mia's deep brown eyes locked with his. Davey stared. His heart tried to do this thing… this thumping thing.

Shaking his head, Davey sucked in a quick breath as he rubbed the heel of his hand over his chest. He wasn't entirely sure what was happening. When he glanced back at Mia, she had her head cocked to one side.

"You okay?" She asked.

Davey merely nodded, still rubbing his hand over his heart.

"It can get pretty hot in here," she offered. "Maybe you should just hang in the shade a few minutes."

"Yeah." Davey cleared his throat and felt his body sinking down beside the trunk of the nearest orange tree. "It's hot."

With a satisfied smile, Mia returned her attention to the row of asparagus she had been tending. In silence, Davey watched her and wondered and watched some more.

His chest was easing now and his pulse was flattening out. For a long time, Davey simply sat in the shade and observed. It was dangerously addicting, watching her. All the while, he knew he should be going. He knew he should be getting up and walking away, but for some reason, he found he was unable.

The blonde, for her part, seemed to ignore him. She kept inching along her row of vegetables with her back to him, humming to herself. It was the most peace Davey had felt since before the war.

The pain of losing his brother was suddenly background noise and Mia was front and center, taking its place.

He wasn't sure if he felt relief at the fact or hatred. All he knew was that this girl was not for him. Anyone that pulled him from his mission was the enemy, and he would be sure to keep that in mind.

As quietly as he could, Davey rose to standing and adjusted his rifle strap across his shoulder. The blonde was still humming happily, not seeming to notice his change in position, but that wasn't surprising. After all, he hadn't survived five years on the outside of the Wall by being a big noisy dumbass.

In silence, Davey pursed his lips and looked down on her. Mia. Yes, she was beautiful *but* she was not for him, he reminded himself. No one was.

With a quick nod of his head, Davey turned on his heel and stalked away.

Bracing his forearms on the tabletop, Jameson frowned down at the papers before him. He'd been called in to work late… again.

Uriah was seated off to his left, at the head of the long mahogany table in the same old meeting room they'd been crammed in for the past several weeks. The usual suspects were taking up the rest of the chairs, with the addition of Liam, Cole and Davey.

It was all hands on deck. Things inside the Wall were shifting. Like everything else in life, change was just around the corner, waiting to flush your happy plans down the shitter.

And on top of it all, this crap was now eating into his time with Cass. Jameson hadn't been able to go home to her last night. It was the first time since she'd moved in. It was the first time in two weeks that she hadn't been pressed against him while he slept. It had him restless.

"As you can see," Hernandez was saying. "The petition is actually quite long. I don't know how we can ignore it."

Nodding his head, Uriah flipped quickly through about a dozen sheets of paper. They were just like the ones sitting in front of Jameson. They were covered in hand written signatures. People wanted what they had before. People wanted to elect a leader. They wanted democracy.

"They're afraid you're a dictator," Malik added, his hands splayed. "If you authorize the election, then maybe that will quiet them down. You could run for office. I think you could win."

Pinching the bridge of his nose, Uriah sighed.

"Newsflash," he stated. "I am a dictator. I'm just a good one."

"Commander…" Hernandez started to argue but Uriah waved him off.

"And I don't want to run for office," Uriah continued. "Democracy worked just fine when the country was huge. We had a lot of moving parts back then and things could move slowly without much issue. But now our world is too small. You can't manage a city of this size without a good leader making quick decisions. It keeps people alive and things running smoothly. If they elect the wrong person, it could sink everything."

"That's why you run for office," Malik urged. A rumbling of assent moved around the table. "We need you, and when the community leaders see that the majority of us living here agree, then things will settle down."

"But what if I don't win?" Uriah's brows rose and he

shoved the papers away from him. "What if they choose some jerk off who can talk a good game, but is completely inept? What happens when one of the other refugee centers decides to fly their jets our way? Will that guy know what to do? Or will he have to take a fucking vote on it while we're all blown away?"

"Sir…"

"And what if the new leader doesn't understand crop rotation?" Uriah continued. "What if he doesn't understand rationing, or the importance of long term storage? What if he thinks every year will be easy, like this one was? What if he gives people too many food credits or not enough?"

"Sir, that's why you need to run for office," Hernandez countered.

The young soldier slapped a palm on the tabletop for emphasis, but no one jumped. They'd had this conversation before. Hell, they'd been having this conversation every day for weeks.

"Alright." Uriah leaned back in his chair and groaned. "So I run and I win. When do I have to do it again?"

"Four years," Malik supplied, but everyone already knew this.

"Let's say I get elected again after that," Uriah reasoned. "Then that's it? Eight and I'm out for life, right? What happens then?"

"We run someone else in this room," Malik said. "And again after that. You'd still be the Commander of the Linfield Army. You'd still have control over all that."

"Ah. Right." Uriah tipped forward in his seat. "The

Linfield Army. Funny. It has my fucking name on it. I'm half tempted to march my happy ass back down to Utah and resume control of my old city. I bet after three years without me, half of the people up here will come running down to live there."

"Then you'd be giving up the weapons bunkers," Jameson said his part, like he had every single time before. "The greenhouses, the apartments, the medical equipment. Not to mention that the vast majority of women and extremely young children will stay here. Will you leave them unprotected?"

Uriah's eyes landed on Jameson and narrowed. It was a sucker punch, but it was also true. The women and kids thing got him every time.

There was also the fact that a whole bunch of soldiers in the Linfield Army had become quite attached to said women, and were currently in the process of making more tiny children. Would they follow their Commander? Would they bring their women with them? Or would they stay?

It was hard to say. The truth was... no one would really know the answer unless and until Uriah decided to leave.

"You want me to run for office?" Uriah's eyes zeroed in on Jameson. This question was for his best friend alone.

The others remained silent. Uriah had never asked Jameson what he wanted before, he never asked anyone what they wanted, in fact. He'd always just said that he wouldn't do it, that he wouldn't run.

"You need to authorize an election," Jameson confirmed finally. "And yes… I want you to run."

The collective exhale from his comrades was audible.

"If you don't get elected," Jameson continued. "Then we can move forward with plan B. We'll have a year to prepare for a move, if one is even needed."

"And you want me to do it all over again," Uriah qualified. "After four years."

"Let's see if we can negotiate the first term at eight years," Jameson offered. "And set no term limits. If you're good, then you can get elected until you die, something like that. I think term limits only became a thing in the U.S. after the first hundred years or so."

"It was over a hundred and fifty years," Malik offered. "The United States didn't have term limits for the President until the 1950s."

"So we'll go with that," Hernandez again, leaning forward. "Let me take some of this to the community members. I think they might agree."

Groaning, Uriah ran a wide hand over his face and sucked in a breath.

"I do not want to be a fucking politician," he said through his fingers. "This is not a country, it's a mid-sized city, and I fucking conquered it. There shouldn't even be a question."

"But there is a question," Jameson cut him off, before adding the obligatory, "Sir."

"You're a testy mother-fucker today, you know that?" Uriah dropped his hand and frowned at Jameson. "You miss one night with her and you're suddenly pushing me to wrap up *the* biggest decision any of us have had to make."

Cole cleared his throat and Hernandez hid his smirk behind his hand. The others all knew that (off the clock) Uriah and Jameson were buddies. But to witness the banter was rare.

Usually, Jameson minded his P's and Q's, careful to keep rank and respect first and foremost in front of witnesses. It was important, he figured, because the soldiers around him would take their direction from his example. He always displayed 100% respect for his Commander in public. And so should everyone else.

"On another note..." Jameson ignored the jab. "How will we know if another refugee center sends its jets our way? We don't use any electronics to monitor the air space."

Lifting a heavy brow, Uriah simply stared at him. Further down the table, Malik shuffled some papers around nervously. This was another longstanding point of debate. Uriah was too paranoid to use technology. Was that a necessary precaution? Or was it excessive caution that would eventually lead to their downfall?

That, along with so many other things, remained to be seen. And bringing it up now in front of every high ranking soldier in the Linfield Army? Sort of an asshole move on Jameson's part. Maybe skipping a night with Cass really did rub him the wrong way.

Leaning back in his black office chair, Jameson gave a

small shrug. It needed to be said. He might as well be the jerk to do it.

"You shrugging at me now, Officer?" Uriah asked.

Sitting up straight again, Jameson composed his features. His hands came up to fold together on the tabletop.

His butt was numb, his back was sore, and his neck had this awful kink in it. He was just so damn tired. It was the middle of the night and they'd been at this for far too long without resolutions. Give him a five day trek in the mud over this bureaucratic bullshit any day.

"No, Sir," Jameson responded.

"Must've been a muscle spasm then." Uriah's lips pressed into a thin line.

"Entirely involuntary." Jameson kept a straight face. "Sir."

"Well in that case you can take your entirely involuntary ass home," Uriah announced. "And that goes for the rest of you, too. Get out. Get some rest. We reconvene first thing in the morning. Take nothing to the community members. I need more time to review."

A chorus of groans rippled around the table as men pushed back and stood up. Papers rustled, chairs squeaked and small conversations began cropping up amongst them. Uriah still hadn't made a final decision. Another day spent debating the same thing and they still seemed no closer to a solution than they had before.

"I need a minute," Uriah said quietly, tapping his index finger at Jameson.

Dipping his head, Jameson eased back in his chair and rubbed at the back of his neck. For several minutes he listened to soldiers approaching their Commander. They asked for this, were given instructions on that. The city still had to run and Uriah still controlled it, even though there was rumbling from some high ranking members of the community about an election.

The truth was, they all just wanted more power. They all just wanted more control. That was all this was to them, but Jameson understood the overall concept meant so much more. Uriah was doing a great job, yes, but what happened if he fell ill? What happened if he suddenly died?

There needed to be some structure in place to ensure that the next leader wasn't the bad kind of dictator. Democracy was the best solution for that, even if it meant a lot of fucking red tape and committees and voting… the kind of monotony that made Jameson's eyes want to bleed.

When the last man had left and the heavy door clicked shut, Uriah rotated around and leaned back against it. Tipping his chin up, he closed his eyes and exhaled a long breath.

Jameson watched him, understanding that the fatigue was bone deep and yet all mental.

Stress. They'd thought they had it when their entire plan was to overthrow this place.

"I don't want to do this," Uriah murmured.

"I know." Jameson sucked in a breath.

"I want to leave," Uriah again, shaking his head. "Just take Ian and Lena and fucking hide away in that compound with my sister. Raise my family. Grow corn or some shit."

"Farmer Linfield," Jameson tried the words on his tongue. "I can see you in overalls now."

"Shut the fuck up." Uriah huffed out a laugh and then grinned. "It'd be good corn, though. Probably."

"You've never grown a thing in your life," Jameson reminded him. "You killed every plant you tried to bring underground in Utah."

"I know, I know." Uriah's eyes popped open as he sighed. "I don't water them enough."

"You water them too much actually." Jameson bit his bottom lip and rocked in his chair.

It was coming. Whatever Uriah really wanted to talk to him about, it was on the tip of the guy's tongue. Shoving off the door, he stalked the perimeter of the room, rubbing his hands together restlessly. Jameson knew enough about his friend to keep his mouth shut.

"You're right about the electronics," he admitted finally. "We're sitting ducks without it… *if* the other centers are functioning *and* they're using their equipment."

"That's a lot of ifs," Jameson remarked.

"Yes, but the possibility is out there," Uriah added. "So it's really just a matter of when."

Rubbing at his scruff of two-day beard growth, Jameson waited.

"First thing in the morning," Uriah continued. "While the others are reporting back here, I want you to go up in the air traffic control tower. Dismiss the soldier we have on watch rotation and once he's gone, you can start testing some of the equipment."

Sitting up straight now, Jameson studied Uriah as he continued to pace.

"Start with the small stuff," Uriah went on. "I'll have Cole and Liam report to the old source office in Building Six. Keep in communication with them. If something gets triggered, then shut down immediately. Understood?"

"Absolutely." Jameson bobbed his head. How long had it been since he had a real assignment? Too long.

Shoving up to standing, Jameson tried to hide the excitement now flooding him. This is what he was really made for, walking the edge, being prepared to strike, not listening to endless reports on the dispute over cafeteria credits.

"And Jameson…" Uriah stepped between him and the door. "I know you miss your little girlfriend so… why don't you take her along on this one? She can help you monitor the radio, just… don't get too sidetracked."

"Yeah." Jameson grinned as he thought of Cass. "Only a little sidetracked. Got it."

She'd felt the moment he crept into bed beside her. The covers puffed up with cool air, the mattress sagged and then his big body was wrapping itself around her. It must've been the middle of the night sometime, because after she inhaled his scent, she'd slipped back into sleep. He was here. She was safe.

In the morning, with the light barely leaking in through their window, Cass rolled over and blinked at a still sleeping Garrett. His face was relaxed, his lips slightly parted as he breathed in and out.

She studied him for a few quiet moments. His brown hair was mussed, his strong jaw was covered in two day beard growth. Reaching up with a hand, she stroked carefully along the bristles, feeling their roughness beneath her fingertips.

That's when he stirred, smacking his lips together and letting out a low groan. It brought a smile to Cass's face.

She'd gotten used to this. Used to his sounds and his stretching. Used to the heat radiating off his body and the weight of his heavy arm as it draped possessively over her waist.

"Missed you," he murmured.

His eyes hadn't opened yet, but he pulled her in closer. Wriggling against him, Cass tucked her face into his neck and exhaled. His chin settled on the top of her head and his hips jumped forward almost involuntarily. She'd gotten used to this part, too. The part where his body woke up before him, and wanted her.

"Good morning," she whispered.

Suppressing a sigh, Cass laid her palms on his chest and pressed her lips up under his chin. Laying slow kisses on his skin, she smiled again as Garrett let loose another long groan.

"Careful," he warned, his voice was still husky with sleep. "Don't start something you can't finish."

"I can finish," she teased and then let out a squeak when he flipped her onto her back.

"Is that so?" Garrett's blue eyes were open now and boring into her.

Nodding, Cass nibbled on her bottom lip. He was so handsome and she hadn't seen him in a few days.

She knew where he'd been, of course. He was busy working, busy with important second-in-command type things. And truthfully, it hadn't bothered her overmuch. She'd spent most of her time at the shop, sewing, creating. It felt good. But then again, this felt good too.

Rolling her hips, Cass wrapped her arms around Garrett's neck and pulled him down to kiss her. He obliged, working his mouth against hers, lazily, slowly, it was early in the morning after all, and he'd been out late.

Sighing, Cass let him overwhelm her. She felt her body light up as tingles rushed through her system. He kept his forearms braced on either side of her head as he ground his hips between her thighs. An aching heat pooled in her core and she let loose a little gasp.

Over the past several weeks they'd done this a lot. Like... A LOT. And Garrett had spent that time learning her. He watched her while they played around, asked her what felt good, what was too rough, what wasn't rough enough. So by now he knew exactly what to do to get her panting for him.

"Mmmm," Cass hummed the word as Garrett's mouth left hers to travel to her neck.

Rocking up on one arm, he used the other to reach under her shirt. His hand cupped her breast. His thumb brushed her nipple. Back and forth, back and forth until she was arching and rubbing against him. A low chuckle rumbled through his chest.

He was all male, all triumph and conquering. Some feline thing inside of Cass caused her to smirk. Two could play at this game, she thought, but only one could win.

"Roll over," she gasped and pushed against him.

"What?" Garrett pulled back slightly and frowned.

"Roll. Over." Cass grinned now as he complied.

Pushing him onto his back, Cass moved on top to

straddle his hips. As usual Garrett slept naked. She could feel his length trapped between their bodies so she ground her core down on him, causing his hands to shoot up to her thighs. His fingers dug into her flesh and squeezed.

"No fair," Garrett growled. His eyes were hooded, lingering on her chest. "You're wearing a shirt."

"I'm wearing *your* shirt," Cass countered, and when he tried to flip their positions again, she stopped him. "Not so fast, big boy," she teased, tugging the shirt off, she tossed it away. "This is my show now."

"Oh is it?" Garrett's eyes twinkled, but he relaxed down to his back once more.

"It is," Cass confirmed, still rubbing herself shamelessly down on him.

"You know, I'm more of a doer than a watcher," he hissed. "Although both is good, I guess."

Humming, Cass leaned down and pressed her mouth to his. Her tongue snaked out, teasing him for a split second before she pulled away.

Frowning, Garrett slid his hands further up her thighs. His fingers began exploring, finding that one particular spot and working it until Cass could feel her heartbeat pulsing between her legs.

He was such an alpha, she thought, sneaking back in to take control. With a tiny gasp she moved away from him.

Sliding down his body, Cass traced her tongue over his chest. Her hands smoothed at his hard abs and coasted to his hips as she continued to move lower. Garrett's head snapped up and his mouth parted as he watched her.

Looking up at him, Cass grinned.

"We should definitely do you first," he rasped.

Coming up to lean on one elbow, his face had grown serious, but his eyes were looking a bit glazed.

"My. Show." Cass repeated, and moving lower, she took him into her mouth.

Garrett swore impressively before releasing a hiss.

His heavy body flopped back to the mattress, forcing Cass to steady herself with her hands on his thighs. She hadn't done this a whole bunch, but she figured the concept was pretty straight forward.

For a few minutes, she played with him the same way he played with her, using her mouth until his hips were jerking and his breath was catching in his throat.

The power was heady. She was so much smaller than him physically, it was a rush to have him writhing just for her. But then he was tapping her shoulder and when she didn't budge he sat up and pulled her off.

Swiping a hand over the back of her mouth, Cass was going to protest, but the look on Garrett's face had her smirking instead. *Point goes to the alpha female.* He looked downright pained.

"Come on Cass baby," he pleaded, and pulled her up onto his lap. "I want to feel you. Let's go together, 'kay?"

"Okay," she echoed but it quickly turned to a moan as Garrett entered her.

Gripping her hips in his large hands, Garrett moved her body up and down, back and forth. He was back in the drivers seat, and in all honesty, he was probably born to stay there.

Biting at her lip, Cass braced her hands on his shoulders, rubbing her chest against his and moaning into his ear.

Garrett remained sitting up, shifting his hips beneath her and working his hands over her until Cass was crying out. Clenching around him, the pleasure overwhelmed her, pulsing and flooding her system until she bit down on his shoulder.

Cursing, Garrett jerked a few times and quickly followed her over the edge. Collapsing onto his back, his arms tightened around Cass and drew her down on top of him.

For a solid minute they were all panting breaths and quick swallows.

When her pulse finally evened out, Garrett began lazily running his hands down Cass's back, then up again, along her spine. It wasn't until he placed one wide palm on the back of her head and peppered her forehead with soft kisses that she completely melted for him.

"You're too much," she said quietly. "You make me so weak for you."

"Hmmm..." Garrett's chest rumbled as he rolled her over onto her back. "Guess that finally makes us even."

Giving him a smile, Cass watched as Garrett pushed away and left their bed. The muscles in his back flexed and moved as he went to grab her a towel. Did she mention he was too much? Too sexy. Too sweet. Too strong. Too gentle.

Taking the towel from him, Cass released a contented sigh. Garrett wiggled his eyebrows playfully before taking the few steps to his closet. Well… except now it was *their* closet. Her clothes were jamming the narrow space to the point of overflowing.

"I'd appreciate it if you wouldn't oogle me like a piece of meat," he teased, stepping into boxers first, then blue jeans. "It's demeaning you know. I *am* more than my body."

"Ha. Ha. Ha." Cass intoned.

Sitting up in bed, she folded her legs beneath her. Was he leaving so soon? It was barely past sunrise.

Seeming to hear her thoughts, Garrett pulled a t-shirt over his head and turned to face her. "I've got some work to do first thing this morning, but I was hoping you'd come with me."

"To work?" Cass frowned, that'd never happened before.

"Yeah." Garrett rubbed at his jaw and eyed her. "I've got to check out some of the equipment in the tower. You could bring a book to read or just hang out. I'll grab breakfast from the cafeteria and we can eat up there. The view is pretty spectacular."

Arching her back, Cass reached her arms up and had a good stretch. Did she want to check out the tower? Sure. Did she want to spend some extra time with Garrett? Absolutely.

Dropping her arms back to her sides, Cass swung her

legs over the edge and popped up to standing. As she passed Garrett on her way to the bathroom, she let her walk sway just a little more than necessary. After all, she was still completely naked and she could feel his eyes searing every inch of her skin.

Glancing back at him over her shoulder, Cass smirked when she caught him staring.

"Hey," she taunted. "I'd appreciate it if you wouldn't oogle me like a piece of meat. Someone told me it's demeaning."

As she closed the bathroom door, she heard Garrett's bark of laughter. It had that same old lightning zinging through her. Damn that whirlwind handsome man, she thought, before turning on the shower.

STARING OUT THE WIDE WINDOW, CASS'S MOUTH PARTED slightly. She'd crawled up on one of the long desks, her legs were tucked beneath her, her hands pressed flat against the wooden surface. The view before her was more than spectacular, it was enthralling. It was life just beyond the Wall.

Mountain peaks, covered in multi-colored green trees. White puffy clouds. The bluest of bright summer skies. A yellow sun, pouring out its heat on everything. It was like a painting. It was like a photograph.

She wished she could capture all the colors in a fabric.

She wished she'd been talented enough to paint.

"Pretty awesome, right?" Garrett was standing just behind her. His hands on his hips. A grin spread over his face.

"Yeah." Cass shook her head slowly. "Pretty awesome."

After her shower in their apartment, Cass had gotten dressed. By that time Garrett had already made it to the cafeteria and back. With their breakfast in hand, they'd walked to the control tower. It wasn't an area that Cass had ever been to before, but the top of the tower could be seen from almost anywhere inside the Wall, so it wasn't too foreign.

Before they'd started their ascent, Garrett had dismissed the soldier assigned to watch, and started a large generator for power. He'd said it needed to be run a few times a year anyway, to keep everything working smoothly.

Then they'd climbed. And climbed. And climbed.

The stairwell was dim and gray, dusty and quiet, so when they'd finally entered the observation room at the top, it had taken Cass's breath away. Three-hundred and sixty degree views, windows taking up every wall, with long tables pushed up against them.

There were rows of desks lined up in the middle of the room with computer equipment seeming to cover every surface. The screens were all dark though, unused.

Garrett had set their bag of breakfast on one desk beside a window and helped her to climb up. She was still frozen in time now, watching a few birds float by on the wind.

"Blueberry muffin for you," he recited. "And a bagel with cream cheese for me."

The paper bag crinkled as Garrett dug around and set the carefully wrapped food beside her. Glancing down at it, Cass plucked the top off of the large muffin and took a bite. It was fresh and warm and delicious.

"Coffee," he announced, and produced two empty mugs and one thermos. "Filled with creamy sugar goodness. Everything's already mixed in."

"Hmmm, I was hoping for black." Cass pouted as he poured coffee into the two mugs. It smelled amazing, though.

"There are some compromises a man just doesn't make," Garrett said seriously. "And how he takes his coffee is one of them. Plus, they'd only give me the one thermos."

Chuckling, Cass picked up her mug and sipped. It was soooooo sweet, but it was coffee, so she wasn't going to turn it down.

Returning her attention to the window, Cass exhaled.

"I'll be checking some of this equipment out," Garrett explained. "Turning it on and poking around. The entire time I'll be in radio contact with Liam and Cole. The whole operation could take hours, maybe even all day. Just let me know if you get bored and I can take a break and walk you down."

"Alright." Cass glanced at him over her shoulder and smiled.

Leaning in, Garrett captured her mouth with his. The kiss was soft and sweet. Pulling back, he grumbled something about getting sidetracked and walked off.

Returning her attention to the view, Cass polished off her muffin and drank from the ceramic mug until the last drops rolled onto her tongue. With a satisfied sigh, she set the cup down and pushed off the table. Garrett was bent over one of the computer screens a few rows away. She could hear the clack of keys as his hands zoomed along the keyboard.

Every once in a while, he would hold a walkie talkie up to his mouth and ask questions. There would be a brief second of static before either Cole or Liam would answer back. It seemed the two of them took turns answering, because Cass recognized Cole's easy joking and then Liam's terse responses. So different. They were so very different.

Strolling around the room, Cass took note of the endless machines and screens sitting vacant beneath a thin layer of dust. Outside the windows, she could see almost every part of the Wall.

There were the fields and greenhouses, the farm with its animals. There were apartment buildings, the medical center, the store where she worked. And then the wide green lawns, the concrete paths, with people riding bicycles and sitting down for picnics.

Weaving around a line of tables, Cass stopped short at a strange piece of equipment taking up space on one wide desk. Unlike its neighbors, this device was free of dust. On the table beside it, was a tripod with what appeared to be a long antenna attached to it.

Stepping closer, Cass bent down and frowned. It was a large rectangular box, about a foot and a half long with a bunch of tiny dials and switches and a little screen. On one side of it, there was something that looked sort of like an old fashioned telephone, but smaller. It had a black spiral cord running off of it.

Straightening, Cass's eyebrows raised. It was a radio, she realized. Like a really, really big radio.

Glancing over her shoulder, she caught Garrett's eye.

"It's a radio?" She asked and he nodded.

Setting his walkie down, Garrett pushed away from what he was doing and crossed over to her. Cass returned her attention to the equipment. Leaning forward she spread her palms on the desk as Garrett came to a stop just beside her.

"It's a long range radio," he explained and switched it on. "Here's how you scan channels. You pick this up and hold it to your ear to listen. If you press this button, you can talk back."

"Cool." Cass accepted the phone type object and held it up to her ear.

"The frequency of each channel shows on this screen here." Garrett gestured to the tiny screen that was now showing the numbers 161.551. "You can listen in on the guard duty rotation, or sometimes the kitchen staff has some interesting stuff to say."

"Oh?" Cass smiled and pushed the scan button.

Static. Voices. Static.

"Just don't answer back," he cautioned. "You can only listen. Okay? You good?"

"Yeah." Cass beamed at him. "Thanks."

Dipping his head, Garrett turned and stalked back to the opposite end of the room. After he'd plunked down in his chair, Cass pushed the scan button again and jumped channels. The numbers whirred until they hit 177.833 and stopped.

All clear Section 4.

Static.

Roger. All clear.

Static.

Nibbling at her lip, Cass leaned against the table and continued to hold the black phone up to her ear. When nothing else happened, she huffed a breath and pressed the scan button again. The numbers whirred until they hit 180.955.

I tell them to bring me three flats of tomatoes. Three. But what do I get?

Static.

Not tomatoes?

Static.

Nice guess. But no. I get one flat. Just one, so now we're out just before the lunch rush.

Static.

So you want me to run and get two more flats? Is that what you're saying?

Static.

You're brilliant Steven. Just a fucking genius. I don't know why everyone isn't working for you. You deserve an award.

Static.

Maybe if you weren't such an asshole, the food runners in the morning wouldn't keep shorting your deliveries. Ever thought of that?

Static.

Snickering into one hand, Cass listened to the roll of expletives that followed. The back and forth in the kitchen was in fact, pretty entertaining.

After another minute though, things quieted down. Steven brought the tomatoes so that was that.

Sneaking a glance at Garrett, Cass hummed absently. He was tapping away at another keyboard and frowning at the screen. His radio squawked beside him. He didn't answer it.

Keeping her eyes on him, Cass pushed the scan button and waited for it to catch onto another channel. It rotated and rotated and rotated. Finding static, catching, then moving forward, not settling and locking onto anything. But then...

If anyone's out there. I'm calling for help. We have women and children in need of food and...

Static.

Cass's heart fell out of her body. It just jumped right through the center of her chest and plopped onto the floor. That voice.

Our location is Hermiston, Oregon. If you can hear this message, please bring food and any medical supplies you may have.

Static.

If anyone's out there. I'm calling for help...

Static.

Static.

Please...

Static.

Cass's eyes flipped to the screen on the radio. Talk. Talk. Where was the talk button? Her heart was thundering and her breath was coming in short. That voice. She would recognize it anywhere, would recognize *him* anywhere.

Jamming her hand on the buttons, Cass let out a shriek when instead of hitting talk, she hit scan again. The numbers whirred and she dropped the phone to the tabletop.

"No! No, no, no, no, no!" Cass ran her hands feverishly over the device.

What channel had her brother been on? What channel had he been speaking from? Oh God. Eli's alive, she thought. Eli's alive and he's out there and he needs help.

"Hey Cass." Garrett was jogging over. "What's wrong? What're you doing?"

"Eli," Cass panted out the word, turning her eyes to Garrett. "He's alive. He's alive and he needs help."

"Wait. What?"

"Eli," Cass repeated. "I just heard him on the… on the radio. He was talking. He was talking and he needs help."

"Whoa, Cass. Slow down." Garrett's hands came to wrap her upper arms and spin her to face him. "What did you hear?"

"I heard Eli." Cass gestured to the radio. "I was scanning channels and then I heard his voice. He said he needs help. There are women and children with him. He needs food and medicine. Oh God. Oh my God, Garrett. He's alive. My brother is alive."

"No." Garrett's hands squeezed her arms tighter and he shook his head quickly. "You're hearing things. It could have been anyone."

"It was him," Cass insisted. "I'd know that voice anywhere. It was Eli. He's in Oregon. A town starting with an H. Hampton? Hemton? We have to go to him. We have to leave right now. Can we leave right now?"

"Cass." Garrett shook her just a little. "It wasn't Eli. Whatever you heard…"

"Hermiston!" Cass cried. "That's where he is. He's in Hermiston. Have you heard of it? Can you get us there?"

"Cass!" Garrett's voice raised and his hands held her fast. "Stop. Stop this. Eli is dead. Cass, he's dead. We aren't going anywhere. We've got to stay right here."

"You don't know that!" Cass wriggled in his grasp, her eyes staying locked on his. "You didn't hear it. It was him."

"It was some guy on the radio that sounded like him," Garrett spat. "It wasn't him."

"It was!" Cass brought her hands up to shove away. "It was Eli! He's alive and I'm going to Hermiston, Oregon whether you like it or not."

"Eli is dead!" Garrett released her and ran his hands back through his hair. "He's dead Cass. Eli is dead."

"You don't know that for sure." Cass stared at him, watching as pain contorted his feautres.

"I just know," he pleaded. His eyes were glassy as they looked at her. "I know that he's dead, okay?"

"He's not," Cass whispered. "I. Heard. Him."

"You heard someone else."

"*Eli* is not dead."

"I watched him die!" Garrett barked. Stepping back, he looked wildly around, as if he wanted to run but had nowhere to go. "I saw him die, Cass."

"Wha... What?" Cass staggered back. The words were like a physical blow. Her knees were weak and her stomach dropped out on her.

"I... I tried to tell you," Garrett stammered, as his eyes came back to rest on her face. "I... I... I killed him, Cass. I killed Eli. He's dead. He's dead because of me."

Garrett's voice was breaking now, cracking and pitching as tears rimmed his eyes.

"You..." Cass's mouth fell open as her heart shattered into a million tiny pieces.

Taking a few more stumbling steps back, she tripped over a chair and slammed sideways into a desk.

Garrett made to follow her. He reached out with his hands, as if to catch her, but she screamed. She screamed at him. Not a word. Not any collection of words. Her body just released sound and had Garrett recoiling.

Then she was running. Cass was turning away from him, like she had so many times before, and she ran. Cass's brain switched off as she flew to the door and pounded away down the steps.

Eli was dead.

He was dead because Garrett killed him.

Garrett killed her brother.

BEFORE

18 months after the start of the war

THE SMOKE WAS GETTING THICK NOW, LAYING LOW IN THE surrounding streets, making it hard to breathe, making it hard to see.

Kneeling down in the middle of the empty roadway, Eli swung the pack off his back and set his rifle aside. His lungs were burning and his throat was raw and his eyes were itching like all get out.

But that was nothing compared to the ache in his feet. He'd been walking for weeks. *Weeks.*

Digging around in his pack, he found his canteen. The thing wasn't nearly heavy enough, but when he held it up to his ear and shook, he could hear water sloshing around.

Yanking down on his thin face mask, Eli twisted off the cap and took in just enough liquid to wet his mouth. God, how he wanted to chug every last drop. But he couldn't, he didn't know where his next source of water might be and he was too close to his final destination to get sidetracked searching the houses in this neighborhood.

Nope. Just one more street up and he'd hang a left and that would be it. Eight houses down on the right and the monstrous two-story that was Garrett Jameson's childhood home would greet him. There might be water there. He hoped there was. He hoped Cass had plenty of water and food, too.

Securing the lid on his canteen, Eli stuffed it back in his pack and grabbed his rifle off the ground. The black weapon felt sturdy in his hands, like an old friend.

Coming up to standing, he swung his heavy pack onto his back and slung his rifle over his shoulder.

Shit it was hot. The wildfires made everything way more miserable than it had to be. Pulling his mask back up over his face, Eli continued walking.

If he'd had any more energy, the adrenaline pumping into his system right now might have had him running. It had been well over three months since he'd last seen his sister and he was worried. But Garrett would've taken care of her, he told himself. They'd been taking turns coming to see her, so Garrett would've stepped up when Eli missed his visit.

Yeah. He could trust Garrett. He was like the brother Eli never had.

Keeping his steps steady, Eli crossed onto the sidewalk and made that left turn. Overhead, heavy clouds of dark smoke obscured the sun. Even so, Eli judged the time to be somewhere in the late-afternoon. He didn't own a watch, and the useless cell phone he'd shoved into his pack hadn't picked up service since the day he'd left.

He'd been assigned to the tank division in the early stages of the war and at first, Eli thought that had been a good thing. Better than standard infantry like Garrett. He'd trained as a driver, but he could also do the gunner's job if necessary.

The guys he worked with were alright, and one in particular had mentioned bugging out to an underground bunker if things got too hairy.

But then they'd been deployed with no notice. They woke up one day and got orders to move out and that was it. Eli had no time to get back to Cass and no time to find Garrett, since he was stationed on a separate base up near Los Alamitos.

So his plans had gone a bit sideways at that point, but he figured their unit would blow the shit out of the enemy and maybe put an end to the whole crazy war business altogether. And Eli had managed to hold onto that pipe dream until they'd crossed into Texas.

It was a fucking wasteland. Dead cities. Dead suburbs. Dead bodies. Everywhere.

The smell, more than anything, would never leave him. That's when he'd ditched. Fuck the mystery bunker and fuck the war and fuck the Command. He was out.

In the middle of the night, he'd packed his bag, stolen extra ammo and MRE's and split. It hadn't been all that hard really. That far into the thick of fighting, communication lines were sketchy at best. He found all he had to do was keep his uniform on and his rifle over his shoulder and no one said two shits to him.

There were just too many soldiers with too many conflicting orders stomping around. No one knew what the other was supposed to be doing.

So Eli'd walked for a few days. Then he'd caught a lucky break, and snagged a ride in the back of a transport vehicle heading for Arizona. Well… he'd thought it was pretty damn lucky at the time anyway.

He'd been sitting on a low concrete wall that ran the length of the highway. Soldiers were everywhere. It was some sort of staging area, so he'd sat his ass on the wall next to a few others and bummed an MRE off one guy. That's when the transport truck had rolled up.

It was mostly empty and the driver had leaned his fat head out and asked where the unit's chief was. One of the guys raised a finger in the air, as if to say, *that's me*, but he kept right on eating.

The driver of the truck huffed a bit, but then started in on his spiel. *We keep having guys walk off the train transpo crews. I'm light four bodies. Can you spare a guy or two?*

The apparent soldier in charge glanced around, swallowed his bite and then shrugged.

Anyone want to go? He asked, like he could give a shit how many soldiers he marched further into Texas.

No one volunteered.

That is… no one but Eli. He'd raised his hand like the naive fuck he was, and the driver in the truck had smiled.

So that was how Eli got a free ride back to Arizona. *Free* being a relative term, because the shit he saw on that ride definitely cost him.

It didn't take long for Eli to learn why soldiers were abandoning their duties on the train transpo crews. And when his stomach couldn't take anymore and his soul had fractured into something dark and bleeding, then he'd ditched too, and walked the rest of the way to California using his own two feet.

Which is why it'd taken him so damn long to get here. But here he was. Finally.

Lifting his head, Eli scanned his surroundings. On his right, the front door to one of the large homes was hanging open. Across the street and to his left, everything seemed in order. Straight up ahead though, there was a hump of something lying on the sidewalk. It was directly in front of Garrett's old house.

Swinging his rifle off his shoulder, Eli brought it up in one smooth movement and made ready to fire. Adrenaline burst into his system, demanding and zinging and painful. *Cass. Fuck. Cass!* His brain was screaming, but he fought his own hysteria and dialed down.

Clamping his lips shut, Eli controlled his breathing, willing his heart to slow and his ears to listen. His senses were on fire now, much like his Godforsaken surroundings, because there was a dead body lying where his sister was supposed to be living.

Eli's boots moved quickly, quietly, deliberately, as he made his way forward. His eyes were on a swivel, darting all around, searching for movement, for signs of an ambush, for signs of anything.

But there was nothing, save that open fancy front door three houses back.

It wasn't until Eli stood directly over the dead body that he shuddered in relief. It was a man, not a woman. It was an old man, with graying hair and wrinkled hands. It wasn't Cass.

Holy. Shit. It wasn't his sister.

Kneeling beside the body, Eli pressed his fingers to the man's neck just to confirm what he already knew. No pulse.

But the body was warm, and the massive amount of blood surrounding him was still wet, tacky, dark and glassy. This was a recent kill. Eli's heart raced and his brain absorbed the scene. A wound to the gut. A wound to the head.

Shoving up to standing, Eli let panic overtake him.

"Cass!" He screamed her name without even thinking, without even caring who could hear him, and what it might cost.

Then he was running. He flew to the front door and was slamming it open. The damn thing wasn't even locked.

"Cass!" He screamed again, yanking down on his face mask to better get the word out.

His hands were shaking and his heart was roaring in his ears. He could hope like hell she'd been the one to kill the guy outside, but they'd left her with a shotgun, not a handgun, and the wounds in that man were not consistent with a shotgun.

Fuck. *Why?*

Why had they let her stay here? What in the holy hell had he been thinking? He should've shipped her off with Garrett's folks when they'd left. Mrs. Jameson had begged him to make Cass go with them. Begged. Him.

But he wouldn't hear of it. No. He'd wanted Cass where he could protect her. What an arrogant brainless fucker he'd been. And Garrett had just gone right along with what Eli wanted, because that was always what Garrett did.

"Cass!" The name sliced its way up Eli's throat as he tore through the house and up the stairs.

He searched the top floor first. No tipped furniture. No kicked-in doors. No messy bed sheets or missing shower curtains or missing anything. Except for Cass. She wasn't there.

Back down the stairs he went. Eli's boots slammed against every second step until he finally jumped to the floor. Her sewing machine and an overnight bag were slumped against one wall. He'd been blind to it before.

"Slow down," he hissed to himself.

Flinging his own backpack to the ground, Eli removed his helmet and swiped at the sweat dripping down his forehead. Adjusting his grip on his rifle, he glanced around again. Quiet. It was eerily quiet, and dark.

Sucking in a breath, he narrowed his eyes. There were drops of dry blood on the wooden floor.

He followed the trail from the front door back through the living room. Still, no overturned furniture. No broken lamps or shredded curtains. That was good right? *Right?!*

"Cass?!" He raised his voice again, even though he shouldn't. He shouldn't be calling attention to his position.

The blood drops led him into the kitchen before they stopped at the side door leading to the garage. Rolling his shoulders, Eli steadied himself and pushed the door slightly open. With a swallow, he stepped just inside the threshold. Empty. Dim.

No cars.

Fuck. Both cars were gone. They'd left her with the Mercedes. Where the fuck was the Mercedes? Where the fuck was Cass? His breath started coming in short. There was something hugging him around the chest now, tightening, tightening.

That's when he heard it.

"Hello!" A male voice was calling from the front of the house. "If you're looking for the girl… I… uh…"

Eli's eyes opened wide and he backed out of the garage like the place was on fire. Bringing his rifle up to aim, he charged towards the living room. The dumbass standing in front of the closed front door had the audacity to look surprised to see him.

What kind of idiot…? But Eli didn't have time to finish the thought in his head.

"I saw him take her," the guy said quickly.

His dark eyes were wide as his hands flew up in defense, after all Eli was aiming his rifle right at him. But the guy's hands were empty. No weapons, no nothing.

This guy wasn't a solider, never had been, Eli figured. He was about middle age, maybe early 50s, with dark skin and dark hair to match his brown eyes. Eli froze in place, keeping his rifle trained on the guy's chest.

"What?" Eli spat. His brain was working on overtime, filled with a million emotions and then dampened by months of war.

"The g- girl. The girl that lives here… Cass…" the guy stuttered a bit.

Eli watched his Adams apple bob as he swallowed. Fear. This guy was afraid.

"How do you know her name?" Eli's voice was steady, it surprised even himself.

"We've been talking for a few months." The guy kept his hands raised, palms facing forward like they were on an episode of Cops.

"You *talked*," Eli repeated the words as a thousand euphemisms for rape zinged through his mind.

This wouldn't be the first guy who'd tried to "talk" to his sister. Well, he'd put this one where he'd put the last one. In the ground.

"Hey, I'm gay." The guy forced a nervous chuckle. "I swear, it wasn't anything more than talking. It gets lonely here day after day."

Blinking, Eli took in the man's appearance. He looked the same as any other guy. There was no rainbow flag, no piercings, no mannerism or voice inflection that would tip the scales one way or the other.

Educated, likely. Rich, probably in a past life. Gay? Who the fuck knew?

"I laid low when you and the other guy would check in," he explained. "She said it was better that way."

Lifting his rifle, Eli changed his aim from the guy's chest to his head.

"Get on with it," he growled.

"The other soldier took her," the guy blurted. "He's never been violent with her before, but this time was different for some reason. I don't know why."

"What soldier?" Eli stepped forward. "What do you mean violent? Where's my sister?"

"Okay, so you're the brother." The guy nodded his head up and down. "Cass's brother?"

"What soldier?!" Eli snapped.

"The other one that visits her," the guy rushed. "You come, then he comes, you and then him."

"Garrett?" Eli frowned.

"I don't know his name." The guy backed a step until his body bumped up against the front door.

His hands were still raised, his eyebrows too. Pleading. Fearful. Truthful.

"He came in and I swear it was like she started screaming right away. You could hear her all the way down the street. There's no other noise around here, you know?"

"Screaming?" Eli gave his head a little shake as his stomach flipped.

"Yeah, man." The guy nodded. "She was screaming and then she was running out on the lawn and he was chasing her down. *Stop. No.* Stuff like that."

"Garrett was…" Eli lowered the rifle just a touch. He couldn't believe this shit. Something was wrong. This couldn't be right.

"The other soldier," the guy confirmed. "Big guy. Young, like you. Brown hair, white guy."

Eli's brow furrowed deeper. His mouth parted, but he had no words.

"She was running and he grabbed her. I saw the whole thing from the house across the street," the guy explained. "I've been staying there for the past few months."

"I don't believe it," Eli huffed the words almost to himself. "It does't make any sense."

"Well he knocked her out," the guy added. "That's when Silas from down the street, he came out and he tried to help her. But the soldier shot him, and then he brought her back in here. He drove away a few minutes later in a white car. I waited until he left to come in and take a look, but she's not here. I don't know what he did with her body."

Dropping the nose of the rifle so that it pointed at the floor, Eli felt his whole body shudder. There was no way Garrett was the soldier behind this. No. Way.

This neighbor guy, whoever he was, simply had it wrong. But that didn't really matter did it? The truth was… the awful sickening fucking truth was, that Cass had been kidnapped by someone. She'd been grabbed by some soldier, some tall, white, brown-haired guy.

Unless it was actually this neighbor guy that had taken her. But that seemed unlikely. He was clean, no blood on him and his energy wasn't right. It wasn't sharp and predatory. He was weak and unsure.

"How long ago was it?" Eli's head snapped up. "How long ago did the car leave?"

"A few hours," the guy answered. One of his hands had dropped limply to his side while the other shot up to press against his temple. "I'm sorry."

In that moment, any last tiny shred of humanity that Eli had clung to, after driving the tank and working the train crew on his way back home, was lost. It simply evaporated from his body. Poof. Gone.

Like sparkly fairy dust, anything good flitted away, replaced by death and destruction and helpless despair.

Outside, the rumble of an engine sounded. It was faint, just a slight revving. Not a truck. Not a diesel. But there.

Rushing to one of the wide front windows, Eli pulled the cream-colored curtain aside and stared. A familiar white Mercedes was pulling into the driveway.

"Yeah." A voice came from just beside him, causing Eli to jerk. The neighbor guy was standing next to him now, looking out the window too. "That's the guy. That's him right there. He took her."

"Garrett," Eli spoke the name of his most trusted friend before turning to storm out the front door.

His heart was leaping in his chest as he charged across the lawn. There was some mistake. Garrett would never hurt Cass, not in a million years, and certainly not like that.

She was probably in the car right now. That guy inside didn't know what he saw. He was just plain wrong.

The Mercedes came to an abrupt stop in the driveway. Eli could see Garrett's face, the shock in his eyes as his mouth dropped open. He looked like shit. His nose was swollen and his face and shirt were covered in blood. *Blood.*

"What the hell happened to you?!" Eli called as he kept jogging towards the car. His rifle was clutched in one hand, held loosely down at his side.

Garrett swallowed hard. Once. Before he slammed the car in park and shoved out of the driver seat.

Sliding to a stop in front of his friend, Eli scanned the car through the windows. No Cass. No nothing. It was empty, and pristine and clean. So there was that.

"Eli." Garrett stood there, wedged between the open door and the car frame, staring.

They were maybe an inch apart in height, but Garrett was much more broad in the shoulders and chest. Even so, they'd always been pretty evenly matched. Not that they'd ever had a real fight, but still, whenever they'd wrestled around as kids, it'd been even.

"What the hell, Garrett?" Eli asked as his breath hitched in his throat. "You're covered in blood, man. Where's Cass? Where's my sister? Where is she?"

"Eli." Garrett closed his eyes as the color drained from his face. "I thought you were dead. I thought you weren't coming back."

"Where's Cass, Garrett?" Eli growled the words as his

fear began to grow. There was no way. This was not happening. "What did you *do* with my sister?"

"I got orders." Garrett's eyes popped open, they were glassy as he met Eli's gaze. "I couldn't keep her safe here anymore. My unit's moving out in a few days. I thought you were dead."

"What. Did. You. Do." Eli stepped closer, until each breath he puffed out was one that Garrett inhaled.

"I did what I had to," Garrett said quietly.

"Where is she?"

"She's safe."

"Where is she!" Eli screamed the words now, spittle flying from his mouth.

"I put her on a transport train," Garrett admitted. "She's going to one of the refugee centers up north. She'll be safe there."

"No." Stepping back, Eli dropped his rifle to the ground. "No, no, no, no. You didn't put her on one of those fucking trains."

"You weren't here!" Garrett yelled finally. His hands came out to gesture around them. "What was I supposed to do? I'm marching out. I wasn't going to leave her here alone. She's safe now. She's getting away from all this."

"Oh my God." Eli's hands shot to his scalp where he yanked and tugged at his own hair. "You fucking killed her! Do you know what happens to the people on those trains?!"

Turning away, Eli tried to suck in air but his lungs wouldn't let him. Images. Terrible images flashed through his mind. All of those bodies. The men and the women and the children.

There were no refugee centers. There was no safety.

There were mass graves. There were cattle cars filled with dead people. There were soldiers with shovels, digging.

There were fires burning.

Stumbling a few feet forward, Eli collapsed to his hands and knees on the yellowed lawn and threw up. His arms were shaking as his stomach punched up into his throat. Again. Then again.

Behind him, he felt Garrett approaching. He could sense his friend. He could hear him calling out to him, but the words he said were jumbled in Eli's mind.

Cass. His sister. His only real family. The little kid he'd taken care of night after night, day after day, for as long as he could remember, was dead. She'd been taken from him, ripped away and delivered to the devil, by his best friend. By Garrett.

"How could you?" Eli rasped the question. His throat burned from the vomit as his sickness gave way to white hot rage.

"I loaded her on the train myself, I made sure it was safe." Garrett was kneeling beside him now. "I swear she's safer now than either you or I could make her."

"Fuck. You." Eli spat the words as he sucked in air. His head was clearing. His muscles were beginning to burn as his hands clenched into fists in the grass. "Those trains go nowhere. Everyone on those trains dies. I've seen it myself. I've buried the bodies."

"Wha... what?" Garrett shook his head. "That's not... no."

Sitting up, Eli wiped the leftover puke from his lips and looked Garrett square in the eye. "Did you hurt her first?"

Garrett's mouth dropped and he huffed a half-indignant breath.

But Eli had known the man long enough. And he'd known the teenage boy version before that. Guilt. Avoidance. There was something here, and it had Eli's whole body priming.

"Look me in the eye, and tell me that you've never crossed the line with my sister," Eli demanded. "Look at me and tell me you've never laid a finger on her."

"Eli... I..." Garrett's blue eyes popped up and locked with Eli's hazel ones.

There.

It was all right there for anyone who wanted to see. Garrett *had* crossed that line. He'd done everything that guy from across the street said he had.

Eli lost it.

He was on top of his old buddy before he even knew what he was doing. His fists rained down on Garrett's face. His legs straddled Garrett's body.

Over and over, he drilled the guy into the ground. Blood began to spray. It was coming from Garrett's face and covering Eli's fists.

Later, Eli would wonder why it had been so easy.

Garrett was a big guy after all, with the advantage in weight, and he'd never stayed on the ground that long whenever they'd sparred before.

Eventually, Eli would come to the conclusion that his best friend had simply refused to fight back… at least, at first.

Was that an admission of guilt? Did Garrett feel he deserved the beating? Did he want to die for what he'd done to Cass? Eli liked to think so, but somewhere deep down, he had his doubts. Simmering, echoing, sad doubts. And questions. He wished he'd asked more questions.

But none of that had registered in the moment. He just kept swinging down until his arms had grown weary from slamming into Garrett's face and his breaths had started coming out short.

Nope, no logical thoughts were getting through when Eli's hands slipped down around Garrett's throat and began to squeeze.

Automatically, he applied pressure. Eli's thumbs dug into the soft flesh of Garrett's neck, until the guy's eyes were bulging and his body was twisting and writhing beneath him.

What happened next was all instinct. After all, in the end, your body just takes over. It wants to live, doesn't it? So the sharp pain that burst in Eli's side was quick and surprising. It was so fast, that it almost didn't register at all.

It wasn't until the pain came again, louder, harsher, more demanding this time, that Eli's grip loosened and he looked off to one side.

Garrett's right hand was clutching a knife now, and it was covered in fresh blood. Eli's blood.

Reaching down, Eli fought the knife out of Garrett's already slippery hand. Then, flipping the thing around, he slammed the handle down onto Garrett's forehead. Once. Twice. Crack. Then his arms were too heavy to move and his own body betrayed him.

Eli coughed and collapsed backwards onto the ground.

"You got him," a voice said. "He's dead."

Looking up, Eli saw the face of the man from across the street. The guy was crouching over him now, his dark eyes were serious, his hands were lifting up the bottom of Eli's shirt. Pain. His entire left side was lancing with pain.

"We've got to get you to the hospital," the neighbor said, and looped his arms around Eli's body. "You've been stabbed."

Letting out a tired laugh, Eli shook his head. The guy was dragging him away from Garrett, across the lawn, back towards the Mercedes.

Garrett was dead. He was just lying there in the grass. His boots were splayed apart. His face was turned to one side.

Smoke was sneaking down the street now and darkness was settling in. Each time Eli tried to suck in a breath, pain rocketed through his lower back and up into his chest. He was bleeding out. He could see a trail of his own blood being left on the crappy lawn.

"Don't bother," Eli croaked, as the guy tugged and rolled

and shoved him up into the backseat of the car. "Hospital's empty. No doctors. Just leave me. I'll die here."

"The hospital has equipment," the guy said. "And lucky for you, I'm…"

The rest of the sentence was cut off. Eli blacked out.

STANDING AT THE DOOR TO APARTMENT 402, JAMESON sucked in a breath. It'd been seven days since he'd last seen Cass and he was bone tired. His muscles were aching and his eyes were burning from lack of sleep. Being without her, having her be in pain because of him, it was torture.

Raising his hand to knock, he hesitated for a few seconds. His head hung down, his eyes focusing on the thin carpeted flooring of the hallway. In his mind, a hundred excuses continued to swirl.

He hadn't meant to do it. He was going to let Eli kill him. He hated himself. It was all a huge fucked up misunderstanding.

But none of that changed the truth. Eli was dead. Jameson wasn't.

They'd fought, for whatever reason, whether justified or not, and Jameson was still breathing today. Eli was not. Because no one could have survived those stab wounds without immediate medical attention.

Jameson might not remember exactly everything, but he did remember that much. His knife sinking into Eli's side, and then again in his best friend's lower back. Then he'd blacked out.

When he came to, there was smoke everywhere. Blood everywhere. It was dark. Things blurred in and out on him. It was hard to focus.

All he could hear was this overwhelming ringing in his ears. Some of the houses down the street were on fire. Their neighborhood was finally burning, really burning.

It seemed so fitting now, looking back on it. He'd just killed his best friend so it made sense that when he woke up, it was in the fiery pits of hell.

But despite all that, his instinct to survive was strong. Somehow, Jameson had pushed himself up and started walking. Walking. His memories of that particular time still cut in and out.

He wasn't sure how long it had taken him, but eventually he'd made it back to his unit. He'd had a busted up face, a broken nose, a severe concussion, but otherwise according to them, he was okay to fight. They'd marched out the following day.

Swallowing now, Jameson fought against the rush of guilt and shame. He should just leave Cass alone already. He shouldn't keep showing up at the door to her apartment and knocking, but he couldn't seem to stop himself. It was a compulsion. His mind was fixated on her, on explaining what had happened, on apologizing.

He thought about Cass all night long and all day long,

too. He couldn't eat. He couldn't work. He was a damn mess.

And sleep? Shit. He couldn't close his eyes without reliving that fight with Eli. He saw his best friend's face, the shock and the rage and the shattered trust. It made Jameson sick to his stomach. Hell, it made him sick all over his body.

Lowering his hand, Jameson stepped back from the door and blew out a breath. Walk away. Go. Leave her the hell alone. His fingers shot up to run through his hair, then slid back down over his face.

With a groan, he tried to turn around and go back to his own apartment. Tried and failed. Sucking in another breath, Jameson stepped back up to Cass's front door and rapped on the surface. There. Fuck. He did it.

Footsteps sounded and he held his breath. *Dear God, please let it be her this time.*

The lock flipped and the knob turned and the door cracked a few inches. Jameson's heart dropped into his toes. It was the roommate again. Not Mia. The other one... Shelby.

"Are you going to do this every day?" Shelby asked, brushing a lock of auburn hair back behind one ear.

She wasn't mean to him. She wasn't snippy. But everyday she answered the door and everyday she sent him away. This five foot three tiny Irish fairy was now the gatekeeper to Jameson's entire life. He was completely at her mercy. A redheaded pixie stood between him and salvation.

"Is Cass in?" Jameson's voice was raspy. He sounded like a crying little bitch. Well, he was a crying little bitch, so there was that. "Can I see her? I just want to talk to her."

Shelby's pale-blue eyes studied him as her head tilted to one side.

"She's not here," she said finally and slammed the door in his face.

The lock snapped into place almost immediately as the words took their time sinking in. She's not there? That was a new response.

Before, Shelby had always said that Cass simply refused to see him, that she was fine, but he wasn't allowed to come in. But this?

She'd left the apartment.

Staggering back, Jameson clutched at his chest. If she wasn't in there, that meant she was out and about somewhere... somewhere he could feasibly track her down.

Whirling on his heel, Jameson jogged to the end of the hall. He was down four flights of stairs in his next breath and bursting out into the sunshine a second after that. It was bright and painful to his eyes but he held a hand up to his brow and kept chugging right along.

Cass. He might get to see her today. If he could find her, then he could *see* her.

His heart was tapping and his stomach was skittering as he began his search. His eyes sought her in every crowd. His head was on a swivel, looking, searching.

But she wasn't at work. Her boss said he hadn't seen her in a week, which made sense because she'd been holed up in her apartment all this time, hiding from Jameson.

But then she wasn't in the cafeteria, or at the gym, or in any of the greenhouses. In fact, according to Mia's manager, the blonde hadn't shown up for work either. They'd sent someone to her apartment, but Shelby had told them all that Mia had left.

"Left?" Jameson huffed the word, his face screwing up, his mind refusing to process.

"Yeah." Her manager gave his head an exasperated shake. "Can you believe that? Just gave up everything here to have some stupid adventure beyond the Wall. It's a crime if you ask me, she's one of the best farmers we have. A real natural."

Jameson's stomach jumped right up into his throat. He wanted to throw up on the guy's dirty boots, but he didn't. He held himself back, fighting the way his head was swimming.

If Mia had gone… and Cass wasn't in their apartment… then…

With a brisk nod, he wandered off and collapsed against a nearby tree trunk where he figured no one would see.

But someone did see.

Jameson should've known. He should've realized Uriah would have him watched.

"Still sick?" Liam crouched in front of Jameson and braced one hand in the dirt.

Swallowing hard, Jameson closed his eyes and tipped

his head back against the tree. He was sick alright. He'd never felt more ill in his entire life. Not even after he'd killed Eli.

Losing Cass like this, it was fucking unbearable. She'd never been his before, not really. And then for a few brief weeks he'd allowed himself to forget who he was and what he'd done. She loved him, he loved her, he couldn't change the past. They'd finally been together after all those years and it had consumed him.

But now... now karma had circled back around and bit him so fucking hard, he was seeing stars. Cass was beyond the Wall, fleeing him and running straight into danger, straight into rape and starvation and death. He'd killed her. Jameson had finally done what Eli had accused him of.

"She's gone," Jameson rasped finally, his eyes popping open to stare up into the canopy of green leaves. "She left."

Exhaling through his nostrils, Liam glanced away for a moment.

Jameson gulped air and tipped his chin down to study his sort-of friend. The guy was thinking. His brow was furrowed and his jaw was ticking.

"Why?" Liam asked finally, his dark eyes came back to lock on Jameson.

And then Jameson's mouth was opening and the whole horrid affair came pouring out. Sentence after sentence. Truth after truth.

They said Liam was one of the most prolific interrogators during the war. He'd successfully elicited information from countless men, and his methods had been reportedly… brutal. He'd liked using knives in particular.

But now Jameson wondered if the knife was even necessary. It was something in Liam's eyes, in the way he didn't talk, in the way he looked at you, and listened, that made you want to confess. In the end, Jameson's whole life story was laid bare before the guy, without him having to ask more than the one question.

When Jameson was finally done talking, Liam stood up and cleared his throat. Shoving his hands into his pockets, the guy cocked his head to one side and stared down at Jameson.

"Have you tried to find the frequency?" He asked. "Have you tried to make contact with the man that Cass believes is her brother?"

"Frequency 131.222," Jameson offered. "It's a recording. It plays over and over for three hours every other day. There's never any response."

"Is it him?" Liam asked quietly. "Is it possible he survived?"

Squeezing his eyes shut, Jameson pursed his lips. By this time, he'd memorized the recording. He'd listened to it, absorbed it. And yeah, the voice was from a man. The age seemed to be about right, but beyond that… who could tell?

"She seemed so sure," Jameson whispered finally.

"But you're not," Liam supplied.

"No." He shook his head and opened his eyes. "I'm not."

"Well…" Stepping closer, Liam reached out a hand as if

to help Jameson get up off the ground. "We better go listen to that recording again, and loop Uriah in. Seems like we need a plan."

Eyeing Liam's empty palm, Jameson frowned.

"We?" He asked, his gaze darting back up to Liam's face.

"Yeah." Liam gave a little shrug, but his face remained impassive. "We better track her down. Just in case this guy isn't her brother. Right?"

Nodding his head quickly, Jameson shoved up to standing and brushed at his pants.

"Yeah…" He cleared his throat as Liam took a step back. "You're right."

CHAPTER THIRTY-TWO_
CASS

GRAVEL CRUNCHED BENEATH HER BOOTS, INTERRUPTED every so often by a wooden railroad tie. Lifting her eyes, Cass watched the empty train tracks stretch on and on before disappearing around a bend.

Thick forest, filled with towering green trees, hugged either side of the tracks. They'd been walking like this for days now, and her feet were beyond sore.

Grasping at the shoulder straps of her heavy pack, Cass let her mouth part just a little. She huffed air in and out. Her lungs were hot, her throat dry. It was summer after all, and the air hummed with heat. Just a bit behind her, she could hear Mia panting too.

When they'd decided to do this, neither of them had understood the reality of what it would be like. But she'd needed to get to Hermiston. She'd needed to get to her brother. Because despite the awful thing Garrett had said, he was wrong. *Wrong*.

Eli wasn't dead. She'd heard him with her own ears. Cass *knew* it was her brother on that radio and he needed her help.

So, she and Mia had left.

Levi and Nolan were still leading a group beyond the Wall and it hadn't been hard to join back up with them. Sure the decision had been a bit rushed, but the girls had trained with that same group for months before, so they all knew each other. Cass and Mia were given twenty-four hours to gather their equipment and that was that.

Right before they'd left, Shelby had agreed to keep her mouth shut. Garrett had already been by the apartment twice by that time, asking for Cass, and Shelby had sent him away each time.

But then the redhead had given Cass this look with those pale-blue eyes of hers and Cass had been forced to glance away.

"What's he done so wrong?" Shelby had questioned. "He looks like he's been crying. Won't you see him?"

"No." Cass had given her head a shake even as her heart plummeted to her toes. "Just do this for me, Shelby. Please."

How do you put words to what Garrett had done? You can't. You don't.

"Alright." The redhead had nodded once and that was that.

She'd promised she wouldn't let him inside their apartment, and if he forced his way in, then she wouldn't tell him where they'd gone.

So the very next day Cass and Mia had walked through

one of the blown out doorways in the perimeter fencing of the Wall… along with fifteen other guys. It had been easy, actually. The guards on duty hadn't even looked at them twice.

Just up ahead now, the group ranged out as they hiked. The guys all varied in size and background. Some were soldiers and some were not. Some were fit and some were not. But even so, Mia and Cass were always bringing up the rear.

The pace Nolan set for them each day was grueling. He didn't like to take breaks, and he didn't like to stop. Occasionally, he'd come to a stand still at the head of the column and turn around to look at the girls. Cass could see his frown from a hundred yards away.

Usually he'd make a show of getting out their only map and checking their progress. Mia would always lean in at that moment and make some sarcastic comment. *Slave driver. Death march. Jerk.* Too often, Cass was too tired to laugh.

By the time the girls would make it up to where the guys were all waiting, Nolan would begin hiking again. It was a bit frustrating, never getting a chance to rest, but Cass always held her tongue. If it meant she got to see her brother again, she'd walk five hundred miles behind Nolan.

Sweat beaded on her brow now, tickling and sticking, making her hair damp. Reaching up, Cass swiped at it quickly before replacing her hand on the shoulder strap of her pack.

Everyone carried their own supplies, their own water,

their own food and sleeping bag. And as if all that stuff wasn't heavy enough, Cass had packed some extra MREs for her brother, some medicine too.

In front of her, Levi slowed his steps. His pack shifted on his back as he turned to glance at her over his shoulder. He carried his black rifle in front of him, clutched in both hands. It was one of six guns that the group had.

Ducking her head, Cass continued to walk. When she finally came up alongside him, Levi smiled and kept pace beside her. His dark eyes cruised over her face before he looked back at Mia.

"You doing good?" He asked.

Pursing her lips, Cass managed a nod. Her mouth was dry and her stomach was clenching. When was the last time they'd stopped for water? Her canteen was empty, maybe she was drinking too much while they walked.

"We're peachy," Mia gasped and came to a sudden stop.

Cass and Levi stopped then, too.

"We'll make camp soon," Levi assured them. "The sun's getting low."

"Thank God," Mia moaned.

Bending forward, the pretty blonde braced both of her hands on her knees. She was trembling slightly.

Cass stole a quick glance at the others. They were all still marching away, following the empty train tracks, following Nolan.

"You guys are doing great," Levi said.

When neither of the girls answered, he ducked down and peered into Mia's face.

"Maybe if you shared a tent with Nolan, you could buy us all some extra time to relax in the morning," he joked.

Forcing a chuckle, Cass stepped closer to Mia and tugged at her friend's arm. This recurring joke about Mia sleeping with Nolan was not new. In fact, it was getting pretty damn old.

Straightening, Mia brushed her hair out of her eyes and gave Levi a sassy smirk.

"That sounds like rest for you all and none for me," she countered and then rolled her eyes.

Laughing, Levi shook his head before turning and hiking away.

That's when Cass and Mia exchanged a look. Not just any look, but *the* look. The one that women give each other when shit is absolutely not funny, even though everyone else seems to think it is.

"This sucks," Mia pouted, half-playfully and half not.

"I'm sorry." Cass squeezed her friend's arm as her heart fell. "Maybe we should go back?"

"No." Mia shook her head. "We can't go back. Your brother asked for help. There are women and children out there that need us. We've got to keep going."

"Okay." Cass nodded her head. "But we're still sharing a tent tonight, right?"

"Yes, silly." Mia played it off, like she always did, and started walking. "I know how you like to cuddle. I won't leave you out in the cold."

Huffing, Cass adjusted the straps still digging into her shoulders, and followed.

. . .

A FEW HOURS LATER, CASS FOUND HERSELF PERCHED ON A rock beside Mia. Darkness had finally fallen and a blessedly cool breeze swept along her forearms.

Nolan had found a small clearing not far from the train tracks and so the rest of them had set up their collection of tents between the towering trunks of trees.

In the center of the clearing, smoke swirled around a small campfire. The burning wood crackled and popped as its small yellow and orange flames danced in the night. Their group was ranged all around it now, sitting on rocks or fallen logs.

Nolan (of course) was planted on Mia's other side, talking to a few of the guys as they ate their dinner. Another night had come, and they were still eating canned beans and MREs. Without taking the time to hunt or forage for food, their supplies were starting to run low.

Cass wondered if they'd have anything left once they finally made it to Hermiston. The way things were going, her little rescue team might just be near starvation themselves by the time they arrived.

"You hear that?" Levi interrupted and everyone paused.

"Hear what?" Nolan looked at Levi.

"I thought I heard a motor." Levi jerked his chin in the direction they'd marched from, but it was dark, no one could see anything.

Another pause ensued. Cass held her breath, listening.

"Nah." Nolan shook his head finally. "You're hearing things. There's nothing out there."

Cass's heart skipped a little in her chest while conversation resumed. She eyed the fire, knowing that they'd been coached not to use one unless absolutely necessary. They'd also been warned not to walk down open roads or paths, too much exposure.

But Nolan had listened to none of those things. He said it wasn't necessary. The area was deserted and they had more than enough fire power to scare anyone off.

The women were also supposed to dress like men, tuck in their hair and wear loose clothing. But that hadn't happened either. It was hotter than heck during the day and so both Cass and Mia were often stripped down to tank tops and jeans. Mia's hair was too short to bind up in a hat and conversely Cass's hair was too thick and unruly to hide.

Had they been watched? Had they been followed?

Frowning, Cass grabbed for her sweatshirt and jerked it on over her head before pulling the hood up. In vain, she attempted to shove her curly mass of dark hair down inside of it. She hadn't heard a motor. She hadn't heard anything when they'd all stopped to listen, but still, her gut churned just a bit as she stared down at her half-eaten meal.

"Hey, you cold?" Levi asked, he was just across the fire, watching her.

"A little," Cass lied as a shiver ran up her spine. It wasn't cold that had her covering up, and it wasn't cold that had her shaking.

Standing, Levi walked over and took a seat just beside her. Cass had to scoot over a few inches on the rock to give him room and that bumped Mia closer to Nolan. As Levi's arm wrapped around her shoulders, Cass cleared her throat and tried to rid herself of the uneasy feeling that had settled in her belly.

"Maybe we shouldn't have the fire," she offered, glancing up into Levi's face.

At that, Levi's mouth opened as if to say something, but after a second he closed it again. Tightening his grip on her shoulders, he drew her in closer to his body and sighed.

"It's a small fire," he said finally, then tipped his head up to stare at the canopy of dark branches twisting over their heads. "And the smoke will get trapped in the trees."

"Okay." Cass worried her bottom lip between her teeth.

There was a little cloud cover tonight, she reasoned, and it was only a quarter moon so maybe the smoke would disappear like Levi said.

Looking around their circle, Cass heaved a sigh. No one else seemed to be concerned. They were all talking again, laughing and joking.

Across the fire, one of the guys was saying something to Mia. He lifted his voice and made some joke and had the men seated beside him hooting. Next to Cass, the blonde ducked her head indulgently and covered her mouth with one hand. Her dark-brown eyes left the soldier across the fire, but his eyes were still glittering, focused entirely on Mia.

Frowning, Nolan looped an arm around Mia's waist. His hand bumped against Cass as he wedged himself between them. His fingers squeezed Mia's side.

Cocking her head, Cass studied their leader for a minute. Conversation continued as if no one had noticed. Mia was tucking her hair behind her ears now and bumping Cass with her pretty shoulders as she shifted. Nolan's frown only deepened as he stared at the guys across the fire. His lips were pursed and his jaw was ticking.

Rolling her eyes, Cass let her attention return to the flames in the center. If Nolan was jealous, then he needed to get over it, and fast. Basically everything Mia did drew male attention. She was gorgeous. Guys reacted to that. Nolan should be used to it by now, Cass figured.

"You should eat more," Levi whispered.

Looking down at the cold MRE balanced on her lap, Cass fought the urge to cry. She was hungry, really she was. But every single time she went to eat, her stomach revolted. It twisted and tightened, making each bite diffi-cult to get down.

And she could say it was because the ready made meals tasted like processed powder, but she knew that wasn't the real reason. It was because they'd stopped walking.

All day long, as long as her body was screaming about its sore muscles and tender feet, then the thoughts were kept at bay. The thoughts of Garrett, the images of him, were over-ridden by her body's need to protest, its need to survive.

But as soon as they stopped, he came flooding back. Memories of him ran inside her mind on an endless loop. No matter how hard she tried to fight it, to shove him away, Garrett just kept coming back.

She could feel him kissing her. She could smell his body lying beside her. She could hear him laughing. She could see him confessing.

It was unbearable and it was all consuming. Closing her eyes, Cass fought against the flood of memories and lost.

But in the next instant, none of that mattered. Her mind cleared instantly and all thoughts of Garrett were replaced by an unmistakeable sound.

The snap of a bullet being racked into a chamber.

It sounded in their clearing. Again. Then again.

Cass's spine snapped straight as her heart slammed to a stop in her chest. Her eyes were wide and everyone had gone deathly still. She couldn't see anyone or anything, save for their group still sitting around the fire, but she knew one thing for certain...

They weren't alone out here anymore. They weren't alone at all.

IT WAS MEANT AS A LESSON. JAMESON HAD AN ENTIRE SPEECH planned about carelessness and idiocy. He'd spent months training these fuckers on survival and yet here they were, shitting all over it.

But as soon as he saw Cass, all of Jameson's snarky words dried up on his tongue.

Suddenly, his chest was heaving. He still gripped his rifle in his hands, the tip pointed harmlessly towards the ground, but inside, his body was zinging. That jerk-off Levi had his arm looped around Cass's shoulders. He was holding her close to him, her side against his side.

It was all Jameson could see. Levi's arm on Cass's body. Her. Him.

Sucking in a ragged breath, Jameson stood there in the dark, just beyond the ring of light thrown by the flames, and stared.

Meanwhile, everyone sitting around the fire was still

frozen in place. A couple of guys had their hands on their holsters, but that was as far as they'd made it. No one dared to breathe. No one dared to blink.

It was self-preservation, Jameson knew. You're supposed to freeze when you hear someone cocking a gun, especially when you can't see where that person is. But, shit. If it'd been him there beside her, Cass would be lying face down in the dirt right now with his entire body on top of hers, covering her, protecting her. Hell, he'd take a million bullets if there was any chance that it would save her.

But that Levi douche just sat there beside her like a little bitch, with both of his palms empty and facing out. Where the hell was the guy's weapon? Probably in his tent, Jameson realized. These guys were sloppy.

Sure, they'd set up two men for watch duty, but the one was already snoring when Jameson had crept up on him and the other hadn't taken more than three seconds for Liam to knock out. They hadn't even made a sound.

Maybe half of these idiots had been soldiers during the war, but it was clear they'd never been on the front lines. They were used to being shielded by a thousand other bodies. They were naive maybe, or stupidly arrogant. Either way, they'd be dead if they kept this shit up.

After another few seconds of silence (wherein Jameson worked for breath instead of providing a lecture) Liam grumbled under his breath and stepped into view.

Keeping his own rifle pointed at the ground, the world's foremost interrogator sauntered into the small circle. The light from the fire illuminated his face. His dark eyes appeared bored as he looked around.

"Lot of good your training did," he remarked. "We could smell that smoke from miles away."

At the sight of him, the men sitting all around the fire exhaled. It was like they issued one collective breath of relief. Liam had been a fixture in quite a few of their training classes, so they recognized him. They weren't all about to be executed. They weren't all about to die.

"Officer Bryne." Nolan cleared his throat and rolled his shoulders. Beside him, the pretty blonde covered her face in both hands. "We're a long way from the Wall. What brings you out here tonight?"

Turning his head, Liam eyed the guy for several seconds. Jameson watched from his position a few yards back, still hidden in the dark. Blinking, he tried to focus. He tried to fight the pull that Cass had over him, the instant spiking in his blood, the desperation.

"We could've killed you all," Liam stated blandly, his voice held about as much emotion as a glass of water. "Stolen all your stuff, fucked your women. It's that quick out here. It goes exactly that fast."

Pursing his lips, Nolan ducked his head in an attempt to hide the anger that crawled over his face. After a beat, he swallowed and lifted his eyes back to Liam. With a forced smile, he tugged Mia in tighter against his side. The little blonde squeaked and looked to Cass.

Jameson's senses sharpened. The two women reached out to hold hands.

"Thanks for the demonstration," Nolan stated finally. "But surely you didn't travel all the way out here for that. What are you looking for? What do you want?"

Ignoring him, Liam turned his back on Nolan and eyed the rest of the men. A few of them smiled at him, tentatively. A few more ducked their heads, still nervous.

"Move." Liam gestured at a few of them.

Immediately, the guys scrambled up off the log they'd been sharing. The thing rolled slightly in the dirt as boots stomped and scurried away. Jameson felt a smile flicker at the corner of his mouth. Liam's reputation always preceded him.

Taking a few steps around the fire, Liam plunked his ass down on the now empty log with a grunt. Dipping his head, he propped his rifle across his lap and began working to clear his weapon.

Nolan would get no answer from him, Jameson knew. He'd seen a similar display before, once upon a time back in Utah. Back then Jameson had been the one wanting to put a bullet in Liam's skull. Now that desire fell to Nolan.

While Liam focused on his weapon, the rest of the men began murmuring. *The hangman. The cutter. The interrogator.* He was infamous. A legend of violent proportions.

Nolan simply gaped. By now he was probably used to being in charge, he was used to having that control. The shift in power from him to Liam was palpable, and it gave Jameson the break he needed.

Giving his head a quick shake, Jameson was able to

gather himself back in, take his mind off of Cass, and make his move into the light.

As if on cue, Davey was right on his heels. The both of them strolled into the ring of light and glanced around. There were just the three of them on this mission, but in reality that's all it would've taken to destroy the camp. Three well-trained men and the element of surprise.

Liam had been right. It would've been a massacre… and an easy one at that.

"Oh, for fuck's sake," Nolan huffed, when he got a look at Jameson. Slanting a look at Cass, he continued, "I thought you said it was over with him."

At the word *over*, Jameson's whole body clenched. He swore right then it was like being kicked in the back, right between your shoulder blades. All the air wanted to leave him in a rush, so he held his breath.

Of course it was done between them, he knew that. After what he'd done, how could he think any different? Still, it fucking *hurt* to hear it out loud. It hurt bad.

Jameson's eyes tracked back to Cass and held. He reminded himself he was not here to win her back. There was no possibility of that and he could accept it, he would make himself accept it. He was here to protect her. He was here to help her get to whoever had made that recording and show her that it wasn't her brother. He was here to make sure she stayed safe.

But in that heartbeat of time, all Jameson could do was drink her in. She stared up at him, those mossy green eyes of hers seemed darker, deeper out here in the forest. A few strands of her curly brown hair peeked out from the hood of her sweatshirt. Her cheeks were rosy, but her face was pale.

Jameson had so many things he wanted to say to her, but he had no right, so he held his tongue.

It took several moments for him to realize Cass didn't answer Nolan. She gave him nothing, she gave them all nothing. Eventually, she squeezed her eyes shut and tipped her face down, towards the ground.

Levi tightened his grip on her shoulders and leaned in to whisper something in her ear.

Jameson forced himself to turn away. Clenching his jaw shut, he stalked around to Liam and took a seat beside him on the log. Davey stayed standing, his hands on his rifle, his eyes boring into Nolan.

"So you've come to take her back?" Nolan asked finally. "Last I checked, she left of her own free will, *after* passing your classes."

"I'm not here to take her back to the Wall," Jameson offered. *Yet.*

"Well, what the hell do you want then?" Nolan asked.

Running a hand roughly up Mia's arm, he quickly dragged his palm back down before giving her a squeeze. The blonde nibbled on her lower lip and blinked up at Davey. He was still standing, watching Nolan with a blank expression on his face.

"Hermiston wasn't your original destination," Jameson began. "The plans you submitted to Officer Hernandez talked about traveling south, to Linfield's abandoned city."

Shrugging, Nolan made a pffft sound. "So?" He asked. "Plans change."

"Well, it's a long trip out of your way," Jameson again, trying like hell not to look at Cass. "We've recently intercepted a radio transmission from that location and Commander Linfield has authorized us to look into it."

"What's your point?"

"We're going that way already, and we have a Jeep to take us there," Jameson countered.

As the words left his lips, it was impossible not to see Cass respond. Her head whipped up. Her hood dropped back. Suddenly, he could feel her eyes on him and it was all he could do to keep his composure.

It was all he could do not to scoop her up and stuff her in that car. It was all he could do not to beg and plead and grovel for her forgiveness. He could be just what he'd been to her before, a miserable guard dog. One that would follow her around and sit outside her front door.

"You're offering us a ride?" Nolan was skeptical, as well he should be.

"No." Jameson's jaw ticked. "We're offering the girls a ride. You all can resume your original plan, head south, or wherever."

Nolan's brows shot up as the word *girls* (plural) sank into his brain. Not only had Jameson and crew waltzed in here to retrieve Cass, but they planned on snapping Mia right up with her.

Beside him, Mia tipped her head up to the sky and let loose a breath. Her face said everything Jameson needed to know. Relief. Exhaustion. Salvation. She wanted out of this situation, and if she agreed to come with them, then Cass would damn sure follow.

Shooting up to his feet, Nolan shook his head and scoffed. All of his men leaned back just a touch, watching the display, excluding Levi, of course, who was now focused entirely on Cass. His hands had moved up to brace both of her shoulders. He was peering into her face, speaking quickly, quietly, convincingly. His dark eyes were wandering all over her face.

For half a second, Jameson actually pitied the guy. He saw himself in Levi just then, about to lose Cass forever. The desperation. The fear. It fucking sucked.

No... scratch that. It fucking obliterated your soul. But that didn't mean Jameson was going to let Levi have her. Nope. Bye bye Levi, he thought, don't ever come back.

"You're out of your damn mind!" Nolan shouted suddenly, drawing all eyes back over to him. "If you think we're going to let you come here and take the girls, you've clearly not thought this thing through."

Jameson cocked his head to one side, frowning.

Liam grew incredibly still.

"There are fifteen of us and three of you," Nolan continued. "You're outnumbered, *Officer* Jameson. And let's face it, the girls do *not* want to go with you. We aren't going to just stand by and let you kidnap them."

Jameson's eyes dropped to Mia then, whose face flushed pink.

"Kidnap seems like a strong word," Jameson offered, still refusing to look at Cass.

One look at her could ruin everything. Jameson wouldn't put it past her to tell him to fuck off that she was going to walk, just to spite him. But Mia. Pretty, pretty Mia was *the* weak link in this equation. And he would exploit that to hell and back to get what he wanted.

"What do you think, Mia?" Jameson asked. "No more walking. You still get where you want to go..."

"Come on, Mia." Nolan reached down and grabbed her by the arm. "We're going to bed."

"Wha- what?" Mia stammered as Nolan yanked her up to standing.

It was rough. Mia gasped in shock, her eyes growing a bit wide at the contact. Nolan held on tighter. His desperation was leaking out from him now.

Out of the corner of his eye, Jameson noted Liam's brows draw together as he watched the exchange. Shit was getting tense, and fast. If there was one thing the infamous cutter of the Nor Side Soldiers didn't like, it was women being shoved around. Call it a trigger. Call it a weakness.

"You can sleep in my tent," Nolan was saying, but his eyes never left Jameson. "I'll keep you safe all night long. I won't let them take you."

"Um..." Mia tried to step out of Nolan's grasp. She was wriggling slightly and glancing around as her voice lowered. "I don't think..."

"Come on," Nolan cut her off and took a step to the side, yanking her along with him as he went.

Mia let out a squeak and stumbled.

"But I sleep in Cass's tent," she protested.

Her words fell on deaf ears. Nolan wasn't listening. Tugging her another step, Nolan kept his gaze focused on Jameson.

"Come on baby, it's time to go," he said.

"No, Nolan. I sleep with Cass," Mia tried again, but this time her words were breathy and quiet.

Cass shot to her feet then, as if to intercede, but she was too slow.

Way too slow.

In two quick strides Davey closed the distance between himself and Nolan. Raising his rifle in both hands, he flipped it butt end first and popped the guy square in the face. You could hear the crunch of bone as the stock of the weapon impacted with flesh.

Nolan dropped like a sack of corn, slumping to one side as his eyes rolled back in his head. Out. Quick as that.

Mia gasped as the hand that had pulled her now fell away. Rocking to one side, she tripped into Cass. Both women bobbled, but managed to stay upright. Their eyes flipped from Davey to Jameson.

He firmed his lips. *Come on Cass baby. Come on.*

"No means no asshole," Davey spat, then lifted his face to eye the women. "Are you two coming with us or are you gonna stay with the pushy douche?"

Mia's mouth dropped open then, and she huffed out a breath. Davey blinked at her, his expression unreadable in the flickering fire light.

"We're coming," she said finally, and squeezed Cass's hand. "Aren't we?"

Swallowing, Cass's gaze moved from Jameson to her best friend. They were doing that girl thing, where they speak mind to mind without uttering a word. The seconds dragged on like hours as Cass hesitated. Jameson could feel his heart beating way up in his throat, where it absolutely did not belong.

But then she sucked in a breath, and lifted her chin.

"Yeah," she said finally, but refused to look at him. "We're coming."

Inhaling, Cass closed her eyes. She was riding in the backseat of a car. She couldn't remember the last time she'd ridden in a car. Well… that time in Garrett's trunk didn't count.

Opening her eyes, she tried not to glare at the back of his head. He was sitting shotgun, with Liam beside him at the wheel, and it was completely silent. They bumped and jolted along the train tracks, moving pretty slowly, but still way faster than a person could walk.

Dark trees rose up on either side of the Jeep. The forest was thick here as the train tracks continued to snake perpetually downward. Their headlights were off, so it was hard to see much further than that.

"I thought you said we should stay off the roads," Cass spoke finally.

Shifting in his seat, Garrett's body tensed, but he didn't respond. Cass narrowed her eyes, fighting the mix of hatred and anger and hopeless love that swirled inside of her.

He was lightning. He'd always been like lightning to her, and now she'd had a taste of being electrocuted. She should've known better.

Beside her, Mia's head was beginning to droop. She was falling asleep, wedged in the middle with the Jeep's heater blowing warmth in her face. Davey was on the far side, his knees drawn up tight because Garrett had scooted the passenger seat as far back as it would go.

"The advice was to stay off the main roads as much as possible," Liam volunteered finally. His eyes glanced at her in the rearview mirror. "It's easier to do that when you're walking, not so much when you're driving. As soon as it opens up at the bottom, we'll find a spot to get out of sight and take a break."

Nodding her head, Cass pursed her lips and let her gaze drift out the rear passenger window. Her body rocked with the constant bumping of their tires traveling over railroad ties. She braced one arm on the window sill and kept her other arm folded in her lap. Mia's shoulder pressed against Cass's shoulder, her leg ran the length of Cass's leg.

Silence resumed.

They'd been driving like this for about an hour now. After Davey had knocked Nolan out, the girls had packed up their stuff and left.

Levi had been upset, but what else could Cass do? Mia was done. There was no way she could walk another four hundred or so miles to Hermiston.

And anyway, at the rate they'd been going it would take another few weeks to get there. How could Cass pass up a ride? Even if it was with the devil himself, she was on her way to her brother. If things went as planned, she'd be face to face with Eli in a day, maybe two at the most. There was just no question.

"You're fine. Just leave it," Liam's voice rang out in the small space.

Looking up, Cass frowned at the rearview mirror. Liam's dark eyes darted up to the mirror, then back to the road. It took her a second to realize he wasn't looking at her, that he wasn't talking to her.

Frowning, Cass turned to her right and sighed. Mia was passed out now. Her eyes were closed and her mouth slightly parted. A few strands of her blonde hair fell across her cheek as she slumped to the side and slept peacefully on Davey's shoulder.

The blue-eyed soldier sat stiffly, uncomfortably. Cass exhaled through her nose and stuck her tongue in her cheek. The poor guy was already cramped as it was, now he had Mia's weight pressing him up against the window.

"Do you want me to move her?" Cass asked quietly. "We can tip her towards me."

"No," Liam's voice sounded again. "She stays exactly where she is. She's comfortable."

"But he's not," Cass countered, and watched as Davey stared at the rearview mirror, his throat bobbing and his eyes wide.

Liam remained unperturbed. His hands were loose on the steering wheel, his shoulders relaxed.

After a few minutes of silence, Cass realized that the discussion had ended. Davey didn't even utter a word, he just sat there quietly now, his eyes having dropped to the floor.

Shaking her head slightly, Cass glanced back up to the front seat. Liam was grinning. A rare sight indeed.

But then Garrett was looking back over his shoulder and his gaze locked instantly on Cass. His blue eyes were piercing in the dark, boring right into her.

Lightning flashed through Cass's body, and she quickly looked away. Folding her arms over her chest, she purposefully shut her eyes and leaned back into her seat. She was not going to engage with him. She could not afford to engage with him.

He claimed to have killed her brother. And no, she hadn't stuck around to find out why. She didn't need to know why. All she knew was that Garrett believed with every fiber of his being that he'd done it.

Did it really matter if Eli had survived? Did it matter if Garrett hadn't actually finished the job? That he was wrong?

No. No, it did not. It *shouldn't*.

Squeezing her eyes tighter, Cass held back the tears that wanted to flow. A thousand questions screamed in her mind, demanding to be let out of her mouth. He'd known all along. Garrett had known the entire time what he'd done, and yet... he'd still...

And she'd liked it. No. More than that, she'd loved it, and she'd loved him. He was the only person in the entire world that she'd ever said those words to. His betrayal stung way down deep, making it hard to breathe, making her chest ache and her throat burn.

Rotating towards the window, Cass pressed her forehead against the glass and folded in on herself. Tears dripped from between her lashes to dampen her cheeks. She sniffed and rubbed her fist angrily beneath her nose.

No one said anything. The engine just kept humming. The Jeep just kept bumping. The heater just kept blowing.

And eventually, Cass stopped crying.

And then, just like Mia, she fell asleep.

CHAPTER THIRTY-FIVE_
JAMESON

Staring out the front windshield, Jameson felt his body shudder along with the Jeep as Liam brought them to a stop. A dark meadow rolled out before them. It's tall grasses were still in the faint moonlight. There was absolutely no wind.

"This should work," Liam said.

Throwing an arm across the seat backs and shifting to look behind him, Liam smirked. When he spoke, it was to Davey.

"Don't move. Don't wake them."

"I can't do this," Davey hissed, keeping his voice whisper quiet as the two girls continued to sleep.

Liam's smirk turned to a wink. "We'll set up camp and come get them when it's ready."

Clamping his jaw shut, Davey turned his head away to look out his window. Jameson sighed. He wasn't sure exactly what the deal was here, but if the tension from Davey continued, he'd be forced to address it.

Pulling carefully at his door handle, Jameson moved his oversized body out of the vehicle as quietly as possible. Liam did the same.

Since collecting the girls at their camp, they'd driven for a little over five hours, bumping incessantly down the train tracks. This was the first break in the forest that they'd found. Without even a question, Liam had turned off the tracks and skirted the wide pasture before finding a spot to back the Jeep into the tree line.

With any luck there'd be a source of fresh water nearby. They'd find out soon enough, when dawn broke over the mountain now looming at their backs.

Stretching his arms up to the starry sky, Jameson bit back a groan. His body was buzzing from being bounced endlessly down the train tracks for so long. That, and listening to Cass cry herself to sleep made for a pretty damn miserable trip.

"I'll grab their stuff from the back," Liam spoke quietly as he moved to the rear of the vehicle.

Jameson nodded his response.

The girls had one small tent that they'd apparently shared (thank fuck for that) and two sleeping bags. Both of their packs were filled with unnecessary clothing and a few too many meals. Jameson could wonder why they'd taken the extra things that they had, but he didn't need to.

Eli. It was all Eli.

Cass believed that voice on the radio was her brother, so she was bringing the extra things that women and children might need, just as the voice had requested. It didn't occur to her that it might be a trap, that it likely *was* a trap.

A part of Jameson wished that Cass was right. He wished Eli had somehow survived and through some miracle it was his old friend on that recording. Although common sense and his memory knew otherwise.

Moving around to the rear of the vehicle, Jameson caught the items that Liam threw his way. The tent. The sleeping bags. Then together, they found a reasonably flat spot free of rocks and debris and began to set up the tent.

"What's Davey's deal with Mia?" Jameson asked after a few minutes. His head was half-stuck inside the tent as he worked.

"No deal," Liam answered.

Backing out of the tent, Jameson braced his hands on his thighs and lifted an eyebrow at him.

"He's been dead a long time," Liam admitted. "That girl's waking him up."

"He looks uncomfortable," Jameson countered.

"Yeah." Liam bobbed his head and tossed Jameson one of the girl's sleeping bags. "Looks that way."

"Probably *is* that way. Would he hurt her? Lash out or something?" Jameson took the bag and crawled back into the tent to unroll it.

He already had his hands plenty full managing Cass and he didn't want to have to add watching Mia to the mix, but he would if it was necessary. If this tension thing with Davey was a threat to her, then he'd have to neutralize it.

"Nah, he'd never lay a finger on her." Liam sat back on his haunches as Jameson scooted out of the tent for the last time. "It's how she makes him feel that's got him all screwed up."

"And how's that?" Jameson asked, dusting his hands together.

"Alive," Liam answered. "He forgot what it's like to be alive and he's fighting it."

Pushing up to standing, Liam cut their conversation short. He had a habit of doing that, of controlling what was being said and for how long. Jameson sucked in a breath and held back another sigh. He was suddenly so unbelievably tired. His body ached and his eyes were burning.

Rocking back on his heels, Jameson stood up too, and retreated a few feet before leaning back against a nearby tree.

Liam walked to the Jeep and, without warning, he yanked open the rear passenger door. With a scowl on his face, Davey shoved out not two seconds later.

"Don't do that again," he muttered before stalking away.

Liam ignored him. He just stood there holding the door open as first Mia and then Cass emerged. At the sight of her, Jameson folded his arms over his chest and stared. She was sleep mussed and beyond pretty in the dark. Would she ever look that way for him again? Hair all tangled, eyes hooded.

No. Jameson gave his head a shake. He couldn't let

himself go there. He had to make it how it was before; him keeping her safe while still keeping his distance. At the realization, a part of him wanted to die right then. His heart bobbed in his throat and his nostrils burned.

For her part, Cass just walked right past him and followed Mia into the tent. She didn't speak. She didn't so much as glance his way. It's like he didn't exist.

Then the zipper of the girls' tent was sliding shut. Sleeping bags rustled, and one of the girls murmured something, but he couldn't quite make out the words. Then silence.

Lifting his head, Jameson met Liam's gaze. The guy was standing by the front of the Jeep, one elbow propped on the hood, one ankle crossed casually over the other. Tipping his chin up, he signaled for Jameson to come over. Jameson heaved a breath and glanced away, back to the tent.

He didn't want to do this. His instincts were screaming at him not to do this. If he'd had his way, they'd of scooped the girls up, turned that Jeep right around and dragged them both back to the Wall. But he'd been outvoted, he'd been overruled.

Uriah and Liam seemed to think Jameson's track record of forcible rescue with women was... *how'd they say it?* Oh yeah... unsatisfactory. So he'd been allowed on this mission as a subordinate, not a team lead. Liam had the ball. This was the interrogator's show, not his.

Kicking off the trunk of the tree, Jameson squared his

shoulders and stalked over to his apparent boss. Liam watched him come on.

"You're going to have to tell her," Liam said quietly. "She deserves to know what happened with Eli."

"She's not speaking to me," Jameson bit out.

"It makes a difference, *how* it happened," Liam insisted. "You couldn't help it."

"I could've."

"Oh?" Liam's brows raised. "So you should've just let him kill you then?"

"Yes," Jameson hissed. "I should've."

Bobbing his head, Liam pursed his lips and looked out into the meadow.

"We've got another three hours or so before daybreak," he said finally. "I'll take first watch, then Davey, then you."

"Got it." Jameson ducked his head.

"I figure we can hang here for half the day," Liam's gaze swung back over to Jameson. "Let the girls rest. Eat. I need to radio Uriah and give him our progress."

"Alright," Jameson agreed, as if he had a choice.

Fetching his bedroll out of the rear compartment, Jameson scanned the area with his eyes. Davey was already laid out on the far side of the Jeep, his eyes closed, his mouth parted in sleep.

Liam had stalked away and taken a seat leaning against a nearby tree trunk. His rifle was slung across his lap and his eyes were watchful in the dark. Between the scattering of stars and the quarter moon, Jameson could just barely make him out.

With a sigh, Jameson walked back over to the girl's tent and stared down at it. He could hear her breathing in there, if he held his own breath. Exhaling through his nostrils, Jameson retreated a few feet into the trees and made his own bed on the ground. He would be close enough to hear them if they woke, but far enough away that Cass wouldn't murder him the second she came out.

Unlacing his boots, Jameson slipped into his own bedroll and laid down on his back. Branches, thick with summer leaves, twisted overhead. Beyond them, a million tiny stars winked and glittered in an ebony sky. Closing his eyes, Jameson tried to relax. Sleep came to him faster than he imagined it would.

HOURS PASSED, BUT THEY SEEMED LIKE A SINGLE BREATH. And just like he'd planned, it was the girls who woke him.

There was the rustle of the tent, then a low groan. Feminine whispering followed, definitely Mia, Jameson thought. It was muffled, but there. Opening his eyes, he inhaled the cool morning air. The sky was the lightest shade of gray, just now tinging towards blue.

Sitting up in his bedroll, Jameson froze when the zipper of the tent whizzed up. Mia pushed out first, still a little groggy. She didn't even see him.

But then Cass was coming out behind her and she stopped short. The calm expression on her pretty face fell as her gaze locked with Jameson's. It was like she could sense him staring.

Frowning, Cass ducked her head and turned away from him. The two women made their way over to the Jeep. As quietly as they could, they opened the back and began murmuring to each other. No doubt they were looking for food.

On the ground a few feet away, Liam stirred. Jameson studied the guy a moment, but Liam didn't wake. At least, his eyes remained closed and his breathing even.

Davey was the one posted up by the tree now. His rifle was clutched in his hands, and his eyes were watching the meadow.

Jameson swallowed, but it was impossible to rid himself of this feeling in his gut. This sinking, awful sensation just wouldn't leave him. Shoving up to standing he pulled on his boots and walked over to Davey. The guy glanced up at him, then back to the field.

"My turn yet?" Jameson asked.

"No," Davey answered, and shook his head. "I just started."

"Alright." Jameson sucked in a breath, his shoulders rising with the movement. "I can't sleep anymore. You wanna go back down?"

"No." Davey's brow furrowed.

"Okay." Jameson rubbed the back of his neck and glanced to the Jeep. The girls were sitting in the back of it now, eating something.

"I was thinking I'll take a hike around," Jameson continued. "Maybe try to find us some fresh water before we head on. You going to be okay?"

Keeping his face to the meadow, Davey's mouth firmed but he nodded.

"Which way are you gonna go?" He asked.

"East." Jameson gestured with his left hand as he looked into the woods. "I'll follow that little rise and see if I can look down on anything. Maybe we'll get lucky with a spring or a creek."

"Maybe," Davey conceded, and that was that.

Sucking in a breath, Jameson walked over to the Jeep to retrieve his canteen. The girls' whispers fell to silence when they spied his approach. Cass looked away from him, out the opposite passenger side window. Mia, however, maintained eye contact with him, a tiny frown creasing her face.

"I'm going to look for some fresh water," Jameson explained as he dug around for his canteen. "Would you like me to get you some, too? I can take your canteens."

"Um…" Mia's eyes shot to her friend then, who still sat stiffly, refusing to acknowledge Jameson. "No thanks."

"Alright." Jameson ground his teeth together before stalking away.

THE FOREST WAS COOL AS HE ENTERED IT, ALTHOUGH AS soon as the sun rose higher, it would turn warm. As he picked his way around the towering trunks of trees, Jameson's boots marred the soft dew that still covered the grassy ground.

Inhaling, he could almost taste the moisture on his tongue.

The incline was gentle at first and he let his body choose the path of least resistance. Soon enough, he located a small game trail and followed it. The surest way to find water was to follow the path animals took. It would either lead you to their source of food, their shelter, or water. He was hoping for the later.

All the while, his brain was clicking through memories. He was swamped with them. He saw Eli on the first day of football practice. He saw Cass in those hand-me-down clothes and worn out shoes. He saw his parents leaving, and his neighborhood burning. Then he saw men that he'd killed during the war, and still others that he watched die right beside him.

He wasn't paying attention to what was around him. He wasn't focusing like he should. The canteen clicked at his side. The trail kept winding up.

When Jameson reached a small stream, it came as a surprise. He should've heard it before he saw it. The gurgling water churned over gray and black rocks on its way back down the hill.

Jameson came to a stop and huffed a breath. He couldn't even tell how far this was from camp. It didn't feel far, but his mind had been elsewhere.

Crouching at the edge of the water, Jameson unscrewed the cap of his canteen and dipped the thing in the stream. It was icy, sharp, biting water. Cold from its trip down from the north, or maybe it had come right out of the ground not a few hundred yards up from here.

Lifting his head, he narrowed his eyes and traced the path of the stream until it disappeared in the trees. He could hike further up and try to locate the source of the water, but they weren't staying here for that long, so what was the point?

Returning his focus to the stream in front of him, Jameson blanched when he heard the snap of a gun. It was sharp and unnatural, making his whole body tense.

The canteen fell from his grip, knocking against the rocks where it bobbed a few seconds before sinking. Jameson swallowed hard as his stomach turned. He was out here with someone else, and that other person had a gun on him.

Chancing a peek over his shoulder, Jameson spied Davey standing just a few yards behind him.

Relief.

The flood of it hit Jameson full force. His shoulders fell and his face relaxed, he glanced up to the sky a moment as his heart skittered in his chest.

"Holy shit you scared me," Jameson heaved the words out and shoved up to standing.

Rotating around to face the guy, he stopped short and frowned. Davey hadn't moved. He was still standing there, aiming his 1911 directly at Jameson's forehead.

"Hey man." Jameson held his palms up in defense and gave his shoulders a slight shrug. "You okay? It's just me."

"Yeah." Davey's throat bobbed. "It's just you."

"Well…" Jameson huffed a nervous laugh. "Then I guess you got me, buddy. I don't know what's going on."

"Of course you don't know what's going on." Davey kept his arms outstretched, his eyes narrowing as he continued to hold his weapon true. "You're used to getting away with everything. No one ever holds you accountable."

"Alright." Jameson licked his lips as his heart began to pound harder. What in the hell was going on?

"You kill that girl's brother?" Davey asked.

Swallowing, Jameson wracked his brain, trying to keep up.

"Cass?" He asked finally.

"That's the one." Davey nodded. "You killed her brother. You kidnapped Lena and Hannah. You killed my brother, too. Hell, you even killed Flynn. Maybe you don't think she counts because in the end she shot herself. But her blood is still on your hands."

"Wait." Jameson's brow furrowed. "I think you've got me mixed up with someone…"

"No." Davey gave his head a quick shake and took a step closer. "I've got the right guy. You led the raid on our compound. Am I right? That was you."

Squeezing his eyes shut, Jameson felt his stomach roll. Fuck. Yeah, he'd led that raid.

"Get on your knees," Davey demanded.

Jameson's eyes flew open and he glanced around. There was no one else here and he had nowhere to go. He could try for the weapon at his own hip, but Davey would for sure drop him before he got to it. The guy was fast. He was wicked fast.

"On. Your. Knees." Davey repeated through gritted teeth.

He motioned with his gun, and Jameson complied.

Dropping to his knees on the rocky ground, Jameson kept his palms facing Davey. He'd been in this position so many times in his life. So. Many. Times. Maybe this was finally the end. Maybe this was how it was supposed to be.

"Before you do it…" Jameson sucked in a ragged breath. "Promise me you won't hurt the girls. I don't know what's going on with you and Mia…"

"Hurt the girls?" Davey's eyebrows raised and he huffed a laugh. "I'm not a psycho killer like you. I don't run around murdering anyone that suits me for no particular reason… especially women."

Clamping his mouth shut, Jameson's jaw ticked. This guy. He was fucking delusional. Davey was a member of Strike Team Three. Bullshit, he didn't go around killing people for no good reason.

"Whatever." Jameson slammed down on his own anger and fear, shoving both emotions to the bottom of his body.

"Oh, you don't believe me?" Davey took another step forward, his fingers tensing on his weapon. "Is that it? You think… what? I'm like you?"

"You're exactly like me," Jameson bit out. "But this time, you're the one with the gun."

"Fuck. You." Davey shook his head slowly side to side, but all the while his eyes were locked on Jameson's. "There are things I need to know first. There are things you're going to tell me."

"What the hell could I possibly tell you?" Jameson was incredulous.

"The raid." Davey let the barrel of his weapon travel from Jameson's head down to his chest. "I want to know everything. I want to know what my brother's last minutes were like. I want to know the last thing he said, the last thing he saw. You're going to tell me."

"Jesus." Jameson whispered.

"*That* will not be the last name on your lips," Davey said and he tipped his chin at Jameson. "Ryder Arthur Wells. Before I end you, you're going to have my brother's name burned into your soul. Ryder Arthur Wells. Got that?"

"Alright." Jameson raised his hands a few inches. "Fine."

"How did you find the compound?"

Sucking in a breath, Jameson worked to steady his nerves. So this would be an inquisition *and* an execution. Great. The raid on the compound felt so long ago now. Like it happened a lifetime ago. Years and years.

"I was given orders," Jameson managed. "To retrieve two women who were being held somewhere in the mountains several weeks hike from Linfield's city in Utah."

"Good ole' Uriah Linfield give you those orders?" Davey asked.

"Yes," Jameson confirmed, hoping his buddy wasn't next on Davey's hit list. "I took a crew of six men with me. We loaded into a 4Runner and headed out. It took us four days to locate your compound. By then it was starting to snow."

Davey blinked, his lips were now pressed into a firm line as he listened.

"The reports said the women were being abused... badly."

"I don't want your excuses," Davey cut him off. "I just want the truth."

Exhaling through his nostrils, Jameson bit back the string of words he wanted to say. Excuses, every single one of them...

It was dark.

They couldn't see into the compound through the perimeter wall.

Snow was starting to fall.

They heard female voices; the first female voices that any of them had heard in over three years.

The decision was made for them, right then.

They didn't wait to see if the women were actually being hurt, they didn't wait to listen to it.

"I heard Lena and Hannah talking," Jameson explained. "But I couldn't see them, and I couldn't hear exactly what they were saying. I gave the order to breach the compound wall, and that's what we did."

"Sloppy," Davey sneered.

"Desperate," Jameson countered. "I lost five good men that night. Your side wasn't the only one taking casualties. Those were the first female voices any of us had heard in over three years. I don't regret giving the order."

"Ian Chan." Davey spat. "That baby you hold all the

time? Lena's kid? That boy was named for a man *you* killed."

Sucking in a breath, Jameson glanced to one side. He gave the order, so yeah, ultimately everyone who died in that raid was blood splashed all over Jameson's hands.

But was he the one to actually pull the trigger? No. No, he was not.

"Just do it already." Jameson's eyes danced back over to Davey and locked. "Ryder Arthur Wells. There. I said your brother's name. Now end this. You've left the girls unprotected for too long. Liam's asleep. You abandoned your post."

"What were his last words?" Davey's voice was strained now. "Did he say anything?"

"I don't know." Jameson gritted out.

"Did he say anything?" Davey repeated.

Taking another step closer he moved the barrel of his 1911 from Jameson's chest back up to his forehead.

"He looked like me. Just like me, but younger. Blonde hair, blue eyes. Can you remember?"

"I don't know." Jameson shook his head.

"You've got to know!" Davey screamed now.

"But I don't!" Jameson shouted back. "I wasn't there!"

Davey's face contorted with anger and frustration as he took another step closer. "You led the raid! How could you not know?!"

"I was the last one to enter." Jameson's hands were shaking now as he held them in the air. "I never even got a shot off, okay? I followed Meeks down and to the right. He shot a soldier, I'm not sure who. We breached a building, and dumped a smoke bomb in the cellar.

That's when we heard the girls again. Lena... she started choking and crying because of the smoke. Meeks... he wasn't thinking. He just jumped down there to get to her."

Jameson closed his eyes, remembering. It was such a shit show. The guys he'd brought with him, they were the best that he'd had at the time, but they were no Strike Team.

"Hannah shot him." Jameson opened his eyes again, and stared at Davey. "Hannah killed Meeks. She shot him three or four times at point blank range, then she passed out. The smoke was going to kill them, so I dragged her and Lena out of the cellar.

By that time, the rest of your crew and the majority of mine were all dead. The other woman... Flynn? The redhead?"

Davey swallowed and nodded. Tears were pooling at the corners of his eyes.

"She had no pulse. She was gone by the time I got up there. They all were." Jameson sucked in air, his heart pounding, his body trembling for what came next. "That's it. There were no last words, no nothing. And that's the truth."

"*Fuck!*" The word tore from Davey's lungs as tears leaked onto his cheeks. "You're leaving something out. You shot him. You did it."

With each sentence he jerked his gun. And every time Jameson flinched, waiting for the shot.

"I didn't shoot your brother." Jameson's eyebrows raised. "But it doesn't really matter, does it? I gave the order to breach."

Lips trembling, Davey's finger held steady on the trigger. His furious blue eyes danced all over Jameson's face as he shifted his feet beneath him. The entire time, Jameson's heart was beating between his ears. One. Two. Three.

Then, just over Davey's shoulder, something moved.

Jameson's gaze was dragged up and to the left as a slender figure appeared from between the trees.

Mia. *Oh. Shit.*

Jameson's gut dropped as his eyes frantically searched the area for Cass, but she wasn't there. Thank God. It was just the leggy blonde, clutching a pair of canteens. She'd come for water, Jameson realized, because they'd been too proud to let him get it for them.

"Run," Jameson forced the word to pass through his mouth. "Get out of here, Mia. Just go."

"What?" Davey's head whipped around until his eyes locked on the girl.

Mia squeaked when she saw the gun and froze in place. The canteens tumbled from her hands as her lips parted.

Davey held the gun so that it was still trained on Jameson, but now his eyes were focused just over his shoulder, on the blonde.

Jameson could try to run, or he could try to tackle

Davey, but each action was a risk to Mia. He had to escape if he could, but first he had to help her walk away.

"Turn around Mia," Jameson called. "Just walk away like this never happened. Davey's not here to hurt you. He doesn't hurt women. Isn't that right, Davey?"

Davey didn't respond. He just stood there, keeping his weapon on Jameson and his eyes on Mia. The blonde's mouth snapped shut and she looked worriedly between the two men.

"Are you going to k- kill him?" She asked, her voice stuttered on the word.

"Let him do what he has to do," Jameson called again, trying to get her to save herself. "Just walk away now. Don't watch, Mia. Just go."

"Is this you?" Mia asked Davey, those chocolate-brown eyes of hers shone as she dropped her arms to hug herself. "Are you going to shoot him like this?"

"Fuck." Davey swore before lowering his weapon. He did not spare Jameson a glance.

Turning fully towards Mia, Davey took a few steps closer to her, and leaned in as he passed. "Yeah, this is me," he growled.

Mia rocked back a step, her mouth parting in an O shape, as Davey brushed past her and stomped into the cover of the woods.

Just before he disappeared from view, he threw a parting look back at Jameson. It was filled with disappointment. Those fierce killer's eyes had dissolved now. All that was left was emptiness and loss.

Jameson knew that look well, because he'd stared at it in the mirror after he'd finally told Cass the truth about her brother. Some things you just can't get back. Once they are gone, they are gone forever. Mostly those things are people. Jameson would never get Cass back and Davey would never get Ryder.

Falling forward onto his hands, Jameson's breath left him in a whoosh. His nerves were zinging and his heart was slamming against his ribcage. It was a familiar reaction. His body did this every time he almost died.

"Are you okay?" Mia was crouched down at his side now, her soft hands trembling on his back.

Shaking his head side to side, Jameson fought the urge to pass out and instead spat saliva onto the ground. Without looking up, he spoke to her.

"I'm fine," he managed.

"You're fine? He just tried to kill you." Mia's voice shook as her hand paused on his shoulder.

"But he didn't go through with it," Jameson said quietly. "So we better get back down to the Jeep. We've gotta get back to Cass."

"But…" Mia swallowed. "What if he tries it again?"

"I don't think he will." Jameson rocked back on his haunches and blew out a long breath.

Even before Mia had interrupted them, Davey had hesitated. He'd had all the information he wanted and Jameson at his mercy… yet, he still hadn't pulled that trigger. In the war, it was like that all the time. That victory you thought you wanted, the one you craved above all else, when you finally got it, it had a way of turning sour in your mouth.

"I don't understand." Mia's brow furrowed.

"That's okay." Jameson shoved up to standing and dusted at his jeans. "We need to get back now though. Liam was asleep and we need to check on Cass."

"She really means that much to you?" Mia asked, leaning back to peer up into Jameson's face. "That you would risk being shot just to see her?"

"Yeah." Jameson stared down at the pretty blonde. "Yeah, she does."

IT WAS GETTING DARK OUT, BUT THE JEEP JUST KEPT trekking right along. Cass sat in the backseat, her shoulder bumping occasionally into Mia's shoulder. Their seating arrangement hadn't changed from the night before.

Garrett was once again riding shotgun and Liam was driving. Davey was wedged on Mia's other side, and the tension inside the small vehicle was palpable.

Something had happened.

When Davey and Mia and Garrett were all in the woods together that morning, something had gone down. Cass just wasn't sure what. No one was talking. No one was saying anything at all.

Staring out the rear passenger window, Cass watched as the wilderness gave way once again to what remained of civilization. They'd long ago left the incessant bumping of the railroad tracks and traded it for the smooth glide of the highway.

Liam wasn't entirely comfortable with their level of exposure on the open road, so he drove like a bat out of hell. That big foot of his just kept jamming down on the gas pedal, making them fly by old towns and zoom past broken farms.

Earlier in the day, Cass had seen a few men standing a little ways off the road. They held no weapons in their hands. They just stood there and gawked as Liam sped by.

Despite their protests, Garrett made Cass and Mia duck down at the last minute. The guys had armored the doors of the Jeep back at the Wall, but the windows weren't bullet proof, and he said they weren't taking any chances.

But no one fired at them. Maybe they appeared and disappeared too quickly for that. Maybe the shock of hearing an engine again after living for so long without one, held the men in a state of awe. Whatever the reason, Cass was grateful. She just wanted this to be over. She just wanted to get to Eli.

"We're close," Garrett announced, his face was buried in a huge paper map that unfolded in a million different ways. "How far out do you want to stash them?"

"One mile?" Liam asked as he slowed the Jeep. "Two? How fast can you run if things go sideways?"

"Wait." Cass leaned up and laid one hand on Liam's shoulder. "What are you talking about? Why can't we just drive into Hermiston? We have all the supplies in the back."

Liam and Garrett exchanged a quick glance. Cass's stomach dipped.

"We need to scout it out first," Liam offered, his eyes

flicking up to look at her in the rearview mirror. "You and Mia will stay hidden with Davey and the Jeep. When the coast is clear, we'll come get you."

"What? No." Cass shook her head and frowned. "That wasn't the deal."

"That's the only deal," Garrett growled, as he folded the map back up. "Turn here."

Returning his attention to the road, Liam pulled off the highway. The Jeep bumped and hiccuped along a rutted dirt road for what seemed like several minutes before pulling into a stand of trees. There was an old farmhouse off in the distance, but it had no lights to illuminate the windows and the sun had disappeared now.

"Stay," Garrett instructed and had Cass crossing her arms over her chest.

"This is ridiculous," she protested. "There are women and children that need help. We're wasting time."

"The recording claimed there were women," Garrett corrected, turning now in his seat to stare at her in the dark. "What better way to lure men and supplies to this location?"

"Eli would never..." Cass started, but Garrett cut her off.

"Regardless, we're going to check it out," he continued. "And for the record, I hope you're right."

Cass's mouth dropped open with another string of protests, but Liam and Garrett were already shoving out of the Jeep. Davey rolled his shoulders before popping open his own door and sliding out. They were all careful to close their doors so they didn't make hardly any sound. Just a soft thump and then the snick of the handles catching.

Mia exhaled and leaned her head back against her seat.

"Just let them do this," Mia coached, and grabbed Cass's hand. "Okay? It's nighttime anyway. We'll go see your brother first thing in the morning."

Pursing her lips, Cass let Mia pick at the fingers of her clenched fist. Uncurling those fingers one by one, Mia remained silent. When the girls were finally palm to palm, Cass let loose a sigh.

"Alright," she relented. "We sleep here tonight and prove all of these guys wrong tomorrow."

"That's the spirit," Mia intoned before groaning and running her free hand down her face. "I have to pee and I am so freaking tired of driving."

Cass huffed a breath. She had to pee, too.

Looking out her window she watched the guys disappear into the woods. Each one of them took a different direction, stalking off with their rifles clutched in their hands. Was it really so bad out here? She hadn't seen any evidence of that. Maybe the guys were just stuck in war mode. It seemed calm to her, calm and unbelievably empty.

Several minutes later, Davey returned. He walked to the Jeep and rapped a knuckle on the window without looking inside. Mia glared at him through the glass.

"You can get out and set up camp," he said, his eyes continued to scan the area. "It's as safe as it's gonna be."

With that, the soldier walked away.

"He's dangerous," Mia hissed and had Cass frowning.

Mia's lips firmed and she turned her whole body towards Cass. Reaching out, the blonde clutched both of Cass's hands in her own and drew in a breath.

"I mean it," Mia said, her eyes serious, her brow furrowed. "When I went to get water this morning, Davey was…"

Pausing Mia nibbled on her lower lip. Her eyes flitted up and away a moment before settling back on Cass's face.

"He was going to kill Jameson," she finished finally. "He was going to shoot him."

"What?" Cass's face screwed up in confusion. "I don't understand."

"Davey was pointing his gun at Jameson." Mia squeezed Cass's hands tighter. "Jameson was on his knees. He was going to kill him."

Cass's mouth dropped slightly and she ducked her head. A sick sort of panic swirled through her as the information sunk into her brain. Davey was going to kill Garrett.

She shouldn't care. She knew she shouldn't care whether Garrett was hurt or in danger of being shot. After what he'd done (or claimed to have done) to Eli, Cass shouldn't be feeling this way. But she was.

Her heart picked up the pace now, beating faster as her lungs drew in air.

"Did you tell Liam?" She asked, her eyes shooting over to watch Davey in the dark.

"No." Mia shook her head. "We've been stuck together this entire time. I haven't had a chance. I just barely got a moment to tell you."

"Okay." Cass licked her lips. "Alright."

Flicking her eyes up, Cass tried to think of what to do. As much as she hated Garrett for what he'd done, she didn't want him dead. And that exact realization had her heart leaping onto the next truth. As much as she hated him, she still loved him too.

Garrett was like lightning to her. He struck her down and lit her up all at the same time, no matter how much she fought it, no matter how wrong it was.

At the edge of the small clearing, another soldier stepped into view. It was Garrett. Cass knew by the set of his shoulders, by the way he carried himself, by the way he moved.

Davey was sitting on the ground now, his back was leaned up against a tree not five yards away. The men eyed one another briefly, but said nothing.

Making his way to the Jeep, Garrett peered through the window glass at the girls and slipped the strap of his rifle over his shoulder. Cass's eyes shot over to Davey who was now looking away. His hands were loose and empty, his weapon was balanced easily on his lap.

He could kill Garrett right now if he wanted, and yet he didn't. And what's worse... Garrett knew it. He knew Davey could shoot him, yet he gave the man his back, and focused his attention entirely on the girls instead.

"I don't get it," Cass breathed the words as Garrett stared at her through the window.

His blue eyes were scanning her face. His head was cocked to one side. He said nothing.

"I don't either," Mia responded. "But I had to tell you. I don't know what to do."

Popping open her door, Cass stepped out as Garrett backed up a tiny bit to give her room. Even still, he lingered in her space, hovering, silent and watchful. Cass could feel the energy around him almost as if he was touching her. Tipping her head back, she huffed a small breath into the night air.

"Um…" Cass swallowed hard and kept her voice low. "He wants to kill you? Davey does?"

Firming his lips, Garrett glanced to Davey and then back at Cass. His expression was difficult to read in the dark, but the black pupils of his eyes glistened at her.

"Yeah," he admitted finally. "He did, maybe he still does."

"Why?" Cass asked, it was all she could do to keep her hands off him, to keep her palms from gripping his arms, from gripping his jacket.

Clearing his throat, Garrett's eyes fell to the ground. Cass ducked her head, trying to catch his gaze. After a few seconds he bobbed his head as if coming to some sort of conclusion, and looked at her.

"Because I killed his brother," Garrett said.

That singular statement had Cass's heart exploding.

It was so familiar, too familiar. How many brothers had Garrett killed? Or tried to kill? What sort of person was he really? She didn't know. For the first time since they were kids, Cass truly didn't know.

Tears pooled at the corners of her eyes as heat flooded

her face. Bringing both of her hands up she slapped at his chest once... then again, harder.

Garrett just stood there and took it. He said nothing, and he didn't try to stop her. He just let her hit him over and over until she finally shoved away and stumbled to the side, into Mia.

Her friend had been waiting there, for who knows how long. Enveloping Cass in her arms, Mia stroked a hand over Cass's hair and shushed her while she crumpled and cried.

"You're a glutton for punishment, you know that?" Liam whispered.

They were lying side by side on their bellies in the dirt. Liam had a pair of night vision binoculars held up to his eyes as he scanned Hermiston's Main Street. Jameson looked through the scope of his rifle.

Dawn was approaching, and they'd been out here all night, perched on a small hillside adjacent to the town's main thoroughfare, hiding under a thick copse of bushes.

Jameson shifted slightly, trying to ease the knot that had formed between his shoulder blades. There were definitely men living here, but the jury was out as to the rest of it. He hadn't seen Eli and there were no signs of women or children.

That didn't mean the women didn't exist, of course. It had been nighttime after all, maybe they were all tucked up inside one of the buildings, sleeping.

"There's a fancy psychology term for what you're doing," Liam continued, his eyes didn't stray towards Jameson, he just kept scanning the town and talking. He never talked this much. Never. "It's called a martyr complex... and buddy, you've got it."

Rolling his eyes, Jameson bit down on his lower lip, stifling any number of responses he wanted to give. Liam had returned to the Jeep last night just in time to witness Cass's breakdown. That led to questions about Davey and what had happened at the stream, and *that* information led to Liam chewing everyone's asses. He was an interrogator after all... it wasn't a pretty sight.

"What?" Liam hissed. "You think I'm too dumb to go to college? Think I'm too dumb to learn big words?"

"Oh for fuck's sake," Jameson grumbled. "You were a psyche major? That's all I need."

"You refuse to tell Cass the whole story about her brother," Liam continued. "Then you tell her that you killed Davey's brother, when in fact, you didn't actually pull the trigger. You hold back important details to increase your own suffering. Martyr complex. Boom. You owe me like a grand in therapy fees."

Sighing, Jameson let his eyes flutter closed a moment. It all made sense now, why Liam was so damn good at interrogation. The guy had an education in reading people. Yeah, he was a natural, and cruel in ways most men weren't, but underneath it all... he'd had a head start.

"For the record," Jameson countered. "Martyr complex

is not a big word, and I'm fresh out of cash. You'll have to bill my insurance."

Chuckling quietly, Liam let the conversation die. The sun rose slowly, spreading its warm rays out towards the sleepy town. Liam adjusted the binoculars so he could see in the light. There was an old drug store, a local bank, a few touristy type shops and a gas station.

Dusty cars lined the roadway and crowded the pumps of the gas station. It was a familiar sight. Abandoned cars waiting to be filled with gas until the last drop had been pumped out of the ground or the electricity gave out.

Thankfully their crew didn't have to worry about fuel. They'd hauled enough gas in canisters on the Jeep to sustain them. Here and back... and a little extra, just in case.

"There," Liam spoke suddenly. "Leaving the coffee shop."

Tensing, Jameson focused once more on the scope of his rifle. He could see a man walking along the street. He had on a pair of faded blue jeans, a cream-colored long sleeve shirt and a red ball cap. It was pulled low over shaggy mouse-brown hair.

"No visible weapon," Liam recited. "Probably has a knife in his left pocket."

"You can tell that?" Jameson's brow furrowed as he examined the man.

"And we've got two more," Liam announced. "Both male, one appears older."

Jameson's muscles tightened as he moved his sight to scrutinize the new arrivals. His heart tapped at him a bit and he hated himself for feeling hopeful. But then in the blink of an eye, his stomach twisted once more and he blew out a breath.

"Negative," Jameson said. "They aren't him."

For the next two hours, they waited. They watched men come and go. Heard them laugh, watched them eat. None of them carried guns and none of them were women.

Jameson's muscles were cramping now and his body was heavy with exhaustion. The sun had crested up into the sky and the air all around them was warming. Hidden under the bushes next to the cool dirt, it was a bearable sort of heat. It wouldn't have been unpleasant at all, if you were wearing shorts and a t-shirt. But the bullet proof vest strapped to Jameson's chest was uncomfortable as hell. Stifling and sticky, but necessary.

"Well?" Liam lowered his binoculars and rolled carefully onto his back. "What do you say? Now's as good a time as any."

Following suit, Jameson released his rifle and laid his head on the ground. All of the muscles in his neck rippled, then relaxed. He breathed quietly, letting his shoulders go slack and his eyes rest.

"Yeah," he said finally. "You'll cover me?"

"Yup," Liam confirmed. "Leave the rifle. Take a radio. Same scenario we talked about."

"Shit, I hate that part," Jameson confessed.

They'd agreed he would carry only a knife and his handgun down with him. His rifle would remain behind, with Liam.

"They'll take it from you regardless," Liam reasoned for the hundredth time. "I'd rather have it up here with me, then in their hands."

"Yeah." Jameson fought his immediate groan. "Agreed."

"No need to fuck with the radio unless they take you inside," Liam went on, rehashing their strategy. "Then I'll need a click every minute or so. If I don't get one, then I'll one-click you…"

"If I don't answer, then hell fire and sniper shit and all that," Jameson cut him off. "I got it."

"I'm not as good a shot as Davey, but I couldn't very well have him covering you," Liam confessed, half-joking. "He may just decide to take that shot on you after all."

Opening his eyes, Jameson stared up into a million tiny green leaves and twisting thin branches.

"You're sure the girls are safe?" He asked.

"Absolutely." Liam turned his head to the right and stared at the side of Jameson's face. "I've known him for a long time, he'll protect them with his life. And to be honest, I don't think he'll try to kill you again.

I'm not one-hundred percent on that, but you weren't what he was looking for by that stream. You weren't involved enough in Ryder's death to satisfy him. At least, that's what I think."

Huffing a short laugh, Jameson turned his face to the left and locked eyes with Liam.

"Why are you doing this?" He asked. "You've got a wife and baby on the way. You should be building a crib or something."

Liam pursed his lips and frowned.

"Truth?" He asked finally.

Jameson nodded.

"I miss this," he admitted. "I miss the missions, the ops. It's part of who I am."

"But…"

"And Hannah's got Cole," Liam continued. "He'll make a great dad whether I'm there or not. Me being able to leave… it's sort of a weird perk of our situation."

"Dude." Jameson turned his head to stare back up into the tangle of leaves. "Your *situation* is beyond me."

"Yeah." Liam snickered and Jameson could feel a smile break out on the other guy's face. "It's beyond me too, man. So, enough of this Dr. Phil shit. Are you gonna go or not?"

"I'm going. I'm going. Pushy prick." Jameson rolled onto his belly and began to scoot his body backwards, out of the copse of brush.

As Jameson emerged from the bushes, he continued to crawl. Dragging his body along, he waited until he was out of sight of the town before lifting his head and looking around. When he was sure the coast was clear, he stood up and dusted himself off.

He didn't want to reveal Liam's position, so he took his

time circling around. He picked up a backpack they'd stashed along the way and flung it on his back.

They'd agreed he would approach the town from the opposite side. Just because the men weren't carrying guns openly, didn't mean there weren't guns present. It made sense, if you were going to set up a distress call and lure people in, then you had to look the part. You had to look unassuming and approachable.

And that radio recording? The one that Cass was so sure was her brother? It was still being broadcast. They didn't dare listen to it when they had Cass with them, but when Liam had made radio contact with Uriah yesterday, Uriah had confirmed it was still airing, and there was still no response to inquiries.

Use caution. Uriah had said. *This whole thing smells like shit.*

Clearing his throat, Jameson adjusted the pack of supplies on his back. It was filled with MREs and some clothes and even a few vials of medicine. Cass had insisted they bring it, and Liam had agreed it would make sense. If you believed the call and were coming to help, then you would be bringing something with you. It would be better to have something to give, than nothing at all, *if* this was just a robbery.

The feel of asphalt beneath Jameson's boots had his pulse jumping a bit before it finally evened out. Keeping his eyes steady and his head up, Jameson did his best to absorb all the tiny details around him while still looking casual. The weight of the 1911 tucked into the holster at his hip felt comforting.

Liam was right. Liam was crazy, but he was also right.

There was something about an op that got your blood heating. There was something about running a mission that got you high. It was addictive, in its own way. Jameson felt more alive in this moment than he had since Cass had left him.

Controlling his breathing, Jameson let a small smirk tug at the corner of his mouth. This felt good. Fuck it. Maybe he was crazy, too.

All the while, Jameson's boots kept thumping down the middle of Main Street. He weaved through broken down vehicles, and sidestepped debris. But the moment they spotted him, the energy in the air changed. It was hard to describe the sensation other than that they knew he was here now and he knew they knew.

As if on cue, two men appeared about one block up, standing on the corner of the sidewalk. One was tall and lean, the other seemed to be of average height.

Jameson's eyes focused on them. He'd seen both of them through the scope of his rifle not half an hour ago and so they were familiar in that way, but nothing more.

Resisting the urge to glance up to where Liam was hiding, Jameson lifted a hand casually and waved at the men. He kept his eyes on them, even as more guys appeared at his flanks. First the left side, then the right.

There were still no weapons visible… but he got this

uneasy feeling. The men were being too quiet. The smiles on a few of their faces were strained.

Swallowing, Jameson once again refused to check the copse of bushes on the nearby hillside. He had to believe that Liam was still there, and he didn't want to give away his position. This part was all about trust.

"Hey fellas." Jameson gestured to the walkie talkie fastened to one of his own belt loops. "This is Hermiston, right? I got your transmission."

"That's right." One of the men stepped forward and nodded his head. "Thanks for coming. You all alone?"

"Yep." Jameson came to a stop a few yards from the sidewalk and gripped the straps of his backpack. "You said you have women and some kids? Wow. Kinda hard to believe, you know?"

"Yeah." The tall guy rubbed at the scruff of his chin and smiled. "Crazy right?"

"Yeah," Jameson echoed him and then glanced around.

Rocking back on his heels, Jameson kept his body loose and relaxed. He counted five bodies total, plus the two men directly in front of him. Returning his gaze to the tall one, Jameson lifted his eyebrows and waited. It was their move. He wasn't sure what would come next.

"Where you from?" The tall guy asked.

"Originally? Southern California," Jameson answered.

"That's a nice piece you got there." The guy nodded to the gun on Jameson's hip. "You a soldier?"

"I was in the war," Jameson conceded, and glanced over

his shoulder. Were they getting closer to him? A little. "What about you guys?"

"Same." The tall guy lifted his chin. "What's in the pack?"

"Some supplies." Jameson kept his eyes on the tall guy. "Some food and stuff for the kids... and the women. You said you needed help."

"Let's see it." The guy gestured for Jameson to open the pack.

With an easy smile, Jameson kept the pack where it was, zipped safely on his back.

"Well I was kinda hoping to see those women first. It'd be a pretty easy thing for you guys to just take everything for yourselves. You know?"

"You're right." The tall guy pressed a hand to his heart and bent forward a little, as if he were about to bow. "They're just inside the bank."

"Oh." Jameson turned his head to look at the old building. The window glass reflected in his eyes. Between that and the distance, it was impossible to see inside.

"You'll need to leave the gun, though." The tall guy spoke once more, drawing Jameson's attention back over to him. "You understand."

"Yeah." Jameson fought the spike of adrenaline that cruised through his body at the thought. "Sure."

Reaching for his weapon, Jameson pulled the 1911 from its holster and handed it over. One of the other men stepped forward to take it. He shoved the thing unceremoniously into the pocket of his pants.

Jameson blinked and worked on keeping any signs of strain from his face. *Stupid. Never ever give up your damn weapon.*

But in this case it was necessary. Jameson had to play along and he'd known that going in. If these idiots had any brains at all, they'd search him right now and find his knife. But apparently they were dumb as rocks.

"Alright," tall guy said. "Let's go."

Turning around, Jameson followed some of the other men towards the bank. They were grouped together now, with two of the men walking side by side and another one trailing a bit behind them. When Jameson looked back over his shoulder, he noted the tall guy was coming along too.

Together, they weaved through the cars in the street and stepped onto the sidewalk. Three buildings down and on the left, was the bank. At the entrance, the men in front didn't hesitate. The four or so guys that were ahead of Jameson pulled the door open and walked inside.

Swallowing down his fear, Jameson followed.

The stench inside hit him like a ton of bricks. It was rancid and sour, smelling of sickness and decay.

Stopping short, Jameson glanced around. Despite the smell, the place was pristine. It looked just the way a small town bank should. There was a wide open lobby with thin brown carpeting and a line of teller windows along one side. The rest of the space was consumed with wooden desks and empty computer monitors. Silent phones sat unused on the desk tops.

It was a blast from the past. Minus the customers and employees, of course.

But that smell. Where the hell was it coming from?

"Did you strip him of his… stuff…" the familiar voice trailed off at the end, causing Jameson's eyes to dart to his right.

Eli.

Mother. Fucker.

Jameson's mouth hung open at the sight of his old friend. How in the hell?

Jameson stared.

For his part, Eli was frozen in place. He was halfway across the lobby, with a rifle clutched in his hands and the long sleeves of his shirt rolled up to his elbows. Large black tattoos ran from his wrists up along his forearms before disappearing under the beige material.

Jameson frowned. Those were new. Eli didn't have those tattoos the last time they'd seen each other.

Blinking, Jameson couldn't help but focus on them. They were code. The tattoos were made up of thick blocks, thin rectangles and tiny dots. Command code was printed all over Eli's skin.

"Nope, that's your job." The tall guy was talking now, answering Eli's question as if nothing strange was going on. "Boss's orders and all that."

"Right," Eli answered, tearing his gaze from Jameson.

With a quick shake of his head, Eli resumed walking towards them. He was still tall and muscular, but leaner than Jameson, like always. His mop of short brown curls, so like his sister's, tumbled down to sway at the tops of his ears. Those hazel eyes of his were darting all around, looking at every face in the place save for Jameson.

"What's a matter Eli?" The tall guy asked. "Looks like you've seen a ghost. You feeling alright?"

"Yeah," Eli managed before rolling his shoulders and aiming the rifle right at Jameson's head. "I'm fine."

Tipping her face up, Cass opened her mouth as fresh water poured down from the brass shower head.

"This is amazing," she said, as the water dribbled down her chin and chest. "Cold, but amazing."

"I know, right?" Mia's voice echoed in the small bathroom, she'd already finished her shower. "Best decision we made all day."

"All week," Cass corrected.

Reaching for a small bar of white soap, Cass sighed. It'd been well over eight days since either of the women had had the opportunity to bathe. They were sticky and stinky and beyond uncomfortable. So when they'd woken up first thing in the morning, and Davey mentioned that the farmhouse across the field was indeed abandoned, they just couldn't resist.

Despite his numerous protests, both of the women had

marched over to the two-story house with the extra wide porch, and investigated for themselves. And... what do you know? The place had a gravity fed water tank, which meant... showers. Real, live, running water, showers.

Bliss.

Heaven.

"Hurry the fuck up!" Davey's fist pounded on the carved wooden door, sending it rattling, and not for the first time. "We should never have left the Jeep."

"Calm down!" Mia called, she was standing over the bathroom sink, combing through her wet hair with a brush she'd found in one of the drawers. "We're almost done."

So *not* almost done, Cass thought. But she wasn't about to tell Davey that.

Lathering up her body, Cass scrubbed and sudsed and rinsed. Mia hummed to herself. The click of the brush hitting the granite counter sounded so normal in the small space, Cass almost forgot where they were and why they were here.

"I'm serious, Mia!" Davey slammed his fist against the door again. "We've been here long enough. Let's go."

"Fine!" Mia snapped the word before dropping her voice to hiss, "He's an ass."

Twisting the faucet off, Cass pulled the shower curtain aside and stepped out. Mia handed her a baby-blue colored towel which smelled stale, but looked clean enough. As she dried herself, Cass watched Mia's reflection in the mirror.

The blonde was already dressed in a pair of skinny

jeans and a pale-green tank top. Her oversized bullet proof vest was still lying on the floor where she'd dropped it to take a shower.

Hefting it up now, Mia grunted as she put the thing on and fastened the straps tight. It was one condition of the guy's leaving that both she and Cass had readily agreed to. Liam had brought them extra vests from the Wall, and since they were now hiding out so close to strange men, they had to wear them, just in case.

"Aren't you monitoring the radio?" Cass called.

Despite her relief at showering, she still felt a twinge of worry. If anything went wrong with Garrett and Liam, then Davey should know right away. They would have plenty of time to prepare because of the radio.

But nothing was going to go wrong, she reminded herself. Eli was the voice on that recording and he wouldn't have lied like that. There were women and children here that needed their help. Cass couldn't wait to be proved right.

"Yes," Davey admitted, his boots stomped a short path back and forth on the wooden flooring just outside the bathroom door. "But this is still a bad idea. I should've tied you both to the damn Jeep."

Rolling her eyes, Cass let loose a long breath. They had time. Everything was still okay. Tucking the towel around her chest, Cass reached for the brush Mia had discarded and began to attack her tangle of dripping curls. She missed shampoo. She missed conditioner.

"Stop fear mongering," Mia chided. With her vest now secure, she stepped into her brown leather boots.

"Fear mongering?!" Davey's outraged voice sounded louder as his boots came to a stop just outside the bathroom door. "Blondie! I swear you are the biggest naive pain in my ass. Get. Out. Here. Now."

"We're coming," Mia grumbled.

Folding her arms over her chest, the blonde leaned back against the nearby wall and watched Cass. Two seconds later they heard Davey release a string of curses and stalk away.

Returning her attention to the mirror, Cass worked the tangles slowly but surely out of her hair. When she was done, she got dressed in her own set of dirty blue jeans and wrinkled white t-shirt. The heavy bulky uncomfortable bullet proof vest came next, and after stepping into her own set of boots, she was done.

"Ready to face the wrath?" Mia asked, her head jerked towards the locked bathroom door.

"You first," Cass teased and had Mia rolling her eyes.

Reaching for the door handle, Mia twisted the little lock on the brass knob and pulled the door wide. Davey was standing directly in front of the opening now, his muscular arms folded over his chest, his blue eyes glaring.

At his waist, the black walkie talkie that was fastened to his belt loop let out a single click.

All of their eyes traveled down to it and held. Davey's hand shot to the radio and he adjusted the volume. There should be an answering click. If everything was okay, then that's what they should hear next.

Cass's heart began to tap, thickly, slowly at first, then faster as the silence dragged on. Looking up into Davey's face, she couldn't keep the worry from her expression as he held a single finger up to his lips.

Silence. He said it without saying it.

Beside her, Mia swallowed.

Then another click finally came from the radio and both the girls sighed. That was the signal. One click, then a response. All clear.

"So it's good?" Mia managed. "That's what it means right?"

The expression on Davey's face was not one of relief. It had Cass sucking her bottom lip between her teeth. He didn't like something about this.

"Come on." Davey motioned with one hand as he stepped to the side. "Let's get back to the Jeep."

Throwing Mia a questioning glance, Cass did as instructed. They moved through the quiet farmhouse with its dusty kitchen and unused living room. Out on the porch, the hot air simmered. The sun was well up in the sky now, turning the field of forgotten weed-riddled plants into a sea of greens and golds.

Birds chirped in a nearby fruit tree, fluttering and singing in the most magical way.

"The ground is good here," Mia commented, as they descended the wooden porch steps. "It wouldn't take much to get it producing again."

Pursing his lips, Davey scanned the open area before yanking the rifle off his back and holding it carefully in his hands.

"Let's stay as low as we can," he said quietly. "And make straight for the tree line."

"Is everything okay?" Cass ventured, as they entered the field. "The signal was good right? All clear."

"The gap between clicks was longer than I'd like," Davey admitted. "It means one can't see the other."

Focusing on the ground, Cass placed her boots carefully in one of the old furrows. The weeds and wild mix of plant stalks had the brush coming up just to her hips. Mia walked along behind her, and after the blonde came Davey. Cass could hear their breath puffing out and the shuffle of dry old grass beneath their feet.

Then the radio sounded again. Two clicks this time. Like a rapid double beat, one right on top of the other. Cass glanced over her shoulder as Mia's face paled.

"Move," Davey growled. "Now."

Frozen in place, Cass watched as Davey stepped out from behind Mia and grabbed the blonde's elbow in one hand. That was the distress signal. Two clicks one on top of the other. That meant something was wrong.

"Go!" He shouted, and broke Cass's trance.

Turning away from them, Cass began to run. Her boots hit the uneven furrows in the field, causing her to stumble, but she didn't fall. She just kept running for the trees, pumping her arms and refusing to look back. Davey had ahold of Mia now, so she knew they were both coming too.

Overhead, the sun continued to shine down, but the song of the birds no longer filled her ears. It was all blood pounding and breath catching instead. Adrenaline spiked through her body, causing Cass's vision to narrow even as her eyes grew wide.

The trees seemed further away than before. How was that possible? Out of the corner of her eye, Cass spied Mia. She was running as hard as she could now, with Davey trailing close behind her, both of his hands were on his weapon as he looked behind them.

"Keep moving," he called. "Straight to the Jeep."

Cass did as she was told. Entering the woods, she tore down the faded path that they'd used to get to the farmhouse not two hours before. When the Jeep appeared in the small clearing, Cass nearly wept.

Sliding to a stop, she fought the clenching in her side and the throbbing in her head. Cass braced one hand on the side of the Jeep and sucked in oxygen.

Mia slammed to a stop beside her as a single gunshot echoed through the air. It sounded far away, but unmistakeable.

"Get in," Davey commanded.

Yanking open the drivers door, he leaned in to set his rifle inside. Once done, he straightened up and fumbled around in the back pocket of his jeans.

Cass popped open the rear door and crawled onto the seat with Mia following closely on her heels.

Another gun shot went off then, which was quickly answered with a short burst of return fire. Again it sounded far away.

Heaving a sigh, Davey drew out a jingling set of keys and flashed the girls a wicked smile. Cass's mouth dropped as a scary sickness pooled in her gut. How could he be happy in a moment like this?

"We're out of here," Davey commented.

Sliding into the driver seat, he pulled his door closed and shoved the key in the ignition. Cass held her breath until the engine roared to life. Mia threw her head back on the seat and let out a small cry.

"Get down," Davey instructed, turning to look at them over his shoulder. "We'll be clear of this place in a few minutes."

"What?" Cass recoiled as if she'd been slapped. "We aren't going to go help them?"

"My orders are to evacuate you if it goes to shit," Davey explained. "It's gone to shit. We're out."

"No." Cass shook her head. "We can't just leave them. You've got to go help."

Scowling at her, Davey kept one arm slung over the seat back as he spoke.

"This is what you wanted," he said. "This is the risk you were willing to take. The guys knew that going in. War's a bitch. We're. Out."

Rotating away from her, he jammed his feet on the pedals as his hand fell to the gear shifter. Cass's heart pounded and pounded as sweat poured from her forehead. Had she really got them killed? Had she really brought

Liam and Garrett all the way out here to die? Because of what? Why?

Sucking in a breath, Cass yanked at the rear passenger door and flung it open. Davey roared and slammed on the brake, as she hopped out and took one giant step back from the vehicle.

"I can't," she almost whispered it. "I can't leave them like this."

"Fucking son-of-a-bitch damn fucking it." Davey released a string of curses as he threw the Jeep in park and stepped out.

"Get in this car!" He screamed.

They were on opposite sides now, with the Jeep rumbling between them.

"I can't." Cass shook her head.

Davey's hands were splayed over the hood now, his driver side door hanging open, and she could see how this was going to play out.

His eyes were boring into her, filled with anger and frustration. He was deciding how best to chase her down and capture her. His fingers twitched and his shoulders bunched with intent.

All the while, the motor continued to rumble.

But then a single gunshot exploded in their clearing.

Boom.

It was so unbelievably close, and so unforgivably loud.

Cass flinched and she heard Mia scream. But it was Davey's eyes that rolled up into the back of his head as his body gave out. Cass watched as the soldier collapsed in slow motion. His face flew forward, smacking hard against the hood of the Jeep before he slid down to the ground and out of sight.

Mia screamed again. She was still sitting in the backseat of the Jeep, but she had a better view than Cass.

Cass's mouth dropped as she stood there in shock. Men were entering the small clearing now. Two, no three. Walking out from amongst the trees, they approached the Jeep. They were unfamiliar. She didn't know them.

Taking a step back, Cass tried to suck in air. But her lungs weren't having it.

Even before the single arm snaked around her neck, Cass couldn't breathe. That's why it took her a moment to register what was happening.

There was a man standing just behind her. He was pulling her up against him now, holding her tight as she clawed at his forearm. He was wearing long sleeves though, so her nails didn't make much of an impact on him.

"You're not going to believe what we found," he was saying. "Women… and I'm not fucking joking this time."

Jerking her head to one side, Cass spied a handheld radio. The man holding her was talking into it. Her eyes were wide and her mouth was open, gasping for air. She was so useless, that he could hold her tight using just the one arm.

On the other side of the Jeep, one of the men was yanking open Mia's door. Reaching inside, he wrestled with her a bit as she kicked and fought him. Screams bubbled up her throat and Cass could feel Mia's terror in every inch of her own body as the guy grunted, but finally succeeded in dragging her out by her ankles.

Mia landed on the ground with a thump and the guy landed on top of her. Her screams turned silent and all the others just stood there with gaping mouths, watching.

Twisting and writhing now, Cass worked hard to draw in air. She shoved her fingers between the man's arm and her neck, trying to gain space so that she could breathe. Just beside her head, the radio crackled with a familiar voice.

"Do not touch the women," Eli instructed. "Bring them directly to me. Boss's orders."

With a grunt, the man holding her snapped the radio back on his waistband and began to tug Cass to one side. He half-dragged, half-carried her around the side of the Jeep until they'd rounded the corner of the hood.

Davey was lying belly down on the ground. His head was turned to one side, away from Cass. There was no blood pooled around his body, so maybe the shot had impacted his vest, but he wasn't moving, so maybe it had got him after all. Cass couldn't tell.

Mia, on the other hand, was fighting hard. Her back was twisting in the dirt as the man on top of her held her in place. One of his hands was tugging at the waist of her tight jeans. The sound of them ripping made Cass want to throw up.

"Do… something…" she gurgled, imploring the man who was holding her.

Twisting in his grip, she tried to look at his face.

"What do you want me to do?" His voice was low and gravelly.

"Stop… them…" she choked out.

"There's three of them and one of me." He gave a little shrug and began to pull her away. "I"m just doing my job."

On the ground, Mia began to scream again.

It was Davey's name on her lips this time.

It had Cass's heart shattering in her chest. Mia was calling for the unconscious man lying not two feet away from her. Cass could see the blonde's arm snake out and slap at the dirt just in front of Davey's face.

He still didn't move.

Squeezing her eyes shut, Cass felt the heels of her boots dragging along in the dirt. She listened as Mia continued to call out for Davey. Over and over, it was pitiful as the man on top of her swore.

Still struggling, Cass moved to wedge both of her hands against her captor's forearm. Finally, she was able to draw in a full breath. Oxygen flooded her system, and with it, adrenaline.

Her heart was pumping and her muscles were zinging. That's when her brain remembered the knife in her pocket. The one Liam that had insisted she carry at all times.

Letting her body go limp, Cass slumped forward as if she'd passed out. It had the desired effect. The man holding her loosened his grip and stopped dragging her along.

Quick as she could, Cass's hand shot to her own pocket and drew out her knife. Flicking the blade open, she gripped the handle and twisted her body to one side.

Without hesitation she thrust the knife deep into flesh. She heard a cry of surprise and kept going.

At first, Cass stabbed at the man blindly. She'd been facing away from him, flopped onto her side and she couldn't quite see him properly.

But Liam had taught her to strike fast and not stop. Faster. More. Again. There was no overkill when you were Cass's size, so she did what he'd taught her.

Yanking the blade out, Cass opened her eyes wide and kept going.

Stab. Pull. Stab. Pull. Stab. Pull.

Over and over she sunk her blade into any available surface. The man cried out, then he stumbled back and fell onto his butt in the dirt. Cass turned on him and kept coming. She kept stabbing until he stopped moving, and the knife began to slip in her hand from all the blood.

Glancing over her shoulder then, Cass saw the other men coming for her. Their weapons were up. Their guns were trained on her. Their focus was entirely on her.

Cass's heart kicked up into her throat as she turned to face the men. She could feel slick hot blood covering her wrist and hand.

Out of the corner of her eye, she saw Davey stir on the ground.

"Davey!" Mia screamed his name again.

This time, she got a response.

He was up and off the ground in the next breath. Throwing himself forward, Davey knocked the man off of Mia and onto his back. The guy's breath exploded in a grunt as Davey got on top of him. His fists rained down on the guy as Mia scrambled up and away.

The men in the clearing were lost in momentary confusion. The guns that had been trained on Cass now swiveled away, towards Davey, then a little to the right onto Mia, then back to the left, on Cass. They didn't know who to aim at.

Gripping her knife tightly in her hand, Cass began to run forward. After all, Liam had said never to stop. Just keep coming. Faster. Sharper. More. So Cass chose one of the men, the one on her right, and she charged him.

Seeing her, the man swung his gun towards Cass and pulled the trigger.

Boom.

The gunshot exploded through the air. Cass could hear it zip towards her, then a slice of hot pain stabbed deep into her right thigh. Her eyes opened wider. The knife fell from her hand.

Tripping forward, Cass stumbled. Her right leg collapsed. Her left knee hit the dirt, then her chest, then her face.

Another gunshot rang out. Then another, and another.

Rolling onto her back, Cass's mouth hung open as her vision blurred in and out. She could hear Mia screaming again, and Davey cursing, and more men shouting.

One gun shot turned into two, and that turned into twenty-two, until each individual sound was unrecognizable.

Sucking in a breath, Cass felt her body start to float.

Her leg was cold and leaking. She blinked up as her vision turned white and all she could hear was one giant roar filling her head.

Her eyelids fluttered.

Then blackness.

Her mouth went slack.

Then silence.

Swallowing hard, Jameson slowly lifted both hands in the air. The men standing around him continued to banter in the way that men do, but Jameson only had eyes for Eli. His former best friend, his lover's brother, the man he'd stabbed to death on the front lawn of his childhood home.

Did Eli recognize him? After so many years?

As Jameson stared into those hazel eyes of his, he knew the answer. Eli most definitely remembered him, but he didn't say as much to the others. The black rifle Eli held was steady, his hands gripped it firmly as his mouth pressed into a thin line.

"Dibs on his boots," the tall guy commented.

"Nah." Eli gave his head a quick shake. "You got the last guy's stuff. This one's mine."

"Fine, I'll take his pants," the tall guy conceded.

"Nope," Eli replied calmly. "You can have his pack and whatever's in it."

With a shrug, the tall guy seemed to agree. Eli tipped his chin at Jameson

"Take off the backpack," he instructed. "Just let it drop to the floor."

Doing as he was told, Jameson shifted his shoulders so that the straps of the pack slid down his arms. Slowly, deliberately, he let the bag drop to the floor. All the while, he kept his eyes locked on Eli. His lungs were burning and his throat was tight. That's when he realized he was holding his breath.

Sucking in air, Jameson kept his palms facing forward in defense. The handheld radio attached to his side clicked. All eyes in the room dropped to it.

"He's not alone," Eli announced.

Gesturing with the barrel of the gun, he went on, "Take it from him. What frequency are they using?"

One of the men stepped forward and relieved Jameson of his radio. Holding it up to his face the guy sighed.

"Ten," he said.

"Alright." Eli nodded as his gaze cruised over the other men in the room. "Let's keep ours on six and see if we can track 'em down. I'll be out in a few minutes."

As the other men filed out of the room, Jameson remained perfectly still. Circling around him, they each grabbed a gun from behind one of the old wooden desks before pushing out the double glass front doors.

When the last one had left, Jameson's radio released another click. The guy who'd taken it off of him had left it on one of the desks when he'd grabbed his gun. Jameson's heart was racing as his pulse skittered and jumped. Liam wasn't getting the responses they'd agreed to. Shit was about to go sideways, and fast.

"I killed you," Eli spoke finally. His rifle remained pointed at Jameson's forehead. "I watched you die."

"I could say the same thing about you," Jameson countered, his voice came out rough, almost gravely.

Dipping his head slightly, Eli pursed his lips.

"I came close," he admitted. "I almost bled out. But you… I guess you just rose from the damn dead. I strangled you with my bare hands, I crushed your skull in. I felt the crack. I went back there… after… but the whole area had burned to the ground."

"We heard your recording," Jameson interrupted, he didn't have time for this little trip down memory lane. "There aren't any women or children here, are there?"

"Nah." Eli shook his head as a pained expression crossed his face. "We just march poor schmucks like you into the bank vault and shoot them in the head."

"Why?" Jameson asked. So, that's where that awful smell was coming from. Decaying bodies in the back.

"Boss's orders." Eli's jaw ticked as he spoke. "It's how we eat. It's how we survive. We just move from town to town, until the area is empty of men."

"Your sister…" Jameson licked his lips and took a tentative step forward. "Recognized your voice. I didn't believe her."

Jerking his rifle slightly, Eli's face grew hard.

On the table, Jameson's radio gave up a double click.

"How dare you talk about her?" Eli accused. His voice was raw now, his face pinched, his eyes glittering. "After what you did? You're gonna make me kill you all over again. I've already had to live with it once."

"She's alive, Eli." Jameson's brows raised, imploring. "Cass is…"

"How dare you?" Eli's voice broke as his chest heaved. "How dare you say something like that? There are no women left. None."

"There are…"

"Who the fuck are you?" Eli took a step forward. "I thought I knew you, but then you took her and you… you…"

"Eli…"

"No!" Eli shook his head. "Now you offer her up to me? Use her memory like that?"

The sound of a single gunshot exploded.

Zip. Crack.

Squeezing his eyes shut, Jameson swore his heart stopped beating completely. His stomach clenched and his muscles zinged with a heavy dose of adrenaline. He'd come all this way, after all this time, only to be executed by the man he thought he'd murdered?

But then he sucked in a breath and opened his eyes. The bullet he'd anticipated never entered his brain. Eli was still standing there, aiming his weapon at Jameson's head. The gunshot had come from outside.

"How many guys do you have out there?" Eli asked. His eyes skipped to the door, then back to Jameson.

"They aren't just guys, Eli," Jameson said. "Cass is out there, too. I swear to God, your sister is out there."

Another gunshot sounded, then a barrage of answering fire. Sweat broke out along Jameson's forehead as the gun in Eli's hands wavered. His eyes turned pleading then, threading with panic.

"You're lying to me," Eli whispered.

"I'd never lie to you about that," Jameson countered, as a wave of fear hit him. He had to get to her. He had to get out of here and get to Cass.

Sniffing suddenly, Eli's eyes slammed shut and he turned his face to one side. Jameson could see the glisten of a single tear leaking down the guy's cheek. The air in the building felt suddenly stifling as sweat slipped down Jameson's spine. He kept holding his hands out, waiting for Eli to come to some sort of decision.

Suddenly, the barrel of Eli's weapon dropped towards the floor, and the guy's arms went limp. Giving his head a quick shake, he took a step back.

"Okay," Eli managed, clearing his throat and returning his gaze to Jameson. "But if Cass isn't out there, I swear I will gut you like a fucking fish this time, and I won't leave until I watch your body burn to ash."

Exhaling in a whoosh, Jameson ran his hands back through his hair. The radio attached to Eli's side burst with static and then a voice began talking. Reaching down, Eli adjusted the volume up.

"You're not going to believe what we found," a male

voice said. "Women... and I'm not fucking joking this time."

Yanking the radio up off his belt loop, Eli's eyes shot to Jameson. Shock. Fear.

"Do not touch the women," Eli ordered. "Bring them directly to me. Boss's orders."

The radio burst with static. There was no answer.

Jameson's gut dropped as terror flooded him. The girls had been found. Whirling away from Eli, Jameson nearly tripped over his backpack and fell to the ground. The tall guy had just left it sitting there, fully confident in his ability to come back and retrieve it.

"Where are they?" Eli's voice was strained as he shoved past Jameson and headed towards the front doors.

"Can you trust your men?" Jameson barked, as he kept his body moving forward. "With a woman? Can you trust them?"

Coming to a stop at one of the desks, Jameson searched frantically behind it. He selected an old rifle and held it up, checking the magazine. It was loaded. Reaching for his radio still lying on the desk, Jameson snatched it up and turned to stare at Eli. The guy looked stricken.

"No." He shook his head and turned once more for the door. "No. I can't."

Fuck. *Cass.*

Depressing the call button on his walkie, Jameson practically shouted into it as he made for the door.

"Two blues coming out!" He prayed Liam could hear him. "Code Eli. I repeat, Code Eli. But we've got problems.

Cass's been found. I repeat, the girls have been found. We've got to go now!"

Shoving the radio into his back pocket, Jameson charged out into the sunlight. Eli was already a step ahead of him.

Darting across the sidewalk, they both ducked their heads and dove for cover beside the nearest vehicle. Crouching down, Jameson's shoulders heaved as he sucked in panicked air. The two men eyed one another, and counted breaths. No bullets chased them. They took no fire.

Giving Eli a brisk nod, Jameson shot to his feet and began running. His boots pounded the asphalt, taking him as fast as they could go across Main Street and down a narrow alleyway. The radio at his side crackled and he could hear Liam's voice, but between the blood now roaring in his ears and the sharp gasps of his own breathing, Jameson couldn't understand what exactly he was saying.

Behind him, Eli kept pace. Jameson could feel his former friend at his back, sense his presence just off his left side. Together, they tore away from the town, running along paved roads and jumping through fenced yards until the asphalt gave way to dirt.

The sound of a woman screaming in the distance had Jameson's heart popping up into his throat. He could hear the rumble of the Jeep's engine as the woods where they'd hidden the girls came into view.

Throwing a quick look back at Eli, Jameson's panic spiked even higher.

"Go!" Eli shouted, motioning with his rifle as he ran. "Fucking, go!"

Jameson went. He tore across the field and entered the woods. A single gunshot echoed through the trees.

Charging into the clearing, Jameson had just enough time to witness Cass fall. She'd been shot. Suddenly everything went silent. His heart no longer pounded in his ears. His lungs no longer churned out air.

Davey was on the ground a few feet away, whipping the shit out of some guy. Mia was leaning against the Jeep, her pants yanked down to her thighs, her mouth hanging open. Surely, she was screaming. But Jameson could hear none of it.

All he saw was Cass tumble forward… and blood… lots of blood.

It happened in slow motion. But it also happened in the blink of an eye.

Jameson's rifle was up and firing before he could even think about it.

Boom. Step. Boom. Step. Boom. Step.

It was so fucking fast.

The strangers, Eli's men, dropped to the ground, or they ran.

Absently, Jameson's brain registered that Eli was moving past him, running, firing his own weapon, gunning down his own men. But when Jameson got to Cass's body, he abandoned his rifle and slid to his knees beside her. She was rolled onto her back. Her eyes were flipped up into her head. She wasn't moving.

"Come on Cass baby," Jameson hissed.

Running his hands over her, he searched frantically for a pulse. His hand was shaking so damn hard, he couldn't feel anything. Fuck.

His eyes dropped to her blood-soaked hand, then to her bloody shirt and jeans. There was one leg in particular that was injured, oozing out crimson like no other.

Diving for the wound, Jameson ripped at the tear in her pants until he located the hole in her thigh.

"No," Jameson whispered the word under his breath. "No, no, no, no. You can't do this to me."

Slamming his palms down over the wound, Jameson leaned all of his considerable body weight on top of her. He was trying to stop the bleeding, but he didn't know enough about this shit. He only knew to apply pressure, beyond that he was utterly useless.

But then Liam was sliding to a stop across from him and Eli was dropping to his knees by Cass's head.

"Move your hands," Liam spat, trying to push Jameson away.

Jameson wouldn't budge. Eli's fingers came down to press against his sister's neck.

"I've got a pulse!" Eli practically sobbed the words. "I've got one. She's breathing. Come on, Sis. Stay with me. Oh my God, she's alive."

"Move your fucking hands!" Liam slammed a fist hard

into Jameson's chest. "Trust me, I know where a damn artery is. Let me check where the shot hit. Move!"

Rocking back, Jameson did the hardest thing he'd ever had to do in his life. He let Cass go. Like he really let her go this time. His stomach pitched and vomit worked at the back of his throat.

Immediately, Liam had his hands on her, assessing her wound. Jameson watched the guy's face as he worked.

"Give me your belt," Liam instructed. "And grab a medic kit from the Jeep. It didn't hit an artery. She's got a chance."

A moment of relief, utter and instant soaked through Jameson, making him feel light-headed. Fighting against it, he whipped off his belt and looped it shakily around Cass' thigh. Liam had his hands on the bullet wound now, applying pressure while Jameson cinched the belt down. Tight. Tighter.

Before he could get up to go to the Jeep; however, the medic bag landed in the dirt beside Liam. Glancing up over his shoulder, Jameson saw Davey. His nose was bleeding. He had a cut over one eye. He was panting hard, but otherwise appeared okay.

"We've got to get out of here as quickly as possible," Eli commented.

When Jameson glanced over at him, Eli's face screwed up in pain, and he sucked in a quick breath.

"You get hit?" Jameson asked.

"Nah." Eli gave his head a shake, but his hands left his sister's body.

Eli was grabbing at his own right hand now, rubbing

hard and applying pressure with his left fingers as if the damn thing was stabbing him.

Jameson frowned.

All the while Liam's hands were flying back and forth from the medic bag to Cass. He was murmuring to himself and injecting her with some shit. There were bandages and gauze and bloody crap being tossed everywhere.

"I didn't know you were a medic," Jameson rasped.

His hands floated to Cass's body where he stroked at her arm and took her limp palm in his own. Limp, unmoving. She was so tiny and fragile and broken just then.

"I'm not," Liam admitted, his brow was furrowed, he did not look up from his work. "But I've cut up enough people to know basically where all the important shit is, and I've watched Ace do his thing a few times too many. Thing is… I'm the best she's got."

"Fuck," Jameson exhaled the word as he closed his eyes.

"We've got to go," Eli again, his voice strained.

Jameson's eyes popped back open. "Can she travel?"

"Yeah," Liam answered. "Tear all the shit out of the back of the Jeep, and fold down the rear seats. Let's try to keep her as flat as possible."

"Roger," Davey responded, and whirled away.

"Let's call it in, first," Liam shouted then. "Before we ditch the radio, set up an extraction with Uriah."

"No time for that," Eli shook his head.

"Why?" Jameson's gaze shot to his old friend, who's face had gone pale. "You know something we don't?"

"Yeah." Eli's lips pursed and he groaned. His left hand

kept working at his right. Pushing down hard on the flesh between his pointer finger and his thumb. "I do."

Jameson's gaze popped over to Liam and he frowned. The interrogator had rocked back onto his heels now. His work on Cass was apparently done. But he was eyeing Eli, studying the guy carefully.

"What's wrong with your hand?" Liam asked finally, nodding towards Eli. "You get shot?"

Sweat had broken out on the guy's brow. The color of his skin had taken on a greenish-yellow hue.

"Not shot," Eli managed.

His breathing was growing shallow now as he glanced down to his own hands. They were trembling. His entire body was trembling. Sweat had broken out on his upper lip.

"Something making you sick?" Liam's voice lowered. "Something in your hand?"

Eli's head popped up then, and his eyes swiveled to Jameson. He looked so pained then, so perfectly wasted in that moment.

"Hold him," Liam ordered.

And before Jameson knew what was going on, Liam was up and leaping for Eli. The two of them tumbled back into the dirt, with Eli fighting and kicking. Liam was on top though, and he was going for his knife.

Jameson's eyes widened and he hesitated, just for a single breath. He saw the flash of a knife in Liam's hand, the blade glinting in the summer sun. But he wasn't going for Eli's throat. He was wrestling to get to Eli's hand.

Jumping up, Jameson moved to Eli's legs and threw himself down on them. Using every bit of his two-hundred and forty pounds, he held his childhood friend as best he could as the guy continued to writhe and growl on the ground.

Liam swore.

"Hold still fucker," Liam grunted. "Almost. Got it."

Then all at once, Eli's body went slack. He just stopped fighting. His legs went limp. His feet fell to the side. The back of his head hit the dirt.

"Is he...?" Jameson sucked in a ragged breath. His hands were trembling as he continued to grip his buddy's legs. "Did you...?"

He couldn't say it.

He couldn't bring himself to say it. Not again. Not now.

Shoving off of Eli, Liam stood up and held the tiniest little piece of plastic up to the light. Jameson's eyes widened, and somewhere several feet behind him, Mia began to cry.

"Know what this is?" Liam's eyes traveled over to Jameson who's mouth dropped.

"A source microchip?" Jameson asked, he didn't want to believe it.

"Looks that way." Liam frowned at the tiny device in his hand and then glanced down to an unconscious Eli. "If patterns hold true, he won't be able to tell us anything about how he got it for several months... maybe even longer."

"He said we should go," Jameson pointed out. "He said we needed to get out of here now."

"Yeah." Liam tossed the chip into the dirt and came to kneel beside Cass once more. "Let's get the fuck back to the Wall."

A CHILL RAN THROUGH HER. IT WAS SO COLD. INHALING, Cass licked at her dry lips and let her head loll to one side. There were voices around her, and a distant rumbling. When her eyes fluttered open, her vision was a bit cloudy.

Blinking, Cass tipped her head up and to the left. Her body was rocking gently, she was lying flat on her back, with her hands limp at her sides. She could hear sniffling, then the sound of a woman crying.

"I know that was scary," Davey's voice was quiet. "But he didn't get you. You're gonna be fine, blondie. It's over now."

Frowning, Cass worked to focus her eyes. Davey was riding in the shotgun seat of the Jeep, with Mia curled into a tiny ball on his lap. His hand was stroking down her short hair, over and over as she pressed her face into his neck. Out the window, trees flashed by.

"Let her cry," Liam instructed, his voice came from the opposite side. He must be driving.

Squeezing her eyes shut, Cass shuddered. Why was it so cold? It was summer, right? The Jeep had a good heater, it shouldn't feel this cold.

"She's shaking," Garrett said. Cass felt his large hands come down to brace her arms.

"She's in shock," Liam replied.

"Well… what do we do?" A familiar voice spoke in the cramped space and had Cass's eyes flying open once more.

Angling her head to the left, she saw her brother. Eli. Someone had laid the rear seats down flat in the Jeep and he was crouched against the passenger window. His impossibly long legs were folded beneath his body and his hazel eyes were looking directly at her.

"Eli," Cass breathed.

Shifting a bit closer, Cass tried to lift her hand to touch him, but Garrett prevented her from moving. Swinging her head to the right, she frowned. Garrett was crouched on her other side, his head bent, his shoulders practically touching the ceiling.

"Shhhh," Garrett's gaze swept down to her face. "Stay still, Cass. Don't move, okay?"

"I told you it was him." Cass smiled before looking back at her brother.

Eli lifted his eyebrows in question and glanced up at Garrett.

"That's your name," Garrett offered. "Elijah Roe. This is your sister, Cass."

"Oh." Eli dipped his head and cleared his throat. "Alright."

Cass's stomach twisted and her heart thumped in her chest. Something was wrong. He didn't know her? But then the Jeep took a hard right, causing Cass's body to shift and slide a few inches in the rear compartment. A shock of pain burst in her leg. Waves of hot needles radiated throughout her body.

Turning her head back towards Garrett, Cass threw up.

"Shit." Garrett swore and gripped her arms tighter.

"A little warning next time?" He called to Liam.

"She's in pain..." Liam answered. "Give her another dose of morphine. We shouldn't be far now."

Closing her eyes, Cass worked to draw in air. Her stomach was clenching and pain kept rocketing through her. All of sudden it was like she could feel every bump, every turn, every jarring movement of the Jeep.

Somewhere near her feet, a bag rustled. Garrett murmured a few words under his breath, then she felt a quick pinch.

Relief came quickly. And she faded away.

WHOOSH. WHOOSH. WHOOSH. THERE WAS A THRUMMING. The sound pulsated around in Cass's mind. It was a familiar sort of sound though... an *old* sound. It was a helicopter.

Trying to open her eyes, Cass found they were glued shut. Well... they felt like that anyway. It was like her eyelids were just too heavy. In fact, everything about her felt heavy, and slow and drawn out.

When she sucked in air, it was like her lungs fought against her. They didn't want to open and let that oxygen in. But she needed that oxygen. It was precious.

"On my count… One. Two. Three."

The voice was unfamiliar, Cass thought, as she felt herself being lifted into the air. Then her back was impacting something flat and hard. Pain lanced through her once more.

She wanted to groan. She wanted to protest. But she couldn't get the words to come to her lips. And even if they did, she wasn't able to open her mouth.

Internally, Cass frowned, but the expression didn't translate to her face. Her muscles didn't obey her here. She thought: eyes open. But they didn't. She thought: mouth open. But it didn't. And soon… she gave up trying.

Slipping beneath the blackness, Cass let go.

All the sounds disappeared.

WHEN CASS'S EYES FINALLY FLUTTERED OPEN AGAIN, SHE WAS somewhere new. Overhead, lights were racing by. There were rectangles of fluorescent brightness that would pass her, then disappear, replaced by a few white ceiling tiles. But then another rectangle of light would appear and so on and so forth.

Groaning out loud, Cass let her head fall to the right. At least she could make sounds this time, she thought.

Blinking dully, she realized where she was. She was in a hospital hallway, on a gurney, and people were running beside her. Doctors. Nurses. Garrett.

"I'm sorry Officer, but you've got to stay here," Doctor Collette was saying. "We're taking her to surgery, you can't come any further."

"Please," Garrett's voice cracked. "I'll stay in the corner, out of the way, I swear."

"No." Doctor Collette gave her head a firm shake.

She was small, but mighty, Cass remembered absently. Of course, Garrett kept begging. He was running beside them too. His face was scruffy and so very pale. Poor guy, Cass thought, what had happened to make him look that way?

Exhaling through her nose, Cass felt disconnected and floaty. The gurney lurched a bit, and then the entire thing seemed to slow. Cass's eyes grew heavy again before they dropped shut of their own accord.

But her ears still worked. She could hear a door opening. Some machine beeping. Garrett kept pleading. Then another voice, Liam?

"I've got you buddy," the voice said. "You've got to let go, now. Let them help her."

"I can't do this," Garrett protested.

Then the door slammed shut and the gurney picked up speed. Cass could hear one of the nurses shouting and the doctor responding.

"We won't know if we can save the leg until we're in

there," Doctor Collette was saying. "Get me Doctor Jarvis. Stat. I need his hands on this one."

Then everything went black once more.

THE STEADY BEEP, BEEP, BEEP, WAS THE FIRST THING SHE heard. It was a heartbeat monitor and it was counting *her* heartbeats, Cass figured. Inhaling a slow breath, the air was pleasant, warm even. It was the first time she'd felt warm in… well, a long time.

Her throat was dry. She was thirsty, but when she tried to lick her lips, her tongue would not obey her. The steady beep, beep of the monitor continued. That's when Cass heard the rumble of male voices. But when she tried to blink open her eyes, they refused her.

She should feel panic at this. She should feel the overwhelming need to struggle. But for some reason, Cass felt none of these things. Her lungs continued to take in air and then release air. She felt no pain whatsoever. So she lay still and listened instead. It was all she could do.

"I'm glad you came to see her," Garrett was saying. He cleared his throat. "She would like that."

"Yeah," Eli answered. A chair squeaked. Was he sitting down? "Of course. Thanks for the picture by the way… it helps."

"That was her picture," Garrett supplied. "She left it in my apartment a while ago."

"Oh yeah?" Eli again, his tone teasing. It made Cass want to smile too. "You two… were you guys a thing?"

"For a short while…" Garrett cleared his throat again. He was uncomfortable. "Yeah."

Eli chuckled.

Cass loved that sound. The sound of her brother laughing.

"You look nervous," Eli commented finally. "Would I not have liked that? You and my sister?"

"Well… you tried to kill me over her once," Garrett supplied blandly. "So no, I don't think you would've approved."

"Kill you?" Eli responded. Cass could practically see her brother lifting his eyebrows. "That seems extreme. In this picture, we look like friends. Younger… but happy. Were we?"

"That picture was taken back in high school, we played football together. And back then, we were best friends," Garrett answered. "But your sister was off limits to me, and at the time I did my best to respect that, to respect you."

"High school." Eli repeated the words, smacking his lips as if they had a taste. "I don't remember what that is. But I do remember football. Isn't that weird?"

"They say it's typical for what happened to you," Garrett again. "Removing that chip from your body scrambled your memories, and how you recall things. Hopefully, everything will come back in time."

"Yeah." Eli sighed. "I hope so."

Beep. Beep. Beep.

The sound of the heart monitor filled the room as the

guys' conversation died. Cass tried to open her eyes once more, and this time she felt just a flicker of movement, but in the end… nothing.

One of the guys shifted their boots along the floor. Cass could hear the shuffle. She wished she could see which one it was.

"So…" Eli began again. "You said you two aren't a thing anymore, but yet here you are. You haven't left her side. Why's that? Should I be escorting you out of here or what?"

This time it was Garrett who laughed. Cass's insides turned to fluttering butterflies at the sound. God. She loved him.

"Well…" Garrett released a long breath. "I wasn't kidding when I said you tried to kill me. It was during the war and you confronted me about her. I'd just shipped her North on a train without your permission. Looking back, I think you thought I hurt her. You thought what I did caused her death."

"I don't get it," Eli admitted. "A train… I feel like I hate that word, but I don't know why. I don't know what it is."

"Someday you'll remember everything." Garrett shifted in his seat as he spoke. The sound was off to Cass's left side, so that's where he must be sitting. "So while I've got you listening, just let me tell you a few things. That okay?"

"Yeah, please do."

"You tried to kill me, like for real." Garrett sucked in a breath. "You had me on the ground, choking me and I was going to let you. I swear to God, I was going to let you do it, but right before I passed out, I stabbed you. I didn't even think about it, my hand just did it. You probably have two scars from it, one somewhere on your left side and then another one maybe on your lower back."

"Shit." Eli whistled.

"I thought for sure you'd bleed out," Garrett continued. "When I woke up, I was confused. Turns out you gave me a pretty good concussion when we were fighting. I didn't see your body, but I knew that I'd killed you. I just knew it. I got out of there, and I never went back."

"Oh, fuck." Eli sighed. "So then what?"

"Well, we didn't see each other for four or maybe five years," Garrett supplied. "I thought you were dead, and I think you thought I was dead, too. Eventually I found Cass and… well, I…"

"You couldn't keep your hands to yourself?" Eli offered.

"It's not like that," Garrett countered. "I tried to just stay friends with her. I tried to protect her but keep my distance. I tried to respect your memory. But the thing is… I'm so crazy about this girl. When I found out she loved me, too… I just went for it."

Cass's heart pounded in her chest suddenly and she swore the heart monitor began to speed up.

"Love, huh?" Eli chuckled again.

"Yeah, I'm in love with her." Garrett's hand came to rest on Cass's. She could feel this thumb stroking gently along her skin. "*This* is the part that I most want you to remember when someday you know everything again and maybe you want to kill me. I'm not ashamed of how I feel about your sister. I'm stupid in love with her, and even if she won't have me, I don't think anything will ever change that."

"But she doesn't feel the same way about you?" Eli questioned.

"Well, the thing is... I told her that I killed you so..." Garrett let his voice trail off.

Eli burst out laughing this time. Full, robust, loud.

Cass's body filled with such happiness that her eyes fluttered a moment. She was getting movement back. She was so close to moving.

"Alright." Eli regained his composure. "So I guess as a brother I'm supposed to say something like... if you ever hurt her, then I'll do a better job of strangling you next time."

"I know this doesn't really count," Garrett cut in. "But is that you giving me your permission?"

Cass's eyes flickered open and she watched as her brother smiled. It was a crooked smile, all charisma and slyness.

"Yeah," he said, and rubbed at the back of his neck with one hand. "Why the hell not? I mean, if she wants to be with you, and all that."

Clearing her throat, Cass turned her eyes to lock on Garrett. His mouth dropped open in shock and he stared down at her.

"I want to," she whispered. "Be with you... and all that."

There were more words that she wanted to say.

Things like: *I'm in love with you too,* and *I feel the same way,* but she didn't have time. Before she could work the sentences up her throat, Garrett's mouth was covering hers. His lips were consuming hers and in the background Cass could hear her brother groan in protest. It made every fiber in Cass's being light up.

Lightning. Garrett was like lightning to her, and she loved every second of it.

"WHAT DO YOU MEAN YOU DON'T KNOW WHAT IT SAYS?" Uriah's voice was impatient as he leaned forward in his chair.

They were in the private meeting room with a dozen top level soldiers sitting around the long mahogany table. Uriah was positioned at the head, with Jameson seated just on his right. There were papers and maps and lists scattered all over the surface of the table, but it was Cole's turn to be grilled by their Commander.

"Code reading is very complicated," Cole countered, leaning forward. "The source developed it for use with electronic scanners. The actual physical reading of it can be open to a lot of interpretation."

"So interpret," Uriah growled. "You read all of the source imprints on people's spines from inside the Wall. You read all of their stats back when we first took over with no problems. How is this any different?"

"For starters, the tattoos on Eli's forearms are all hand done," Cole explained. "The code on everyone's spines was computer generated and applied with a laser.

Secondly, Chan was the expert code reader, not me. He taught me enough to get by, but not everything. If you would just turn on one of the scanner machines, we might be able to use the equipment on Eli's arms…"

"Absolutely not," Uriah cut him off with a slice of his hand. "I'm not opening a potential portal to the source and scanning code into it. What if the tattoos are some sort of trigger? It's not worth the risk."

Leaning back in his own chair, Jameson sighed. They weren't getting anywhere.

It'd been two weeks since they'd all returned to the Wall with Cass dying and everyone scrambling. Thank God Uriah had received their distress call and arranged for a rescue helicopter.

At that time, Uriah was willing to risk using those electronics because he hadn't known about Eli. Davey had conveniently forgotten to tell him during his radio call for help.

And thankfully, the source hadn't shown up. Well, at least the pilot hadn't noticed any irregularities in the computer system while flying the helicopter. But as soon as they'd landed and Liam was debriefed by Uriah, shit hit the fan.

Because the truth was shocking. Somehow, someway, the source had implanted a microchip in a South West Side

Soldier who had never had any contact with the Wall. None. How in the hell did that happen?

It was a puzzle that they'd all spent the past few weeks desperately trying to figure out.

Cole had inspected and traced and played around with the code tattooed on Eli's arms every single day. Unfortunately, he wasn't able to interpret it, and that left them all feeling exposed. Eli didn't remember a damn thing and the entire situation was beyond frustrating.

"All I can promise is that I'll keep trying." Cole's shoulders sagged. "If you know of any other code readers that were trained and not eliminated during the war, then let me know. Maybe we can try to track them down."

"There was a code reading school," Uriah acknowledged. "I'll see if the library here has any information on the subject. Until then, you all can go."

Letting loose a breath, Jameson pushed back his chair and shoved up to standing. Like always, he waited for the others to file out first. Uriah stood silently beside him, his jaw clenching and releasing until the last man left.

"What do you think?" Uriah asked finally, still staring at the closed door.

"You're making the right call for now," Jameson assured him. "Let's just take one day at a time."

Nodding slowly, Uriah seemed to agree. Then, with a quick shake of his head, the Wall's Commander slipped out of leader mode and into best friend mode.

"How's Cass?" He asked. "How's the new apartment?"

"It's good." Jameson let himself smile. "She's good, still

using the crutches of course, but with physical therapy she should regain full use of her leg."

"And her brother?" Uriah tried to look innocent. "You're keeping tabs on him, right?"

"He's still living with us," Jameson confirmed what Uriah already knew.

As soon as Cass had been released from the hospital, the three of them had moved into a ground floor apartment together. It had three bedrooms and a full kitchen, which was awesome. Cass wanted to spend as much time with her brother as possible, and frankly Jameson wanted to be with his old friend, too.

Plus, it was easier for Cass to come and go with her leg injury because there weren't four flights of stairs to navigate.

Thankfully, Eli (in his current memory-wiped state) was pretty damn relaxed about pretty much everything. He moved in with them without fuss and seemed to sleep solid every night.

Their new apartment also happened to be directly across the hall from Uriah's place.

Convenient? Definitely.

Calculating? Probably.

But still the guy needed reassurance that Eli wasn't going anywhere.

"You hear anything about Davey?" Jameson asked. Mia had been wondering. The guy had saved her one day, then ghosted the next. "He make it back to the compound with the PRC-511?"

"Yeah, we got radio contact from him just yesterday," Uriah confirmed. "All good there."

"Alright, well I'm gonna head out then," Jameson said. "Unless you need something."

"Man, Cass got you whipped quick, didn't she?" Uriah teased. "What's that girl got that I don't?"

"Everything," Jameson answered with a smile, and quickly crossed to the door.

He was out of that conference room, down the stairs, and stepping into the sunshine in no time at all. His lungs sucked in warm air and his heart felt lighter than it had... maybe ever.

Crossing one of the wide green lawns, Jameson didn't bother with sidewalks or paths. He cut a straight line to his apartment building, he cut a straight line to Cass, weaving around buildings and people and trees.

When he rounded the last corner, Jameson stopped short. Cass was sitting on a bench with Mia curled up beside her. The two women held hands. The sun shined down on them, making Cass's hair shine.

Cass's bad leg was propped up on the bench seat. Her crutches were lying flat in the grass not a few feet away.

It was perfect.

Despite the mystery of Eli, his tattoos, the microchip and the possible threat of the source, Jameson had never felt so easy in all his life.

Picking up his feet, he crossed the last expanse of grass quickly and knelt down directly in front of Cass. She and Mia both sat up straighter when he put his hands on either side of Cass's face and gave her a long, slow kiss.

He could do this whenever he wanted now. Because she was his. She'd agreed to be his.

Pulling back, Jameson looked into Cass's eyes and rubbed his thumbs gently over her cheeks. She smiled then, her smooth skin flushing a shade of pink that stirred him.

"I love you," she said simply.

"I love you, too," Jameson replied, and went in for that next kiss.

A word from the author:

There's a fifth book! TAKING TOMORROW (Davey and
Mia's story) will be making its debut August 18, 2020.
Order now!!!

Book hangover much?
Might I suggest my completed series…
THE CAPTIVE BORN
It'll be right up your alley… wink, wink.

Join my email list...
LK MAGILL NEWSLETTER

Join my ARC Team!
ARC TEAM - LK MAGILL

Reviews, pretty please...
Each and every positive review makes a huge difference.
Be it Amazon, Kobo, iBooks, Barnes and Noble; no matter
the retailer, I read and appreciate them all.
Thank you and I hope to see you in the future.

Websites:

www.lkmagill.com

Facebook:
https://fb.me/LKMagill1

Instagram:
https://www.instagram.com/lk.magill.author

Amazon page:
http://amazon.com/author/lkmagill

ALSO BY LK MAGILL_

Standalone novels:

VANISH ME

The Captive Series:

THE CAPTIVE BORN - Book One

THE CAPTIVE MISSING - Book Two

THE CAPTIVE RISING - Book Three

Outlasting Series:

OUTLASTING AFTER - Book One

CHASING TRUTH - Book Two

SURVIVING THE WALL - Book Three

BREAKING BEFORE - Book Four

TAKING TOMORROW - Book Five

FINDING FOREVER - Book Six

www.ingramcontent.com/pod-product-compliance
Lightning Source LLC
Chambersburg PA
CBHW031607180726
48284CB00005B/1439